FORBIDDEN PASSION

"You love me, Cassie," he whispered. "You cannot turn your back on that and walk away."

"Oh, yes, I . . ." she began to protest.

"Look at me."

She wanted that least of all, and would have turned her head away, but his gentle, persistent hands held her shoulders immobile until she could find nowhere else to look and had to look up into those silvery, moonlit eyes.

"Cruz."

Her resistance melted. She was betrayed, not by him this time, but by her own body and soul. She cried out his name once more before she opened her arms to him. Propriety fled from her mind, along with any thoughts about tomorrow.

Seeing the shimmering sparkle of love in her eyes, Cruz grabbed her, taking her lips in a slow kiss that unleashed a burst of sweeping desire. The tension of past days when they'd tried to stay apart, tried to deny what they felt, exploded around them . . .

CAPTURE THE GLOW OF
ZEBRA'S *HEARTFIRES!*

CAPTIVE TO HIS KISS   (3788, $4.25/$5.50)
by Paige Brantley
Madeleine de Moncelet was determined to avoid an arranged marriage to the Duke of Burgundy. But the tall, stern-looking knight sent to guard her chamber door may thwart her escape plan!

CHEROKEE BRIDE   (3761, $4.25/$5.50)
by Patricia Werner
Kit Newcomb found politics to be a dead bore, until she met the proud Indian delegate Red Hawk. Only a lifetime of loving could soothe her desperate desire!

MOONLIGHT REBEL   (3707, $4.25/$5.50)
by Marie Ferrarella
Krystyna fled her native Poland only to live in the midst of a revolution in Virginia. Her host may be a spy, but when she looked into his blue eyes she wanted to share her most intimate treasures with him!

PASSION'S CHASE   (3862, $4.25/$5.50)
by Ann Lynn
Rose would never heed her Aunt Stephanie's warning about the unscrupulous Mr. Trent Jordan. She knew what she wanted—a long, lingering kiss bound to arouse the passion of a bold and ardent lover!

RENEGADE'S ANGEL   (3760, $4.25/$5.50)
by Phoebe Fitzjames
Jenny Templeton had sworn to bring Ace Denton to justice for her father's death, but she hadn't reckoned on the tempting heat of the outlaw's lean, hard frame or her surrendering wantonly to his fiery loving!

TEMPTATION'S FIRE   (3786, $4.25/$5.50)
by Millie Criswell
Margaret Parker saw herself as a twenty-six year old spinster. There wasn't much chance for romance in her sleepy town. Nothing could prepare her for the jolt of desire she felt when the new marshal swept her onto the dance floor!

Available wherever paperbacks are sold, or order direct from the Publisher. Send cover price plus 50¢ per copy for mailing and handling to Zebra Books, Dept. 3948, 475 Park Avenue South, New York, N.Y. 10016. Residents of New York and Tennessee must include sales tax. DO NOT SEND CASH. For a free Zebra/ Pinnacle catalog please write to the above address.

Kristal Leigh Scott
Santa Fe Surrender

ZEBRA BOOKS
KENSINGTON PUBLISHING CORP.

For Mary Vanecek, who knows
the true meaning of friendship.

ZEBRA BOOKS

are published by

Kensington Publishing Corp.
475 Park Avenue South
New York, NY 10016

Copyright © 1992 by Kristal Leigh Scott

All rights reserved. No part of this book may be repro-
duced in any form or by any means without the prior written consent of the Publisher, excepting brief quotes used
in reviews.

If you purchased this book without a cover you should be
aware that this book is stolen property. It was reported as
"unsold and destroyed" to the Publisher and neither the
Author nor the Publisher has received any payment for
this "stripped book."

First printing: October, 1992

Printed in the United States of America

Chapter One

Santa Fe. 1845.

Cassie McPherson Layton shoved her shoulder against the heavy wooden door of her log cabin, fighting to keep it shut long enough to drop the bar into place, securing it against the fierce buffeting of the blizzard raging outside. The solid door shuddered under the attack of the howling winds and her breath came out in harsh gasps from the effort.

Snow dusted the floor inside the cabin where it had been driven indoors by the unrelenting wind. In five winters spent in Santa Fe, this was one of the worst storms she'd seen.

It was also the earliest, only a few days into the first week of October. When she had left town that morning to ride the five miles to the summer cabin she and Cameron had built two years ago, she never dreamed she'd be stranded out here by a sudden, freak storm.

Only intending to prepare the isolated cabin, nestled in the shadows of the Sangre de Cristo mountains, for the coming winter, she'd planned to ride back into town within hours and had brought only

5

enough provisions for the day. Now she faced the troubling possibility that she could be stranded here for some time.

Cassie and her young husband had wanted the cabin to be rustic without many luxuries, since they used it mainly for excursions in the summer or for weekends when they needed to escape town or whenever the weather was nice.

Luckily, there was some hay and a huge stack of split firewood in the barn, no doubt put there by Cameron in the last weeks of his life, and a few essential supplies in the kitchen. She would be able to get by for a short time, until the weather improved.

After shoving the heavy bar into place to keep the door from blowing open again, she made haste back to the fireplace and coaxed the kindling into a comforting blaze after a couple of awkward attempts, since she was unwilling to remove her gloves from stiff fingers, numb from the cold. She stood as close to the fire as she dared, holding her hands out in front of her, gradually absorbing its warmth.

Fingers tingling from the gradual return of feeling, she worked her fleece-lined gloves off, one finger at a time. Thankfully, she had worn her heaviest coat and lined gloves, but several trips to the barn for wood in the harsh cold of early evening had chilled her thoroughly from her head to her toes.

Maybe she would be lucky and the storm would blow out as rapidly as it had blown in and she could quickly get back to town. Early storms were known to do just that, but she was more than a little afraid that this was a vain hope. She could be trapped out here for days, dependent on the meager vittles she'd brought and the small stash of canned goods and dried foods left in the cupboards of the cabin's kitchen.

She would have to make the best of it, she decided, slipping out of her coat and shaking the snow off it. She hung it on a hook beside the door and quickly backtracked to soak up the welcome heat of the fire. Piñon logs crackled and popped, burning brightly and cheering her a little with the cozy glow and fragrant aroma.

A fire of piñon logs was one of the things she associated in a pleasant way with New Mexico winters, one of the things that helped make them bearable. She and Cameron had carefully designed the cabin so that the one fireplace would open into the two main rooms of the cabin, heating the living area as well as their bedchamber. She loved that arrangement, and it was one of her favorite things about the cabin.

After she thawed out some more, she unwrapped the small dinner she'd packed and ate it standing close to the fire, turning every so often to warm her opposite side, being at once too hot and too cold. The cold chicken and fresh bread tasted heavenly, though. She hadn't realized her exertion had left her famished until she took the first bite. She ate slowly, wanting to draw out the pleasure. She was all too aware that what she would have to eat for the next twenty-four hours or so would not be nearly so tasty.

Some time passed before she was warm enough to move a few feet away from the fire to the big chair Cameron always favored. She curled up in it under a heavy comforter they'd brought out West with them.

She reached for a well-worn book on the table, one she'd already read more than once, but would nonetheless make good company for her again on a long and lonely night. Cassie took a great amount of pleasure in reading and had a small, but highly prized, personal library of books. She had brought most with her when she and Cameron made the trip West from Boston to Santa Fe.

Today, though, the words ran together after awhile and she found herself rereading the same passage several times. Warm and content at last, she nodded once or twice and drifted off to sleep, the book in her lap falling shut with a soft rustling of its pages.

At first, she was sure she was dreaming; the loud noises she heard were only in her mind, until very real, frightening sounds awakened her.

The distinctive noise of gunfire boomed through the stillness of the late evening. Her head shot up in shock and fear, her eyes wide open and staring. The sound of angry shouts and hoofbeats pounding fast and hard, though somewhat muffled by the drifting snow, had her on her feet and reaching for the rifle she'd left standing by the door. She had felt more than a little silly for bringing it, but experience had taught her to be cautious in this sometimes lawless territory.

No one should be riding like that in this blizzard. It was suicidal or, at the very least, foolish.

Her feeling of smugness for having wisely brought the firearm faded when she realized she'd completely overlooked loading it. There should be some ammunition in the cabin somewhere, but where had Cameron kept it?

Cassie dug frantically through the shelves in the kitchen, in the wardrobe by the bed, and finally remembered the metal box behind a loose brick on the side of the kitchen stove where they had often hidden valuables.

Fingers shaking, she pulled a handful of shells from the box and loaded the gun as Cameron had taught her. She stood, listening, in the middle of the room, uncertain what to do next. She was unsure of the nature of the threat to her or what form of attack to expect. Even with a loaded gun in her hands, she was ill equipped to face a large group of armed men.

When the sounds grew less distinct and she could tell that the riders had passed by without stopping, she let out her breath and walked hesitantly to the front window to open the wooden shutters a crack.

Dimly, through the curtain of thick snow, she caught a glimpse of red uniforms. It had to be the Spaniards, and they were in a tearing hurry, despite the weather conditions. More than likely, they were in pursuit of someone, some poor soul who was no doubt running for his life.

With little cause to respect the Spanish officials, she unconsciously placed herself on the side of the fugitive, whoever he might be, and wished him luck in evading his pursuers.

Her imminent danger apparently over, she started to return the gun to its resting place near the door; but then, on second thought, decided to keep it closer at hand. There was always a chance they would come back.

In vain, she tried to calm her shattered nerves. The

quiet that marked the passing of the band of soldiers was, in a strange way, almost as threatening as the noise had been. She wrapped her arms around herself, wondering what could still be wrong, why she felt this continued uneasiness.

Cassie added another couple of logs to the fire and tried to get back into her book, a task that had become impossible after the excitement of a few minutes earlier.

What had the soldiers been up to, way out here, and in the middle of such a terrible storm? Spaniards usually kept to their quarters during bad weather, drinking and playing games of chance, when they weren't chasing the skirts of all the single or married women of Santa Fe.

Whatever had brought them out must have been important. A matter of life and death, perhaps. Had the person they'd been chasing been able to get away? She hoped with all her heart that he had, for she knew the justice of the Spanish government could be swift, harsh, and violent.

She slapped the book shut impatiently, giving up for the time being. She leaned back with her eyes closed, not unwilling to resume the nap that had been interrupted earlier. Sleep was elusive and the unnerving quiet continued to disturb her.

Coffee! Yes, that might be just what she needed. She threw the covers aside, stood up and stretched out some of the kinks. After pausing long enough in front of the fire to warm one side, she went through the arched doorway to the kitchen and brought the kettle to hang over the fire.

She added coffee grounds and a tantalizing aroma soon filled the cabin. The boiling of the water whooshed into the silence, bringing comfort of a familiar kind.

Before she could pour a cup and sit down to enjoy it, she remembered that she had not put hay down on the barn floor for her horse. On such a cold night as this, it would be cruel not to provide the animal with bedding.

Scolding herself for not tending to that chore when she had been in the barn to get the wood, she strode quickly over to the door to retrieve her coat, woolen scarf, and gloves.

As soon as she got this task over with, she could return to her book and cup of hot coffee, perhaps even the nap she had begun.

She almost changed her mind about going out when she opened the door to a driving snow that had increased in its intensity. The wind shrieked, throwing waves of snow in its path. Cassie could not even see the barn. She would have to follow the rail fence by touch, though she was fairly certain she could get there, even if she wasn't able to see the shape of the barn from the house. She had made the short journey enough times in the past to feel safe in trying it, even in these conditions.

Hunching down into the upturned collar of her coat, she struck out, head down to protect her eyes from the snow that felt like tiny darts where it hit her exposed skin. She made quick work of spreading the hay, spared only a moment and an affectionate pat for the animal and was making her way back, inching along the fence, when she heard a noise.

At first, she thought it was the cry of an animal in distress. She stopped, head inclined in the direction from which the sound had come. Long seconds passed and she heard nothing more, though she listened quite intently.

It had only been the wind after all. She breathed a relieved sigh and continued making her way toward the house, step by careful step, holding onto the fence with all her might. She reached the door and had her hand on the latch when the haunting cry came again, more clearly this time.

Only it didn't sound like an animal now. It sounded human. Though it was so muffled and covered over by the whistling of the wind, she couldn't be sure.

"Just go inside, Cassie Layton, and tend to your own business. There's nothing out there, most especially nothing . . . or no one . . . who needs your help! You're always too nosy by a long shot, anyway. Listen to your better judgment for once!"

Her lecture didn't work, of course. She could not go inside and turn her back on someone who might need her help. On the other hand, she would surely be putting her own life in jeopardy if she ventured any farther away from her front door than she already had. Before she committed herself to such a foolhardy act, she had to at least know for sure whether someone was out there.

With a worried sigh, she pushed open the door. Propelled by the wind at her back, she stumbled inside. Closing the door behind her, she had every bit as much trouble with the latch as she had the first time.

12

When the door was fastened, she shuffled over to the fire with toes so cold she could barely feel them. Cassie was determined to convince herself she had heard nothing and that it wasn't necessary to go out again on a night like this. She shivered.

The tempting aroma of the coffee beckoned, and her book lay invitingly on the table where she had left it. Like a statue she stood, not removing her coat, not making a move toward the book or the coffee.

There was no way she could be sure it hadn't been a human cry. She couldn't live with the possibility that she had left someone out there to freeze to death. She had to go out and try to help.

Cursing herself for being a fool, she bundled up as much as she could while still being able to walk. She couldn't help anyone if she froze to death before she got to them.

Then, she snatched the lantern off its hook and set off on a rescue mission that could leave her with a miserable case of frostbite, or at the very least searching aimlessly and feeling entirely foolish. The worst scenario, that she could die in the attempt, she wouldn't even think about.

The gale wind struck her with intense force, and a driving sheet of snow nearly sent her running back inside for cover. Instead, she trudged off in the direction from which the sound had come, or at least from where it had seemed to come.

She thought she'd been near the well when she'd heard it, so she would use that as a place to begin her search.

Because of the nearly impossible conditions, she

would not be able to go far, but surely the weak sound she heard could not have traveled over much of a distance and still have been heard over the howling of the wind. If someone was out there and in trouble, that person couldn't be far from the cabin. She pushed on through the deep snow, holding the lantern precariously in front of her, just a bit above her head.

"Is anybody out there?" she called out, her words seized by the wind before they were out of her mouth.

No answer. No cry or moans of pain. Nothing.

She was a fool and it was past time to turn back. There was no one out here. What she had heard had been only a distortion of the wind, a wild animal, or a figment of her active imagination. Nothing more.

In spite of her more sensible nature urging her to go back, to seek the easy way out, she took a few more tentative steps away from the cabin into the swirling, dark void of the snowstorm.

Then she heard it! From her left and a bit in front of her, surely no farther than a few feet, came a very distinct, though quite weak, cry for help.

Her legs had grown heavy from lifting them time after time to plow through the ever increasing depths of the snow. Still she found the strength to increase her pace, moving as fast as she could, in the direction of the sound.

"Where are you?" she cried out again, sure that it was futile and there would be no answer.

Again, she doubted she'd ever heard anything in the first place. She had surely only imagined it. She should go back now, while she still could and forget the whole thing.

14

But no, she was only fooling herself, trying to find an easy way out. That last cry for help had been clear enough. Someone was out there. *And in trouble*.

A cry that was either weaker or more distant than she'd thought reached her ears, compelling her to keep going, leaving the warmth and safety of her home farther and farther behind.

She tried to shout in answer. With the wind blowing into her face, her voice quivered and was so raspy she was certain the sounds would never reach the person who so desperately needed her help.

Cassie grew nervous about how far away she'd come from her cabin. What if she couldn't find her way back? She would die out here and no one would even know until spring. But, whatever the outcome, she couldn't turn back.

Picking up first one foot and then the other, she commanded her limbs to obey as she dragged them wearily out of the snow. Then she planted them again, though her muscles ached unbearably and the wind stole the very breath from her lungs.

Her legs felt like lead, as though they might give out on her at any moment. Somehow she found the strength to keep on going, even when she would have liked to quit.

She stumbled over something. With arms flailing, she landed flat and hard on the ground, the lantern dropping out of her hands and rolling to one side.

Tentatively, she reached out to touch the obstruction that had sent her tumbling, almost afraid of what she might find. At first, she wasn't sure what it was, covered as it was with a thick layer of snow. But when she had brushed most of it away, she felt the contours of a very still body.

She had found him! But it might very well be too late.

"Oh no!" she cried, trying to scrabble back to her feet, terribly afraid the man who had called out to her was already dead. She looked at the still body that hadn't moved, even as she'd tumbled over it, and she nearly cried from frustration.

Squatting in the snow, she shoved her hand down into the snow-covered collar of the man lying there, seeking a pulse. Unable to feel anything through the layers of the bulky glove, she pulled her hand back out and peeled the glove off. She held it in her teeth, while she put her icy fingers back inside against his skin.

For a few seconds, she still could not make out a pulse, but assumed that was as much due to the loss of feeling in her fingers as to anything else.

Cassie waited, while her hand warmed to the point that her fingers tingled painfully. Then she was finally able to detect a faint pulse. Or, at least, she thought she could.

It was enough to galvanize her to action. She had to get him back to her cabin without delay or she would be dealing with a corpse. Probably, he had already been out here too long, but he was warmly dressed and the covering layer of snow might have helped give him insulation. There was a chance he would live, though it was a slight chance.

Dear God, please let him live, she begged. She began to shake his shoulders, trying to bring him back to consciousness, to rouse him from the slumber that was too like death.

"Wake up! Wake up! You have to help me. You'll die out here!"

The body remained as still and slack as death.

"Please!" she cried, bending over and breathing into his face.

The lantern lay on its side and, remarkably, still cast a bit of feeble light. She wouldn't be able to carry it and support him, too, so she would have to make her way back in the dark, relying on her instincts. There was no way she could manage that task if he couldn't help her, even if just a little.

"God help me!" she breathed, without thinking about how long it had been since she'd prayed, since she'd practiced the religion of her childhood.

She reached behind his head and raised it, brushing the snow off his eyes and mouth, anxious for some sign of life. She shook him, terrified that he would die right there in her arms . . . if he hadn't already . . . and more than a little afraid that she could die with him!

"Please wake up! You have to help me!"

When she tried to raise his body, she became aware of what a big man he was. It would be physically impossible for her to get him back in this unconscious state.

Had she imagined it, or had there been a slight response from him? She was almost sure she'd seen his arm move and then his legs.

"That's it! Come on . . . wake up! I'll help you, but you have to do your part."

His lips were closed in a thin, tight line of pain, but his eyes blinked open, as though in answer to her command. He seemed to see her, but said nothing; closing his eyes again just as quickly as he had opened them.

She felt him push with his arms against the ground under him, and she put both her hands behind his back, pulling with all her might until he was sitting up.

His head hung down and she thought he might have passed out again, but his legs moved against hers. He was trying to stand up! For the first time, she had hopes they might both make it back alive. She clung to him tightly, determined not to lose the small progress they'd made.

One of his arms fell heavily over her shoulder and she put both arms around his chest. She could feel the bunching of his muscles to help her. Straining, yet working together, they pushed and pulled until she dragged him to his feet. He wobbled and leaned heavily against her. They swayed and almost went down. She stumbled and almost fell under his weight, but she could tell he struggled to support himself as much as he could. She was not about to give up . . . not now.

The weather was not cooperating. The storm had not lessened in its intensity and the snow still fell steadily. At least the wind blew from behind them as they took the first difficult steps in what she hoped was the direction of her cabin.

Tediously, they took one slow step and then another; their progress punctuated by an occasional grunt of

18

pain from him or a breathless word of encouragement from her.

Sometimes, they staggered like a pair of drunken sailors. Once, he lurched sideways, his hold on her loosening, but she clung to him.

"My place . . ." she said between gasps of frigid air, "is not far. I think . . . we can make it. Hold on, do you hear me? Hold on!"

When she felt him losing contact and the strength in his arms ebbing, she shouted at him over the screaming winds, "Hold on, damn you!"

The command in her voice jerked him back more than once from the void of unconsciousness. He clutched her like a drowning man would grasp a life preserver.

Cassie felt him shivering from the cold, his body practically in spasms. She had to get him to shelter soon. He already suffered from overexposure to the elements and he was weakening with each passing minute. He probably hadn't eaten in some time, and he might even be wounded.

She stopped briefly to catch her breath and to still the runaway pounding of her heart. Her deep breaths drew the frigid air painfully into her lungs and her head felt light. His arm tightened around her in encouragement and, taking strength from that, she discovered to her surprise that she could go on.

How in the name of all things holy had this man gotten himself into such a predicament? Alone, with no horse, no gear and no supplies, and on the run from the Spaniards, he had been several miles short of town when he'd landed in the ditch where she'd found him. He hadn't been there very long, but any time at all in this frightful weather could be life-threatening.

Her arm tightened around his waist. The snow fell faster and a white curtain of it isolated them until it was impossible to tell north from south, east from west. Cassie knew they weren't far from her cabin and hoped with all her might that her good sense of direction wouldn't desert her now when she needed it most. The wind was still at their backs so they had to be going in the right general direction. Didn't they?

Impatiently, she brushed the snow from her nose where it clung tenaciously to her eyelashes. She pushed ahead, step by torturous step, through the ever deepening snow, her burden becoming heavier with each step.

"Keep going . . ." she urged her sometimes reluctant, faltering companion.

"It's not far . . ." she promised and hoped she was telling him the truth. It couldn't be far now. It had to be just up ahead somewhere.

But what if she had become disoriented, veered off course and missed it altogether? They could wander around out here for hours, or probably not even that long, until they were both dead.

Her heart banged against her chest and her breathing came in painful gulps. Her fingers were numb. Freezing snow clung to her brows and eyelashes until she could barely see.

More than once, a wave of blackness moved through her, leaving her dizzy and afraid. If she passed out, they would both die within minutes.

She sniffed once, then again. Yes! It was the fragrant smoke rising from the piñon logs in her own fireplace. They were very close.

Still, she couldn't see a thing. Was it straight ahead as she thought, or more to her left? They could miss it by a few feet and be just as lost as he had been before. She'd heard tales of people who froze to death mere steps away from their own front doors.

She wouldn't let that happen. It had to be right up in front of them. It had to be!

Her decision made to keep going straight ahead, she pushed him forward in that direction. Desperately trusting that she was right, that her instincts hadn't deserted her, Cassie needed them more than she ever had in her life.

A dark outline loomed in front of them. Yes! It was the cabin. They were almost there.

"A few more steps, that's all. Come on, now. I told you we'd make it!" she cried, relief sweeping through her. "Here it is. . . ."

With a shoulder into his chest, bracing him against the rough outer wall, she freed one arm to reach for the latch that held her front door. It was wedged tightly shut! Though she shoved against it as hard as she could, it wouldn't budge.

It was frozen shut! She had nothing to beat against it except her gloved fist, which was what she used. The action brought tears of pain to her eyes. After a few blows with the side of her hand, the ice fell away and she was able to lift the latch.

A welcome current of warm air and golden light from the fire spilled out into the white funnel of snow swirling around them. Once more she anchored him

21

to her side with both arms, and edged them both inside. With a sigh of relief, she kicked the door shut behind them, praying it would stay. His body was very nearly a deadweight against her now. He seemed finally to be giving up the struggle he'd put up to help her, and giving in to his weakness.

She propelled him toward her settee and, as gently as she could, dropped him against the cushions. With a grunt of pain that made her wince, he went limp, his eyes closed, hands falling limply to his side. He was unconscious and made no response when she bent over to brush the snow from his lips and eyes and hair. He trembled violently and she knew his sodden clothing had to come off.

Frantic and with numbed fingers, she set to work. Sliding his buckskin coat off and down his arms, she was amazed at the width of his shoulders and the muscles in his arms that were smooth without bulging, the same arms that had barely been able to cling to her. She had to give him credit for a lot of grit. He could easily have given up at any time during the torturous trip back through the storm, but he hadn't.

As she'd half-dragged, half-carried him back to the cabin, she'd been aware of his size, but now she could see that he was at least six feet, perhaps a few inches over. His body was slender and well-proportioned.

He mumbled something unintelligible and she thought he looked like an innocent young boy in his semiconscious condition.

Rubbing her hands together until the numbness was gone, she knelt in front of him and pulled off one calf-high boot and then the other. These she sat beside the front door, then she hung his coat on a hook along with the hat she'd taken from his head.

Jet-black hair fell rakishly over his forehead. She smoothed it back, glad to note that though it was damp, it wasn't thoroughly soaked. In spite of herself, she also noted that it was soft and velvety to the touch, and as black as the darkest night.

His eyes, the majestic clear blue of a New Mexico summer sky, blinked open and studied her briefly. He smiled his thanks; the brilliance of the unexpected smile washing over her before his weary eyes dropped shut again. He drifted off, his full lips closed and quiet.

Cassie thought he was the most handsome man she had ever seen. Suddenly, she felt shy about the task of removing the rest of his sodden clothing, but steeled herself to do what must be done.

Trembling fingers reached for his collar, then fell back.

"My God!" she cried out loud, then slapped her hand over her mouth to cover the exclamation.

The man she'd just risked her life to save, the same one she'd begged God to spare, wore the clerical collar of a priest!

Chapter Two

"A priest!" she exclaimed. "God help us!"

A priest should not have dimples or eyes that blue! And surely priests were supposed to be soft and portly, not slender and muscular and so very tall. She chuckled at her irreverent thoughts.

"A priest!" she muttered again.

"And a priest who's nearly dead," she rebuked herself, remembering her only goal, to save his holy life.

"Sorry, Father," she apologized, as she unbuttoned the clerical collar and dropped it to the floor, trying not to think how much better he looked without it.

The flush on his cheeks alerted her to the presence of a fever. She placed a cool hand on his forehead. Sure enough, he was burning up.

Keeping her eyes carefully averted from his bare, bronzed skin, Cassie managed to remove the rest of his wet clothing. Now she had to get him quickly into bed and under a layer of warm blankets, in order to deal with his rising temperature.

His head lolled back on the calico fabric of the settee, and his long legs were extended in front of him.

It would be difficult at best, perhaps impossible, to move him to the bedroom by herself. Once again, she needed help. He would have to help her.

"Come on!" she urged, bending over and putting both arms around his bare chest and heaving. "We can do this together, but you have to help me."

Although he didn't open his eyes and gave no other outward sign of a return to consciousness, she felt him trying to help.

"It's not far." She echoed the same words she'd promised him earlier out in the snowstorm, but this time she knew they were true. The bedchamber lay only a few short feet away from them.

But his legs were like jelly and he fell back. She collapsed, sprawled across him and the couch. Struggling to ignore the sensations his bare skin aroused in her and the way the firelight danced across the planes of his attractive face, she lay there, considering their dilemma, while trying not to look at him.

"Damn it! You have to help me. Oh, sorry, Father!" she quickly apologized for the curse word.

His eyes blinked open and though they were glazed with pain, he managed a small smile. He had heard her apology.

"Are you an angel?"

His voice was soft, but she clearly heard every single syllable.

Cassie chuckled nervously, afraid she might somehow reveal the impact his deep, rich baritone voice had on her. It was like a golden warm brandy, and the hint of a Spanish accent only made it more mysterious.

"Are you?" he repeated, his breath brushing her ear.

"What?"

She could only hope she didn't sound as stupid as she felt. From the moment he spoke, she had been irrevocably lost, caught in a spell he wove without being aware of it.

With a start, she realized she hadn't moved, but was still lying stretched across him. Self-consciously, she scrambled to her feet and stood looking down at him.

"I . . . think . . . I can help you, if you'll let me, and if you can help me just a little."

His body made an instinctive effort to help her as she tugged on his arms and, with his assistance, hoisted him to his feet and half-carried, half-dragged him to the bedroom.

Her arms ached and her stomach was queasy, her head spinning wildly from the effort. They weaved together across the floor, step by awkward step, tilting first in one direction, then the other.

Once she stumbled and almost went down, but she kept them upright and never loosened her hold on him for a minute.

Panting from exhaustion, she dropped him to her bed and swung his legs up. He seemed to be unconscious once more. She rushed to gather the blankets and quilts left behind in the cabin and threw them over him, tucking them in tightly to conserve his body heat.

Frowning, she stood back and watched him, not sure what to do next. She had never had to take care of anyone who was so ill and the burden of it weighed heavily on her narrow shoulders.

He was still and peaceful enough. Maybe he would be all right, and she wouldn't have to make a decision about what to do next, except for getting some nourishment into him when he awoke.

Dear God, she prayed once more, please let him wake up.

But as she continued to watch, his body twitched and he shuddered hard. Then he began to shake as though he were freezing, even under the heavy layer of blankets.

His body shook so hard her bed rocked like a storm-tossed sea, and he threw his long arms and legs first one way and then another. His lips spoke a nonsensical stream of disconnected words in his delirium.

Every time his restless body tossed the covers off, she piled them back on top of him; willing the awful fever to break its hold; the forceful, chilled trembling to stop. But nothing worked.

His condition reached something deep inside her, compelling her to do something more, to find a way to help him further. But what else was to be done?

She wrapped her arms around herself in her distress and felt the heavy pounding of her heart, the warmth of her own body.

"That's it!" she cried.

Her body heat could be used to warm him. But that would mean she had to crawl into bed with this handsome stranger . . . who just happened to be a priest, in the bargain!

Cassie Layton had never been in bed with anyone except her husband Cameron. She didn't think she could possibly do it. It wouldn't be right. There had to be another way.

She fetched a cool cloth and bathed his forehead which had grown hotter to the touch. He was burning up, his temperature rising steadily, harsh chills still shaking his body, even as she stood there arguing with herself about what she could, or would, do to save his life. Nothing she had done thus far had had any effect on his temperature nor had she found any means of stilling the appalling shudders that swept through his body from time to time.

How selfish it would be to let her modesty get in the way of doing what she knew she should do, or some misguided loyalty to a husband who'd been dead for well over six months.

Finally, ignoring the implications and the consequences of her actions, whatever they might turn out to be, she stripped off her outer clothing and sensible boots and climbed into bed beside his shaking body, snuggling close to him, pulling him close to the length of her body and wrapping herself around him.

She rubbed his shoulders, his back, and his arms, all the while trying not to notice the rock hard, smooth strength in him. She told herself she was performing a necessary function to save his life. She valiantly tried to ignore his masculine, outdoors scent and the way her own body reacted to his proximity. Her heart pounded in her ears and her breathing soon became as erratic as his.

This mysterious priest was so different from her

husband Cameron, and she'd never been so close, so intimate, with any other man. She discovered she had desires she hadn't been aware of, feelings that lay dormant until being fully aroused by this strange priest.

And he is a priest! she admonished herself, shaking her head in dismay.

She could not deny she had felt something primitive and at the same time spiritual. Cassie Layton, who had always been in control of her feelings and actions, was appalled by her unexpected response to this stranger.

Soon his harsh shaking quieted somewhat, but she found that she could not leave him, regardless of what his closeness did to her tormented feelings. He still needed her warmth and she needed something from him, too, although she wasn't sure what that was.

He murmured now, but his wild delirium seemed to be lessening. He nestled against her, his arms going round her instinctively, pulling her up close to him. Her breath caught in her throat and now she felt her own body shake, but not from cold.

Climbing into bed with him may have been the right thing to do for him, but she hadn't counted on what it would do to *her*. She didn't have a clue how one was expected to deal with the emotions boiling through her.

"Dear God," she whispered and then chuckled at herself. "Imagine that," she said to him, "my talking to your boss about you."

The relief sweeping through her with the realization that he would be all right had made her giddy. But she felt better than she had in a long while. With a smile on her lips, she drifted off to sleep in his arms.

Exhausted from the fear and tension as much as from the physical activity of a very long day, Cassie fell into a heavy and deep sleep, but not a dreamless one.

Her exhausted body with its sore, complaining muscles failed to find the rest it needed. She moaned and cried out in dreams that tortured her.

She saw Cameron with blood seeping and spreading over his chest, soaking his white lawn shirt; his face pale as death, his arms reaching out for her.

Dead. In minutes, he was gone, shot down, lost to her forever. Overpowering grief swept over her and tears dampened her cheeks.

Thankfully, that dream ended and another took its place, this one of a happier time.

The two of them had taken a picnic lunch to a nearby mesa. An afternoon of laughter and companionship gave way to the twinkling stars of evening. They made love on the blanket they'd spread out on the ground.

Cassie recalled the emotions, the sensations of bare skin, a mass of curling hair across his wide chest . . . his hands on her body bringing her pleasure.

Her body arched in response, needing more of the caresses and her hands reached for him, smoothing their way over his chest, down across a taut stomach, tracing the silken line of hair down even farther. She took him in her hand and relished the satiny hardness, felt it grow stiffer in her hands.

His fingers, too, sought hidden places, teasing and pulling, circling, then pushing into her and withdrawing, in a simulation of the act of love they would soon share. A hot shiver of pleasure spoared through her, sending her pulses racing. Her nipples tightened and puckered against his chest.

He rolled over and she felt his weight on top of her, his fingers now in her hair, and his body sliding sensuously up and down across hers, felt him enter her and the gentle stroking continue, bringing her immeasurable joy and a blessed, sweet release.

He cried out his own pleasure and kissed her forehead, her nose and her mouth, the kisses immeasurably sweet and tugging at emotions deep inside her.

"Ah, my love," he murmured as he rolled to his side and gathered her into him spoon-fashion, her back curled into his stomach. It was in this position that sleep overtook them. She remembered waking up in his arms the next morning at dawn's first light.

The same sigh of utmost pleasure escaped her lips now.

But the arms wrapped around her this early morning were dark and covered with fine, black hair, not the light golden hair of Cameron's arms.

Completely awake in the instant of that awareness, her eyes blinked open. Cassie lay there, aghast at the

31

reality of her dreams and the position she now found herself in. She lay secure in a man's arms.

The present crashed down on her.

Cameron was dead! He was gone from her forever. It had been a dream. Nothing more.

The arms around her belonged to the unknown priest who'd invaded her life, her home, and her bed. She remembered rescuing him, tending to him and, finally, climbing into bed with him to share her body warmth with him.

She did not remember removing her chemise and her drawers and was shocked to find herself lying naked in his arms.

What was happening here?

The priest lying beside her moaned, still deep in sleep and rolled over, removing his arm that had been resting precariously close to her bare breasts, freeing her to slip out of bed.

There was simply no way the dream could have been real, was there? He'd been ill and injured and his sleep had been deep. Surely, he would not have been able to. . . . No, that wasn't possible. It had been only a dream.

Hurriedly, before he could turn and see her, she pulled on her chemise, her drawers, and a day dress of peach-colored cloth. She bent to tie a slipper onto each foot and then stood looking down at him for a very long time.

It had been a dream, hadn't it?

It only seemed so very real because it had awakened her and she remembered it so vividly. Anything else was unimaginable, unthinkable, beyond the scope of her experience or her ability to cope with it.

Even the shock of being in bed with a strange man with no clothes on was too much for her to deal with right now. She shoved it to the back of her mind, deciding not to let herself think about it anymore.

Tomorrow, when all of this was over and done, maybe she would think about it tomorrow.

Careful not to disturb his sleep, she slipped out of the room. She would do her chores and come back to check on him later.

Before going outdoors, she arranged his clothing so that it could finish drying in front of the fire. In doing so, she dislodged a piece of folded paper that fell to the floor. Reaching down, she retrieved it to return it to the pocket of his jacket. On the top she read the name Antonio de la Cruz Santiago Reyes. Was that the name of the man she'd rescued and in whose arms she had spent the night? Apparently so.

Her eyes drifted down over the lines of Spanish in a slanted handwriting, words she didn't understand for the most part. But she did recognize the signature at the bottom. It was signed by none other than the president of Mexico!

It seemed to her highly unusual that a priest would carry on his person such a document, but it was none of her business anyway. Hurriedly, she stuffed it back into his pocket. She shouldn't have been reading his private papers and felt a flush of shame creep up her face.

Dropping his things, she pulled on her outer clothing and fled out the door.

Like a Mexican jumping bean, his mind refused to focus, hopping from one place to another, one time period to another. It displayed a kaleidoscope of impressions and striking visual images that would not cooperate and that refused to make any kind of sense.

First, he was a young boy in his family's village in Spain; then he was a strapping lad setting off for the New World and an American college. Later, he was standing in front of Mexico's supreme ruler and accepting his commission to the territory of New Mexico.

He'd left the Mexican capital in plenty of time to reach Santa Fe before the first snow. Having been warned of the dangers of raiding Comanche along the Santa Fe trail, he had decided to take the long way through San Antonio and across country. That had been his first mistake, and there had been others.

At first, he'd appreciated the stark beauty and vivid colors of New Mexico. Soon all the rounded red hills and juniper-studded arroyos had begun to look alike, until he'd had to admit to himself that he was hopelessly lost. He had been foolish to think he could find Santa Fe with only an ancient map, and no guide. But desperation had driven him into the heart of a deadly situation, and there'd finally been no turning back.

Then that storm had unexpectedly screamed down out of the purple mountains, enveloping him in a white nightmare of gigantic proportions. His head spinning, he was doubly lost in the snowstorm. He remembered shouts and shots from behind and his headlong flight for his life. His horse stumbling, falling.

Then blackness. . . . The next thing he remembered was looking up into the face of an angel, the only thing between him and a long sleep with no morning. Even when she'd uttered curses at him, he thought he'd never heard a sweeter voice, a voice matched by the golden beauty he'd glimpsed in his dreams.

But it was those remarkable eyes that had the most impression on him. Her eyes were soft and brown and filled with a tender kindness he hadn't seen since he'd last looked into the face of his mother more than a dozen years ago.

He'd noticed the way her eyes had twinkled with good humor when she muttered to herself about something, even as she had worked to tend to his needs, thinking him still unconscious.

Hours had passed in a feverish blur, but vivid images flashed through his mind. In the midst of the blackness, an angel of mercy lying beside him . . . with exquisite cheekbones . . . upturned nose . . . full, red lips.

Had he died and awakened in heaven? For surely that vision of loveliness had been an angel. But were angels so soft and sweet smelling and possessed of such a charming sense of humor? Were they possessed of courage that sent them out into the night on a mission of mercy?

Were angels allowed to feel so good to mere mortals? Surely not. And yet . . . the sensations he recalled were sensuous and most pleasant . . . a soft, cool hand on a fevered brow, surprisingly competent arms that had supported his weight and then patiently nursed him back to health.

Was he totally deranged, or did he not also remember soft womanly curves nestled against him, a silken length of leg next to his, the body heat of another warming him back to life?

No, he could attribute the ravings of his mind to the delirium of the fever. None of it had been real. It couldn't possibly have been real. His angel of mercy was not a real, warm-blooded woman who would crawl into bed with a man and make love to him while the storm raged outside.

He blinked his eyes open to a cozy and apparently deserted room. Through the door, he glimpsed another room, warm with a blazing fire, fragrant with piñon logs. Over the fire coffee steamed, its aroma bringing an answering, hungry rumble from his stomach.

It had not all been a dream, then! Someone had gone to the trouble of rescuing him and bringing him here, to this place of refuge. Not heaven, but close enough.

But was his rescuer also golden and beautiful, as he remembered? And if so, where was she now? The rooms seemed to be deserted.

"Anyone out there?" he called, and it seemed to him years since he'd heard his voice or any other. Had he been unconscious for a very long time?

"Hello. Is anyone there?" he repeated. No voice,

soft and feminine or otherwise, answered. It seemed that he was very much alone, at least for now.

Resisting a returning blackness, he rolled to the edge of the high bed and slid his long legs out from under the covers, letting them drop heavily to the floor. The sight of his own bare legs startled him and a glance down confirmed his first impression . . . he had no clothes on! Even his long underwear had been removed!

"Hell's bells!"

He muttered an unpriestly oath, pulling the covers back over himself and looking around self-consciously.

But whoever had taken him in and undressed him would surely not be too shocked to see him in his current seminude condition. And he'd never really been one for excessive modesty, he thought with a grin, relishing the idea of the golden beauty who'd shimmered in his dreams undressing him. An intriguing thought!

He put his feet on the cold floor and tried to stand, but his knees buckled and he fell backwards onto the bed. Dizziness swept over him, making him sick to his stomach. Horrified, he was afraid he was about to be sick all over the bed. He lay very still until the feeling passed.

Then he sat up warily, moving much more slowly this time. He tested putting weight on his feet, then stood shakily, supporting himself with his hand braced against the wall. He might be able to make it to the other room where his clothes were spread neatly in front of the fire; if he could maintain contact with his hands on the wall and his feet on the floor, and not the other way around!

A few more careful steps. He stopped and rested in the arched doorway, arms spread out to either side, holding him up. The short trip across the room had been taxing in the extreme, and seemed as far as the endless trip across Mexico to the Texas border.

The fire beckoned and his confidence grew as he put one foot in front of another, enjoying the warmth of the room and the very good feeling of being alive after what must have been a close call.

Reaching for his trousers, he was surprised momentarily by the sight of the collar and cassock. He still was not accustomed to them. Hastily, he jerked his long underclothing, his pants and shirt back on, everything except for the collar and clerical robe.

His great coat was dry and his boots, standing near the outer door, had been painstakingly dried and rubbed down. Someone had not only saved his life, but also had given him the best of care. But who? And where was that person? Now that he was awake and able to show his appreciation.

"Hello?" he called out again, anxious to see if he had been dreaming indeed, or if it all could possibly have been real.

Outside, Cassie found trudging about in the deep snow quite tedious and her legs grew tired from the exertion long before her chores were done. She felt satisfaction in what she'd done for the priest, but it had left her exhausted and bruised. She hadn't

38

thought to eat anything herself and was now feeling the effects of it.

After two days of round-the-clock care, his fever had finally broken. She had gotten some broth into him and felt reasonably certain he'd soon be as good as new.

There had been no outer wounds that she could find. His head boasted a huge knot and his ribs had been badly bruised, but otherwise he seemed to be uninjured. The fever brought on by exposure and the blow to the head had been his biggest problems and the greatest threat to his life.

The sacrifice she'd reluctantly made in sharing her body heat with him had done the trick, she thought with a smile, and it had not been nearly as traumatic as she'd feared. In fact, it had been downright pleasant. She tried not to let herself think of it overmuch.

Her too predictable life had been turned upside down by his dramatic entrance into it. She'd felt something in her soul, deep and indescribable, when he'd smiled up at her and called her an angel, then recovered because of her efforts.

But in the process, she had felt more than she'd ever wanted to again. Feelings only led to pain; this was a lesson she thought she'd learned well.

Nothing was changed in her life, not really, as a result of her face-to-face encounter with and rescue of this much too handsome priest. After all, he was obviously a priest and inaccessible, regardless of how attractive he might be. The instant, overwhelming feelings she'd had for him would have to be set aside. She could try to dismiss these feelings from her mind, to pretend she was no different than she'd been two days ago.

It had been touch and go for a while though, and she had been truly afraid she might lose him to the fever and delirium. He'd said some strange, nonsensical things as he'd thrashed about. But during the past night, all that had changed and this morning she tiptoed out and left him sleeping peacefully, his temperature normal once more.

She felt as though she'd been hit with a bat and not entirely because she'd been without a goodnight's sleep for over forty-eight hours. She couldn't erase from her mind the impression of his clear blue eyes looking up at her, the deep timbre of his voice when he'd called her an angel, the sincerity in his glance that said he meant every word, even though she doubted whether he'd been in his right mind at the time.

Her mind still on her unexpected guest, Cassie made her way back toward the cabin. Her heart pounded from the exertion, but she suspected it beat from another cause as well.

Had it beaten in normal rhythm at any time during the two days he'd been her guest?

The moment she lifted the latch and put up her hands to open the heavy door, it swung inward as though of its own accord. Caught by surprise, she stumbled forward from her own momentum, losing her balance, but was saved from pitching headlong to the floor by a pair of surprisingly strong arms.

"Oh!?"

Her part question, part exclamation was the best

she could manage as he righted her, steadying her against the solidity of his body, his arms holding her securely.

A deep chuckle rumbled through his chest. She had heard the remarkable sound of it sometime during the night she'd spent in his arms, and it was strangely familiar now, like the laugh of an old friend.

"I am sorry," he apologized, setting her away from him so they could both breathe normally. "I heard you coming and I only thought to assist you. But I haven't, have I?"

His wide smile was heartstopping . . . and that voice. It was distinctly unfair that it should belong to a priest! She felt as though she could sit at his feet for hours and soak up the cadence, the deep timbre of the voice with that marvelous Spanish accent.

"Are you all right?" he asked.

Concern creased his forehead and she noted the crinkling around the eyes that indicated his age to be beyond what she had first assumed. He was a bit older, perhaps, than she had thought, but not one whit less handsome.

"Uh . . . yes, I'm fine." Why did she have to sound like such a ninny every time she talked to him?

She stomped the snow off her boots and slipped her arms out of her long coat.

"Please. Allow me to help."

Before she could stop him, he'd eased the coat from her shoulders and was carefully hanging it on the hook beside his own.

Oh, Lord! she thought, that voice could just be

her undoing. And the touch of his large, gentle hands on her shoulders had brought her a surge of unexpected warmth. Again, she was helpless as he knelt in front of her. With one hand on her calf, he easily slid off first one wet boot and then the other.

"I . . . could have done that," she croaked.

"I know."

"Thank you."

She couldn't get much beyond sounding like a bumbling idiot when she talked to him. And she just wanted to make him hush, to stop her own reaction to that remarkable, caressing voice.

"You are most welcome."

The lilting Spanish accent gave the words a formal quality, but his eyes were much more intimate and personal as he continued, "But surely, it is I who should thank you . . . for saving my humble life. You are indeed a most beautiful angel of mercy."

She didn't think she'd ever felt less beautiful; her hair mussed and her face red and raw from the wind, but the sincerity in his eyes almost convinced her of the truth he spoke.

"No, no!" she denied. "I was lucky to have found you, that's all. Anyone else would have done the same, I assure you, Father."

He glanced over at his clerical frock and a shade dropped over his intense blue eyes, as though he might have forgotten for a minute who and what he was.

"Perhaps," he agreed, "but it was not someone else, was it?"

"What are you doing out here, alone and on foot

in such a storm?" She ignored his question and blurted out the question that had bothered her since she found him.

"It was not the smart thing to do, I admit." He had a rueful grin on his face.

"No," she answered slowly, noticing that he hadn't answered her question, either, and wondering even more about this mysterious priest, this priest who carried such important, official papers from none less than the president of Mexico himself.

"Not smart. Not smart at all."

To the contrary, she thought he looked quite intelligent and his clothes had the cut of someone of wealth.

"I was on my way to Santa Fe and I became lost. My horse threw me into that ravine and ran off."

His cryptic explanation didn't include mention of the men who had been chasing him, causing him to be more hasty and foolish than he otherwise would have been.

"Where do you come from?" She noticed his omission, but didn't comment on it, though it made her wonder.

"San Antonio," he answered. It was only a small evasion of the truth, but one that made him very uncomfortable.

"Oh. . . ." She had expected him to say from somewhere in Mexico and was surprised by his answer, but her face gave away none of her doubts.

"I must continue my journey right away. I have pressing business in Santa Fe." His voice was deep and urgent.

"I'm afraid you won't be able to find your way there. The snow has covered the road and any landmarks you would need to assist you."

The blizzard that had roared through the night she'd found him had blown itself out after dropping two feet of new snow. This was common of early New Mexico snowstorms, but it was still cold enough that the snow remained, piled in deep drifts.

"The roads will be impassable for some time yet," Cassie elaborated.

"Oh. . . ."

She saw his disappointment and could almost feel his desperate need to reach Santa Fe.

"How far is it?" he asked.

"Only five or six miles, but in this weather that might as well be a hundred."

"I am not accustomed to such storms."

An understatement of some magnitude, he thought.

"No. I understand San Antonio has mild winter weather."

"Uh . . . yes." He had hesitated only an instant before responding, but she noticed that pause.

She looked him over, surprised at how quickly he'd seemed to recover from his ordeal. His face was perfection from the fine arch of black brows to aristocratic high cheekbones, a finely shaped nose and those incredibly hypnotizing sapphire blue eyes filled with a warm sincerity and just a hint of rich, good humor.

A shock of glistening blue-black hair waved across his forehead and reached down to his collar in the back. She vividly remembered its silken texture, the way it had felt against her fingers. His skin was bronzed with the natural coloring of his people.

While she studied him, he strode to add a log to the fire. She took note of the understated elegance and potent masculinity in his movements.

"I made some soup."

She shook off her lethargy and sprang to her feet, anxious to be moving about, to be away from the magnetism of his presence.

He turned to her, flashing the brilliant smile that had been her undoing earlier. She almost dropped the pot filled with thick stew.

"Allow me."

He covered the distance between them in long strides, and eased the pot from her fingers, leaving a tingling in her grasp. He hung the stew on a hook over the fire, where it was soon bubbling, its tempting aroma filling the room.

Cassie took the ladle and two bowls from the shelf. Before she could dish up the stew, a loud knock sounded on the outer door.

The priest jumped, his eyes widening in alarm. Neither of them had heard a sound outside, and both were startled by the hammering on the door. They stood without moving, looking at each other. Clearly, she saw the alarm in his blue eyes and sensed the alert readiness in his stance. He suddenly appeared to be a dangerous man, a man who would do whatever it took to survive. She saw that he had no weapon, but found herself thinking that he was so strong and quick, he mightn't need one.

He seemed to make a decision and put his finger to his lips, eliciting her silence, his eyes entreating her to keep his secret. She shook her head, thoroughly confused, and opened her mouth to say something. He flew at her and with one arm around her shoulders, clamped a hand over her mouth. They stood thus, while the knocking continued, growing louder and more demanding. Spanish words were called out, and someone was entreating them to open the door.

"Whoever it is, don't tell them about me! Do you hear me?" he whispered. He released his hold on her mouth, grabbed her by the shoulders and shook her, harder than he intended, to emphasize the importance of his words.

At her frightened nod, he let her go, grabbed his coat, his collar and robe, and disappeared into the bedroom and out of her sight.

Chapter Three

Independence, Missouri. A Few Months Earlier.

"Independence, indeed!" muttered Sarah McPherson.

In her less than gentle estimation, this city surely did not live up to its proud name. Everything here was apparently done according to a rigid schedule and she'd not glimpsed a single sign of freedom since her arrival there the previous evening.

Frantically, she'd pursued every avenue she could, trying to arrange transportation West. But, even though it was only the middle of the summer, all of the traders were too afraid of early winter storms to set out for Santa Fe, New Mexico, at this time of year.

"But you don't understand," she patiently explained to the third wagon master she'd approached in as many hours. "I really have to leave here *now*. You see, my sister is out there all alone. I have to get to Santa Fe as quickly as possible, and persuade her to come back with me."

"You won't catch no caravan settin' out from these parts until late next winter, early spring, young woman. It's jest a sight too risky."

The old man spat a stream of tobacco juice and fervently wished he could have the pleasure of the attractive redhead's company on the two-month trip. She was just about the prettiest little thing he'd seen in all his sixty-two years. But even if she promised to share his blanket, he wouldn't journey across the Santa Fe Trail this late in the year. He'd been caught out there in a blizzard once and that was enough for him. He'd never admitted to a living soul how scared he'd been. They'd had to unload most of the goods intended for sale just to get across one of those bloomin' mountain passes and he'd barely made five hundred *reales* on that trip. He'd vowed never again. He was a fair weather merchant, and that was that!

"No, ma'am. You won't find a soul a'leavin' this here town for parts West this time o' year. Not now and not for many months."

Sarah couldn't believe her ears. She'd already traveled hundreds of treacherous, difficult miles to get here from Boston, and she wouldn't stop now because a few traders were afraid of a little snowstorm. She would find a way to get to Santa Fe, if she had to walk . . . or crawl . . . every step of the way!

The old man grinned at the indignant fire of youth that blazed in her green cat eyes and again bemoaned the fact that he wouldn't be the one to have the pleasure of her company.

"Only one man even crazy 'nough to *think* about goin' West right now."

"Who might that be?" she asked, her eyes lighting with renewed hope.

"Don' rightly know as you'd be wantin' to go all that way with an old coot the likes o' him, though."

"Who is it?"

She was not moving from the spot where she stood until he told her, and her squared shoulders confirmed her resolve.

"Emerson Smith. Folks 'round here call him 'Emo.' "

"Where is this Emerson Smith?"

"He used ta be a trader. He was one to go any-wheres, any time. Not now, though. Prob'ly down at the cantina. Spends a lot o' time down there these days, he does."

Sarah's heart accelerated. This was the closest she'd come to finding a guide. She made up her mind to hound this Mr. Smith like a dog would a bone until he agreed to take her.

"Which way?" She grimaced, noticing that she was even starting to talk in the same abbreviated style as the old man and others in this part of the country! The soft, lazy patterns of Boston were disappearing quickly. Then she grinned at herself, glad she hadn't lost her sense of humor.

"That-a-way. 'Bout three blocks."

With a brief word of thanks, she whirled and strode away from him. He didn't have a chance to tell her the cantina was no place for a lady. He doubted whether it would have done any good anyhow. This particular redhead put him in mind of a mule he'd once owned, stubbornest creature the world had ever seen. Still, he cast a longing glance at the provocative sway of her

49

rounded hips as she walked away and clamped his teeth down a little too tightly on the stump of a cigar in his mouth.

Sarah McPherson had the red hair and the pugnacious spirit of the Irish. She walked with a jaunty but determined step, unaccustomed as she was to being turned down. She'd left home against her parents' wishes and without any financial help.

Though they, too, longed to have her sister Cassie back home in Boston, they had been adamantly opposed to her making the dangerous trip alone. They had done everything they could to stop her, and finally their health had not been good enough to allow them to accompany her. So, in the end, she'd done just what she wanted to do, as she always did. Or, as she'd told herself, just what she had to do.

Now she was more than ready to begin the last leg of her trip. All she required was a guide, and she'd find one before this day was over!

"Cantina" was a delicate name for the dump the old man had directed her to. The dirt-floored hovel was dark and smoky, and the rancid smell of liquor mixed with unwashed bodies assaulted her nostrils as she neared the doorless entrance.

Her silhouette in the doorway quieted the boisterous sounds inside. Every eye turned to study the out-of-place intruder encroaching on their seedy, but predictable, world.

"What'll it be, miss?" snorted the bull-necked bartender. "Tea and crumpets?" He howled at his own crude humor and slammed a dirty glass down on the low plank that served as the bar. " 'Fraid we is fresh out, today!"

A loud guffaw burst out of an oversized mouth filled with a motley assortment of brown, misshapen teeth. Greasy strands of grayish-brown hair slithered over his forehead while his portly body shook with unkind mirth at her expense. Sarah thought him quite the ugliest man she'd ever laid eyes on. Surely no person in this establishment could be trusted to guide her over one thousand miles westward.

What could she be thinking? She turned to leave. Then stiffening her spine, she spun back around to face the hostile bartender and his few patrons. She had come this far, and she wasn't about to back out now.

Only two other people occupied the small room. One of those was an overweight middle-aged woman who spread over a stool, mounds of fat hanging off on every side.

The other person could barely be seen in the dim light, but he was grinning and seemed to be enjoying the confrontation.

Emerson Smith, in his younger days, had been a trapper and wagon master *extraordinaire*. Now, as he rolled on toward retirement and his sunset years, he could pick and choose the projects he wanted to do. For the most part, he chose *not* to do anything! His life was slow and completely without stress. He liked it that way. He had no family and no obligations except to keep his own stomach satisfied, and generally that was not a difficult task. The little cash he had stashed away for emergencies gave him an easy feeling of security.

A couple of straight whiskeys during the long after-noon had left him feeling no pain, but able to appreciate the delicate young beauty who stood defiantly in the door.

Observing the bartender's reaction to her and hers to him, Smith chuckled. "Come on in, miss. He really won't bite!" He motioned for her to come back to where he sat.

Sarah took a hesitant step inside, not wanting to get too far away from the door.

"Are you Mr. Smith?" she asked. "Emerson Smith?"

His bellowing laughter filled the corners of the room. "I 'spect I just might be at that. But most folks call me Emerson," he said with an exaggerated wink, pulling out a rough-hewn bench for her. "What's your business with an old codger like me?"

"Mr. Sm . . . er, Emerson," she began. "I have a desperate need to reach Santa Fe as soon as possible and everyone seems afraid to make such a journey. I was told you were the man for such a job."

He saw that she made no apologies for appealing to his sense of pride, and he knew he should get up and leave her without another word or a backward glance. But something nailed him to the splintery bench and he didn't move. It could have been the quiet desperation in her vivid green eyes; it could have been memories of another young redhead he'd loved so long ago. It could just have been because he knew beyond question that if anyone could get her there at this time of year, it was none other than himself.

He liked the musical quality of her voice and kept her talking, explaining her reasons and importuning him; even though he'd already made up his mind, almost from the very minute she'd sat down with him and made her straightforward request. Emerson Smith would take her to Santa Fe.

"Now, tell me about this sister of yours," he encouraged, leaning his chair back on two legs and chewing on a wooden stick.

"Her name is Cassie . . . Cassandra McPherson Layton. She is a widow now and all alone. She went to Santa Fe with her husband Captain Cameron Layton, who worked for the U.S. Government. But then he was killed. Cassie thinks he was murdered."

"How so?"

He'd heard of the much admired Army officer and the suspicious circumstances of his death. Gossip was cheap in New Mexico, and he made regular trips to Santa Fe. However, he wasn't nearly ready to tell this young woman what he knew.

"No one seems to know. Or at least no one will admit it if they do. There was an investigation and then the case was officially closed. But Cassie won't let things lie. She's very headstrong and determined not to leave Santa Fe until she learns the details. If it was a murder as she suspects, she will never leave until the person or persons responsible are brought to justice. I'm so afraid she's in over her head, perhaps even in great danger. She never said this in so many words, but there was something between the lines in her last letter, the one I received just before I left Boston. I have to get to her right away, before it's too late."

Emerson thought the young Miss McPherson could very possibly be right. The Western frontier was still uncivilized and no place for ladies, most particularly not for a lady alone. Her sister, the young widow, could very well be in over her head and in a whole passel of trouble.

"Well," he drawled, "if you're hell-bent on gettin' out there, I reckon I'd be the one to take you."

"I reckon you would!" she echoed with a big smile. Then she went on, her eyes wide, "You mean you will!?"

At his affirmative nod, she went on breathlessly, "When can we leave?"

"No sooner than tomorrow morning."

"That suits me! What will we need?"

"I'll take care of all that."

She pulled out a small roll of bills, and his bushy eyebrows shot up before he brushed her money aside.

"I've got purt-near everything we need already. You can take care of my fee after I get you safely to Santa Fe."

Relieved, she stuffed the bills back in her small bag and bestowed a brilliant smile on him.

"Best get a good night's sleep . . . in a bed. It'll be your last chance for a while."

"How long?"

"Best I can figure, 'bout sixty to sixty-five days, give or take, and if we're more than a little lucky."

Sarah passed a trembling hand over her forehead. She was already bone weary, and she hadn't even begun the hardest part of the trip. Her emotions showing clearly on her face, she wondered for the first time if she were really doing the right thing.

Maybe her parents had been right and she was on a

fool's errand, but she couldn't turn back now. Cassie would do the same for her, if she ever needed her sister's help. Sarah straightened her shoulders with new determination.

For a minute while he watched her, Emerson was sure she was ready to back out. He had been hopeful in fact that she would do just that. Then he'd be off the hook. Then, he saw the steely determination settle back into her green eyes. There'd be no talking her out of it now.

"I'll walk you back to your room," he offered.

"Thank you."

He left her on the front steps of the boardinghouse and ambled off down the road. He wouldn't get much sleep this night. They had to leave no later than sunrise; even then, the trip would be risky at best, deadly at worst. It was quite possible they would never make it.

Sarah's eyes were closed almost before her head hit the goose down pillow. She slept deeply and dreamlessly, awakening refreshed and feeling ready for the adventure, her spirits revived.

The sun edged its way up past the horizon, suffusing the rough and tumble town with a golden glow that made it seem more beautiful than it was, or perhaps ever had been. The air even felt fresh as she walked out onto the porch with her overstuffed satchel to find Emerson and his wagon waiting for her.

A couple of saddle horses were tied to the back of the wagon. She hoped they were for emergencies, and that she wouldn't actually be called on to ride one of the creatures. She'd never been in a saddle. Of course, she'd never ridden in any kind of contraption that vaguely resembled the one waiting for her now.

"Mornin', ma'am."

"Morning, Emerson. All ready?"

"Sure enough. Climb aboard, Miss Sarah."

As soon as she had done that with his help, he slapped the reins and the yoked animals pulled in unison.

The wagon rolled down the rutted roads, its iron wheels clanking noisily. They reached the edge of town in a very few minutes and were on their way.

Open prairies waited ahead, and at the end of the trail . . . Santa Fe and Cassie.

Chapter Four

Shocked at the abrupt and almost rough actions of the priest, Cassie stood motionless after he'd gone into her bedchamber, trying to steady her breathing, until another more impatient rattling shook the solid door.

"Abierto!" someone shouted, pounding firmly and repeatedly on the door.

"Just a minute," she called out, stalling, though she wasn't sure she knew why. Did she hesitate to give her patient enough time to hide, or because she dreaded finding out who was outside?

Nearing the door reluctantly, she asked, "Who is it?"

"Lieutenant Mendez of the governor's staff, ma'am. Please open up." He had switched to English now, which he spoke quite well.

The heavily accented Spanish voice rang out with the authority of his position. He would not be patient if she tarried any longer.

She knew the young lieutenant, newly arrived in Santa Fe, from a recent *baile* at the Governor's Palace. He'd seemed a nice enough young man and

57

he'd danced beautifully. She couldn't imagine what he might be doing so far out of town and in this weather. Had he been with the company of men she'd seen earlier, one of the men who had been pursuing the priest she'd rescued and taken into her home?

Opening the door, she looked out. Seeing that he was alone, she invited him in.

"You must be freezing. Would you like some coffee?" she asked, motioning him to the settee in front of the fire.

"Yes, *Señora*. That would be most welcome."

He seated himself gingerly and sat nervously, his hat in his hands, accepting the steaming cup she held out to him with thanks. While he sipped the warming brew, his eyes scanned the room, peering into every corner.

Cassie watched him studying her home. He was looking for some sign of the priest! Alarmed, she noticed the two bowls she'd set out on the table. Afraid he would see them too, if he hadn't already, she edged her way over to stand in front of the table. Making small talk all the while, she tried to keep his attention on her rather than on the table with the telling evidence.

With her hands behind her back, she felt for the bowls and wrapped her shaking fingers around one. Carefully settling it inside the other, she prayed its soft clink hadn't given her away.

What was she doing? Without a conscious thought about why she was doing it, she realized she was protecting the man in her bedchamber, certain now that he was the reason for the lieutenant's visit.

Feeling the same sympathy she'd felt for the fugitive fleeing the Spanish a few days before, she'd chosen sides with the priest against them in an instant; a decision based purely on instinct and not really a conscious one.

His heavy-handed treatment of her, that followed the knock on the door, had no doubt been brought on by a high level of stress and very real fear for his life. She thought that she would most likely have done the same under similar conditions.

"What brings you out here, Lieutenant?" she asked, even though she was sure she knew the answer to her question. She was only surprised that it had taken him so long to arrive at her door. Perhaps they hadn't located her house in the snowstorm and had come back later to seek it out.

"Please sit down, *Señora* Layton."

Her moving about seemed to make him nervous. He went on, "I hate to tell you this, but we have been in pursuit of a dangerous criminal. I was afraid he might have stumbled in here and troubled you. A woman alone is not always safe, you know. You should stay in town where you would have the protection of the government troops."

His lifted eyebrows and pointed words reflected the general feeling in town about her remaining alone in the house she'd shared with her husband before his death. She'd always felt more than secure and well able to take care of herself.

"I take care of myself quite well, Lieutenant." She echoed her thoughts, squaring her shoulders proudly, though she was amused to think what the lieutenant's reaction would be should he discover that there was a strange man in her bedchamber at this very moment.

"And, as you can very well see, no one has been 'troubling' me, nor would I ever allow a stranger in my home. I have my rifle for protection, and I know how to use it," she said pointedly.

"Yes, ma'am. I can see that," he agreed, but his eyes continued their surveillance of the cabin, lingering on the closed bedroom door, not certain he was ready to accept her story.

She was afraid he would demand to search the bedchamber, but apparently that would be going too far for the timid young officer. He stalled, sipping the dark fragrant brew and asking questions about what she might have heard or seen out of the ordinary.

"We passed very near here, and it is hard to believe that you heard nothing."

"Well, you must believe it, Lieutenant." She hoped she wasn't painting herself into a corner she might never be able to cross.

"You don't intend to stay out here for the entire winter, do you, *Señora?*"

"No, Lieutenant. I will return to Santa Fe as soon as the weather clears up. I wasn't expecting this storm when I rode out here a couple of days ago."

"None of us were. My men and I were caught off guard, as well. We would have caught him except for that damnable snow. Sorry, ma'am." He had been thinking out loud and apologized for the inadvertent curse.

"That is perfectly all right, Lieutenant. Who is this man, anyway?"

"I am not at liberty to say."

Actually, although he would never admit it to her, he didn't even know the man's name, only that he was to be stopped from reaching Santa Fe.

"I find it strange that you would chase a man through a blinding snowstorm whose name you don't even know, Lieutenant." She softened the direct words with a slight smile, intended to charm.

He seemed not to take offense, but smiled in response.

"I only follow orders."

"I see," she said, and she did.

The lieutenant's obsequious behavior around the general's staff since his arrival only a month or so earlier had been more than a little obvious. He was the kind to carry out orders without question, and he would constantly strive to please his superiors for his own advancement.

An ambitious man could be a dangerous man. Cassie had heard that somewhere and wisely made a mental note to avoid him whenever possible and to be careful what she said to him.

At the moment, she just wanted him out of her house as quickly as possible.

"Well, as you can see," she said, indicating with a motion of her hand, "there is no one here."

She stood up then, hoping he would take the hint, but he remained seated.

At last, when he could seem to find no reasonable excuse for extending his visit any longer, he stood up slowly.

"I'll be going, then, *Señora.*" With a nod in her direction, he settled his hat back on his head and squared his shoulders.

Her relieved sigh was inaudible or at least she hoped it was, as she took the coffee cup, accepted his thanks, and escorted him to the door.

"Good luck in apprehending your 'criminal,' Lieutenant."

"Thank you, *Señora.* Keep your door latched."

Was his voice cooler than it had been at first? Had he noticed the two bowls, her nervousness, the closed bedchamber door? Was he suspicious?

"I certainly will, Lieutenant Mendez," she answered.

But, she wondered, would she be locking a dangerous criminal inside?

She closed the door and glanced down to see a pair of men's boots in plain sight beside the door. Even if he'd missed seeing the two bowls, he must have seen these.

The lieutenant and his men would be back.

When she turned to face her guest who was emerging from the bedroom, her confusion must have shown clearly in her face.

She had no clear-cut answer for the question apparent in his eyes.

Why had she covered for him? Was it because he'd threatened her, or because she'd had problems with the Spanish herself and didn't see the need to help them? Or was she protecting him for some other reason?

"I really don't know," she said in answer to the question he hadn't asked. "I suppose you just don't look like a criminal." She smiled a tight smile, as dissatisfied with her answer as he was.

His face, however, was very serious. There was no answering smile on his lips. "I must thank you yet once more. And I apologize for my behavior earlier. It was inexcusable."

"No, that's not necessary. Please. I understand." He was so contrite, she rushed to reassure him.

"Oh yes, I most certainly do have to thank you." He swept her hand up in his and to his lips. "Dear lady," he murmured, as he gallantly kissed her hand. "Now you have saved my worthless life twice over. I shall be forever in your debt."

How could a courtly kiss on the hand, so routine among Spaniards, be such an intimate thing? Why did the tingle travel from her hand all the way down to her toes, when she should be angry with him for his behavior earlier when the knock had sounded at the door . . . and for drawing her into this impossible situation?

"I cannot allow my presence here to bring you any further trouble. The lieutenant will soon be back with his men."

Cruz knew the officer had not been alone, and he

was certain he would be back with reinforcements soon. He only had minutes, probably less than an hour to be gone before he would be apprehended. "I have to go."

The hard, dangerous glint in his eyes, now the silvery blue of mercury, revealed a side to this man that she'd only seen once before, when he'd given her shoulders that hard shake upon the lieutenant's arrival. He was in flight, but he would fight bitterly for his life.

"You'll never find your way alone," she countered.

Why had she said that? The last thing she wanted to do was to ride into Santa Fe with this man!

"Perhaps not. But I must try. I bring grave danger to you by remaining here, Mrs. Layton."

She was momentarily stunned at his use of her name, but then remembered that he must have overheard the Spanish officer use it. Though he knew her name, she had not yet heard his.

"Cruz Delgado," he replied before she had the opportunity to ask. He had an uncanny knack of reading her mind. She found it strange that the name he gave her was not the same as the one she had seen on the presidential papers.

"Well, Mr. Delgado . . . *Father!* I will go with you."

She couldn't believe she'd said that! But he would never find Santa Fe alone.

"I could never allow it." He headed for the door.

"Hold on! What horse do you intend to ride into town?"

He hesitated and his face reddened. "I shall have to use yours. I am sorry, but I will send it back for you as soon as I can."

"And in the meantime, what am I to eat? What am I to do out here all alone? That soup represents the last of my supplies. With no horse, I will be stranded here."

"But I must go. The lieutenant will be back with reinforcements. We will not have a chance against them."

Simultaneously, they realized that she was in as much peril as he, for having harbored him and for lying to Lieutenant Mendez to cover for him.

"Damn!" he muttered an unpriestly oath, looking long at her, studying her as though their lives depended on it.

This woman had found the courage to venture out in a blizzard and pull him bodily from a snowbank. Single-handedly, she'd saved his life, nursing him through the fever. She had covered for him with the officer and now she stubbornly insisted on accompanying him to Santa Fe. He had never known anyone quite like her.

Her soft honey-blond curls, big round brown eyes, petal-smooth skin and fragile body hid a backbone made of pure steel. She possessed a streak of toughness not to be expected in a woman; in her it was beguiling and not unfeminine.

He could not leave her out here, with no food and no horse, to face the soldiers alone and answer their questions about him.

Cruz wondered how she'd come to be way out here by herself, but he didn't question for a minute how she'd managed to make it on her own. He'd seen the kindness in her as well as her strength and understood that once more she was willingly putting her life on the line for him. Despite her protests to the contrary, he understood her real reason for insisting on going with him.

He fumed, impatient to be gone, uncomfortable with the decision to be made before he could leave. To be honest, he had to admit that he did need her. "Are you sure you can find the way in this storm?"

"Perfectly," she replied.

"Well, then," he said at last, "we should prepare to leave quickly. They will be back soon."

The men who were after him would have no qualms about killing the both of them, if they found them and realized she had been hiding him. But if he could reach Santa Fe, he had friends waiting there. His enemies could not afford to tip their hand publicly, and would not dare to make a scene. Besides, it was entirely possible they wouldn't be looking for a priest. His identity had remained a well-protected secret until now, or at least he hoped it had. The men chasing him had seen only his backside which was covered by his heavy coat, as he'd fled the band of Spaniards.

"We should eat the soup before we go. It could take a day and a half to reach Santa Fe and we will need the nourishment," she pointed out.

"No. I am afraid there is no time." His voice was

brisk now. He wasn't happy about the decision he'd made, but he would have been even less content to leave her behind. "We have to get away from here as quickly as we can. Bring some bread and the coffee. Nothing more."

"I have to see to the fire and store away the blankets, and—"

"Wait! There's no time for all that."

His voice rose in his anxiety to be leaving quickly. "Really, *Señora* Layton," he continued, forcing himself to speak in a calmer tone. "We have to go *now*. Get your coat on. I'll saddle the horse. Leave the fire. It will burn itself out, and it just might mislead the soldiers and lull them into thinking they have longer to make their move."

"All right, then," she agreed reluctantly, thinking him to be the bossiest man she'd ever known. Ordering her about like that, with not a word of thanks to her for offering once again to save his mangy life!

Cassie stuffed the few items they might need into her bag, but then stubbornly rinsed out their dishes and wiped them dry, putting them away neatly in the cupboard. She spread the covers carefully up over the bed, after stripping the linens.

He was shouting to her to hurry before she even started to put on her coat. Within minutes, he stood in the doorway, legs spread apart, hands on his hips and glowering at her.

After only a few minutes more, she was ready.

"Come on! We have to get moving." His words were clipped and the frown on his face forbidding, to say the least. Agitated at the delay, he pivoted and stalked out the door.

She followed in his wake, taking her time to close and fasten the door behind her. Looking up at her big bay gelding, she was taken aback by how they would be riding. She hadn't really thought about having to ride double with him, but there was only one horse, one saddle.

He vaulted into the saddle and leaned over to offer her his hand. With a strong pull, he hoisted her off the ground and onto the horse in back of him. Ever since she'd been forced to share his bed and had to deal with her own runaway emotions, she had carefully avoided touching him. Now she was pressed snugly against his back. He wrapped her arms tightly around his waist, and she was keenly aware of every inch where their bodies touched.

As they galloped away from her cabin, Cassie marveled at her own foolishness. She had vowed to stay as far away from him as possible. Now here she was, as close to him as one could get, considering the layers of clothing they wore.

She wriggled, trying to put more space between them, but he was having none of it. Even the horse got into the act; its jouncing, uneven gait threw her forward so that her breasts flattened against his broad back. She had to cling to him more tightly to keep from sliding to the ground. She grimaced. It was shaping up to be a very long ride into Santa Fe.

This stranger who had tumbled into her life was

overbearing and might even be a criminal. He was mysterious and perhaps dangerous. But, above all other things, he was a *priest*. He'd already brought confusion and upheaval into the pattern of her life. She just didn't need any more trouble. As soon as they arrived safely in Santa Fe, she would leave him and do her best not to cross his path again. That would be best for both of them.

But on the long and tedious trip, her mind would have plenty of opportunity to replay the events of the past few days and to question his motives as well as her own. What was he really doing here? Why were the governor's men on his trail? What could a priest have to hide, or to run away from?

One question led directly to the next, and it all added up to uncertainty. This remarkably handsome man had trouble written all over him. So what the devil was a sensible woman like Cassie McPherson Layton doing riding double with Cruz Delgado, a band of Spaniards on their trail, toward an uncertain welcome in Santa Fe?

"Divine intervention," she said, her words snatched away by the wind without his hearing. She chuckled, always quick to laugh at herself, and held on a little tighter. She wondered what she'd done to deserve all of this, how she'd managed to land squarely in the middle of a situation so impossible.

Though he rode silently, his back straight as a board, Cruz Delgado, too, fought his own personal battle with the sensations her nearness brought. She was so slender and fragile. He wondered how she had ever managed to get him through the blizzard back to her cabin. It must have taken an extreme amount of physical exertion and more than a little courage.

In the fog of his memory, he recalled little about that, except for her agitated voice exhorting him to hold on and help her. He had leaned on her, supporting as much of his own weight as he could, and he'd found her to be much stronger than he would have imagined, given her size.

Afterward, everything had gone completely black. But in the midst of that endless night, images and sensations came to mind that were very real.

A satiny length of leg next to his, the scent of camellias, a soft murmur of encouragement and the clasp of arms around his middle, a cry of ecstasy. . . . Cassie Layton did not seem the promiscuous type. He would have bet all he owned that she had been sleeping on the settee while he occupied her bedchamber.

So, what was going on in his head? Had he imagined the whole thing? He would ask her, but a little later when she was in a better mood. Now he looked around, judging the New Mexican landscape, on guard for the unexpected.

The trail they followed was harsh and brittle, like a frustrated old maid. How could he ever have found this country beautiful? Of course, snowcapped mountains still rose majestically on either side and in the distance up ahead, but all around them was barrenness, trees stripped of every leaf, drifts of deep snow and patches left bare by the winds. Huge boulders rose like sentinels along the trail. A man with a high-powered rifle could be waiting behind any one of them.

He'd never been so jumpy, so much on edge before. Was it due to his close call with the lieutenant's band of men? Or because he was now responsible for someone other than himself, for the beautiful woman riding with him?

He shook his head in an attempt to dispel the cobwebs of thought that crowded it and threatened to slow his reactions. Both their lives depended on him, and he knew it. That responsibility was the heaviest load he'd carried in a very long time.

All that would change, though, when he had her safely in Santa Fe and a comfortable distance away from him. He hunched his shoulders under his coat, and with his free hand shoved his hat down farther over his forehead.

She surely was not a comfortable distance away now, he mused with a scowl. She was much too close. Her soft breasts were snug against his back, and her arms wound around his waist, her hands woven together over his stomach. He had seen a bruise on one of those delicate hands and wondered if she'd gotten it in rescuing him. He owed her much . . . his very life, in fact.

No, there was not one comfortable thing about her nearness. Nor was it comfortable the way his arousal pressed tightly against the fabric of his pants. The beautiful widow was entirely too close and he knew it, but there was damned little he could do about it. He smiled. He couldn't very well tell her she would have to walk. After all, it was her horse they were both riding on.

Damned uncomfortable, though.

Cassie had felt him stiffen as though to pull away from her and she'd loosened her hold the slightest bit to accommodate him, though she didn't understand his withdrawal. If she relaxed her hold on him any more, however, she would be on her rear on the muddy trail. She needed the anchor he provided since the uneven gait of her horse and her position behind the saddle had combined to make her bottom numb and to make her legs feel like two sticks with twenty pound boots on each one.

From time to time, her head reeled from lack of sleep and the constant stress of the past few days. Once or twice, she had needed to lay her cheek against his shoulder to calm the whirling. It had worked remarkably well, but now he seemed not to welcome that intimacy.

So be it.

She straightened and arranged herself stiffly so that she was hardly touching him and tried to hug the horse's flanks with her uncooperative legs to keep herself from sliding off.

What was wrong with that man, anyway? He had

to be the strangest, the most standoffish man she'd ever known. Sometimes, he seemed concerned about her welfare and her feelings; other times his eyes had a faraway, haunted look. His face took on that harsh stillness that was warning enough to anyone with good sense to keep their distance.

With all of that, she was supposed to accept at face value that he was a priest? It was no easier for her to think of him that way than it had been that first night when she'd dragged him back to her cabin from the snowbank. In fact, it was much harder now. And if he were really a priest, he was that and a whole lot more . . . of that much she was certain.

The rocking motion of the horse beneath her and the solid back of the man in front of her were too much temptation. Her head bobbed a couple of times, her eyes drifted shut, and she could resist no longer. With a moan of protest, then one of pure pleasure, she lay her head against his shoulder, entwining her fingers tightly in front of him. She gave herself up to the deep sleep that had been tempting her for the last hour or more.

His back was firm and yet intriguingly soft where she lay her cheek against it. Though the rough material of his overcoat scratched her cheek lightly, she paid no attention, settling against him and drifting away into her dreams. She hadn't felt so good in a very long time.

Cruz was aware of her resisting their closeness and

then giving up, relaxing against his back. And then he became aware of something more.

The damned woman was asleep!

He hadn't a clue how she could sleep in their predicament. At first, he was angry and ready to shake her awake, knowing that he would need her direction before long. He was firmly convinced that they couldn't afford to be lost out here.

He went from cursing her to cursing himself when he recalled her nursing him through more than one pain-filled night and the sleep she must have lost, though she hadn't complained once. She had to be exhausted and it was a wonder she'd been able to make it even this far without sleep.

He felt like a cad.

A sudden burst of tenderness caught him off guard. Her small hands in his and her slight body leaning into him were nearly too much. She hadn't done anything to deserve the trouble he'd brought to her doorstep. Well, he would let her sleep as long as he could. He would just keep on following the trail, and they should be all right.

Her fingers loosened and she tilted precariously to one side as she fell into an even deeper sleep. With a muttered oath, he clasped both her hands in his and secured her more tightly so that she was in no further danger of sliding from the horse.

When Cassie awoke, her head felt like a wagon had run straight over it. Her thoughts were cloudy, and long minutes passed before she was oriented enough to know what was going on, to remember where she was and who she was with.

It all came back in a rush. The two of them were on the run, trying to get to Santa Fe before being overtaken by the lieutenant and his men. It was up to her to get them there. She blinked once and then again, trying to clear her vision, to see where they were.

Nothing looked familiar. This was not the right way! What had happened? She knew the answer. She'd gone to sleep like a fool, and he had gotten off the trail.

Alarmed, she looked about them and realized they had missed the fork in the trail that led directly into Santa Fe. How could she have gone to sleep like that, she berated herself.

"Stop!" She pulled his sleeve, nudging him in a not so gentle way to rein their mount off to the right through a stand of trees.

"What's wrong?" he asked.

"I don't know where we are." Her voice was soft, apologetic.

"Whoa," he commanded, his voice harsh.

"What do you mean, you don't know where we are? I thought you knew the way to town 'perfectly.' " He hadn't meant to be sarcastic with her, but they were dealing with a life and death situation. A mistake could mean the end for them both.

"Well, I do know the way, but I . . . I went to sleep. We have missed the fork in the road that leads to Santa Fe. We'll have to go back."

Forgetting his earlier, kinder thoughts, he cursed colorfully under his breath. "We cannot go back. The lieutenant's men are back there."

He spoke patiently, as though explaining to a child and his tone made her furious. She was not accustomed to being talked to in that way.

"If we don't go back, we'll never find Santa Fe and you did seem awfully anxious to get there." Her brown eyes snapped angrily at him. "And I would appreciate it if you didn't curse at me." How could she ever have thought his voice was wonderful?

"I was not talking to you." He spoke through gritted teeth, uncomfortable with the way she talked back to him.

"There doesn't seem to be anyone else here," she pointed out.

He started to say something else, but bit off the words before they were out of his mouth. "Let's go then."

"Do you think we might stretch our legs for a minute? I can't feel mine from the hip down," Cassie challenged.

To her surprise, he readily agreed, even looked a little chagrined for his unreasonable anger. But their time on the ground was very short, before he gave the order to mount up once more.

This time he settled her on the horse first, sitting in the saddle, and threw himself up behind her, reaching around her for the reins. She figured the only reason he'd gotten down as she asked was not out of sympathy for her discomfort, but because he wanted to change places with her, a feat that would be hard to accomplish without getting off the horse.

"You'll be able to see better this way," he said, speaking softly into her ear.

"I am capable of handling the reins myself," she told him.

"But then what would *I* do?" he asked softly, the rancor gone from his voice, as he flicked the reins, his arms snug on either side of her waist. He turned their mount back in the direction from which they had come.

She had some vivid thoughts about what he might do, but none was worth mentioning, so she placed her hands on the saddle horn and kept her mouth shut. She bit back the angry words, with only the greatest effort on her part.

"How far back is it?" he asked.

"Only about a mile or so, I think. I will find it this time. You don't have to worry."

"Good."

He was so smug, she wanted to smack him. Instead she gripped the pommel tighter, straining to see the snow-packed trail, doing her best to be sure they were going in the right direction.

If they could reach the fork in the road before the Spaniards, they still had a chance to reach Santa Fe ahead of them. She studied every tree and the snow-capped peaks on either side of them, hoping to reorient herself and lead them to safety. Nothing looked familiar though, and she was desperately afraid that they might be lost. Perhaps they weren't even on the trail any longer.

He yanked back on the reins and the horse slid to an abrupt stop. "Do you hear that?" he demanded.

She listened, but heard nothing, except his breath as it formed white puffs in the air and the snuffling and stamping of the horse. "No."

They remained thus, motionless; he listening alertly and she straining to hear what had disturbed him. Finally, she heard the jangle of spurs, the steadily pounding hoofbeats.

"It's them," she observed quietly.

"Yes, I'm afraid so, and they're not far away. We have to find a place to hide and stay out of sight until they've passed by." He spoke with urgency.

With a worried frown, he searched the terrain around them. Though there were scrub bushes, a few tall trees and misshapen clumps of boulders, he could not see any place where they could wait.

Although still not in sight, the Spaniards were rapidly approaching and would be upon them at any time.

Cassie put her hand over his on the reins and yanked to the left, off the trail, kneeing the horse at the same time.

"I know a place," she assured him over her shoulder. "There should be a cave not so very far from here."

The prospect of facing their pursuers had galvanized her memory. In an instant she had known exactly where they were, and remembered a place where they could hide, a place used for picnics in earlier, happier times.

The noises of the approaching band of Spaniards grew louder, masking the sound of the galloping bay beneath the two of them as they disappeared over a rise. Her eyes searched the rolling hills, squinting; then she spied the entrance to the cave which was only a few hundred yards up ahead of them. It was covered by brush, and Cassie had to find it by walking the last part of the distance on foot with him close behind, leading the horse.

"Here it is!" she called after a few minutes of looking and doubting whether she even had the right place. He moved up beside her and pulled the heaviest of the brush out of the way. He was as relieved as she to see the yawning mouth of the cavern open up in front of them.

Walking behind her, he led the horse inside and carefully pulled the brush back in front to hide the entrance. He hoped the Spaniards were not good trackers and would assume they had taken the fork toward town as Cassie had originally intended.

Would the soldiers see signs they might have left behind in their haste and spend some time searching the area? Or would they somehow discover that they hadn't taken the fork in the road and come back after them? They would be sitting ducks if they were discovered to be hiding in the cavern.

"I think we should stay here until dark. Can you find the way then?" he asked, his voice not holding a clue about his feelings.

"Yes, I'm sure I can." Her voice, too, was non-committal.

Now that she had her bearings, she knew exactly where they were. She was confident she would be able to find the way with no problems, although she'd never travelled it at night.

"All right."

He breathed a sigh of relief, unsaddled the horse, and settled back against the smooth stone wall of the oversized cavern, crossing his feet in front of him. Dim ribbons of gray light filtered in through the brush stacked up at the entrance, just enough that they could still see each other. He found himself studying her as she joined him on the ground, her legs pulled up under her.

Surprisingly, she looked none the worse for the wear, he thought. As a matter of fact, she was hauntingly beautiful in the dim light. He dragged his eyes off her and turned to the bag that held the supplies she had carefully packed for them. "How about something to eat? I'm starving."

"Me, too. I wish we had some of that hot soup."

His stomach rumbled as though in reply, and they both laughed. The laughter relieved the tension that had been building steadily between them since morning.

"Can we have a fire?" she asked.

"Yes, just a small one. We don't want to send up a smoke signal. The smoke from a small fire will get lost in the cavern. Even if they pass nearby, they won't see it or smell it."

He coaxed a reluctant and feeble fire from some scattered bits of kindling. They heated the coffee in the small pot she'd brought along. As soon as that was done, Cruz extinguished the fire. She broke the bread apart and they shared it and the warming brew.

In the light of early evening, they sat with their stomachs full, reasonably sure the soldiers were no longer nearby, but content to wait until dark to be sure before moving on.

"We'll be here for a while, so we may as well be as comfortable as possible."

The earlier strain between them had eased somewhat. They sat in comfortable silence until she felt the crazy need to know more about him.

"So, Father . . ." she began, eager to open up some topic of conversation.

"Please," he said, raising his hand, "I . . . it's Cruz. I haven't been a priest for very long and I still have not grown accustomed to the title. Do you think you could just call me Cruz?"

"I suppose so. If you're sure it's proper."

He smiled. "It's proper."

His rich, sultry voice made it sound anything but proper, she thought.

"Cruz," she said, testing the name on her lips and liking the sound of it. "And your family is in San Antonio?"

A look of pain darkened the silvery blue of his eyes. "No," he answered, speaking slowly. "My family . . . my mother, my father and my brother are all dead, for many years now."

"Oh! I am sorry. How sad for them and for you. Was there an accident?"

In her mind, Cassie pictured some kind of natural disaster that might have taken the lives of his family members, or perhaps a shipwreck.

"No," he said shortly. "It was no accident. They, like your husband, were murdered."

"Oh, my! But how did you know about Cameron?"

"You must have mentioned it in your discussion with the lieutenant," he explained quickly.

"Oh," she said, but wasn't at all sure she had. Still, she could think of no other way he might have known.

"It's hard to lose someone you love, isn't it?"

"Yes," he replied, and she felt the bitterness in him and the anger at whoever had killed his family.

"Were the murderers punished?" she queried.

"No. They were never found." His jaw hardened and twitched.

Maybe they weren't so very different after all.

"And your husband?" he asked. "His murderers still roam freely, too?"

"Yes," she admitted, "but I'm determined to change that. I'll see to it they're brought to justice no matter how long it takes."

"That could be a dangerous undertaking for a woman alone."

"Perhaps, but that doesn't matter to me. All that matters is clearing Cameron's name and bringing to trial the men who did that to him."

"Was your husband accused of something then?"

"They tried to say he had something to do with the disappearance of the army payroll intended for the soldiers and stolen artwork from the parish church. But Cameron would never have done that. Never!"

Her defense of her dead husband was admirable, but it could be misplaced loyalty, he thought. A wife was sometimes the last to know. Still, he had to admire her for it, even if such loyalty had been undeserved.

"Is that why you stayed on here after he died?"

"Yes, it's the main reason."

But not the only one, she realized as she thought of the children she taught each day, and the good friends she had in Santa Fe.

"Perhaps you should give up and go home to your family," he suggested mildly.

"No! I will never leave here until I know for sure what happened."

They were in similar circumstances, for he was committed to the very same thing.

Cassie was exhausted and her head reeled. She regretted initiating the conversation: she'd learned more than she wanted to about him, had been surprised by the pull on her heart when he spoke of the loss of his parents. She knew what loss felt like, but she didn't know or understand the bitterness or the hard edge that followed his loss.

The more she knew about him, the more of a mystery he became to her. Like an unread book, there was much more to him than he would allow anyone to see.

The strong coffee had made her feel much better for awhile, but now it all caught up with her again. She grew weary, her head was throbbing miserably, and her legs wobbled as she tried to stand. She shook her head, only to be sorry immediately when it pounded painfully and images swam before her eyes.

She slumped and would have crashed back down to the floor except for the strong arms that caught and lifted her to cushion her against him, keeping her from a collision with the unforgiving rock of the wall or the packed dirt underfoot.

Later, cool fingers brushed across her brow and massaged her temples as she rested in the comforting circle of his arms. She slept like a baby until he awakened her to tell her it was time they moved on.

· Watery daylight had given way to intermittent moonlight that cast weakened beams of light across the outstretched blackened arms of the trees. It was eerie and unsettling. Cassie was glad for the comfort of Cruz's presence, as just being with him made it less frightening.

The remainder of the trip passed in silence with no further sign of the Spaniards.

Chapter Five

Three centuries earlier, Don Pedro de Peralta had chosen a site along the Santa Fe River for the settlement that would come to be known as La Villa Real de Santa Fe . . . the Holy City.

Surrounded by the majestic snowcapped peaks of the Sangre de Cristo mountains, the area's winding river provided meadows and farmlands with ample water.

Mountain foothills furnished hunting and wood for fires and construction, as well as a shield from attackers. Santa Fe would become the northernmost outpost on the Camino Real, a one-thousand-mile passageway north from Mexico City.

The Palace of the Governors was begun in 1610 and a Spanish government set in place. In 1680, a bloody revolt of the Pueblo Indians brought about the exile of the Spanish colony. In 1693, the city was once more captured for Spain. Political unrest and espionage marked the next century.

In 1821, two events occurred that were to have a very marked effect on the city's future. Mexico declared its independence from Spain, and the Santa Fe

Trail opened commerce between New Mexico and the rapidly expanding United States. For the young nation, New Mexico became a vital link to its western coast and expansion in that direction. Santa Fe became a bustling center of commerce for the West.

Cruz and Cassie reached the outskirts of the city without any more sign of the Spaniards. He brought the horse to a stop; the cathedral spires and rooftops of Santa Fe visible up ahead, and turned to her.

"How far is it to your home from here?"

She pointed, indicating that it was not very far.

Cruz Delgado had ambivalent feelings about his arrival with the beautiful young widow in Santa Fe. He hadn't found the trip nor the company at all unpleasant and, in fact, regretted its end. However, he had to leave her, and the sooner the better.

Cassie Layton was lovely almost beyond belief, resourceful, and kind. He had no business dragging her into his increasing difficulties. On the ride in and during the time they'd spent hiding out in the cavern, he'd had plenty of time to question his motives and the wisdom of riding into town with her. But she had really given him no choice; she was one opinionated, stubborn woman.

He grinned, feeling her soft body pressed closely to his. He found himself wishing Santa Fe was on the other side of the distant mountain range or the other side of the country, so he'd have more time to get to know her, more time to be close to her.

Hold onto yourself, Delgado, he cautioned.

They rode on for a while in silence until they were within sight of her home.

Aloud he said, "Then I'll get off here."

"What!?" she asked, surprised at the abrupt remark.

"I will walk the rest of the way into town."

"But why? It's still a long way on foot."

"It is best if no one sees us together. And it would be best if you said nothing about having met me or helped me. I will watch you until you reach your door to be sure no one bothers you."

He was hiding something and in some kind of trouble, but there was little else she could do. She had gotten him safely to Santa Fe. She could not stop him from doing what he seemed so set on doing. Perhaps he was right and it would be best if they parted company now. He had not threatened her, but had asked for her help in keeping his secret.

"All right," she agreed reluctantly, as he slid to the ground.

Shocked, Cassie realized as she rode away from him, that he'd never said or done a single priestly thing: no blessings, no prayers, no sign of the cross, and no prayerbook. Devoid of clerical trappings, his eyes had nevertheless seemed to probe into her soul. Despite that, he was not nearly so strange a priest as Father Auguste, who drank like a fish and gambled away the church's offerings every Saturday night. She could find little to admire in that elderly priest. She had been forced into an association with him by her desire to help the children of the parish in their efforts to learn to speak English.

Faithfully and painstakingly, she instructed the children, drawing on her limited knowledge of the Spanish language and teaching them history, English, literature, and mathematics. The lessons had become her passion and a driving force in her life since Cameron's tragic death. She loved the children as if they were her own.

Her other goal and reason for living was to unravel the mystery behind her husband's murder and to bring the perpetrators to justice. Certainly, local officials showed no inclination to do anything about it. They seemed more than content to sweep the whole troublesome matter under the rug and forget all about it.

She was determined not to allow that to happen. Every door had been slammed in her face, though, and she'd gotten absolutely no cooperation. It was clear that if anything were to be done, it would be up to her. She was making no plans to leave Santa Fe . . . not now, perhaps never.

Cruz stood ankle deep in the wet snow, his blue eyes trained on her slender, straight back as she rode away from him. He'd practically ordered her to do just that; he had given her no choice in the matter this time. And even though her big eyes had softly questioned his motives and perhaps even his sanity, she'd left him there.

The first part of his mission was now accomplished. He'd arrived in Santa Fe, in one piece and still breathing, though his ribs ached like the dickens and he was more than a little unsteady on his feet.

What he couldn't understand was the sudden,

empty longing in his heart. Revenge and the ideals of a just cause had driven him through the impossible odds of arriving safely in Santa Fe, with the Governor's men hot on his trail. He had tortured himself with vivid memories of the violent and tragic deaths of his family. These fatal visions had spurred him on: The horror of the unprovoked ambush . . . flashes of fire in the dark of midnight . . . the deafening roar of heavy-duty artillery . . . screams of panic . . . blood everywhere . . . the lifeless eyes of his father and brother.

Though his mother lived on for a little time after that, she had never recovered from the trauma. All the love he'd ever had was taken from him in that one horrible night. He would never forget and never forgive. And the angry, harsh face he'd seen for years only in his nightmares had recently been seen in person leaving Mexico City, the ugly evil face of the man with one finger missing.

That man was reportedly now in Santa Fe, in a position of influence in the local government. Cruz would make him pay, for all the dreams he'd killed, for all the destruction to one family that he'd caused in that long night.

He would have come to New Mexico regardless once he knew where that loathsome man was, but the mission he'd been assigned by the Mexican ruler had given him a cover and another just cause added to his own personal need for revenge. He had adopted the name Cruz Delgado, for that man would be sure to recognize his true family name. Now he would not rest until he'd run the beast to ground and finished him off, made him pay for all the grief he'd brought the Reyes family.

Greed. For that reason alone, he had seized the family's lands and holdings. *Greed.* It had been no more than that. For that alone he'd taken the lives of three good, innocent people. He had also given one small lad enough nightmares to last a lifetime.

But for the past forty-eight hours, a beautiful angel of mercy with soft, healing hands and warm, womanly eyes had almost driven those thoughts from his mind. Her presence had chased dark memories away, memories he was not prepared to relinquish, memories he dragged out and hugged to himself now like a well loved quilt.

He cursed his weakness and wondered how a woman who'd been a complete stranger to him only a few days before could have wormed her way into his consciousness so thoroughly in such a short time. He must find a way to deal with such thoughts. They were not permissible. He would put them aside.

Dragging his eyes away from her, as she grew smaller in the distance, he forced himself to look elsewhere. Out of sight, out of mind. In the same way he'd put her on a path steadily moving away from him, so must he deal with these renegade thoughts of her. He must not see her again. Whatever it took, he would work to ensure that their paths never crossed again and to keep himself as far away from her as possible.

He had a job to do in Santa Fe and nothing would stop him. *No one. Nothing.*

As he trudged through the damp, clinging snow, he

repeated this litany over and over, as though by saying it, he could make it so. Those two words summed up his life, didn't they? He had no one. Nothing. All that he loved had been taken from him. Even the inheritance, the wealth he'd been promised since his early childhood in Spain, had been snatched from him.

Fair enough. He could start over. But, first, the man who had done this to him and his family would pay. If, in the process, he could assuage some of his own powerful feelings of guilt, so much the better. Those who knew him insisted none of it had been his fault. After all, he'd only been a boy. But he could not make himself believe it. Surely, he could have done something to prevent the tragedy. He should have done something. Maybe it wasn't too late to right at least some of the wrong that had been done.

One fact remained: Antonio de la Cruz Santiago Reyes would never allow an innocent person to be hurt by his actions again. The widow Layton was as innocent as she was good and kind, sweet, gentle and beautiful. . . . His mind wandered off on that tangent again.

Control yourself, he cautioned, leery of dead ends and trackless seas, tempests and turbulence that could drive him off course. In a short time, this young widow had moved him in ways he'd never have thought possible.

More than likely, she had already dismissed him from her thoughts as a good deed that was well done. The flare of interest he'd seen in her eyes had been effectively doused by the reality of the clerical frock he wore.

A steady stream of colorful oaths now punctuated his measured tread. His breath snatched away by the frigid air, he stopped and grinned widely. For some reason, he felt a bit better after the outburst and set his sights on the town up ahead.

First, he must find a room and then locate Evan Hamilton who should have been in Santa Fe for several days, waiting for him. The American officer was a good friend, and Cruz was anxious to see him and work with him again. It had been several years.

In another part of town, a young officer addressed his superior, clicking his heels together in proper military fashion.

"Your excellency."

"Lieutenant."

The voice was deep and commanding and brought an unwelcome shiver to the erect spine of the nervous lieutenant, who had less than acceptable news to report.

"Reporting as requested, sir. Our small party found the trail of the emissary from Mexico. We almost had him, but then the storm came. We lost him, sir, but it is unlikely that he survived. No one could live without shelter in such weather."

"Were there not homesteads in the area?" The commandant's black eyebrows raised in question and the frown on his swarthy features deepened.

"We checked with the widow Layton whose house lay very near the place we last saw him. She seemed quite safe and very much alone."

He would not tell his superior about the two bowls on the table, or the pair of men's boots he'd noticed near the door. Nor would he mention the fact that when he rode back with his men to check, there'd been no one at the small cabin, though a fire still burned in the fireplace. He'd only recently been promoted and didn't want to jeopardize his position, or perhaps even his life, for his commander could be a vindictive and sometimes violent man.

"If he still lives, he will now be in Santa Fe, no doubt," the officer growled. "Keep your eyes and ears open and enlist the services of the venerable Father Auguste."

The younger man smiled at that. "Father Auguste knows everyone and everything in Santa Fe. A stranger asking questions will be easily located, your eminence."

"Yes, even so. Keep an eye out for just such a one and we shall have our man. The Americans would very much like to get their hands on him first. They constantly look for anything to stir up trouble." He slapped his hand on the smooth, varnished oak of his desk, effectively ending the tense interview, much to the lieutenant's relief.

Cassie was tormented by ghosts from the past every time she entered the stucco house she and Cameron had built a few blocks off the plaza in Santa Fe, yet she loved it and was always glad to return to it.

The house exemplified the Santa Fe style, built of adobe bricks with pine beams holding up the flat roof, sheets of mica used for windows and leather hinges for fastenings. Strings of dried red peppers still decorated the front door, though they were very dry by now. A small corral with stake fences in back made a temporary shelter for her horse since the weather had improved somewhat. She would take the gentle bay to the town stable in the morning.

After she had carefully tended to the animal, she stomped the mud off her high-topped leather boots and hesitated before entering the house that held so many bittersweet memories of the past. Cameron was gone and she had to go on . . . alone.

That fact was all too plain and obvious. Yet being alone felt so much more barren now, and the hurt she'd been holding at bay swamped her, burying her under layers of lethargy and fear. Had her brief encounter with the intriguing but untouchable priest done this to her? She'd tried so hard to keep a distance between them, to maintain the appropriate attitude toward a man of his position, but she'd failed miserably and completely.

Unfastening the latch, she stepped inside, leaving the door ajar for the moonlight reflecting off the snow. She shuddered. The interior of the house was very dark and as still and quiet as a crypt.

Once more, she shivered and wondered what was wrong with her. This had been her home, a place of love and laughter, but tonight it felt unfamiliar and almost hostile. She was suddenly very uneasy and afraid.

Hurriedly, but efficiently, she started a fire using the neatly stacked wood ready and waiting in the corner fireplace. The warming glow it brought was comforting and she closed and bolted the door, feeling a bit better.

She'd been unnerved by the lieutenant's visit and knew she hadn't heard the last of it from the governor's office. Even before the unexpected arrival of the priest, she'd had an uneasy relationship with the political powers in Santa Fe. They didn't like her constant attempts to find out more about the death of her husband. They had told her in no uncertain terms, on more than one occasion, to "let sleeping dogs lie."

They hadn't counted on her stubborn intractability. Lately, their attitudes had taken a gradual turn from impatient aloofness to something more sinister. She worried about their reactions should she really uncover something substantial in her investigations.

She lit the brass candlesticks on the wall and slipped out of her heavy coat. She needed rest to heal her tired and battered soul. But a deeper and more encompassing need was to find her husband's murderers, so that she could put the past behind her once and for all.

Her rumpled clothing replaced by a fuzzy robe and slippers, she curled into a tiny ball in the curved end of the settee. Her eyes intently watched the rosy patterns and occasional bright sparks from the fireplace. She intended to sit there for only a few minutes before retiring to her bedchamber, but the hectic pace of her life over the past few days again caught up with her. She dozed.

A sound brought her awake instantly. Was it her horse stomping nervously in the corral out back? Or, had it been a footstep outside the room's only window?

Almost without breathing and trying not to make a sound, she listened, plagued by the fear and the near certainty that someone was out there. Someone had been watching her as she slept. She shivered, pulling her robe around herself more tightly, holding her arms close to her sides.

Legs trembling, she forced herself to her feet and reached for the omnipresent rifle in its rack over the fireplace. Its cold weight felt foreign to her, but she cradled it in her arms, checking its chambers to be sure it was loaded.

A shuffling of feet outside brought life and reality to her fears. There *was* someone out there! But, apparently, he watched as she grabbed for the gun and was now making a hasty and rather noisy retreat.

When she summoned the courage to look out, she could see nothing at all. She dropped the curtain over the window and held her weapon tightly while the sounds of running steps became more distant and at last were stilled completely. Whoever had been there was gone, vanished into the night.

Even though she felt sure he wouldn't return this night, she still spent the remainder of it sitting upright on the settee. Her pillow was positioned on the carved mahogany of the armrest; the comforting weight of the loaded gun nestled on her lap.

The morning brought her scratchy eyes, tired from lack of sleep, and stiff, complaining muscles. How she'd longed for a good night's sleep in the feather mattress Cameron had bought them before they were wed, but it had remained vacant and unruffled through the long night. The sight of it now brought back a heavy measure of pain mixed with intense longing.

"Oh, Cameron," she whispered, a tear slipping from beneath long lashes and sliding down her cheek. "I need you so."

Cassie was not a woman who could happily spend her life without a man. Though Cameron's inheritance from his wealthy family and his small military pension took care of her financial needs, she needed the companionship and the emotional support. Yes, she also needed and longed for the loving, too. She'd been fooling herself into believing anything else.

It had been the mysterious priest who'd brought back all these buried and thoroughly unwelcome longings. A *priest*, for Heaven's sake! she rebuked herself. How could she have such unholy longings for a man of the cloth?

She smiled. It was certainly unfair of such a man to be so appealingly good-looking. But it hadn't been only his looks, there had been something else. Something indefinable. Something elusive. She'd seen in him an unusual gentleness and a concern for her well-being.

Yet he'd been on the run, obviously hiding something and hiding from somebody. This priest was in a lot of trouble, and he hadn't wanted her involved in it. He had carefully pulled himself apart from her once they'd neared the outskirts of town. That obvious need to protect her had tugged at her heart in an unexpected way. There was more to this man than was apparent on the surface.

Cassie had had the feeling, too, that he would fight to the death for what he believed. Cruz Delgado was an unusual man, if indeed that was even his name. He was an intriguing man with many secrets.

More than anything else, Cassie wanted to see him again. She longed to know him better, and she even found herself wanting to help him. Her nurturing instincts were fully aroused by him. Too bad those were not the only instincts he'd aroused. She chuckled.

It was not like her to allow her mind such freedoms. She had always been carefully proper. Even in her thoughts, she was decorous and respectable to the extreme. Boring. Respectable. *Prim,* even.

Once more, she chuckled, more than a little surprised at the changes in her over the past few days.

Cassie dismissed her fears of the night before, unwilling to put any credence in strange noises in the night and certain there had to be a logical explanation for what she'd heard. In the bright, pleasant sunshine of a New Mexico winter morning, it seemed more than a little foolish to linger over such thoughts. She was not about to let them mar her day.

She needed friendship and companionship. She knew right away who she had to visit. Lucita! Santa Fe had its share of mavericks, eccentrics and mercenaries, along with a respectable collection of politicians and priests. It also boasted a few seers or fortune-tellers who, for a few *dinero,* would read the cards or palms, and predict future events.

Though Cassie put little stock in such doings, her

best friend, Lucita Chavez, made her living that way. Luci was a loner. Her family had been killed in an Indian uprising, along with a number of other Spanish settlers in the area around Santa Fe when she was a young woman. She had chosen her life-style then and had not altered it since. Like most Spanish women in Santa Fe, she was granted a degree of independence. If people found it strange that she lived alone, they never said so openly.

Lucita was warm, sincere, and a loyal and trusted friend, though her humor sometimes tended toward the bawdy and she continually gave Cassie insight into her future whether she wanted it or not.

After the restless and disturbing night, Cassie naturally found herself at her friend's *casa*, which was only a few blocks away.

"Cassie! Where have you been?" Lucita greeted her. Without giving Cassie a chance to answer, Luci went on, "You left town without letting me know. I've been worried sick. I asked around. No one knew where you were. Then I checked and found out your horse was gone and I guessed you had ridden out to the cabin. A foolish thing to do alone and with a storm coming!"

It wouldn't do a bit of good to point out to Luci that there'd been no sign of the storm when she rode out of town. Her friend never slowed down long enough to listen to reason. Once she got started, she was like a runaway freight train.

Lucita Chavez was beautiful with her midnight black eyes, ebony hair, and dusky skin. She was a little plump, but her curves were womanly and sensuous. The soldiers were always making passes at her, though she brushed them off without a second thought, usually with a chuckle or a risqué comment.

"Oh well, I guess it doesn't really matter, now that you're back safely, does it? No, it's all over and you're here! But look at you. You are much too thin and you look tired. Where did you get those awful dark circles under your eyes? Of course, you haven't been sleeping well since Cameron died, have you?"

Cassie decided not to worry her friend by telling her of the events of the preceding night. There was nothing Luci could do about it. It would only worry her and fuel further conversational fires.

"Well?"

Lucita stood with her hands on her hips, silent, waiting for an answer. Cassie honestly had no idea which question to answer from the stream of dialogue.

"Oh, Luci!" she cried, hugging her friend to her. "It's so good to see you. I've missed you terribly."

And she truly had.

Luci held her out at arm's length. Her eyes now dreamy, with that far away look Cassie knew so well, she began to speak. "I see the arrival of someone dear to you, someone you do not expect."

The enigmatic priest? . . . Cassie had certainly never expected him, but neither was he dear to her.

More often than not, though, Lucita might be half right in a prediction. It was sometimes uncanny. Lucita winked at her. "Could this 'guest' be tall, dark, and handsome, no?"

For the past couple of months, Lucita had lobbied on behalf of several available young men in Santa Fe, hopeful of drawing Cassie out of her widow's garments and away from her obsessive and dangerous quest to find her husband's murderer.

"No such luck," Cassie replied with a grin. "Probably only creditors."

"No, you are far too beautiful, my friend. The right man is just around the next bend in the road. When you find a way to let go of the past, then you will find your future."

Once more, Cassie's mind flew to the charming and handsome priest. Should she tell her friend of her recent adventures? No, perhaps later. He had requested her silence, and she'd give him that for now.

Would she see the mysterious Cruz Delgado again? Santa Fe was too small a town for him to disappear completely. They were almost certain to meet, a circumstance she both dreaded and longed for. Much against her better judgment, she'd thought of little else since she'd left him at the outskirts of town.

"A dark, tall, handsome man," her friend repeated, as though reading her mind, "will enter your life. He will bring you love, but much trouble and much danger." Lucita's brow clouded with worry at the words she'd uttered and she wished she could snatch them back. Trying to soften the prediction, she went on, "But is there not always trouble accompanying love? Is it not the very danger in itself that makes the love more exciting?"

Cassie considered that the part about trouble was true; the part about love was impossible!

"Aha!" Lucita was watching her much too closely. "There *is* such a man, is there not, Cassie?"

"I can't talk about it now, Luci."

"Aha!"

"Will you *quit* saying 'Aha!'?"

"Mmmhmm."

"That's just as bad!" Cassie laughed.

"Beware, my friend. Before the morning comes, there will be a long and starless night filled with many tempests and storms."

Cassie really hated it when Lucita talked in platitudes and paradoxes. She felt like making the childish gesture of putting her hands over her ears.

"Come to the plaza with me. I have some shopping to do," Cassie suggested, having had her fill of Luci's predictions and warnings.

A raised eyebrow, then a hearty nod of her head met Cassie's suggestion. Luci could always be persuaded to go shopping. It was one of the true passions of her life.

"As soon as my next customer, an important client of mine, leaves," the young Spanish woman promised.

Even as she spoke, the outside bell rang, announcing the arrival of her next client.

"Wait for me in there." Lucita nodded her head toward the kitchen. "This will not take long. Or perhaps, you would like to listen?"

A wave of her hand indicated another room, a door through which Cassie had never been before.

"I believe I'll have a cup of coffee and wait for you in the kitchen." She couldn't imagine eavesdropping on one of her friend's sessions.

"Don't be long," she urged as Lucita went to open the door for her next appointment. A masculine voice was met by Lucita's higher pitched words of welcome.

After that, Cassie heard only murmured two-sided conversation, with occasional raised voices.

Cassie shook her head, constantly amazed at her friend's chosen profession. She couldn't understand why so many wealthy and influential Santa Fe residents paid good money for prophecies that might or might not come true. She chuckled again, thinking how close Lucita had come to predicting the priest's arrival into her life. It had been too close for comfort, entirely too close.

The session was over in less than a half hour, and they left soon after for the plaza. Lucita seemed nervous and distracted as they made their way toward town.

"Did something happen in your session that has worried you?" Cassie asked, wondering again about the "important client" her friend had seen earlier.

"No, nothing really."

Cassie was not surprised at the noncommittal answer; her friend rarely discussed her business or her clients. She had been shocked when Lucita offered to allow her to listen in on the session that morning. Had she been worried then?

Cassie almost wished she had agreed to listen since her friend seemed so nervous and reluctant to discuss it now. She was too sensitive to Lucita's feelings to push it, though. So Cassie did the next best thing, she changed the subject in an attempt to get her mind off it.

"I'd like a nice, warm shawl," she remarked, linking her arm with Lucita's. "Maybe red and purple, or do you think black and green?"

"Sounds warm, all right!" Lucita answered with a chuckle, the mood broken. "Personally, I could use a nice, warm drink!"

"Me, too. First things first. We'll stop at the hotel."

Warmed by the drink and the companionship, they once more trod the cleared walkways bordering the central plaza, intrigued by the bustling crowds, the exotic aromas and the raucous sounds, all common at that spot. The two young women enjoyed themselves immensely, speaking to acquaintances, gossiping and laughing as they strolled the plaza's perimeter, all cares forgotten for the moment.

As the day wore on toward the noon hour, clouds skittered away toward the distant mountains, replaced by a brilliant sunshine that reflected off the pristine banks of snow piled to the sides of the walks and roads. Unexpectedly, it had become a gorgeous winter day. Cassie breathed the crisp air, impossibly glad to be alive, her problems and worries eased by the grandeur of nature's beauty.

Lucita's body tensed at the same time that Cassie caught sight of the one man in Santa Fe who was capable of ruining her beautiful day. Juan Perego!

Oblivious to their distaste for him, the Spaniard, dressed in his official uniform as one of the governor's trusted advisors, hurried toward them. His wide smile revealed very white, widely spaced teeth that seemed too big for his mouth. His black mustache was manicured to perfection, and his black hair slicked back from a slanted forehead. His ears flared out at right angles to his head, becoming more obvious when he doffed his hat to bow in a courtly fashion before them.

This man had the annoying habit of standing entirely too close when he spoke with someone. Cassie felt his fetid breath before she took a couple of cautious steps back.

"Good morning, ladies."

Even though he addressed them both, his eyes never moved from Cassie's face. Without blinking, he stared at her and the smile that crawled across his face caused her to shiver in revulsion. He noticed, but attributed her reaction to the weather.

"A little cold for my taste, though," he went on.

Cassie nodded, reluctant to pursue the conversation, anxious to get away from the distasteful man.

"It's been some time since I have seen you in town," he remarked.

"Yes." She was determined not to encourage him. His nearness made her feel as though she were suffocating. But then she forced herself to remember his importance to her in the search for her husband's murderers. He had the ear of the government and much power in Santa Fe. "I've been busy and the weather—"

"Of course, I understand, but our town has suffered from your absence at our social events. I hope you plan to attend the governor's dinner party tomorrow evening?"

"No, I don't think so. I only wish to speak to the governor himself at the first opportunity."

"Perhaps I can help, in that event. If you would be so kind as to pay me a visit in my office tomorrow afternoon?"

Often, it was difficult to arrange an appointment

with the chief magistrate. It couldn't hurt to have one of his staff in her corner.

"That would be very much appreciated." She tried to smile, but was afraid that it became more of a grimace. Still, this man was much too thick-skinned and self-centered to notice.

"Anything for such a lovely lady," he replied with a lecherous grin. "If you could tell me something of your business with the governor, perhaps?"

"I am sorry, but I think I should first take it up with him, though I appreciate your concern."

The man frowned and they could see that he was unhappy not to have been taken into her confidence.

Lucita took her elbow and tried to steer the two of them around the enormous man who effectively blocked their path with his legs wide apart.

"We have shopping to do, so if you will excuse us . . ." Luci began.

The big man swung his head in her direction, black eyes boring into her. "I'm sure there remains much daylight for your 'shopping excursion' as soon as Mrs. Layton and I have completed our discussion."

The words were sharp, pointed, and spit out in her direction without apology. His attitude showed that he felt no need to be polite to this peasant, friend of the widow, or not.

"Oh, I do think we have said everything that needs to be said," Cassie said sharply, stepping around him and holding Lucita's arm firmly so she wouldn't do anything foolish. Lucita hated the Spanish official perhaps more than Cassie did, and only tolerated him from a safe distance.

"Come on, Luci," she urged, even as the fortune-teller glared back over her shoulder, about to issue a curse, or something worse in his direction. "Good day, sir, and once again, your help will be appreciated."

Juan Perego stuffed his hat back on his head and watched while they walked away from him, his eyes on the firm, round bottom of the widow Layton. He did not look in the direction of the priest who was standing in the shadows.

Cruz had witnessed the encounter and his fists were tightly clenched. He had watched, hearing bits of the tense conversation and longing to intervene. He itched to knock the huge man onto his fat rear end right in the middle of the street. Only the need to maintain his priestly decorum and to remain unnoticed had prevented his doing just that. He breathed a sigh of relief when the two ladies walked away without further incident. If the man had overtly threatened them, he would not have been able to curb himself. He would have recklessly put his mission in grave danger.

He slipped back into the depths of the alleyway, cursing softly under his breath, desperately wanting to help her. If he could only use them, his connections with the government might be of assistance. That was most certainly impossible, at least for now. Still, he would keep an eye on her and try to protect her from the attentions of men like that pompous Spaniard.

Chapter Six

More than a week had passed since Cassie had been to the church to work with the children. Normally, she met with them several times a week. She could hardly wait to get back to them after her extended trip out to the cabin. Since there were no free public schools yet in Santa Fe, the children had only the mission to depend on for their education. Many of their parents were beginning to see the need for more than this. When Cassie volunteered to supplement their usual training with instruction in English, mathematics, and the fine arts, they gladly accepted. The small group was comprised of enthusiastic students, and she felt they gave her much more than she could ever give them.

More than one of the youngsters had stolen away pieces of her heart, bit by bit. Manuelito . . . Carmelita . . . Josephina . . . she ran a list of the well-known names through her mind, even as she quickened her steps toward the church. She longed to see them again and to begin their lessons.

Another name came to mind that did not bring her

pleasure . . . Father Auguste. He was as crude and un-righteous as a priest could be. There'd been times when she'd felt him staring at her in a decidedly unpleasant way. He was, however, a necessary evil.

If she wanted to be allowed to continue working with the children, she had to associate with him and at least be civil to him. He could cause her a lot of trouble and she was acutely aware of that. She'd kept her distance as much as possible.

"*Señora* Layton!"

A small, excited voice drew her attention from her troubled thoughts to a nearby *casa*. A dark-haired, big-eyed young boy propelled himself out of the gate and straight into her outstretched arms.

"Manuelito!" she exclaimed. "How good it is to see you. I've missed you so."

"I . . . have . . . missed . . . you, also," he managed, speaking slowly and stuttering over the still unfamiliar English. He was rightfully proud of himself for his ef-forts, his pleasure evidenced by his wide smile.

"You've been practicing," she said, smiling in encour-agement and hugging him tightly.

He shook his head up and down, even while he clung to her, repeating his much practiced sentence.

"I . . . have . . . missed you, *Señora*."

He backed away and stood looking up at her with ad-oration clear on his dark-skinned face.

"Are you ready to go to the church for our lessons?"

She motioned, indicating that he could walk along with her. At another affirmative nod, she went on, "Let's stop for Carmelita, too, shall we?"

"*Sí*. Yes!" he said, correcting himself. "Carmelita!"

She took his small hand in hers and they continued

to walk toward the large church that towered in front of them.

With much the same flurry of affection and excitement, Carmelita joined them, clutching her prized possession, a small bag tied with a blue ribbon. Cassie held one of their small hands in each of hers, and they laughed and talked as they walked toward the church.

The threesome arrived at the front portico of the church where several other bright-eyed children awaited them. Word traveled fast in the community and Cassie was not surprised to see them all there, waiting for her. They had heard that she was back in town and ready to resume their regular lessons.

Her class had grown to seven, sometimes eight, children now. She knew that several other families were considering allowing their youngsters to become a part of the group. She wished to help them all, but there was still some resistance to Americans and their ways in some quarters. It was hard to convince many of these people that she really wanted to be of service to them.

Cassie herded the children into their allotted schoolroom, bare except for the long wooden bench for the children, a chair for her and a plank shelf to hold their few supplies. These consisted of pewter mugs, a small slate and precious bits of chalk and charcoal, a few of her own books, and a priceless set of *McGuffey's Readers* from which the children learned and practiced their ABCs.

Under the shelf were hooks where they hung their coats on cold days. Beneath that, their small lunch parcels sat in a neat row on the floor.

Cassie began their instructions each time they met. Then, the older ones would take over and help the younger ones. They were bright children and memorized quickly. Best of all, they were so willing; they brought their own special sunshine into her life when she was with them.

Today, they began their lessons by each reading a paragraph and then passing the reader on to the next impatient set of hands. Every half hour or so, they rotated seats so each could be near the fat-bellied black stove for a time, since it didn't heat the entire room.

Later, they would work on penmanship and the little ones would copy and practice their numbers. On days when it was fair enough, they went outdoors for rowdy games of tag and tug-of-war. Their happy giggles would fill the somber yard of the church building.

Today, the effects of the storm lingered in a chill wind and muddy ground, so they remained inside for their lesson break. Cassie smiled as she watched Carmelita carefully untie the blue ribbon and take her penny doll from the tiny bag she always carried with her. Made of china with moveable arms and legs, black hair and black eyes, and a tiny red mouth, it was so dear to her that the child was never without it. Polite and loving, Carmelita was everything Cassie could ever think to ask for in a child of her own. She was sorry that she and Cameron had never had a child who could fill the lonely void his death had left in the center of her life.

"How is little Maria today?" she asked softly, pointing to the doll. Cassie sat beside the child on the bench while the others played in a huddle on the floor close to the stove.

"Oh . . . she is . . . fine!" Carmelita beamed at her teacher's interest and her own answer.

"And how are your mother and father?"

"They," she began and then frowned as she struggled with words. "They . . . work . . . and . . . sleep."

Cassie knew that even Carmelita's thirteen-year-old brother Thomas must work, making and selling handmade rugs and capes in the plaza so the family could eat. In addition, they grew all their own food, so they often spent hours in the field and tending to their livestock. One day, Carmelita was expected to join them, but Cassie hoped to help the little girl find a way to make a better future for herself. She hugged the child then and turned her attention to the others for a few minutes before calling them back to their lessons again.

The days passed quickly for her when she was with the children. She found delight in each one of their successes, both small and large. The earnest faces and busy hands of the children, as she created assignments and walked among them, completely occupied her mind. They ended their lessons without having caught a glimpse of Father Auguste, much to her relief. It was a rare day when he didn't find some excuse to interrupt her class or bump into her on some pretext. She hoped she could get away from the church today without coming face to face with him.

Cruz Delgado stood unnoticed outside the doorway to the schoolroom, taking in at a glance the rapt attention and devotion of the children, and the loving and patient way Cassie dealt with them. The young teacher looked so lovely and so innocent that his resolve to stay away from her weakened substantially at the sight of her.

He had wanted to see her again. No, to be honest, he

112

had fairly ached with the longing, but he'd never imagined seeing her here. And he wished her anywhere but here, somewhere far away from the political turmoil that swirled around the parish priest and this church.

What would she think if she knew of the priest's association with Juan Perego? What *could* she think? He wondered whether she had any idea that both men were thoroughly evil, aggrandizing, and lecherous, to boot. Cruz frowned.

Did Cassie have to associate much with the elder priest in her dealings with the children? Had Father Auguste tried to force his attention on the widow Layton?

No. Cassie would not still be teaching here at the church if he had tried anything of the sort. But she obviously loved working with the children, and Cruz knew the older priest's nature all too well. If he hadn't tried something with the beautiful young woman yet, he soon would. That was as predictable as the regular arrival of wagon trains over the Santa Fe Trail. The man should have been removed from his office in the church long ago.

Hurriedly, Cruz pulled himself away from the doorway where he'd stood mesmerized, watching her. He could still feel the warmth of her arms around him and smell the fresh, flowery fragrance that was her essence. In his dreams, he felt the satiny smoothness of her skin against his. But he had decided that the sensation and memory of having been with her on that first night were far too real to be a dream. He still could not understand it, though, for such a thing seemed so very far from what a lady like Cassie Layton would do. His puzzlement aside, he found himself recalling sensations from that night at the oddest times.

He shook his head sharply and the dark inscrutable mask dropped into place over his features once more. He had a job to do in Santa Fe. And she could easily distract him from that purpose. He couldn't allow it.

So intent had they been on their lessons that neither Cassie nor the children had seen him during his momentary presence in the doorway before he continued on his way deeper into the interior of the building for his meeting with Father Auguste.

"Now, children . . ."

The tones of her soft voice followed him down the narrow hall. It would be some time before his business with the priest was done. Cruz could not bring himself to shake the priest's hand as he made his departure much later, but gave him a stiff bow instead. His aversion was total and it was a constant struggle to hide it in some measure. He needed the priest's connections and his assistance, however reluctantly they might be given. Cruz knew exactly what he had to do and was willing to do it, for the success of his mission, a mission both personal and political.

The day was well into evening before he once more passed the schoolroom, by this time quiet and dark. His disappointment in not seeing her again made the evening seem darker still.

Cassie had kept the the children later than she planned, so excited was she at their progress and unbounded enthusiasm.

"Come on children," she said, "I'll walk you home now."

114

Their laughter echoed off the walls as they scampered for the front door. It was already twilight and the darkness would fall fast, so she hurried them along until they reached the adjoining houses of Carmelita and Josephina. The two girls danced off with a wave and a backward glance.

Manuelito was the last to leave her, as his home was the one nearest Cassie's. As they walked hand in hand and the dark shadows lengthened, she thought his hand seemed a bit too warm.

"Do you have a fever, Manuelito?"

She placed a cool hand on his forehead and it did seem warmer than normal. Cassie walked him up to his doorway and in faltering Spanish, with hand motions, tried to explain to his mother about the fever, hoping she would understand and take proper care of the boy. There seemed to be nothing more she could do then, so she dropped a kiss on the top of his head and turned to leave.

During the time she'd been speaking with Manuelito's mother, it had gotten completely dark. She still had some distance to go before reaching her own doorway. She hurried along, not sure what made her so uneasy, but knowing she couldn't get home soon enough for her own peace of mind. She must still be spooked by the noises she'd heard the night before from outside her window. Had there truly been someone out there, as she'd feared?

Trying to avoid dark alleyways where someone could be hiding, waiting for her, she walked faster and faster. The evening grew unnaturally quiet and that only served to make her more nervous.

Almost running now, she felt a little foolish at her

fears. How many times had she walked this way? No one had ever bothered her before. Of course, it had never been after dark. Everything always seemed more suspect, more threatening in the dark.

Was that the sound of footsteps, a little way behind her? She cast a worried glance over her shoulder, but saw nothing, not even one suspicious shadow in the ever deepening darkness. Nevertheless, she quickened her steps, more anxious than ever to get home.

The noise behind her sounded more definite and hasty, as well, in direct proportion to the accelerating speed of her own steps. Now there was no doubt in her mind that she was being followed! When she walked faster, the steps behind her sped up; when she slowed, they followed suit.

Someone was stalking her. But why? Why would someone want to scare her, or do her harm?

Surely, it was not a friend of hers. No one had called out to her or admonished her to stop. She lengthened her stride. Before she realized it, she was running headlong down the road.

Cassie was in full flight, the pounding, running steps behind her added wings to her feet. Thoroughly frightened, she ran as fast as she could, allowing her instincts to rule and, she hoped, keep her from the disaster of falling headlong and being overtaken. She had no idea what this person wanted or what he'd do to her if he caught her.

Nor did she intend to find out.

But she was helpless. She had nothing, no weapon with which to protect herself, and there appeared to be nowhere to hide or find sanctuary. Longingly, she thought of the rifle resting safely on the wall in its hooks above her fireplace.

How much farther could it be now? And how much longer could she keep up this pace, barely outdistancing her pursuer? Her heart pounded so hard against her chest she could scarcely breathe.

A black film came and went in front of her eyes. No! She would not black out. She would, by the strength of her will and determination, keep putting one foot in front of the other until someone came to help. This seemed more unlikely by the minute, but she was determined to reach her own home.

What if she did manage to outrun him and reach her front door? He would be too close behind for her to have time to slide the bolt free and get inside safely. He would have the advantage then, would perhaps even follow her inside.

Frantically, she tried to think of a way to save herself, even as her feet continued their ceaseless pounding, as did the steps behind her, becoming louder and louder.

A shaft of light pierced the darkness in front of her and Cassie thought thankfully of Lucita. Of course! Her friend's house was nearby. Luci's house was a much safer refuge than her own vacant house, if she could only reach there in time.

With a strangled glad cry, she turned sharply to her left at the wooden street marker without looking behind her, ran as fast as she could for the house at the end of the lane. Another hundred feet brought her to Lucita's front gate. Nervous fingers worked the latch.

"Open!" she breathed. "Come on!"

As if in answer to her command, the gate squeaked and swung inward. Headlong, she plunged up the narrow pathway. She fell against the door, hammering with all her might, her lungs drawing in deep breaths and aching painfully from the effort. Long seconds marched quietly by, one by one, like tiny toy soldiers in a parade.

Cassie clasped her hands to still their shaking, even as she heard footsteps pounding, overtaking her from behind. The menace in the air was like another presence in the night. He was only seconds away. He would be upon her.

"One moment, please," the blessedly familiar voice floated out to her ears.

"Hurry up, Luci!" she shouted.

Cassie stepped back as the door was flung open and soft, golden light poured over her.

"Cassie! My God! What . . . ?!"

Weary and breathless, Cassie fell into her arms. They both heard the heavy steps falter, stop, linger for a few seconds and then reverse direction. Their echo died away as they faded into the distance.

Lucita dragged her exhausted friend inside, casting a worried look into the darkness before slamming and bolting the door.

"Was someone chasing you, Cass? You're not hurt, are you? Are you *sure* you're all right? What are you doing out alone after dark, anyway? You know there are too many unscrupulous people in Santa Fe. How many times have I told you not to . . ."

The probing questions continued with no response as Lucita helped her shaking friend over to the security of her settee and the warmth of her fire, slipping her coat from her shoulders and throwing it over a chair.

Cassie managed a small smile as Lucita handed her a

cup of coffee and her prattling went on and on. She thought she'd never heard anything that sounded quite so good, so natural, so wonderfully safe. Thankfully, she closed her eyes and lay her head back on the over-stuffed cushion and breathed a sigh of relief.

She didn't want to think what might have happened if Luci hadn't been there to take her in, if the unknown assailant had caught up with her before she'd reached Luci's house. She shuddered, either from fear or relief.

Warmed by the thick, black coffee and unconditional friendship, Cassie began to unwind and breathe normally. Lucita, unable to wait any longer, began verbally grilling her.

Reluctantly, but knowing it was the only way to stop Lucita's questions, Cassie told her inquisitive friend about hearing noises outside her house the previous night. She continued with her certainty that someone had been chasing her when she'd banged on her friend's front door minutes earlier.

"I'm not making this up, Luci! He was right behind me. Honest!"

"Damned right some bastard was hot on your trail. I heard him, too, you know."

Luci always lapsed into profanity when she was deeply troubled or angered, which was fairly often with her volatile temper.

"But I don't know what I can do about it," Cassie mused.

"You can get some help, that's what."

"Oh, really, where? The officers of the law in Santa Fe are unlikely to be of any help to me. They *want* me to be scared off." She thought for awhile before going on in a determined voice, "But I won't be, Luci. I won't let them do that to me. One or more of them murdered Cameron. He never trusted them, from the time we arrived here. He must have learned something they didn't want revealed to the American authorities. I wish he'd confided in me." She remembered Cameron had seemed nervous and distracted during the last few weeks of his life. He'd spent a lot of his time at the Governor's Palace, talking with officials. He had even made an unexplained trip out of town for a few days. It *had* to be connected with the notoriously crooked leadership in Santa Fe.

"No, they won't run me out of town so easily as all that," she concluded.

"I never knew how thoroughly stubborn you could be, Cassandra McPherson Layton."

Cassie's mouth curved upward. "I think you may have just come to know me a little better, my friend. I'm afraid I've always been a bit hardheaded."

"Well, you have to start being more careful, and there has to be *someone* who could help you. The two of us aren't strong or powerful enough to fight them alone."

"You aren't a part of this." Cassie frowned, her eyes troubled at the thought of her friend's becoming involved in her problems.

"Oh, yes, indeed, I damned sure am! You're not the only one here who has a mulish streak!"

"So I see," Cassie smiled.

"Well, then, what's our plan?" Lucita rushed on. "You know I have ways of learning secrets in my line of work, if I can just attract the right customers in for a session. They tell me everything."

"No, you mustn't. That's much too dangerous."

Lucita shook her head thoughtfully, as though in agreement, but Cassie feared she hadn't heard the last of the foolhardy plan proposed by her headstrong friend.

Cassie's mind flew to a pair of sincere, blue eyes that had filled with concern for her and strong arms that had held her, however briefly. The priest!

She dismissed the vagrant thoughts of seeking his help as impractical. Cruz Delgado was a stranger in Santa Fe and, even if he were willing, there wasn't much he could do to help her. She needed someone with influence, someone with power. But who?

"You've thought of someone, haven't you?" demanded Lucita, who'd been watching her face closely and read her thoughts there as she always could.

"No, not really. I did meet a priest who is new in town. But no, he's not the one I need to help me. Anyway, I'm sure he wouldn't want to be involved in my problems." This particular priest had enough problems of his own.

"You are not telling me everything," Luci accused.

"Yes, I have."

"No, you haven't. Cass, you have to tell me everything. I'm dying of curiosity. Where did you meet this man? A priest, you say? Where is he now? Why would you think of asking him to help? Of course, priests are bound to help their parishioners, aren't they? And I suppose, if he is new in town, we will be his parishioners. So, let's go see him now and ask for his help. Men of God are *supposed* to help, you know."

"That's true," Cassie replied with a chuckle, "but I don't think it's spiritual help I'll be needing. A hired gunman might be more my cup of tea."

"Now you're talking," Lucita beamed.

"I was only teasing."

"Oh," Lucita looked decidedly disappointed.

"Yes!" Cassie laughed and hugged her wonderful friend. "I'll have to think about it. Maybe I *will* ask someone for help."

Lucita's foot tapped impatiently. "I know better than to ask. You wouldn't care to tell me who you are thinking of now, would you?"

"I'll tell you just as soon as I've spoken to him."

Lucita was immensely relieved that she'd persuaded Cassie to ask for help, regardless of whether it was from the mysterious priest or someone else.

"You know I worry about you," Lucita seriously confided.

"I know, Luci, and I'm so glad and so very fortunate to have a friend like you." She meant every word wholeheartedly. Though she had other acquaintances in Santa Fe, Lucita was her only true friend and the only person she could count on.

Even so, Cassie was not ready to reveal that she did, indeed, plan to seek the young priest's help. She had no one else. And he'd seemed kind and interested. Maybe he would help her.

The more she thought of his strength and character, the more she felt sure he had the ability to help her, if he only would. But he had been awfully anxious to get away from her the last time she'd seen him. She had the distinct impression it would be to his immense satisfaction if he never saw her again.

At the same time, she'd been very much aware of his attraction to her and his admiration for her. Would he have cared to be around her more if their circumstances had been different?

No matter, they were stuck in the roles they were in, and that was that. He was a priest and she a grieving widow with enemies and a mission. Perhaps he could be persuaded to help her out of common decency or some sense of duty, if for no other reason.

She wouldn't know if she didn't ask. She took her leave of Lucita with the rising of the sun the next morning, intent upon seeking his help, hoping she could find him and knowing there were only two boardinghouses in town where he might be staying.

Cruz had spent most of the last two days in the thoroughly unpleasant company of Father Auguste. Every minute spent in his company was a torment, though not nearly so much a torment as the way his troubled thoughts kept returning to the lovely widow Layton.

As unreachable to him as the stars high and brilliant in the New Mexico sky, her beautiful image seemed etched in his mind. He could not shake her from his thoughts, no matter how hard he tried. And he had been trying. There was no room in his life for the complications she would undoubtedly bring his way.

"I'll be happy to help in any humble way I can." The oily voice of Father Auguste jerked him back from his fancies. "You have only to say the word."

The man was practically groveling, but his insincerity was all too obvious. He would be the first to stab a person in the back the minute his back was turned, and would seek only his own advantage in any situation.

Cruz had taken the true measure of the man and vowed never to let down his guard with this religious hypocrite. How had a man like that come to have a position as a representative of the Catholic church? It was a crime and disgrace that anyone had to depend on this man for spiritual leadership. But Cruz was not naive and knew there were more than a few such scoundrels in the church who had no business being there.

And Cassie — Mrs. Layton, he corrected himself — had to associate with Father Auguste regularly in her work with the children. He would keep a sharp eye out to be sure she wasn't mistreated by the elderly priest or taken advantage of in any way. He had come to know her as a kind and loving person. He'd seen in her face and her actions how much she cared for these children. She deserved much more than the lonely life of a young widow in this remote outpost.

"I will need you to be my eyes and ears," he explained to Father Auguste. "Let me know the minute anything out of the ordinary occurs or should a stranger be seen near any of the paintings."

"*Si*, oh *si, señor!* It is my most excellent wish that nothing further disappear from my jurisdiction."

It had better be, Cruz thought, but he smiled and nodded his head in agreement.

"Of course," he said amiably.

Several invaluable paintings by Spanish masters had disappeared from the churches in Santa Fe, as well as from several other churches in adjoining parishes. A highly organized ring of thieves seemed to be operating in the area. A portion of Cruz's official mission was to apprehend them and put a stop to the thievery that had been occurring over the past year or so.

He strode out into the bright winter sunshine, glad to have seen the last of the priest for the time being.

Breathing deeply of the crisp, fresh air, he brushed at his sleeves as if he could physically remove any residue of unpleasantness.

He saw her then. In spite of all his best intentions, he broke into a wide smile and quickly covered the distance between them until he stood close enough to touch her.

"Are you all right?" he asked, having noticed the worried frown on her face. At the same time, he was helpless to ignore her loveliness.

"Certainly," she lied. "And you?"

He spotted the lie, seeing trouble and fear in her eyes.

"You are not fine, *Señora*. That is clearly evident. Would you care to tell me what is wrong?"

For a long time her gaze held his and then she bowed her head briefly, before looking back up into his clear blue eyes. Her decision was made, for better or worse.

"You are very perceptive. I've come to you for a reason. I need your help, Father."

His heart soared that she would turn to him above any other, but he was jolted back to earth by the look in her eyes.

"You are in trouble, *Señora* Layton? Is there something I can do? You saved my life two times over. You have only to ask. Anything. There is not anything I would not do for you."

"Will you walk with me while we talk?"

"Of course."

He took her small hand and tucked it inside his elbow where it rested against his side. A feeling of warmth and almost painful protectiveness moved through him. He wanted to prolong the intimacy and

125

the walk for as long as possible. He slowed his steps to match the length of hers and inclined his head in order to hear her soft words.

"I seem to be in a bit of trouble, Father."

An understatement, she thought with an impatient shake of her head. Her voice was stronger when she continued speaking.

"Night before last, I thought I heard someone outside my house. Then yesterday, when I left the church, someone followed me. I'm sure of it. I think he meant to harm me. I was lucky to get away, but who knows what could happen next time?"

"You think there will be a next time, then? That this was not a random thing, or perhaps a mistake?"

His face was filled with concern. Disturbed by her words, he had stopped walking. Taking hold of her arms, he swung her around until he was looking down into her eyes.

"Yes," she admitted.

"Do you know who it is, then?"

"Yes."

"Well, then, you have only to speak his name and I will see that he never threatens you again."

His deep voice was filled with promise and a resolve that comforted her. He would help her! She had known that she could count on him. She felt a huge relief to be able to put her problems into his hands.

"Oh, thank you, Father. The man's name is Juan Perego."

"The commandant's *aesesor?*" A dark scowl changed his features dramatically. It was clear he knew the man whose name she'd mentioned.

"The same. Perego, legal adviser to the governor,"

she acknowledged, watching him closely, wondering about his strange reaction.

He released his hold on her arms and began to walk beside her once more. This time, she felt in him a reserve and withdrawal. What could she have said to upset him so? At first he'd been more than willing to help her. Was it merely the mention of the Spanish official's name that bothered him?

"Do you know him?" she questioned.

"Yes, I know the man. In fact, I have been sent to work with him. I'm afraid I cannot help you, *Señora* Layton, as much as I might want to. If you would ask anything else of me . . . only this man . . . there is nothing I can do. I am sorry. Why do you think he is harassing you?"

"I'm sure it's because of my refusal to allow my husband's murder to remain unavenged."

Cruz had long ago realized that Cassie must be the widow of the man, Cameron Layton, whose name he had heard mentioned in connection with the ring of thieves and politicians involved in the intrigues rampant in Santa Fe. It was suspected that her husband might even have been one of the thieves. Cruz admired Cassie's fidelity to her late husband, in spite of all that.

Cassie watched him closely as the emotions played clearly over his face. "My husband did nothing wrong, *Father.*" Her voice extended the distance growing between them. Loyalty to Cameron still went too deep and she would allow no one to question him or his motives, especially since he was no longer there to defend himself. "He was a just and honest man and because of that, he was killed. Now they want to cover it up. I won't let them do that!"

He admired her courage and wanted to help her more than he'd ever wanted anything in his life. His conscience warred with his heart and won. "I'm afraid my hands are tied. Perhaps you should do as they wish and leave the investigation to the authorities."

"Never! They lie, they steal, and they murder! Cameron got in their way—or knew too much—and was killed for it."

"Are you sure that what you say is true?"

"Absolutely."

She was quiet for a minute and then continued, "But I apologize for having discussed it with you. Since you and Perego are colleagues, you would surely not be the one to help me."

"I'm sorry."

His eyes were a deep indigo and a frown scored his brow. She believed that he was truly sorry. But she could not understand why he wouldn't help her, why he seemed to take Perego's side over hers, after all she'd done for him.

"I shall have to seek help elsewhere, then. Good day, Father Delgado."

"Good day, Señora Layton."

It hurt like hell to watch her straighten those slender shoulders and walk away, after having refused to help her. His eyes followed her until she was well out of his sight. He would not let anything happen to her, he vowed. He would do everything he could to help her, but he couldn't let her nor anyone else know.

Though the incident of the night before worried her, Cassie had an appointment with Perego and she intended to keep it. Surely she would be safe with him in a public place, even if he'd been the man following her. With some haste, she made her way to the Governor's Palace, a flat-roofed adobe rectangle supported by pine pillars and shaded on the entire southern side by a *portal*.

The walk underneath was often used as a public meeting place and extended to a market on its western end. The long and spacious building housed civil offices, including that of the governor, a granary for taxes paid by the citizens in grain, a custom house, a warehouse for items that had been confiscated from its citizens, a jail, and a guardhouse.

On the plaza across the narrow road stood a single pole, proudly displaying the Mexican flag. Relieved, she saw Manuelito playing there happily with some friends. He was all right, then, and the fever had been nothing. She supposed that she would be a doting mother, if she were ever to have children of her own.

She glanced across to the east where the *parroquia* or parish church stood, as though keeping watch on the activities, before she turned to step inside the shadowed interior of the main hall. She was admitted into Perego's office after only a short delay, an unusual circumstance. She had been required to wait as much as half a day on some occasions to see the man so impressed with his own importance.

Sparsely decorated, the large square room boasted whitewashed walls, the lower portion covered with calico to protect clothing from the white dust. Handmade chairs and tables showed obvious imperfections; a *jerga* woolen rug covered a portion of the earthen floor. Brass candlesticks imported from Mexico were the room's only source of light and they flickered dimly.

Juan Perego's huge bulk filled the ornate, carved chair and his hands were steepled beneath his second or third chin as he regarded her steadily. She could not see his face clearly since the light was behind him, but his lascivious intentions were all too clear, as they had been ever since Cameron's death.

He stood and extended a plump hand to her. Cassie forced herself to offer her own in return, and hoped she didn't recoil noticeably when he placed a moist kiss on it. The man was revolting, but he didn't seem to know it. He obviously thought his position was enough to make him attractive to all of the local women.

As quickly as she could without offending him, Cassie pulled her hand away, resisting the urge to wipe it on her skirt.

"Señora Layton, what can I do for you this afternoon?"

She cleared her throat and waited a moment before making her request, a petition she'd brought before this man and others more times than any of them could count.

"As you know, *Señor* Perego, I am very concerned about what is being done to find the murderers of my husband. Has there been any progress since we last talked?"

"Not to my knowledge, but I, of course, am a lowly emissary. The governor himself is involved in this investigation, and has been since the beginning."

Investigation! she thought with some scorn. How could they even dignify their meager to nonexistent attempts with the term investigation? They had half-heartedly done a few things, designed to pacify her more than anything else. Nothing of any substance was being done, however, and she knew that without asking. She was wasting her time here as usual, but she really had no other recourse. She kept thinking if she pestered them often enough, perhaps something might eventually be done, or she might find out something on her own that would lead to the answers she sought. Whatever her reasons for coming, she seemed incapable of stopping herself.

"Well, perhaps I might be able to speak with him personally, then?"

"Oh, I'm afraid not. You see, there is an important dinner being planned for this evening." He paused and looked long at her before continuing, "Please permit me to invite you to the dinner, *Señora* Layton. Perhaps at that time you may have the opportunity of asking the governor personally about your concerns."

If the lovely widow attended the dinner, as his guest, he might be able to make some amorous progress with her. He wanted to get under those very proper skirts, but had been rebuffed by her at every turn. Maybe with a few glasses of the white Bordeaux the governor had imported by mule from Mexico, she would be more malleable. At least, it was worth a try. He grinned when she nodded her head in agreement.

"I shall be happy to attend. Thank you."

For entirely too long, she had been kept at arm's distance from the one person in the government who really counted. This was her chance to corner the governor. She thought it entirely possible that he was even being shielded from her requests by an overly solicitous staff, that he might not even know what she was so intent upon learning.

"May I call for you, then?"

"No, I think not. It would be unseemly for me to be seen in a man's company, even a gentleman such as yourself, with only a matter of months having passed since my husband's death. I'm sure you understand?"

He almost cursed out loud. It had all been turning out so perfectly, but he couldn't argue with her observation about proprieties. He would have to watch for her arrival and be sure that she was seated near him, making his move at a later time. He could and would definitely escort her home, with no questions asked.

"Of course," he said smoothly, but without his ready smile. He had to go along with her, but he didn't have to be happy about it. Since being appointed to his position of prestige in the government, he had been welcomed by any woman of his choosing and was not at all accustomed to being turned down. His pride took a beating each time he spoke with this haughty woman. He would make her pay when she lay beneath him, writhing in ecstasy . . . or in pain . . . he didn't much care which.

"I'll say good day, then." She stood and edged toward the door before he could claim her hand again.

"Until this evening." His words followed her as she made a hasty exit.

"Not if I can help it," she vowed under her breath, hurrying from the building.

She did not see the man who watched her from the plaza across the street, nor did she see him stride into the building she'd just left.

Cassie felt depleted and empty as she did every time she requested help from the Spanish government. She knew in her heart that her visits did little to no good, but still she couldn't stop herself from pursuing the only avenue that seemed open to her.

"Oh Cameron," she whispered, "what am I to do?"

Without a conscious decision on her part, her feet turned toward the cemetery. Before long, she stood looking down on the simple gravestone that marked her husband's resting place. She fussed with the flowers she had left there only the day before, and then knelt beside the slightly raised mound of earth.

"I promise I'll find who did this to you," she vowed. "If it's the last thing I ever do. And I will never leave Santa Fe until I know, and until those murderers are brought to justice."

Cameron would be the first to tell her to go back home and get on with her life, but that didn't matter. There was no way she could do that until the matter was settled for good.

When at last she stood to leave, the sun, diffused by gathering storm clouds, cast long, brooding shadows across the simple headstones. Triangular peaks in the distance topped purple, changeless mountains, standing indestructible and majestic. She loved the mountains and might have enjoyed the beauty unfurled in front of her at some other time. But not today. She was troubled by too many uncertainties.

Chapter Seven

"La entrada de la caravana! Los Americanos! Los carros!"
The arrival of Sarah and Emerson into Santa Fe was heralded by shouts from local citizens who lined the rutted thoroughfare and by "poppers" or noise-makers on the whips wielded by the wagon masters. They had been joined along the way by only a few more hardy souls and hardly deserved the designation of "caravan," but Sarah had been glad of the company of other travelers.

Emerson was muttering under his breath, "Don't take much to get 'em worked up, does it? Some caravan! Huh! Lots of *Americanos!*" But he couldn't hold back a grin, thinking of the goods he'd thrown into the back of the wagon, all he'd been able to get his hands on with such short notice, but still enough to turn a tidy profit in Santa Fe.

At least, he'd have something to barter with. He would sell his items to shopkeepers who would be running low by this time of the year. Since he'd be stuck here at this outpost until the spring thaw, he figured he might as well make the most of it. He had loaded a few beaver pelts, some cutlery and looking glasses, as well as a varied selection of religious medals and colored prints of the saints onto his wagon.

The trip had been without incident and mostly pleasant, in spite of his reservations about setting out so late in the season. His lovely traveling companion had not given him a single reason for concern. She'd willingly pitched in and carried her weight with no complaints. For an Easterner and a city girl, she'd held up remarkably well. A couple of harsh winter storms had hampered their progress along the way, but not significantly.

When he'd told her the night before that they would reach Santa Fe by noon, the relief on her face had mirrored his own feelings. Civilization, or at least as civilized as a frontier town could be, was a welcome change from the long weeks spent coping with the hardships of the trail. Santa Fe didn't rank high on the list of his favorite towns, but it was a welcome sight on this clear, winter day.

"Are you glad to be here?" Sarah asked. She'd been intently watching his face.

"Yes, ma'am!"

Though road weary and longing for the luxury of a nice, hot bath, the sights and sounds and even the smells of the rowdy frontier town energized him as they always had.

"You really like out here, don't you, Emerson?" She grinned at him when he offered her his hand to help her down from the wagon. She enjoyed his contagious high spirits.

"Reckon I do," he grumbled in reply, unwilling to reveal more of his true feelings than he already had. The petite redhead had weaseled her way into his heart on the trip, something no woman had done since his second wife had died, leaving him a widower for the second and last time. He'd had some men friends since then, but had steered a wide path clear of the fairer sex, a task he intended to maintain with the possible exception of the young city girl whose green eyes twinkled up at him in a decidedly female way.

"What say we mosey on down to the hotel?"

"Heavenly idea! I'm right beside you. And I can hardly wait." She smoothed freckled hands down over dusty skirts, thinking with longing of a scented bath in a real tub, a thorough shampoo and clean, fresh clothes. She really could hardly wait and danced out in front of him.

"Wait up! Remember, I'm just an old man, worn out and beat up," he cautioned.

"That's not the Emerson Smith I know," she returned. "What happened to that 'young at heart' routine?"

"Just tryin' to charm a pretty young thing. Can't blame an old codger for tryin', can you?"

"Suppose not." Her bubble of laughter made him feel better than he had in years. They walked companionably side by side, leading their wagon and horses.

They had become friends on the trail West, and

his gap-toothed smile was now as familiar to her as the sunlight. She remembered well the night he'd promised to help her convince Cassie to go home with her, agreeing that Santa Fe was no decent place for a lady alone.

"I can't wait to find Cassie." She could only hope that the long months that had passed since her last letter might have made her sister more amenable to a speedy return home. Knowing how stubborn Cassie could be, Sarah wasn't counting on it.

Sarah looked across at the plaza, teeming with happy and excited Mexicans and Americans. The exotic aromas of steaming tortillas and beans were unfamiliar, but far from unpleasant. Drivers calling out to teams of mules, jingling bells, laughter and boisterous talking made up the steady noises of bustling activity giving the scene its life and vitality.

Across the way, one man stood out from the crowd, towering head and shoulders above the others. He was tall, with sandy-blond hair, dark brown eyes, and the most heart stopping smile she'd ever seen in her life. He was dressed in an American army uniform.

"Oh!" She wasn't aware that her exclamation had been spoken aloud until Emerson questioned her about it.

"What is it, Miz Sarah?"

His worldly wise eyes followed the direction of hers, and his eyes crinkled with his huge grin.

"Oh," he said, thumping her on the back. "Long time since you've seen a fine-looking man, eh?"

She shook her head, but knew in her heart that

137

she'd never seen one quite so handsome as this one. None of the young men back East could begin to compare. Funny she'd had to come way out here to stumble upon the man of her dreams.

His lingering glance in her direction indicated that the attraction was far from being one-sided.

"I'd steer clear of these young fellas, if I was you."

Sometimes Emerson Smith thought he had been born a century too late. When he dispensed his words of wisdom like a harlot sharing her favors, it never occurred to him they might fall on deaf ears. But he could see Sarah McPherson was having none of it this day. He'd seen the inflexible side of her before and knew when to push and when to stand back, so he just shook his head.

Not quite ready to abandon the effort completely, he took her elbow and steered her in the direction of the hotel, though not without her casting a backward glance or two over her shoulder. He decided right then to speed up Sarah's attempts to find her sister and convince her to return home, so the two of them would be safely out of the less than savory atmosphere of this young and bawdy town. It was sure not a place for an attractive, single young woman like Sarah McPherson.

But at the moment, Emerson had himself a powerful thirst. He figured he'd get Sarah settled in her room and head on down to the town's biggest and rowdiest saloon. He had earned himself a big drink.

Sarah had other ideas. Her longing to see her sister, to hug her tightly and share some good old-fashioned girl talk had grown stronger until she didn't think she could wait any longer. Missing her older sister had been a nagging pain over the two years she'd been away, like an unattended toothache. But she had never realized just how much she'd pined to see Cassie until she'd gotten this close. Now, she could hardly contain herself.

"Emerson! Let's go and find her now! I can't wait another minute."

He frowned, but found that he couldn't say no to her. He hadn't been able to since she'd found him in the saloon and talked him into this foolhardy trip.

"All right, Miss Sarah. Just you let me unhitch the wagon and get these tuckered nags to a stable."

The narrow roads that carved their way around the main plaza and angled down into winding pathways bordered by dwellings were more suitable for walking than for a wagon and team, so they wouldn't be needing the wagon.

Sarah knew enough to find Cassie's house with only Emerson's help, or at least she hoped she did. A crude map Cassie had included in one of her letters home more than a year before had showed their town residence to be only a few blocks off the main plaza.

The walk, once begun, covered more territory than she'd imagined, though. By the time they reached a charming house with Layton carved into the gate, Sarah's legs and feet were complaining vigorously, and she was puffing from the unaccustomed exercise. She'd spent far too long in that rickety, old wagon!

Sarah pushed the hat back off her head, her riotous red curls gleaming in the midday sun. Forgetting her own fatigue and the rigors of the rough ride across the country, she burst through the gate and bolted for the door, pounding on it loudly.

"Cassie! Open up! It's me, Sarah!"

Excited, she hopped first on one foot, then the other, her skirts swirling around her. She would push the door down if Cassie didn't open up soon. Before she had a chance to knock again, the door flew open wide and Cassie stood there.

With a gasp of delighted surprise and astonishment, the two sisters fell into each other's arms.

Tears streamed down two attractive faces that strongly resembled each other. They hugged so ferociously that neither could breathe normally, but they didn't seem to care. Neither wanted to be the first to relinquish the other.

Finally with great reluctance, Cassie loosened her hold on her younger sister and stepped back. She still clasped both her sister's hands in her own shaking hands.

"Sarah! I'm so glad to see you! I can't believe it's really you. I've missed you *so* much. Just let me look at you."

Minutes ticked slowly by while the two sisters examined each other thoroughly and lovingly.

"You look beautiful," Cassie said at last, as though in awe. Her sister had grown up in the years since Cassie had left Boston. With her striking red hair and brilliant green eyes, she was a beauty.

"Come on now, Cassie. Nothing's happened to your eyesight. Even though something must have happened to your hands."

"My hands?" Confused, Cassie looked down, noting the bruise and remembering Cruz's reaction to it.

"Seems like they forgot to write!" Sarah teased.

"Oh! I'm sorry, Sarah."

Cassie had been so unhappy and frustrated at every turn by the government in Santa Fe and she'd been so overwhelmingly lonesome for her family and her home since Cameron's death, it had become too painful to write much. She'd let her correspondence slip, feeling terribly guilty, but unable to do anything about it. And now here was her sister Sarah, in person!

"You didn't come all the way out here just because you hadn't heard from me in a while, did you?"

The worried frown on her sister's face had Sarah quickly denying it, even though it had been partially the cause.

"No. You know me. I needed a change of scenery."

"You're not telling the truth. Your eyes always did give you away, even if you could keep that sheepish grin off your face."

"It's not fair to have an *older* sister, who knows you so well. To be truthful, I did come because I was worried, but not because of the letters that did *not* come. It was the few you wrote that concerned me. I could read something between the lines. You were in trouble and I knew it. When you flatly refused to come home, I knew I had to come out here and get you."

"Looks like I'm not the only one with a good set of womanly intuitions." Cassie grinned, so inexpressibly glad to see Sarah that she didn't even know how to show it. "Sarah . . ."

"I know. Me, too."

Cassie's eyes filled with tears again. "I'm sorry. Like a babbling idiot, I'm keeping you standing out here on the porch. Come inside! Do you have your bags with you?"

They both looked back down the walk to see Emerson standing patiently by the gate with Sarah's heavy valise in his hands and another hitched over his shoulder.

"Emerson," Sarah called out. "I'm so sorry. Come up here! I want you to meet my sister. Cassie McPherson Layton, meet Emerson Smith, my good friend and trusted guide."

His chest puffed out with pride at her words. Emerson strode up to the two happy young women, set the battered valise and bag down at their feet, and stuck out his beefy hand.

"Pleased to make your acquaintance, Miz Layton."

"Call me Cassie, please," she responded, taking his hand and smiling into his eyes, her pleasure reaching out to encompass him as well.

"Right! And you call me Emerson. All my friends do."

"And believe me, he has plenty of those," Sarah added, linking her arm with Emerson's. "He's positively the best guide in the whole frontier. And he knows everybody between here and Washington, D.C.! Why, I'll bet he could find his way across the Mississippi river blindfolded . . . and barefooted!"

"I'd sure nuff hate to have to try that!" Emerson

142

laughed heartily while he patted her small, freckled hand. "But we did get here in one piece, didn't we, spite of what anybody said."

"That's right," she explained. "Emerson was the only man in all of Missouri with the courage to set out for New Mexico at that time of the year."

". . . or the cussed ignorance," he cut in with a chuckle.

"The courage," she repeated emphatically, "to bring me out here safely. They all said I'd have to wait for months before it would be safe to travel."

"You both took a big chance, then?" Cassie asked, looking them over, concern showing on her face. "You shouldn't have, Sarah."

"But," Sarah bubbled, "if we hadn't, we wouldn't be here now. Aren't you going to invite two weary travelers inside? We might even be interested in a bite of supper."

"Oh, my!" Cassie's hand flew to her mouth. "I don't know what's wrong with me. Do come in, both of you. Mr. Smith, er, Emerson, just put her bags in the other room, if you would, and come in here and sit down. I have a big pot of beans cooking and some cornbread. I don't know what I would have done with it all if you two hadn't shown up. Do you suppose, I sensed somehow you were coming? We always were good at reading each other's minds, weren't we?"

"We sure were! And it's a pretty dangerous ability at times, isn't it? Do you remember the time Johnny Youngston asked you out and you didn't want to go? I knew it even though you didn't say it. I told him you had the measles, or something? You never even thanked me for that, Sis."

"Oh, Sarah!"

Tears gushed again from two sets of eyes and the sisters fell into each other's arms once more, loathe to let go.

"Ahem." Emerson was getting fidgety, unused to sitting about with nothing useful to do. "Could I build up the fire for you, Miz Cassie?"

They pulled apart at his words, still holding hands.

"Please do, Emerson. And I'll go put some coffee on right now. I know the both of you could use a cup, and so could I!"

"Sure 'nuff."

He bent to add another split log to the dwindling fire and to stir the embers back to life with a poker while the two women went off to the kitchen.

The simple lunch was delicious, and they all agreed it was the most pleasant meal any of them had enjoyed in months.

"I never realized until now just how lonely it is to eat alone," Cassie said, after they had finished and returned to the sitting room to relax in front of the fire.

"Cassie," Sarah began, "I'm so sorry about Cameron. You must miss him desperately."

"I do, every minute of the day. I loved him so much, Sarah."

She turned to Emerson to explain further. "Cameron was my husband. And he was murdered, a little more than six months ago." Her face had stiffened with these last words and her eyes took on a faraway expression.

Then seeming to snap back, she went on, "Of course, no one in the governor's office believes that, or will admit that they believe it. But someone knows and they know *why*. And I will find out who, if it's the last thing I do."

"Cassie . . ."

"No, Sarah, if you've come here to try and talk me out of it, or persuade me to go back, it won't work. Not until I find Cam's murderers and they are punished for what they did."

"Oh, Cassie! Do you really think you can do that?"

"I have to. I can't quit."

"Do you have any idea who killed your husband, Miz Cassie?" Emerson asked quietly. He had heard rumors circulating about the erstwhile officer's demise. Unfortunately, he had no concrete facts.

"Yes. But I can't prove anything."

"Can I help?"

"No, I don't think there's anything you can do, but I do thank you for bringing Sarah here safely."

She would not involve the elderly man in her troubles, troubles that seemed to be becoming more dangerous with each passing day.

"It was entirely my pleasure."

He beamed at the compliment, clearly enjoying the company of the two young women. His devotion to Sarah was obvious, matched only by his growing admiration for her older sister.

"And I will be happy to escort the both of you back East as soon as you're ready to leave. Until then," he said, looking pointedly at Cassie, "I'll do anything I can to help."

"I will, too, Cassie," Sarah added. "Maybe if we all work together, we can get to the bottom of this."

Cassie nodded her thanks, but she knew it wouldn't be that easy. Still, though she was determined not to drag the two of them into it, she was unutterably glad for their kind offers of help and felt much better.

"Oh! I almost forgot. The governor is giving a big dinner party this evening. I think I can arrange an invitation for you two if you'd like to go?"

"Oh, yes!" Sarah exclaimed immediately. "That would be great fun!" The prospect of a party erased any feelings of fatigue. "Do you really think it would be all right if I go along, too?"

"Yes," Cassie said with a nod. "I'm pretty sure it can be arranged. Emerson?"

"No, ma'am," he said, shaking his head from side to side. "That's not my cup o' tea. I do 'preciate the invite, though."

When Emerson took his leave, Cassie pressed a note into his hand and asked him to take it to Juan Perego's office on his way to his own evening's "entertainment."

"That is, if you don't mind," she said, smiling at him.

"No, ma'am. I'd do purt near anything for a lady like yourself. And you two have youselves a high time tonight."

He was whistling when he walked down the walk, and both young women smiled as they watched him leave.

But Perego was not happy when he read the hastily scribbled note. He wadded it into a ball and dropped it to the floor. Her sister, *indeed!* This ruined his plans for the evening, but there was little he could do about it. If he refused, the widow would most likely not come, either. Grudgingly, he penned a reply that included an invitation for the sister and sent it to the widow Layton's house with one of his men.

Chapter Eight

The widow Layton had lied to him! Lieutenant Mendez felt as though he was suspended over a deep pit on a fraying rope about to snap. His superior was not a man to be trifled with; Perego was a man who demanded action and results.

The lieutenant's career, perhaps even his life, would have been over had he admitted how close he had been to apprehending the man they were looking for when he stopped at the widow Layton's. He had no doubt been within six feet of the man! Yet he had let him slip away!

Why had she protected a stranger? Where was the man now? These were questions he fully intended to have answered, and the charming young woman was the key.

By the time he had rounded up his men and returned to her cabin, there'd been no sign of the fugitive nor of the presumably innocent widow. He'd been hoodwinked by the charming young woman, something that had never happened to him before.

He suspected from the moment he arrived there

that she was hiding someone, but was not sure until he had seen the boots on his way out. Thinking that he would surely have time to get his men so that he didn't have to face the fugitive alone, he had opted for the safer course. He had badly underestimated his adversary, though.

There was no way he could tell his commander of her connection with the man they sought without putting himself in jeopardy, so he had decided to pursue it on his own. He was willing to do whatever it took, and he had already begun his campaign of following her. He cared little if he frightened her in the process.

He had been disappointed to find her alone in her house in town the night he'd crept around outside and seen her sleeping in front of her fire, with no sign of the stranger. She was a fetching sight, he had to admit that. His anger toward her had become so intense that he decided he wouldn't mind a little "sport" at her expense in the process of getting the information he needed.

He had followed her the next evening, again without success. He was in a very foul mood when he'd had to give up at the fortune-teller's front gate. Now, *there* was a lusty little baggage . . . Lucita Chavez. She could be of use to him, too, perhaps.

But for now, he vowed to be *Señora* Layton's constant shadow until she led him to the man he sought. Unfortunately the pressure of the past few days had left him weary. He caught himself dozing from time to time while he waited for the widow to make her next move. In that way, he must have missed her departure from her friend's house. Aggravated at himself, he searched for her all over town, locating her some time later at the Governor's Palace, where she had an audience with Perego himself.

After that, she'd gone on to the church. Though there was nothing suspect in that, he wasn't about to give up!

The dinner party might give him just the chance he needed. He had been ordered by the commandant's assistant to escort the lovely widow and her sister to the party that was becoming the talk of all Santa Fe.

Cassie took great care in dressing for the governor's party, giving far more attention than usual to the way she looked. The light rose-colored dress of watered silk taffeta with delicate ecru lace edging the bodice was perfectly fitted and a good color for her.

Her intuition told her this would be an important occasion, for reasons not yet completely clear to her. Her high state of agitation made it hard for her to button the row of tiny, covered buttons down the back of her dress.

At last, with some wriggling, she managed to get the last one fastened and looked into her oval mirror, anxious to see if she looked presentable.

Her hair was lustrous and piled on top of her head in auburn curls, secured with Spanish combs. She added ribbons of rose trimmed in the same ecru as on the bodice of her dress to her coiffure. Curling tendrils escaped to frame her face softly with wisps of bright red-gold. Dainty cameo earrings and a matching necklace on a thin gold chain, a gift from her father many years ago on her tenth birthday, completed the ensemble.

Pinching her already flushed cheeks, she had to admit that she looked somewhat better than presentable, maybe even glowing! Though why she should care, she couldn't imagine. She felt no compulsion to impress the governor nor his lecherous assistants.

Lieutenant Mendez who was to drive her and Sarah to the dinner tonight was handsome enough, but Cassie knew that he realized she'd covered for the man he'd been seeking, though he had never said so. She dreaded the time she must spend in his company. Keeping her distance from his questions seemed the best policy, and she could only hope she'd be able to do that tonight.

Was she more aware than she wanted to admit to herself that the priest would more than likely be included in the assembly of local dignitaries? An invitation to such an affair was a courtesy generally extended to the local religious leaders and Father Auguste never failed to attend. It was common knowledge that he enjoyed a good party.

Why did the thought of Father Delgado make her pulse race faster and her cheeks a bit pinker? With a conscious effort, she forced these inappropriate thoughts out of her mind. Her husband had been dead for only a little over six months, and it was not yet time for her to be thinking of another beau. Besides, this man was a priest. She could not allow it.

Stepping back from the oval mirror, she could see her entire image by shifting first one way and then another and by standing on tiptoe. Satisfied that she looked her best, she added a bit of color to her lips and swept out of the room, her skirts rustling and her heart beating faster than ever, in spite of the sensible lecture she had given herself.

After what she'd been through, she wanted and, perhaps even needed to have a good time, and that was just what she set out to do.

Sarah joined her, eyes sparkling and a happy smile on her face. She was hoping the handsome young American soldier she'd seen in the plaza might be a guest, but she would have gone in any event. So much here in Santa Fe was new and interesting, even exotic, that she didn't want to miss a single thing.

Tonight, she'd chosen one of only two evening dresses she'd brought, a brilliant jade with earrings and necklace of the same striking shade. The effect was dramatic. A smattering of freckles across her cheeks kept her from looking too sophisticated, and Cassie's heart filled with love for her.

Cassie complimented her on the dress.

She, too, was looking forward to the evening, more than she would admit, even to herself. Her heart accelerated as she threw her fine cashmere wrap, a prized possession, over her bare shoulders, pulled on long kid gloves and answered the door in response to an authoritative knocking.

"Good evening, Lieutenant." Her voice held the right combination of reserve and civility, she thought.

"Good evening, *Señora* Layton. You are looking quite lovely this evening." His eyes revealed that he meant the very proper words.

"Why, thank you, sir. May I introduce my sister,

Sarah McPherson. She just arrived in Santa Fe, and I felt certain you would not object to escorting both of us to the governor's dinner this evening?"

"My pleasure," he murmured, extending his hand to the younger sister.

"Thank you, Lieutenant. We are ready to leave now. It is very kind of you to escort us."

He pulled the door shut behind them and followed the two women down the walk. He suspected that the evening would surely not be a total loss, in the company of two such beautiful women, though he would have preferred the widow alone. The sister was a complication to be dealt with at another time.

Conversation was polite and general, with no attempt on his part to question Cassie further about their encounter at the cabin. Cassie was thankful that the trip was a very short one in the state coach and that Sarah was along to keep things on a less than personal basis. On the way, though, she did have time to feel guilty about her anticipation and to remind herself that her main goal was to find Cameron's killers. This dinner was merely another step toward that end, nothing more.

They arrived at the front entrance of the palace which was bustling with activity. Carriages lined the narrow streets and well-dressed couples picked their way carefully across the road, with its remaining few mud puddles, to the wide doorway where they were greeted by a pair of soldiers in the vivid red uniform of the Spanish guard.

Cassie, Sarah, and the lieutenant joined the throng. Once inside, the ladies were soon separated from him, as their places were set in different parts of the room, much to their relief and his great disappointment.

Cruz, too, had mixed emotions about the dinner. It was imperative he attend, but he had no respect for the politicians of Santa Fe. Still, he was forced to be civil to them and to work with them as he tried to carry out his mission in the town. That meant accepting invitations to social events, thus his presence at this party at the Governor's Palace.

He felt the Americans were the inevitability of the future for the region, though their influence had been both good and bad. At least two types of Americans had made their way to Santa Fe. One group was rude, boorish and dishonest. These men shortchanged their customers and sold guns to the Indians and looked down their noses at the Spanish inhabitants. Then there were those who worked to improve the living conditions by serving in municipal offices and as advisers to the governor. Some of these were carpenters, gunsmiths, hatters, traders, and surveyors. They imported goods such as trousers, boots, muslin shirts, furniture, tools, medicine, fabrics and other items that added to the quality of life.

For their part, the Spanish residents of Santa Fe were mostly outgoing and fun loving, favoring church festivals and fandangos, with only a small portion who were selfish and vindictive. Unfortunately, the governor and his staff were, for the most part, among the latter type of Spaniards. Each was concerned primarily with his own advancement and personal fortune, giving little thought to the needs of his constituents.

More than likely, one or more of them were involved in the conspiracy to pilfer from the government payrolls and to steal priceless paintings from parish churches. He would soon find out who was responsible. In the process, he would deal with the nine-fingered man he sought.

The governor's party met all expectations, with its long tables set with snowy linens and the best china and silver to be found in the West laid out. A band composed of fiddles, horns, and guitars featured a soloist with a beautiful clear Spanish voice singing haunting ballads, which alternated with lively dance tunes to set the mood for the evening.

The golden glow from a myriad of candles set in brass holders along the tables and on whitewashed walls was pleasant, though their flowered scent could not quite cover the musty odors of the old building. The Palace was a long way from anything approaching elegance, at least the way Cassie had known it in the East. The previous governor, Albino Perez, had left behind some of the luxuries he favored.

Invited guests were a mélange, representing a cross section of the culture of the diverse town. Minglers included merchants, soldiers, men in colored trousers, and beautiful Spanish ladies in bright dresses with elaborate hairpieces held in place with decorated ivory combs. American soldiers were resplendent in their dress uniforms with gold epaulets and braid, having set their sabers and guns aside to be retrieved later.

155

Perego's wife looked elegant, sitting beside her husband at the head of the largest table. Cassie had seen her several times before and was always struck by her quiet, refined air. She wondered why she was married to the unprincipled man who helped govern Santa Fe. Perego himself cast more than one interested glance in Cassie's direction, but did not seek her out.

When she finally cornered him and requested an introduction to the governor, he brushed her off, saying perhaps later. He clearly had no intention of helping her. And she had no luck on her own in trying to approach the powerful man who was continuously surrounded by a crowd.

Manuel Armijo, the current governor of Santa Fe, was a large, fine-looking man dressed tonight in a royal blue frock coat with rolled collar and cuffs, blue-striped trousers with gold lace and a bright red sash around his waist. Armijo had been governor from 1835 up until his violent overthrowing by a mob of rebels. He had returned to resume governorship in 1838 and had been a decent governor ever since, with only one other interruption in his leadership. Only recently, he had begun his third term. A proponent of literacy for his people, he encouraged teachers like Cassie and had made it possible for her to work with her group of children without outside interference.

His presidial soldiers performed mostly ceremonial duties as guards for him and the palace. With their old muskets and meager amounts of ammunition and sometimes delayed payrolls, they were grateful for sporadic gifts from wealthy Americans, gifts of monies that helped to keep the Spanish government working.

These were not generally discussed openly and did not serve to soften the governor's attitude toward Americans, to whom he had proved to be no real friend.

Neither was the governor's friendship with the infamous but kindhearted *La Dona Tules* openly discussed, but it was common knowledge. The woman was in attendance at most public functions and never far from his side. It was rumored that she, too, contributed to the governor's coffers from her wealth acquired as the proprietress of a successful local gambling hall.

To her dismay, Cassie was seated across from the young priest, Delgado; his proximity gave her a start and then a peculiar mix of troublesome feelings. She was wary but intrigued, feeling a surge of pleasure mixed with a healthy dose of caution. His presence reminded her of his connections with Perego and all the questions she had about him and his reasons for being in Santa Fe. A sweeping disappointment moved through her as she thought of that. She realized that she had put a lot of faith in his willingness to help her, and had been even more let down than she'd realized when he'd refused.

Was he working with the Spanish officials, then?

At the sight of him, she dredged out all her resolves to remain aloof from him and made an attempt to hold them close. Trying not to look in his direction, she had already seen enough to know how dangerously handsome he looked, even in the sedate robes of the clergy. The black was nearly, but not quite, the same lustrous midnight color of his hair and the white collar made his complexion even darker, the light blue of his eyes a sharp contrast to the whole.

"Good evening, *Señora* Layton. You are looking lovely tonight." The disarming smile he aimed in her direction made her feel like a girl of eighteen, and his voice hypnotized her, as it always did.

"Good evening, Father, and thank you. I would like you to meet my sister, Sarah McPherson, from Boston. Sarah, this is Father Delgado." Her voice was purposefully cool and invited no further niceties or intimacies. She hoped it gave no clue to the turmoil within her.

Sarah looked questioningly at her, then held out her hand in greeting to the priest.

"Nice to meet you, Father Delgado."

"And I am delighted to meet you as well." He brought her hand to his lips and Sarah grinned, thoroughly pleased at the courtly gesture.

The priest then introduced her to a handsome, though very quiet, American, who sat on his left whose name was Evan Hamilton. The young man had been staring unabashedly at Sarah since their arrival. The two men appeared to be the best of friends, which Cassie found strange, having assumed that the priest had spent little time among Americans.

"Good evening, Mr. Hamilton."

"How do you do, Mrs. Layton?"

"I'm fine, but call me Cassie, please." She wondered why she had never seen the American before. Perhaps he was newly arrived in Santa Fe.

"Thank you, Cassie. I would be most honored if you and your lovely sister would both call me Evan."

Unconsciously, Cassie compared him to Cruz. He was American, with none of the air of Spanish mystique about him. He had sandy hair, brown eyes, and was well-built, more square and athletic than the priest who sat beside him, but certainly no stronger. He had an honest, open face, and Sarah was clearly smitten by him. Sarah whispered in her sister's ear that she had seen him on her arrival at the plaza. Cassie then pointedly drew her sister's attention away from the priest and his companion, to introduce her to other acquaintances sitting near them at the table.

Dinner was served in an endless series of courses of rich, carefully prepared food. A creamy rice soup was followed by main courses that included roasted meats and a stew thick with big chunks of beef in a fiery red sauce. Vegetables of every conceivable kind, accompanied by yeast bread that was fresh and hot, were served by a large and efficient staff.

When she thought she could not force down a single bite more, a remarkable custard pudding sprinkled with raisins and cinnamon was brought out, along with wonderful fresh fruits pleasingly arranged on a silver platter.

The repartee between the young American Hamilton and her younger sister was lively enough and sufficient to keep her attention from straying too often to the priest throughout the meal. But it had been less than comfortable sitting so near him.

A few older couples drifted out after dinner while the chairs were being pushed back to accommodate dancers. Cassie would have joined them in leaving, but for Sarah, who wanted to stay. She was was not surprised that Sarah seemed to want to get to know Evan better.

"It's been such a long time since I've danced!" Sarah whispered to her. "And he's so good-looking!"

Cassie knew her sister had come a long way and endured a lot of hardships on her account. It was surely a small thing to stay for a dance. She nodded and slipped her arm in that of her sister. "All right. We'll stay for a while." Cassie was secretly glad her sister had persuaded her to stay.

The two priests seemed intent upon staying also, although the younger man appeared to want to keep his distance from Father Auguste, who was already "in his cups."

Eyes bleary and bloodshot and his speech slurred, the elder priest sat slumped in a chair off to the side of the floor now cleared for dancing. He reached out once to grab the arm of a fair young Mexican lass who strayed too near him and tried to pull her down onto his ample lap.

With a playful giggle, she resisted and twisted away out of his grasp. After that, the dancers cut a wide berth around him. He sat alone, his chubby hands clasped over his rotund stomach; his eyes followed the twirling skirts, sparkling with delight at the revelation of a bare ankle or a length of leg now and again.

The punch bowl was refilled as often as it was emptied, as were the cups Cassie and Sarah held. She thought the punch tasted different than usual, but she found it quite tart and delicious.

Couples began to dance, swaying to the exotic music. Laughter and the rhythm of the music filled the room. The handsome young Lieutenant Hamilton claimed Sarah for a dance.

Sometime later, the tempo of the music changed and a beautiful young woman began an erotic fandango near the center of the room. With her dark-hued skin, silken, inky-black hair and sensuous, voluptuous body, a man would have to be dead or blind not to notice her.

Cruz Delgado apparently was neither. He was enjoying the exhibition entirely too much, his wide grin showing off perfectly straight white teeth. Didn't the besotted man remember that he was a priest, and bound by his vows to the church? Apparently not.

Disturbed and trying not to pay any attention to Delgado's reaction to the dancer, Cassie drank several extra cups of the punch, without really being aware of what she was doing until it was too late. Her head began to swim and colors blended and faded before her eyes. She blinked and tried to focus, but to no avail. When she put the back of her hand to her forehead to stop the whirling, it did not the slightest good.

Holding onto the arm of her chair with one hand in an effort to keep herself from floating away, she tried to bring back her sanity and a shred of reasonable thought. Instead, she saw in her mind only fleeting images, brilliant colors and heard the echo of the vibrant, seductive cadence of the Spanish music.

What was happening to her? She'd had punch with spirits before, but had never felt anything like this. She had the strangest feeling, as though she were out of her body, a mere interested spectator looking on with curiosity to see what would happen next.

Suddenly, the air in the room felt close and stifling. Cassie felt faint. She was afraid she would pass out if she didn't get some fresh air soon.

Determined to make a respectable and ladylike exit from the crowded room, she shoved herself to her feet and stood there clinging to the arm of her chair for a minute or two until the room stopped its infernal tilting. She took a tentative step and smiled thinly. She could put one foot in front of the other if she did it with extreme care.

She would walk outside to the garden without weaving or falling flat on her face. But the outer door was such a great distance away, it could have been on the moon. How would she ever get there?

A gloved hand on her elbow impeded her unsteady progress, and an American soldier politely asked her to dance.

"Um, not right now," she said vaguely. She wished with all her might that she hadn't found it necessary to shake her head in a negative way. The movement, although slight, sent pain banging against her temples. It turned her stomach upside down or inside out, she wasn't quite sure which.

Unsteadily, she continued across the room, lessening the distance between her and the door with each careful step. By the time she reached her destination, two more men had requested a dance. She had refused, each time being circumspect in moving only her lips, not her head.

At last! She was outside. The cool air of late evening washed over her and she felt a tiny bit better, though still less steady on her feet than she might have wished.

"Ahhh . . ." she breathed, pleased with what she had accomplished all on her own. But she had to get home and put herself to bed before something awful happened. She was in trouble here and out of control, and she knew it.

Delgado had not been near her since the dinner tables were rearranged. She thought his attention had been trained too completely on the dancer. Why should that bother her? It had been true of every single man in the hall, without exception, even including the young American Evan Hamilton. But Cassie Layton was admittedly angry. She was frustrated and jealous, not to mention being tired and more than a little tipsy.

Memories of long, loving nights spent in Cameron's arms crashed into her without warning. She was defenseless and unable to resist their effect. Feeling alone and dreadfully sad, she dropped her head and grappled with her feelings.

A gentle hand fell on her shoulder. She whirled, pain and confusion in her eyes, fully expecting to see one of the obnoxious Spanish officers. Instead, she looked up into the countenance of the much too handsome priest who was looking down at her with smoky blue eyes. His warm smile crushed her defenses in an instant.

Cruz hadn't wanted to follow her outside, feeling entirely too vulnerable where she was concerned and leery of being alone with her. But he'd been afraid for her to be out there alone. Too many things could happen and he had promised himself, if not her, that he'd watch out for her.

He had been affected by the dance, but not nearly so much as by Cassie's fragile loveliness. Carefully, he'd kept his distance all evening, afraid to get too close. Ironically, he'd thought only of her, even when the dancer had rubbed up against him after the brazen display, offering him more than a dance.

After he'd rebuffed her overt advances, he'd looked around to see if Cassie had noticed, only to see her making her unsteady way toward the door. He had followed her as though he had no choice in the matter.

And he hadn't.

His hand dropped to her shoulder. In spite of himself, his fingers softly massaged her stiff muscles. "Something is troubling you tonight, Cassie?"

"No," she said, denying the truth of his words. She could never admit the turmoil of her emotions, not to him, not tonight.

The blue-eyed devil! She'd seen those eyes that looked at her so tenderly riveted brazenly on the seductive dancer, even though she had done her best not to notice that he was noticing.

"Too much Taos Lightning?" he asked softly. His warm chuckle did silly things to her spine. "It is a most potent drink."

Her head reeled and she found it difficult to maintain her composure, especially with the sound of that voice raising gooseflesh on her arms.

She wanted reassurance. She wanted loving. She wanted things that were taboo, things she'd once had,

164

but had lost for good. She wanted all these things . . . and more . . . so desperately. It was like an ache or worse, something alive gnawing at her insides. She was consumed by a pain and a longing that refused to go away.

Tentatively, she raised her hands and laid them on his arms that were still holding her shoulders and she looked up in to his eyes. Suddenly, she felt so sad, so very much alone. She needed him to stay with her, to be with her, to hold her.

He leaned toward her, saw the need so clear in her eyes and his arms moved around her without a conscious thought on his part. He, too, had longings that were overpowering.

He kissed her then, his mouth moving softly over hers and then demanding more. The musky fragrance she wore, combined with the sweet response of her lips, made his knees weak. His hands stroked the satiny skin of her bare shoulders, then fell to her waist to pull her tightly against him.

Haunting strains of a love ballad drifted out the open door; even the moon was doing its part, dropping golden rays of light on them. The night was touched by magic and the two of them were caught in its spell.

Promise smoldered in her dark eyes, now hidden by the sweep of thick lashes. She seemed oblivious, for the moment, to the priestly garments he wore. Her movements were like those of a kitten, lazy and sensual. With a curse, he gave into his spiralling emotions and swept her into his arms, kissing her deeply.

She moved against him, returning his kiss in an experienced way. He held a woman in his arms, a woman who no doubt knew about making love, a woman who would know how to make a man feel good. He felt her fingers thread through his hair, drawing him closer, and her body meshed with his along its length. She felt warm and lush and smelled of nighttime and flowers. Her soft, pliant response to his caress had more effect on his emotions than the steamy eroticism of the dancer. Even while he'd watched the dancer, his mind had been on Cassie, though he'd not dared to look in her direction. He recalled the way she'd felt in his arms during the long night they'd spent in bed together at her cabin.

But she didn't seem to be aware of what had happened between them that night. In her dreams, she'd reached out to him. That was all. He would be lying to her if he took what she so freely offered now. He couldn't do that in good conscience. He pulled himself back away from her.

"I can't, Cassie," his voice was choked and filled with longing and repressed desire. "I want to, but it's wrong. Don't you see?" His fingers gently stroked the soft down of her cheek.

"I don't *care* about that. I really don't want to care. I just want to feel, Cruz. It's been so long since I've felt such things. Do you understand?" Her voice caught and pain, mixed with desire, filled her eyes.

Yes, he understood. He damn well understood. His hands balled into tight fists while he fought his feelings.

Tears moistened her eyes and her lips quivered. His resolve weakened, just like his knees. He wanted nothing more than to take her in his arms and make sweet, passionate love to her all night long. She needed him, longed for his loving. He knew they could find paradise together. God only knew how very much he wanted her, how much he had wanted her from the first time he'd looked up into the eyes of his rescuing angel.

Now, the opportunity was his. Cassie would give herself to him. He had only to say the word, to make the first move. But he couldn't do this. Not this way.

Regret tinged his words when he spoke slowly, placing his hands so they rested lightly on her shoulders. "I'll walk you home. Stay right here."

He went back inside and asked Evan Hamilton to escort Sarah home whenever she was ready. Then he retrieved Cassie's wrap and reticule and his own coat.

By the time he had told the lieutenant not to expect to be taking her home and returned to the garden, Cassie had been transformed. The sadness and dizziness she'd felt earlier had disappeared, leaving a smiling and very sexy minx. She stood with her hands on her hips, her shoulders back, revealing entirely too much of her bosom.

"What?!" He stopped abruptly, seeing her, started to curse, thought better of it, and then laughed out loud. "Why, *Señora* Layton! I do believe you're drunk!"

"Never!" she replied haughtily, her eyes not quite focusing on him. She made three stabs with her arm to find the sleeve of her wrap that he held out to her. Finally, he took hold of both her arm and the sleeve and put one inside the other, still chuckling.

"I do declare, sir," she mumbled, "that I am quite

capable of *dreshing* myself!"

"So I see." He laughed. "But this is too much fun. Please allow me."

Easily, he slid her other arm into the opposite sleeve in the same way, without any help from her.

"Shall we go?" he asked.

"Go where?"

"I thought that I might escort you home."

"But Sarah, and the *Loo . . . lootenant!*"

"I explained to them that you would be leaving with me."

"Oh?" she said, but seemed to accept his suggestion without question. She fell into step beside him obediently, giggling and holding onto the arm he offered her with both her hands.

"*Ttsh* really a *nish* evening, *ishn't* it?"

"*Yesh!* Yes, it is!" he replied with a hoot of laughter, enjoying himself as he hadn't in a very long time.

It *was* a very nice evening. The weights and cares he'd felt earlier were swept away. He was prepared to enjoy her delightful company, at least for a little while. Before they reached her front steps, she was caterwauling off-key like a tomcat at a full moon on a clear night. She had never looked more fetching, more alluring. He'd never felt a stronger urge to make long, slow love to her for days without end.

"Cassie . . ." he began.

But she interrupted, looping her arms around his neck and planting a sloppy kiss on his cheek. "*Yesh,* Cruz. I want . . . to . . . thank . . . you," she spoke haltingly, trying to be sure of the words, "for escorting me home." She beamed up at him, thrilled with the effort she'd made to say the words just right, and the successful outcome.

She did not move away from him, and her arms remained tightly wrapped around his neck. Her lips sought his and she pulled his head down toward hers.

"Wait . . ." It took all his powers of restraint to set her away from him. "You don't want this."

"How do . . ." she faltered, trying hard to follow her train of thought before going on. "How do . . . you . . ." she went on, poking her finger into his chest, "know what I want? You *don'* . . . you *don'* know me at all."

"You're sure right about that, lady."

There was still humor in his voice, but his body saw nothing funny about it at all. Oh God! He did want to know her, to feel her body beneath him. He wanted to know all about who she was and what made her act in totally unpredictable but utterly charming ways. He wanted to know what she had been like as a child, wanted to know exactly how she looked without a stitch of that proper clothing she always wore on her shapely little body.

He swallowed hard and fought down his intense feelings. If she even had a hint about what he was thinking, all Hell would break loose. He might never be able to break away from her. Looking into her sultry, knowing eyes, he saw her complete awareness of his thoughts and feelings. His sigh was one of resignation mixed with heady relief as he swept her into his arms.

"Ah, my love . . ."

The endearment came from the depths of his soul

169

and he meant it with his whole being. Entranced, she watched the pulse flutter in the vein of his neck and her lips covered it, her tongue tracing its outline, then trailing up to his ear.

He shuddered then, his body moving in response and his arms tightening around her, pulling her as close to him as it was possible to do. She was small and vulnerable and she clung to him. She fit him so well. His fingers of their own accord played through the silken golden curls, loosening more of them to fall freely around her face.

He wanted her. He longed to take what she was so freely offering, but he couldn't do that without giving something back, and he had nothing to give her. His need to bring her pleasure was as great as the need to seek and find his own joy with her. This was not the right time. And he was all too aware that there might never come a right time.

Sanity made a claim on his mind and he tried to push her away, but she was having none of it. Her arms twined around his neck, her fingers kneading the muscled shoulders beneath her touch, skimming down his arms and back up to stroke his neck in a tantalizing way.

"It's not for always, Cruz," she crooned into his ear. "It's just for tonight. I only want what you can give me tonight."

Cassie was sober enough to recognize her words as a falsehood of gigantic proportions, yet she went on, "And don't you *shee* . . . how *mush* we both need it?"

He did. God help him, he did.

"We'll think about tomorrow . . ." she paused, trying to marshal her vagrant thoughts into some kind of sense and then smiled brightly. She had it! "We'll think about *t'morrow,* tomorrow! That's soon enough, *ishn't* it?"

Was it? Damn it it, yes, it was! Why couldn't he let go of himself and take what she offered so willingly? Because only one of them was drunk and, damn it to hell, it wasn't him!

"No, Cassie. This is not right. We can't do this."

Her lips puckered and the bottom one quivered in a maddening way. He very nearly lost control again. Had any damned thing ever been so hard to do in his entire life? To be truthful, he wasn't even completely convinced that she was wrong and he was right.

She slumped against him, her arms sliding down limply. He caught her before she reached the ground, his arms around her waist.

Praise all the powers that be! he thought.

She'd passed out cold and was a deadweight in his arms, taking some of the intense pressure off of his heart. The gut-wrenching decision was out of his hands for tonight. One day . . . or one night . . . at a time!

He had swept her up into his arms with one arm cradling her shoulders and the other under her knees. He stood there, immobilized for long seconds. He enjoyed the feel of her in his arms and was reluctant to put her down. He wasn't quite sure what to do with her either.

Once she'd put him to sleep and now he had the chance to return the favor. Though putting her in bed alone in her state of unconsciousness was the furthest thing from his true desires. It was almost comical. *Almost.*

No smile crossed his scowling face now as he held her in his arms, binding her against his chest where he could feel the steady thrumming of her heart.

Tempting little sprite. So soft. So sweet. So damned appealing. He had to get her to bed as quickly as possible and hope that would put an end to his own agony, but he suspected that it wouldn't help in the least.

He was all thumbs when he tried to unlace her slippers. He was even more inept when he turned her to her side and dealt with the row of tiny buttons down the back of her dress. He slipped the crinkly material down over her shoulders. Putting his hand under her waist and lifting, he was able to drag it over her hips and finally off over her toes. Carefully, he spread the dress across a chair, trying to steel himself to look at her one more time without touching her in an intimate way. His fingers tingled and his arms ached from the need to hold her. He reached to stroke the length of her bare arm, from shoulder to wrist, laying his hand over hers while he watched her, fighting the building passion in his body.

With one finger, he gently traced the soft fullness of her rosy lips. He had seen the spark of jealousy in her eyes during the fandango dance. He relished the thought that she might care enough for him to be angry in that way. He was not inexperienced with women, but no one in his life had ever moved him the way Cassie McPherson Layton could do, with no conscious effort on her part. Somehow, he had to keep his hands off the tempting body clad only in a soft, filmy

172

chemise. He would cover her so he wouldn't be tormented by the sight of her.

Unfortunately for him, she woke up before he could get her covered with the spread and make his hasty exit from her bedchamber.

"I knew you'd come around, Cruz Delgado," she said sleepily. "You want me. *Elsh,* why would you be taking my clothes off?" Her eyes blinked and made an effort to focus, but then drifted shut once more.

She was hauntingly beautiful with the golden light of the candles on the smooth skin of her face and shoulders, lighting sparks in the red-gold of her mass of curling hair that tumbled over her goose down pillow. The rise and fall of her pink-tipped breasts beneath the nearly transparent fabric of her chemise was impossibly tempting.

He smiled and squared his shoulders. "Not tonight, *Señora* Layton."

His murmur was laced with regret and tenderness and he was glad she hadn't heard. Carefully, he tucked the covers in around her, anxious to hide her seductive curves from his own seeking eyes as quickly as possible. Then he turned on his heel and left the room without looking back, hurrying out like a man running headlong from a building on fire.

But Cassie had heard the words and the longing in them. Maybe not tonight, but sometime soon. Sometime soon, she murmured to herself as she heard him let himself out. Then the sweet oblivion of sleep claimed her.

173

Cassie awoke to the aroma of coffee and the sounds of bacon frying and her sister humming. Sarah had fixed breakfast? she wondered, her head still a bit foggy.

So far, Sarah had shown no inclination to be the domestic type. Though she'd helped with the shopping and cleaning up back in Boston, she had made a habit of leaving the cooking to Cassie.

She would have preferred to sleep longer, but if Sarah had gone to the trouble of cooking, she would have to get up and join her. Cassie sat up, swinging her feet out of bed in one motion, just like always, and instantly regretted it. Her head pounded viciously and her stomach rolled.

"Breakfast is ready!" Sarah announced cheerfully from the doorway.

She spoke much too happily, for Cassie's frame of mind, which was less than pleasant, considering the size of her head. Had she really drunk that much at the governor's dinner party?

Somehow she managed to drag herself to the wooden table set with her best china, silver and linen napkins. The bacon was only burned on the edges and the eggs only slightly undercooked, but she didn't think she could manage to keep down a single bite.

"What's the matter, Sis? Not feeling so good this morning?" Sarah laughed, but not unkindly. She gave her sister a knowing wink.

"I . . . feel . . . well, I have felt better," Cassie admitted ruefully.

"Some breakfast will have you on your feet in no time," Sarah promised.

"I don't think so. It looks good, Sarah, but I'm just not very hungry. I'm sorry. Perhaps just some coffee?"

A few sips of the strong brew did make her feel a bit better. She looked across the table to see Sarah smiling widely at her, anxious to talk.

She groaned, putting a hand to her head, longing to go back to bed, to pull the covers over her head and forget the whole thing.

"What's going on with you and Delgado, Sis?"

At the mention of his name, Cassie was instantly alert, but not in any mood to answer questions. "It's *Father* Delgado, Sarah. And nothing is going on. Whatever makes you ask?" She tried to conceal the bright flush that stained her cheeks, but she suspected she was only partially successful.

"Oh, nothing, just the way the two of you couldn't keep your eyes off each other all night and the way you disappeared without saying goodnight to anyone. I noticed that a certain priest, too, was conspicuous in his absence."

"I . . . I . . . wasn't feeling well," Cassie said, averting her eyes from her sister, "and he insisted on seeing me home."

"*And* putting you to bed?"

"Of course not," she snapped. "Why would you think that?"

"A few things around here looked a little unusual, a little out of place, that's all. But if you say it's nothing . . . then it's nothing. We never could fool each other for long, could we, Sis?"

"No." Cassie rubbed her hand across her brow.

"Still not feeling well, eh?"

"No, not particularly. I think I'll take a bit of a nap, if that's all right with you?"

"You go right ahead, Sis. I'm sure you need one, if anybody ever did!"

Sarah spun around on her heel and began to clear away the dishes, her laughter ringing out and not doing Cassie's head a bit of good.

With a moan, Cassie lay across her bed, not bothering to crawl back under the covers, and tried not to think about what she might have done the night before.

Had something happened beyond the point that she could remember? She vaguely recalled coming home and Cruz. . . . God! Sarah was right! He must have put her to bed. Had anything else happened? Surely, even a mind as befuddled as hers would hang onto something like that, wouldn't it?

She frowned and squinted, trying as hard as she could to remember. But after he lit the candles and put her in bed, it was all black. She must have passed out.

He must really think she was something. To get silly drunk, for now she even remembered her awful singing on the way home . . . to get silly drunk and be put to bed by a man who wasn't her husband. Lord, what had she come to?

This was not the prim and proper Cassandra McPherson Layton of old. Her mind toyed with the very slight possibility that it might be an improvement and then discarded it. Her whole life had been built around who and what she was.

One enigmatic priest was not about to change all

that. Not if she had anything to say about it.

Those arms . . . those strong, dark-skinned arms with the fine dusting of black hair that had carried her so easily last night and gently smoothed the covers over her, those were the same arms that had made love to her in her dream.

Not Cameron's arms. . . . Not a dream? Please God, she prayed, it wasn't real, was it? Had the two of them made love that night when she crawled into bed with him to share her body heat? What she attributed to a very realistic dream, had it actually happened? She remembered calling out Cameron's name, and the picnic had definitely been a part of the dream of the past, but after that?

The arms that held her, the hands that stroked secret places to life, had those been the hands and arms of a stranger? If it had happened, he had to know. But he had never said a word. What if it hadn't been a dream? What would she do then? How would she ever face him again?

No, her dreams had just gotten fused with reality somehow and the arms wrapped around her seeking warmth had ended up in the annals of her dream world. Yes, that was it.

Not wanting to think about it anymore, she threw her arm over her eyes and willed herself to sleep a dreamless sleep.

When she went to the church later in the morning, Delgado was conspicuously absent. Cassie watched for him out of the corner of her eye all day long, as she listened to the children reciting their lessons, correcting their mistakes in her gentle voice.

Manuelito was in his place and did the work that was asked of him, but he was not his usual vivacious self.

"Mano, is everything all right? You do not still have a fever, do you?" she asked him when there was a break in the lessons.

"No, *Señora,* I am not sick any more, but only tired, I think." He tried hard for the remainder of the day to act as though nothing was wrong. Cassie was so distracted that he was able to convince her.

A happy smile stayed with Cassie throughout the long day, though its origin was unclear. She wasn't sure why she felt so good when she'd done her best to seduce the priest and he'd rebuffed her at every turn. Even her sister wondered what was going on.

In spite of all that, she felt the satisfaction of a woman who knows that she is desired, his protests to the contrary.

And there would be a tomorrow.

The strong drink had loosened her inhibitions, but had only served to reveal to her what it was she really wanted. She wanted *him.*

God help her, she loved him, didn't she?

"*Señora* Layton?"

"Yes, Juan."

Reluctantly, she set her troubled thoughts aside and turned her attention back to her youngest and most demanding student.

"*Por favor,* would you help me with these sums?"

His English was halting, but improving every day.

178

She smiled brightly at his efforts before bending her head to demonstrate the problem, unaware that Cruz picked that exact moment to leave, passing the door without being seen by her.

A narrow escape! He frowned as he stalked down the uneven steps of the church. The last thing he wanted today would be to come face to face with the seductive woman who had been in his arms the night before. He was equally as afraid to meet up with the staid and very proper widow Layton. He'd swear she had two very distinct, separate personalities, either one able to devastate him and weaken his firmest resolve with only a look, a smile, or a touch.

He couldn't stay away from her, couldn't avoid her forever. He knew that. Santa Fe was too small, and he was stuck there until his mission was done. So he might as well make the best of it.

Why not just make love to her, the thing she'd seemed to want last night and the thing he wanted so badly? It was a near constant pain in his heart . . . and in his lower regions, he thought with a moan slipping past his lips. But he couldn't entangle her in his life like that and endanger them both. It would leave her vulnerable to the man who would kill him without a second thought, if his identity ever became known.

And one day soon his job would be done, his mission complete, and he'd be leaving. Cassie McPherson Layton was not the kind of woman a man could make love to and leave behind.

No. She was the kind of woman a man wanted to cuddle up with on long winter nights, ride with across flower-strewn fields, and take long swims with in the hot summer. She was a woman whose wiles could snare a man so he'd never be able to leave her.

Chapter Nine

The Epidemic.

The next day Cassie made her way to the school-room. When Manuelito did not run out to greet her as was his custom, she was concerned and went up to his door to find out if he was really all right. He had not appeared to be ill during their lessons the previous day, though he hadn't been as vivacious as usual. When she had questioned him, he said he felt fine, but was just a little tired. And when she'd seen him later on the plaza, he had seemed to be fine.

During the night, though, she had awakened in the midst of a bad dream. She was troubled about the young lad, remembering his pink cheeks, his listless eyes, his unusually quiet behavior.

His mother, Maria Sanchez, in her halting English, opened the door and explained to Cassie that he was sleeping. She did not seem overly concerned that something might be wrong. After telling *Señora* Sanchez to be sure to send him on to school as soon as he awoke, Cassie continued down the street, gathering up the rest of the children on her way to the church.

When Manuelito didn't show up all day, though, she had a heavy feeling, a premonition that all was not well and that he might really be sick. She brought an early end to the day, anxious to get back to check on him.

This time, she would insist that Maria allow her to see him, just to be sure he was really all right. It was not like Manuelito to miss school. He was a bright and devoted student, always ready to start early and willing to stay late. He had never missed a single day before this.

A piece of peppermint in her pocket for one of her favorite students, Cassie walked up to the front door of his home and called out. The small dwelling was a typical adobe with brush and mud ceilings over wooden poles, much like many others in the community. Cassie knew something was wrong immediately when the boy's mother met her at the door, wringing her hands and with tears in her eyes.

Cassie put her arm around the plump woman's shoulders and said softly, "Take me to him, *Señora* Sanchez." She followed the woman into the front room where Manuelito's younger brother and sister were eating, sitting on the floor in front of the fireplace. As in many adobe houses in town, the fire served a dual purpose, to heat the dwelling and as a place for cooking indoors.

An unnatural quiet pervaded the small home. The children ate quietly; their big, somber eyes on Cassie who stopped to speak softly to them. Maria Sanchez pulled on her arm, urging her on toward a darkened bedroom lit only by a single candle.

She was startled to see Manuelito lying very still on his pallet on the floor, bundled up in a brightly colored, handwoven blanket. She fell to her knees beside him, very much alarmed at how still and pale he seemed with his eyes tightly closed.

When she put a hand to his head, his brown eyes, glazed over with fever, blinked open and looked up at her. He was burning up. She looked closer while her hand stroked his forehead and was alarmed to see tiny red bumps all over his face.

What could they be? She'd seen measles, but those red splotches looked nothing like this ominous splotching.

He tried to speak, but couldn't utter a word. His tongue was dry and his lips parched. He didn't make a sound, though his mouth worked. His big, black eyes were wide and very frightened.

"It's all right, Mano," she said, soothing him, placing her hand on his cheek that was hot to the touch and flushed with his fever. "I'll be right back and I'll help you. You'll feel better soon, you'll see."

She could only hope and pray she was right, but she was terribly afraid for him in her heart.

Maria shuffled out of the room behind her swiping at her tears. Trying to make the distraught mother understand what she required was too difficult and taking much too long.

Finally, Cassie gave up and went to the well for a cup of cool water. Returning to the room, she bent over and ripped a strip from her petticoat to use as a cloth.

Sitting cross-legged on the floor as near to him as

she could, she gently raised his head and held the cup to his parched lips.

"Drink, Mano. Please. You need this and it will make you feel better. I promise."

He took a sip or two, anxious as always to please her, before his head fell back and his eyes drifted shut.

Cassie poured water from the cup onto the soft lace she held and bathed his face, neck, and small arms and legs with it. She willed the fever to go down, anxious to see his eyes, bright and healthy once more.

Through the long night, the fever steadily climbed and the red bumps increased, spreading over his whole body. Cassie stayed with his mother by his side, the two of them doing everything they could to keep him comfortable and to get fluids and a bit of broth into his system. Precious candles, normally used only when necessary, were kept burning constantly during the endless night.

But they were losing their battle to help the small boy.

"We need help," Cassie said at last to the worried parents. "A doctor! A *medico!* We must have a doctor, *Señor* Sanchez!" she cried out to Manuelito's father who had stood by helplessly, rubbing his hands, through the night-long ordeal. Once, she'd seen him kneeling in front of a *bulto,* the carved statue of some saint, his lips moving in prayer. These were hard-working, religious people who had known trouble and deprivation in their lives, but never anything like this. Her heart had gone out to them.

"*Si, señora.*" He pulled a poncho over his head and let it fall about his shoulders. The stoop-shouldered man

184

left without looking back. She could only hope he'd understood her desperate plea and would bring a doctor back quickly.

Time dragged slowly by. Minutes became hours. Too much time passed. No one came to help.

Manuelito steadily declined, becoming weaker by the minute. He tossed and turned, moaning in his restless sleep, but he did not open his eyes again. Cassie rubbed his hands and spoke to him, exhorting him, begging him to get better, to talk to her, to take a drink or a sip of broth.

She had no idea what the devastating sickness was, nor did she have any knowledge of how to treat it. She could only hope she was doing the right things, that she had sent for the doctor in time. She could only hope and pray.

"Cassie."

A familiar voice drew her eyes to the open doorway. She hadn't heard him come in, but he was there! Her heart soared. His robes wrapped around him and his eyes warm with concern, he was a welcome sight. Surely Cruz—Father Delgado—would be able to help the boy. He did something for her just through his presence in the room, just by being there.

"Cruz."

His name spoken by her lips hung in the air for long seconds before she went on. "The doctor?" she asked. "Did you see him? I sent *Señor* Sanchez for the doctor. But it's been such a long time and they aren't back yet. I'm very worried about Mano. He has a very high fever and these awful red bumps."

"Yes," he replied, putting a comforting arm around

185

her, "I saw Felipe. He's still searching Santa Fe for a doctor, but he asked me to come as he ran past me near the church." His eyes on the boy were compassionate as he moved nearer, without taking his arm from her shoulder, a touch that brought her new strength and hope.

"What can I do to help, Cass?"

"Look at him, Cruz. He's so small, so helpless. What *is* it? What's wrong with him? What can we do for him? Surely there's something more, something I haven't thought of." She told him what they had been doing for Manuelito since she arrived there.

Cruz examined the fevered body of the child, looking at the spots, gauging the fever and gently feeling the swollen glands in his neck, looking in his mouth at an enlarged tongue that was bright red.

He knew what the sickness was immediately. For a year or more, Cruz had considered becoming a doctor. He had taken several medical courses, enough to recognize scarlet fever, or scarlatina, when he saw it. He also knew that there was no cure. Though some people were able to ride it out with no lasting effects, very often patients died from it, developing rheumatic fever or pneumonia, complications that could bring death.

"You know what it is, don't you?" she demanded, her voice cracking, her eyes wide and frightened, at the somber look on his dark-skinned face.

He hadn't wanted to tell her, hadn't wanted to scare her with the mention of the disease, for she would almost surely have heard of it. But he owed her the truth, as painful as it might be. Her eyes told him she

186

would settle for no less than that and they never left his face for a minute.

"It is the scarlet fever," he said softly. "We can only make Manuelito comfortable and pray it does not settle in his lungs. You have been doing all the right things, Cassie. There's nothing anyone could have done, nothing more that can be done."

The words were little comfort. She longed to do more for this child, this small boy who believed in her. Manuelito looked up to her and was, even now, depending on her to do something to help him.

"But surely there's something more we can do."

"No, I'm sorry, Cassie."

Tears rolled down her cheeks, but she resumed her place by Manuelito's bedside. She prayed as hard as she ever had in her life, willing the lad to fight the disease, to get better, to win, to live.

Another long hour passed before the boy's father returned with the doctor. They all stood aside while the elderly man with his thick shock of white hair bent over and examined the young boy thoroughly. When he spoke, his diagnosis agreed with the one made by Cruz earlier. He also prescribed the same treatment: rest, fluids and broth, if possible, along with bathing the fevered skin regularly with cool cloths to try to reduce the temperature.

The doctor checked on the other children in the household before he left. Cassie's fears escalated when she realized from his actions and his warnings that the deadly disease was also highly contagious. It could have been contracted by others in the household.

The other children in her class were at risk, as well.

They had probably already been exposed by being with Manuelito in the schoolroom over the past few days. Panic filled her heart along with an almost unbearable pain.

"What can we do, Doctor, to prevent the other children from getting it?"

"Nothing. Except from this point on, anyone with the disease should be quarantined, or kept away from others who have not been exposed and who might contract it. It is too late for the Sanchez family. They have all been exposed. So, too, have the both of you, I'm sorry to say." He looked with pity from Cassie to Cruz and back again, shaking his head sorrowfully.

The anguish in her wide brown eyes when they met Cruz's tore at his heart. He felt more helpless than he ever had in his life. She'd spent the entire night tending to the child and now she was in danger, too. She could have already been stricken with the disease without knowing it yet.

In that moment, he acknowledged how much he'd come to care for her. His feelings for her went well beyond lust. And well beyond friendship. He knew he couldn't bear to lose her.

Dear God, he breathed. I'm in love with this woman.

In the very same instant, he also saw the hopelessness of such an emotion. The two of them could never be together.

"Cassie, you have to go home and get some rest now."

"No!"

She argued with him, but the doctor joined Cruz in

insisting, and he offered to stay with Manuelito through the morning. Cassie reluctantly went home for a few hours, at last.

Cruz insisted on escorting her home and she drew strength from the strong arm wrapped around her in support and comfort. He had been a tower of strength she'd so desperately needed through the past few hours.

"I will send Emerson to get Sarah and take her to Luci's. Till he arrives she should wait outside. She will need to stay at Luci's until the contagion is over, until the danger is past."

"Oh." Cassie hadn't really understood what being contagious meant until that very minute, when Cruz made it clear she could be a danger to her own sister.

"It is merely a precaution," he reassured her, "and this will soon be behind us."

"I hope you're right, Cruz."

But she felt the danger and death predicted by Luci descending upon them all. She was frightened, but she was too tired and heartsick to think anymore.

They bid goodbye at her front door, and she thanked him for his escort home, a small thing after all they'd been to each other and what had happened over the last few days. Sarah, once warned, slipped by her with a squeeze of her hand and was soon gone.

Cassie was once more in her empty house alone. Making her way to her bedchamber, she fell across her bed and was almost instantly asleep. She had not even taken time to remove her shoes or her heavy skirts. Troubled dreams robbed her of restful sleep. In less than two hours, she was on her feet again and on her way back to the Sanchez home.

That afternoon, the nightmare continued and grew worse. Two more children were stricken with the fever. Cassie and Cruz divided their time between the homes of the three sick children, doing everything they could to defeat the disease. They struggled to keep it from spreading any further, and worked to calm confused and fearful families.

As days blurred in passing and as Manuelito clung tenaciously to life, others contracted the disease. Some who were less sturdy or determined to live than he lost the battle.

Three children were buried during the second week of the scourge, and hearts were raw and bleeding from their terrible losses. Five others were known to have scarlatina and scores more had been exposed, despite their best efforts to confine the disease.

Cassie dragged through the days in a haze of fatigue and pain, but she wouldn't quit. There were too many who needed her help. She went tirelessly from one home to the next, doing what she could. She took time out to sleep only when she knew she must, or collapse and be of no use to anyone.

Each time she saw the young priest who battled the disease alongside her, she was comforted to know she wasn't in this alone. He had been there every step of the way, to comfort and console the bereaved, to encourage and to tend to the sick children. He'd also been there with the families at the graveside as they buried their children. And he'd been there for her.

Together, the two of them ministered to the sick; together, they prayed over all the children and for all the families, doing their best to support each other.

Terrified, they watched for signs of the illness in themselves. Each day that there was no sign of it was a small victory.

But each time another child fell victim, they suffered and grieved. Sometimes the parents asked unanswerable questions when they turned to Cruz and Cassie for help or consolation.

"Our children are dying, *Señora*. What are we to do?"

Cassie had no ready answers to the desperate plea of Juanita Gonzalez, whose eldest son lay in a shallow grave and whose youngest daughter, the lovely Carmelita, hovered near death. Wracked with a blazing fever, her small body was covered with the despicable welts caused by the hideous, pitiless disease.

Scarlatina. Not a disease native to New Mexico. It had been imported, brought here by Americans, her own people.

"I am so sorry, Juanita. It is a terrible disease. We are doing everything we can."

They had applied cool cloths, kept the room darkened and supplied the child with fluids which she promptly threw up. Carmelita was not strong and was gradually losing her courageous fight.

"There is nothing more, except prayer."

Together, Cassie and the middle-aged Spanish woman knelt on the hard-packed dirt floor and offered up their prayers for mercy from a God who seemed very far away.

"The *padre*," Juanita said, scrambling to her feet with new hope on her lined face. "I shall call Father Delgado right away. He will pray with us."

And he had.

But it hadn't been enough.

The final toll of the terrible disease was the deaths of four children and one adult. Miraculously, Manuelito had survived and was recovering. Others, too, had fought and won, so there was victory intermingling with devastating defeat, a tiny silver lining on an ominous, black cloud.

Cassie never let herself stop—or even slow down—until the crisis was past. She never gave in to the grief that set so heavily on her heart continually, nor the exhaustion that weighted her limbs and threatened her own questionable health. Only when it was over, did she feel close to a total collapse and admit the need to sleep for days.

Cruz, too, was exhausted. They both had been worn to a fine edge by days on end of doing battle with the unthinkable, desperately working to spare one child, even one life from the deadly killer. Nerves and emotions were ragged, and fatigue claimed their bodies.

He felt a momentary surprise at himself. How easily he'd set aside his mission for the past few days to concentrate on bringing comfort and medical attention to these families stricken by disease. He was strangely starting to think and feel very much the way a priest should. He cared for these people, and he shared in their pain and in their victories. Had he taken on the character of his disguise? Or, had that caring part of him always been there, but subjugated to his hatred?

Even if Cassie had not been in the middle of it, he still would have been there, doing all he could. In his heart, there had been no choice to make. He had learned something about himself and he felt better than he had in a long time. Before he'd concentrated solely on revenge, now he discovered that by helping others, he could honor the family he'd lost in some way.

As had become his wont, Cruz walked Cassie home, her arm held securely in his. He adapted his pace to her shorter strides. They didn't speak and felt no need to break the silence that was a companionable one. They had come to have a new respect for one another and a new ease of friendship through the hardships they had faced together.

Still uptight and needing something before seeking the oblivion of sleep, the two of them sat alone in her parlor, candlelight flickering across their faces. The fire that Cruz had built crackled, its fragrance filling the room.

He poured coffee liberally laced with whiskey into an earthenware mug, put it in her hands and held them around it. He guided the cup to her lips and saw that she drank of the warming liquid. Her eyes were glazed with hurt and the fear that had not gone away . . . that might never go away. She looked very much like a little lost child herself. He found himself wanting to hold her forever, to keep the world outside.

"You did all you could, Cassie. No one could have worked harder or longer or sacrificed more for them than you have."

"But it wasn't enough, was it?"

In her mind's eye, she saw one after another succumbing to the scourge and then their tiny, lifeless bodies laid out so carefully in those obscenely small coffins. She heard the mournful cries and sobs of helpless parents who had been confronted with the worst that life had to throw at them.

They had all lost so much in those few days.

"It's a disease brought here by my people, Cruz. I feel responsible. Those innocent children," she paused, her voice choked with pain, "those innocent babes have done nothing to deserve such sickness and death. There was such bright promise in their smiles and their happy laughter. I'll never hear them laugh again." Her voice choked up with her pain and she couldn't go on, but his arm went around her shoulders.

She thought of little six-year-old Carmelita, buried with her precious penny doll. And others, just as young and just as special, lying cold in the ground.

"It's just not fair! Could I have done something more? Could I, Cruz?"

Cassie was shaking and crying, having let go finally after holding herself together for so long.

Cruz could see that the whiskey had not had time to have any effect in easing her pain — perhaps it was not even strong enough for that. He took her in his arms, hoping to absorb some of the hurt into himself, make her load lighter if he could.

Sobs tore out of her, and she pounded on his chest in her sad frustration. He covered both her hands with his, pulling her even closer to him; he stroked her back, her arms, her hair, wiping away the tears with a sweep of his thumb.

"No, love, none of it was your fault. How can you think such a thing? You brought them love and knowledge, not disease, not death! Do you hear me, Cassie?"

He set her away from him and shook her shoulders gently, forcing her to look up into his eyes. His voice was firm when he spoke again.

"You have to listen to me, Cass. You have to believe what I'm saying. It is the truth, my love. It is God's own truth, I swear."

He felt the shattering, how near she was to breaking. Fine tremors shook her as she clung to him again, trying through touch alone to absorb comfort from him, to take the healing he offered her.

Cruz had watched her with the children, patiently teaching them about life and giving them much more than lessons. While they'd labored together trying to snatch the children back from the deadly grip of the disease, he'd seen her keep going for days with no sleep, seen her hands redden and had watched her body grow thinner from the strain and from not taking care of herself.

Worse, he'd seen her grief and despair each time another child had been lost to the deadly disease. She had suffered greatly, but he'd never known quite how much until this moment when she sought comfort in his arms.

"Juan had the brightest eyes and the most promise of any of them," she went on as though unable to stop talking about the children. "He had such beautiful dreams for the future. And his smile . . ." Her words were broken off by the anguish that tightened around her throat, and her eyes held the sheen of more tears, yet unspilled.

His gut twisted at the evidence of her pain, a pain that mirrored his own. Yet hers was much greater and more deeply felt, for she had known them all longer, loved them all more.

"Cruz, the children—"

"I know, love, I know. Come here."

She heard the words and reached out again for the healing waiting for her in the warm circle of his arms.

"Cassie, love," he murmured, dropping kisses on her forehead, her closed eyes, her upturned nose and finally on quivering lips that responded, moving with his, drawing from him all he was able to give her. He was willing at that moment to give her everything she needed, for now and for always, if only he could.

Tonight, she needed the life-affirming benefits of loving, the assurance that life would go on. Even in the face of terrible tragedy, victory could be found, some hope for a better future.

He swept her up into his arms and cradling her gently strode into the bedroom, kicking the door shut behind them, locking the world and all its anguish outside.

He had been inside her bedchamber before without paying much attention to the furnishings. But for some reason, the room seemed familiar tonight, like an old and dear friend. It wrapped around them in welcome.

Cruz glanced about, noticing the high bed with its wooden bedstead and thick mattress where he'd reluctantly put her to bed and even more reluctantly left her alone the night of the dinner party. He glanced at the American clock on the wall above, a rarity in Santa Fe, that must have been brought out here by her and her husband. His eyes lingered on the handmade quilt and embroidered pillows, and he wondered if she had crafted those herself.

He wanted to know everything about her. He wanted to know her favorite color, her preferences in music and literature. He wanted to know about her childhood and he wanted to share with her his own.

Lord help him, he wanted to be a part of her life.

Inside the sparsely furnished but comfortable room were only the two of them now, man and woman, with needs and desires that could be satisfied only by the other. He held her in his arms, reluctant to put any space between them, his steady heartbeat blending with hers until they seemed to beat as one.

When he could postpone it no longer, he turned back the cover and lay her tenderly on the bed. His arms felt empty without her in them.

Then, he turned to light several candles in their brass candlesticks on the wall and to stoke up the fire in the fireplace. He was thankful it opened into the bedchamber as well as into the front room, since it gave a pleasant warmth and a cozy feeling to the large, high-ceilinged room. Determined that everything should be perfect for this one night, he set a bucket of water over the fire to heat for the bath he knew she'd find welcome. It would ease her aching muscles and tired body and would bring a measure of peace to her troubled mind.

The exhaustion and the pain would be pushed aside for a more basic and elemental need. He wanted her more than he had ever wanted anything. His body ached with his need to make her his, to lose himself in her warm, moist center. He was sure he'd seen the same desire building in her eyes.

He began to undress her tenderly even as her wide eyes watched him, beckoned him. Her clothing made a small pile beside the bed. His eyes filled themselves with her golden beauty and the cloud of red-gold fire that was her hair fanning out around her.

When he bent toward her, she reached up for him and drew him down until their lips met in an affirmation, a declaration that at least for this one time, they would be one. They would make love until they were satisfied and had found in it some release from the relentless pain of the past few days. It seemed to be as good a reason as any for a physical union that they had longed for and fought against for weeks. Now, they willingly reached out for it.

Cassie knew she was not thinking clearly, was not being sensible, but she'd never wanted anything so badly. It was a deep, gnawing ache inside, her need for him. All she had to do was say one word and he would stop. She knew that. And she knew that she should say it. Now, before it was too late. But just this once, couldn't she do something entirely for herself? She would reach out and take what she longed for.

And the consequences be damned. For she knew there would be consequences, even if no one besides the two of them were ever to know what went on in this room, this night.

He kissed her long and deep, but with a gentle tenderness that spoke of his delight in her and his need for her, a need that went deeper than desire and physical longing.

With a soft curse, he dragged himself out of her arms and set about hauling in the tin tub and filling it with the water he'd warmed over the fire.

He put his elbow in to be sure it was a comfortable temperature and, satisfied that the bath was just right, he scooped her up in his arms and strode across the room. She was so light, he was hardly even aware that he carried her. She had lost weight over the ordeal, and she had always been small and fragile.

Gently, he eased her down into the warm, scented water. Her sigh of contentment brought him an intense, burning pleasure. He took a soft cloth and the slippery bar of fragrant soap, giving his full attention to the task and trying not to let his fingers linger in tempting, secret places.

There would be time for that later.

She lay her head back against the rolled towel he held in place for her and settled down comfortably into the water, giving him beguiling glimpses of golden skin and soft, womanly curves. These visions fairly took his breath away.

Did she have any idea what she was doing to him? He had to have relief from the unholy torment that loving her purely had brought him. But could he take what she offered him, even if he wanted it more than his life, more than he wanted to live for the next twenty-four hours?

"Mmmm," she murmured, as his hands slid down her arms and brushed across her hips to massage their way down her legs, treating each long leg to special, individual attention.

The smile that curved her beautiful lips told him she just might very well have some notion of the effect she was having on him.

"Feel good?" he asked, his question sounding silly in his own ears. He smiled.

Brown eyes with tiny flecks of gold blinked open and looked up at him. There was no smile on her lips now, just a sensual heaviness in her glance.

His eyes darkened and his hands stilled their gentle torture while only their eyes spoke.

"I want it too, love. Soon," he promised. "Slide down a bit and tilt your head back, just so. I'll shampoo your hair for you."

"Ah," she responded as his fingers moved easily through her tangled curls, separating each one and combing through the thick burnished gold mass ever so gently with his fingertips.

"No one ever did that for me before." Her voice was silky, like her hair and it wrapped its tendrils around his heart until there was no escape for him. Even if he wanted to now, he knew he couldn't leave her.

"I'll do things for you that no one else has ever done," he vowed, his voice a caress. "I will love you as no one ever has."

And he knew he could. He'd never wanted anything

so much in his life, and she wanted it, too. He bent his head and captured her lips, savoring the softness and the sweet freshness of her response.

The kiss deepened and his tongue stroked and teased and tasted. Tentatively, she did the same, exploring first his lips and then slipping her tongue inside to dart lightly, as she shyly returned the favor.

He held her captive with his mouth, loathe to let go, his mouth moving over hers. He wanted her so desperately, it was an aching hurt inside him that cried out for release. With a groan, he pulled away, ran fresh water over her hair to rinse it, squeezed it gently dry with his fingers and wrapped it in a fluffy towel that had been warming near the fire.

Putting his hands under her arms, he raised her until she was standing calf deep in the tepid water. He couldn't keep his eyes from her smooth, glistening skin and the shadows of her curves. Water clung to her in the most maddening places, drawing his eyes like a magnet to the rosy nipples and lower to the elegant rounding of her hips and the long, sensuous line of her legs. He might have stood there staring at her for a much longer time, but she shivered from the cold air brushing across her bare, damp skin. Quickly, he wrapped another heated towel around her shoulders and lifted her easily from the tub, holding her to him for a moment longer than necessary before releasing her.

He stood her on a woven rug near the fire and, taking his time, dried her all over, his hands stroking hypnotically, the activity stoking the fires of his own hunger. He loosened the towel from her hair and rubbed its silky red fullness until it was nearly dry as well, and it gleamed brightly in the firelight. He stepped back to look at her and inhaled sharply, fighting the need that coursed through him, the fine-edged desire that spread through his body, consuming him in its intensity.

She shivered and he snatched a night rail from the back of a nearby chair where he'd put it earlier after locating it in one of her bureau drawers. He slipped it down over her head, watching it slither over the delightful planes and curves of her long-legged body.

Her eyes showed her gratitude mixed with disappointment and confusion. He hastened to reassure her, "Not quite yet, love."

With one hand, he pulled his shirt up and off over his head while his eyes never left her. Efficiently, he reached down and slid his feet out of his boots.

Warm desire darkened her eyes while she watched as he unbuttoned and dropped his trousers and then stepped out of his long underclothing.

Her pulse beat like a moth fluttering near a candle while she stared at him. He had a breathtaking body, long and sleek with tension rippling along his muscles. His skin was as bronzed beneath his clothes as his face. She'd always loved that natural tan that set off his eyes so startlingly. He was beautiful. She felt the most extraordinary torment at the sight of him.

He stepped into the lukewarm bath and sponged himself all over while she watched with a deep satisfaction. He did not tarry but was quickly out, had dried himself, and joined her once more.

At last, all was ready.

The room was cozy. They were both warm and relaxed, their exhaustion and pain forgotten for the time. He lifted her in his arms and kissed her in a long, heated kiss before he gently laid her down on the bed where the covers had been turned back invitingly.

Cassie was feeling languorous and refreshed from the most memorable bath of her life. With a glad cry, she took refuge in his loving arms, open and welcoming, waiting for her.

Her experience with lovemaking had been more limited than she'd ever realized until this moment. She had just boldly watched Cruz get out of his clothes. Without any feeling of self-consciousness, she had enjoyed the sight of his beautifully sculpted body as he'd bathed himself.

But she couldn't remember ever once watching Cameron undress, even though they had been married for a handful of years before he died. She would have been much too embarrassed. The two of them had always gone to bed in their nightclothes, removing them only after the candles had been extinguished and they were under the covers. Her husband had never looked at her like something good to eat, his eyes devouring her as Cruz had done this night.

And he'd surely never tended to her needs in such a tender and seductive way. She could still feel the warm gentleness, the sensual stroking of Cruz's hands on her tired body, the silken fragrant warmth of the bath, his hands massaging her head so luxuriously when he'd shampooed her hair.

He'd restored her life and her will to live, as well.

He built fires that she'd thought long turned to ash, but that even now burned deep inside her and refused to die.

She would never be the same person after this night. She never wanted to be. He made her feel womanly and desirable, attractive in a completely new way.

She nestled against him and felt the rightness of it, the perfect fit of this man with this woman. Her head fit neatly into his shoulder just below his chin, her breasts rubbed the downy hair of his chest, causing a distinctive tingling between her legs. Her heart thrummed against her chest, echoing the rapid beating of his.

The hard length of him pressed into her and she moved against him, her hands exploring the muscular masculinity in his shoulders, his lean, long back and firm buttocks that rotated in an evocative and irresistible way against her fingers.

His hands, in turn, were doing unbelievable things to her, sparking flames everywhere they fell until she felt the lightning heat of a building inferno, the sweet warm fire of loving.

"Ah, my love," he breathed.

That mystical voice speaking words of love was her undoing. She would have given him anything, done anything he asked, gone with him anywhere in the world in that moment. She was his as surely as if a claim had been duly staked out in her heart.

"My sweet," he went on, murmuring endearments even as his hands moved magically across her bare skin. He chuckled and she knew he was pleased by the obvious and uncontrollable response of her body to his.

"Cruz—"

"Say it," he demanded softly.

"My love," she whispered in answer.

Any other words were lost in the thunderous beating of joined hearts.

Playfully, he nipped at her neck and then his lips nuzzled and tugged on her ear, the dark hairs on his chest tickling her. She couldn't resist stroking there with her hand, enjoying the feel of the soft, springy curls beneath her fingers.

He lifted her over him and settled her easily on top of him. The kiss they shared was moist and slow, his teeth softly grazing her lips before his tongue dipped inside to caress her in a new and intimate way.

Pulling away, he looked long into her eyes, the turbulent fires blazing there. He rolled to one side and eased her off him and onto her back, before lowering his head over her chest. His tongue flicked across her nipple that hardened and tightened at his touch. His hands worked a magic of their own, finding the silken nest of hair between her legs, his hand cupping her warmth and stroking, before his fingers dipped inside.

Tremors shook her. He quieted the gasp of pleasure that escaped her lips with his mouth on hers once more. But his gentle torment was not done. His tongue traced a line down over the other breast, to which he ministered in much the same way, dragging a sigh of wonder from her. But he wasn't through. His tongue traced a line down her midriff, dipping into her navel and then slipping lower still, stroking her satiny skin, lighting blazes along the way.

She called his name once and arched against his mouth, into the caress of his lips and tongue, accepting gladly the delights he brought her until she could stand not one minute more. He held himself back from her, but she knew there was more loving to come.

Wanting to love him the same intimate way in return, she rolled over and out from under him. She climbed up to straddle his midriff and bent over him. Her hair cascaded around them in a brilliant red-gold curtain, shutting out the world, sealing them in a private nest of touching, of sensation, of loving.

Her tongue licked at his flat, masculine nipple, drawing an unexpectedly fervent response from him. He held onto her tightly and moved his head back and forth, enjoying what she was doing to him, and wanting so much more.

Intrigued, she continued her gentle torture, slipping lower until her hand cupped the nest of hair between his legs. Her lips traced the firm, smooth length of his shaft, standing at attention for her, eager for her.

"Ah, Cass, my love, you do try a man's endurance," he moaned, pulling her back up his body until he filled his mouth with her puckered breast and suckled. She moaned, her hands on his shoulders and then she bent to kiss him.

She began to set the pace, playing the role of the enchantress. With a sigh, he lay back then and stretched his hands over his head, allowing her to orchestrate the lovemaking. This time, the seduction would all be on her part. The power this gave her came with an excitement of its own that she transmitted to him.

She brushed the silken raven hair back from his tanned, unlined forehead and placed kisses on his eyelids, his nose, his cheekbones. Her lips traced a path over to nibble on his ear, much as he had done to hers, and then back to claim his lips in a hot, open-mouthed kiss that had him writhing, begging for more.

"You torment me, Cass!" he cried. "But I swear that it is the sweetest agony I've ever known."

"I know," she answered with a chuckle, her voice husky. Her pulses seemed to beat in the strangest places: in her neck, behind her knees, fluttering like a butterfly in her side. A spreading hollowness made her feel weak, and desire flowed through her veins like rivers of molten lava.

When he could resist no longer and when she was ready to take him inside her, she sank down over him and he entered her. They moved together in a dance as timeless as the mountains. Rocking together, they blended into one complete whole. Their bodies rose and fused, and wave after wave of crashing pleasures shook them in a mindless ecstasy that seemed to go on and on, with no end.

Afterward, their bodies were still entwined, still intimately joined. Neither seemed inclined to put an end to the embrace, to the loving they'd shared.

Gradually, their breathing returned to normal, but no words were spoken. Giving in to her utter exhaustion and replete from the loving, Cassie slept peacefully before very many minutes had passed, cuddled against him, secure in his arms.

Long after he was sure she slept soundly, Cruz eased himself out of her arms, and drew the covers carefully up under her chin. He looked long at her loveliness, noting the flush that lingered on her cheeks, the rosy fullness of her thoroughly kissed lips, the wild flame of her hair spread over the pillow. She was the most beautiful woman he'd ever seen.

He pulled on his clothes hurriedly, spun on his heel and left quickly, while he was still able to move away from her.

Whatever the cost to his heart to leave her, he knew he couldn't stay. He would never bring her ridicule or have her asked uncomfortable questions by Sarah, or anyone else who might notice that he had spent the night in her home, in her bedchamber.

Later, when he was alone in his hard, narrow bed, he would have time to wonder just what he'd wrought by his actions this night. Had he taken advantage of her vulnerable condition after all she'd been through? Probably so, but he'd felt battered, too, and had needed her as badly as she seemed to need him.

Would she look him in the eyes when they met on the morrow? Or would shame keep them apart? He fell into a troubled sleep at dawn with these questions still on his mind.

Chapter Ten

Weeks of mid-winter went by and little changed. The weather steadily worsened, becoming colder, and snows fell more heavily and more frequently. It was very much a typical New Mexico winter. Hearts in Santa Fe were heavy from the loss of the children, but life went sluggishly on. Those most affected, did their best to cope with the tragedy, to make some sense out of it, to comfort each other when they could, and to live each day as it came.

Cassie's and Cruz's problems had worsened and were complicated further by what had happened between them after the crisis was past. They studiously avoided being alone together, although she noticed that he was never far away. He seemed determined not to let anything happen to her, to be there should she need his protection.

When they were together, she tried to act naturally, but her increased awareness of him made that task exceedingly difficult. It was hard to see him without thinking of what he'd looked like that night in her bedchamber when he'd stood before her, naked and proud, with love radiating from his intense blue eyes.

Cassie fought the desire to curl up in his arms and recreate their night of loving. She wanted nothing more than to be with him, to be loved by him; the need was a constant ache. But it was hopeless. They both acknowledged that. She did not regret what had happened, though. It had given her back her life and the will to live after all the sickness and dying. Because of it, she was able to go on.

Emerson called on Cassie and Sarah at regular intervals, entertaining them with tales of his exploits in marketing his wares in town and with words of wisdom for them that neither of the young women chose to heed. Still, he was a constant, bright spot in their lives, and his humor gave them laughter and hope. The older man had become like a father to them both.

Evan Hamilton courted Sarah. As they became closer, Cassie tried not to be envious of their developing relationship. When they were together and laughing, she did her best to hide her feelings, but it was so difficult. Evan promised to use his connections to find out what he could about Cameron's death. She had the distinct impression that he had a purpose for being in Santa Fe other than a routine military one, but he never admitted as much.

As hard as she tried, she could not keep her mind from straying to what she and Cruz had shared, to what might have been for the two of them, if only. . . . But he was a priest, and that was the end of it. They could never allow a repetition of their night of lovemaking to occur. It was a sin. And it was over.

He had sought to comfort her, and she had reached out for that comfort.

Could that be so wrong? Yes, it was wrong.

No more troubling incidents had occurred, but Cassie was no closer to discovering the truth about Cameron's death than she ever had been. She did not feel that she was in any kind of immediate danger, since apparently she was no longer being followed or watched. But the men who opposed her were no less serious in their campaign to shut her out, to keep the truth from her. There seemed to be a conspiracy of silence.

The children who had survived the epidemic thrived and continued to learn from her eagerly. A few new students had hesitantly joined them. Cassie's greatest joy was found in their small successes and their unquestioning companionship and love. As always, the parents of her students brought her gifts of fresh eggs, hams, bacon, and other items as tokens of their appreciation for what she had done, not only during the epidemic but in the weeks that followed when she continued her students' education. It was the only payment she received and more than she had ever asked for or desired. She would have been content just to help them and to see their progress.

The last time Cassie had seen Lucita, her friend had seemed nervous and agitated, but excited about something she wouldn't discuss. She brushed off Cassie's attempts to find out what was going on, saying she would find out in due time. Since then, she'd seemed to be constantly busy with her customers. Cassie had seen little more of her since then.

Cassie tried not to think about her encounters with

Cruz Delgado on the night of the governor's party and most especially, on the night after the epidemic when they had made love. She was only successful at suppressing these recollections for small periods of time. When she did remember, it was with a longing so intense she didn't know how to cope with it.

She was also burdened with an excruciating weight of guilt. She felt that somehow what had happened to the children was her fault. Added to that was her guilt for having made love to a priest. She carried a heavy load that she shared with no one.

Cruz had made it clear by avoiding her that what she felt was one-sided, that what they'd shared that night was only a reaction to what they had been through together. His attitude said plainly that there was no place for her in his life. He was a *priest*.

She'd seen him regularly in the company of the oily and untrustworthy Juan Perego and even more often with Father Auguste, which she had to admit was not that unusual, since they worked together at the parish church. But both men with whom Cruz was associating were unsavory, and their motives and activities questionable.

How had she dared to imagine for even a brief instant that Cruz might not really be a priest, that it was somehow just a disguise? It had only been a vain hope, at best, mere wishful thinking on her part.

In his dealings with the parishioners, Delgado had shown himself to be a man of a different caliber than Father Auguste, and the people had willingly turned to him for leadership. He was unfailingly kind and considerate with them all and seemed genuinely concerned about their problems. He counseled them in their loss and was always there when he was needed, not just in the confessional booth like Father Auguste, who had more and more of late been missing from the church and had been acting in a most suspicious way. The children in particular clearly adored Cruz and he them. He spent as much time with them as he could, but always when Cassie would not be there.

Tensions in the politically divided town had heated up. The Americans who arrived now turned their eyes and hearts toward an imminent American takeover. Spanish officials by their actions showed that they would resist such action. Violence could be the only end for such a conflict, with innocent lives taken on both sides.

Helpless to alter the outcome, Cassie was frustrated and dispirited. She watched the men who'd wronged her and her husband ever more closely, still hoping they would divulge the truth for which she had searched so diligently, and that some peaceful solution might be found to the political problem.

Cruz fought a constant battle with his own demons. He was drawn to the parishioners in a way he had never expected to be, and discovered he was becoming caught up in their lives. It made his job infinitely more difficult to do, and it would make his leaving harder.

Though he sincerely cared for the people, he was an imposter in the role he played and felt true guilt over this. He'd even had to assist in giving communion and had been called on to hear a confession or two. The guilt he felt was a heavy weight on his shoulders, but he was trapped in this lie and there was no way out, at least not now.

His mind was filled with images of Cassie: adorably tipsy as she'd been after the governor's party, sleeping peacefully when he'd left her that same night, working diligently with the children, lying satisfied in his arms, happy and laughing in the company of Sarah and Emerson.

She was everywhere, occupying the empty spaces of his mind. She was everywhere, except in his arms, where he most wanted her to be. Where she could never be. Their paths led them in different directions and, just as they'd had separate pasts, so they must have separate futures.

To see her was to ache inside and to be away from her was misery of an even more painful sort. She was a magnet, drawing him, her pull on his emotions stronger than anything he'd ever felt in his life.

She'd made him feel like a man again and he'd felt alive for the first time in years. He desired her and hungered to make love to her again in a painful way. But the physical side of love wasn't all he needed from her, was perhaps even the least of his need.

Was this growing love for her stronger than his undiluted need for revenge? Surely not. It couldn't be. He'd vowed that nothing could ever get in the way of that, and he'd never broken a vow, most particularly one he'd made to himself. He'd have to stiffen his resolve to do what had to be done.

Could he walk away from her now if it were demanded of him? A jagged, excruciating pain pierced his heart at the thought. But wasn't that just what he had to do?

He would speed up his covert activities in an attempt to flush out his adversaries and put a quick end to his reason for being in Santa Fe. And then he would be on his way as quickly as possible.

Evidence he'd recently unearthed pointed at Cameron Layton more and more as having been a participant in the scheme he was investigating. He knew Cassie would never forgive him if he brought any disrespect or cast doubt on her dead husband's character or reputation, yet he couldn't help himself. He had to learn the truth, whatever it might be. And he had to settle accounts with the man who had ruthlessly killed his family.

A note fastened to her door with a hunting knife was waiting when Cassie returned from the church, tired and hungry, wanting nothing more than a meal and a good long night's sleep.

"Just when I thought my life had returned to normal," she muttered.

Sarah, walking beside her, saw the note only after Cassie pointed to it. The younger sister was quite alarmed, even more so after Cassie read aloud the words printed boldly in charcoal.

"Mind your own business," she read. "Let sleeping dogs lie."

Let them lie indeed! She snatched the paper off the knife and wadded it angrily into a ball. With her other hand, she reached for the shaft of the knife and yanked until it pulled free of the slatted wood, leaving a jagged, ugly scar behind. Its ivory handle felt evil and out of place clutched in her hand. It clattered onto the wooden porch when it fell from her fingers.

"Cassie! What is the meaning of this?"

"It's just a harmless threat, Sarah, nothing to worry about." She reached down and retrieved the knife, still holding it like a snake that could strike at any moment, but trying to keep her concern from her sister.

She uttered the sensible words entirely for Sarah's benefit, knowing she had more than a little cause to worry. She was suddenly terrified, but she was not about to stop probing and asking questions. If they thought a knife stuck in her door would do the trick, they were sadly mistaken.

But whoever had done this meant business, and they would be back. Did it mean she was getting closer to the truth? Possibly. It certainly showed some fear on the part of her adversaries. At least, she hoped it did.

"I wish Emerson were here," Sarah said. Emerson, too, had been trying to learn some things to help her from some of his friends in the business community in town.

"Me, too," Cassie concurred.

"And Evan."

"Mmmhmm." And Cruz, Cassie thought but the words were unspoken.

She was distracted and only half listening to her sister, already thinking about how she could find out who'd left her the warning.

"Evan's going back East in a couple of months. He says he's about finished with his business here. He'll be in Washington for a while."

"That's not far from Boston," Cassie said, turning to her with a smile.

216

"Not too far," Sarah agreed with a smile of her own. "You really like him, don't you, Sarah?"

"I really do. He's the finest man I've ever met. He's such a gentleman. And he's so good-looking!"

They both laughed at that, remembering it had been Sarah's first comment about the young American. Cassie had to admit the young officer was nice-looking, but she wished they knew a bit more about him. The fact that he seemed to be a friend of Cruz's was recommendation in itself, though, so there was probably no need for concern.

Through the rest of the evening spent in front of the fragrant fire, Cassie tried to downplay the importance of the warning, and Sarah tried her best to believe her. Cassie was glad to have her sister back home, now that the scarlatina epidemic was behind them. She needed the joy and laughter Sarah brought with her. Tonight, she needed the comfort of her presence.

Another warning came from someone close to her when she'd gone to Luci's house for lunch. She needed to visit with her friend, even if it was only for a short while.

Luci was delighted to see her and, since she was between customers, they had some time to visit and catch up on the time they'd been apart.

Without preamble, Luci blurted out unexpected words of advice. "Cassie, my dear friend. You must be very careful. I see trouble and death. Bad signs surround Father Delgado and they are dangerous to you, as well. You must not be near him. Please stay away from him, Cass!"

Luci was frowning, her ever present happy smile wiped off her face. Usually animated, she seemed more disturbed than usual today. Cassie frowned, trying to decide what to make out of her heated warning.

It was strange that Cruz had told her nearly the same thing, back when they'd first arrived in Santa Fe, warning her to stay away from him, saying they would be better off apart.

Why didn't she have the sense to listen to either one of them? Because she was a stubborn fool, that's why!

"Cass, you're smiling! This is serious! Will you listen to me for once? For one time in your life, take some good advice. That's the only kind I ever give, now, isn't it?"

Luci, too, was smiling. They knew each other entirely too well and liked each other far too much. She shrugged. She had shared her warning and that was all she could do.

"Oh, Luci!" Cassie said, taking her friend by the hand, "what would I ever do without you? My life would be so dull. I need someone like you to give me advice, whether it's good or not, *occasionally!*" She pointedly emphasized the last word, her eyebrow raised.

"Even if you never take it? And you never do, Cass. No matter what I see, you ignore it and go right on your merry way, running blindly into all kinds of trouble. Which brings me back to the priest, where this all started. He is trouble of the worst kind for you, Cass."

"I remember not so long ago, your saying something about some dark and handsome stranger coming into my life?"

218

"Forget about that!"

"What?" Cassie asked with a chuckle. "Forget about one of your predictions?"

"Well, I can't always be right, can I?"

"You are not right this time. Cruz would never do anything to hurt me. He's not a violent man. He's a good and decent man."

Cassie recalled his loving touch as he'd soaped her back and shampooed her hair when she'd been too tired to do it for herself, the way he'd cared for the sick and dying children, the way he'd comforted their families, the way he'd been there for her when the ravages of death and disease had brought her to the edge of collapse.

"All right. I won't say any more on the subject," Luci grumbled.

"Of course you won't."

"At least, not today."

Once more the women were smiling, their somber mood broken. A knock on the door had Luci on her feet, but her conversation continued, with her talking back over her shoulder even while she walked over to the door.

Sarah entered the room with a small bag in hand.

"Oh, my!" Luci exclaimed in mock alarm. "You're not back!"

Sarah laughed. "Not on your life! I just came to collect a few things I left behind. I thank you again most heartily for your hospitality, Luci, but it's ever so much quieter at Cassie's. Still," she went on with a wink in Cassie's direction, "it was an experience staying here. Cass, you wouldn't believe the fascinating people who regularly come and go around here.

219

It's better than the Governor's Palace, I swear!"

"You are exaggerating, Sarah. Why, if I were that busy, I could surely afford more luxury than this," she said with a wave of her hand to indicate her humble adobe house.

"Come back with us," Cassie urged, "and have dinner. I've already invited Emerson and Evan Hamilton."

"Anyone else?" Luci asked, eyebrow lifted.

"No, that's all. There will be five of us, if you'll come, too, that is."

"All right, then. I accept."

Luci got her wrap, Sarah gathered up the few things she'd left there, and they happily left her house together. Wrapped up in their happy conversation, they didn't see the crowd that began to gather. Before they could turn the corner, they were accosted by an angry group of people.

"*Bruja!*" they were shouting. One of them pointed a finger at Luci and accused, "Our children are *muerto* and you are to blame! You have cast the *malojo*, the evil eye, on our little ones. Leave Santa Fe now, before it is too late. You are no longer wanted here!" Their anger was directed at Lucita, who was in a state of shock while they railed at her, and completely unable to defend herself.

"What is the meaning of this?" Cassie demanded, stepping between her friend and the angry crowd. "Lucita had nothing to do with the deaths of your children. She is *not* a witch! Your children died from a disease brought here by the Americans. There was no spell put on them!" Her voice softened as she went on, "I know your losses are great and you have suffered much. But you must not blame her."

"*Señora* Layton, do not put yourself in the middle of this. Our problem is with your friend. She has a *pactado con el diablo,* an agreement with the devil. You have done only good for our children. You teach them. You are there when they are very sick. You and Father Delgado bring only good to us. But she . . ."

The older woman who was speaking pointed a gnarled, bony finger at Luci. "*She* is the one to blame. She brought this terrible thing upon us with her spells . . . and her potions!"

"No, that isn't true!" Luci burst out, tears in her eyes. "I would *never* do anything to hurt the children. I know nothing of any spell. You believe me, Cassie, don't you?" Her voice broke as she went on, "You know I'd never hurt the children. I love the little ones as much as you."

"Of course you do, Luci."

Cassie put a protective arm around Luci, turned to the people gathered around them and ordered, "Go home, all of you. Now you see! She had nothing to do with any of this. Leave her alone. Do you hear me?"

"*Si, Señora.*"

The fight and fury had gone out of them and they once more looked like the bereaved parents they were, before they drifted away, one by one, their heads down, not meeting Cassie's eyes as they passed by her.

"Luci, please don't be hurt by this. They would not have done it on their own. Someone has incited them to act this way and I think I know *who!*"

She had always been afraid that Luci, being her friend, might also become a target for her enemies.

221

Cassie was angrier than she'd ever been in her life. It was one thing for Perego and his henchmen to harass her, but another entirely for them to turn on her best friend, to bring trouble to Luci, who had done nothing to bring on this attack and did not deserve to be treated like this.

"Cass, it's all right, really." Having seen her friend's growing anger, Luci tried to soothe her, to keep her from doing anything foolish. "They didn't mean anything. They're just hurting, that's all. They need someone to blame besides themselves. This will pass."

Cassie nodded her head in agreement, but thoughts still swirled through her mind. He would answer for this. She would confront Perego about this and he would answer to her. She would order him to leave Luci alone.

The happier mood they'd shared earlier was ruined by the confrontation; the three women continued on their way without speaking. The loud pealing of the church bells would have made conversation difficult, anyway.

The dinner they shared that evening was much more subdued than usual. Evan and Emerson expressed concern when Sarah told the two men what had happened, but there was little they could do without knowing who was behind it.

Cassie chose not to tell them.

The strident ringing of the church bells had continued to echo in Cassie's mind long after they were still, after her guests had left and Sarah was well asleep. It had been such a long time since she had been in a church, other than to instruct the children. Her faith had faltered and she hadn't seen the need to go in a very long time.

But now, something inside her longed for forgiveness. It had begun with Cameron's death. She had felt responsible, as though she might have been able to do something to prevent it if she'd been more alert, more involved in what was going on with him. She hadn't been able to tell him goodbye and had even argued with him on the last day when he'd left her side, the day he hadn't returned, the day he'd been murdered.

Now, she felt guilt for what had happened to the children. She should have watched more closely, sent for the doctor sooner, tended them more carefully. She replayed each hour over and over in her mind, seeking what she might have done to save even one more of them. Her grief was not lessened and her pain seemed to grow greater with each passing day.

The night she'd spent in Cruz's arms had been only a temporary healing and had left its residue of guilt behind, as well. What must he think of her? But his opinion was not even as important as what she thought of herself. She needed forgiveness. And she made up her mind what she would do about it.

Her resolve faltering, Cassie almost turned back before she reached the church. She hadn't been able to talk to anyone about what she'd done or the burgeoning guilt she'd been feeling. But she needed absolution, something to take away the heavy load of guilt she carried. It had been years since she'd been to confession and she wasn't sure she could even go through with it. But her need was so great, she had to try.

Hesitantly, she entered the confessional, sat down on the hard bench, and arranged her skirts around her. She heard the distinctive rustling of the priest, taking his place on the other side of the petition.

"I have sinned, Father . . ." she began.

He was silent for so long, she wondered if she'd really heard him come in, then she heard a muffled sound as he cleared his throat.

"My child," he said in a gruff voice.

"I . . . I have done something terrible. Something perhaps unforgivable."

"Ahem . . ."

She went on, in a rush to get it all out before she changed her mind and backed out of making the confession.

"My husband has been dead for several months, you see, and I . . . I . . . have never been with another man."

He started to reply, but she hurried on, "Until . . . until last week. And, Father . . . I . . . I . . . you see, we had taken care of the children together. We'd shared so much, pain and trials and suffering . . . it seemed a natural thing. Inevitable. He was gentle and kind and I needed him, needed what he could give me. He needed me, too, I think. Nothing seemed wrong about it at the time. It all seemed so right. And it healed my heart, in a way, gave me reason to want to go on living . . . and loving."

He cleared his throat a couple of times before he spoke at last, his voice barely above a whisper, "Say no more."

He went on hurriedly to offer her penance and the

promise of forgiveness, almost as though he wanted to hear no more, as though her confession was painful for him, too.

Cassie bit her lip. There was no way she could have completed her confession, anyway.

How could she tell a priest that she had made love to a priest? Especially since this might compromise Cruz?

It was not possible. She'd really known that from the beginning, but she'd had to make the attempt. And she did feel better. She'd wanted to tell the priest of her feelings of guilt about Cameron's death and what she might have done to prevent it, and her guilt about the children, but that would have to wait for another time.

She made the sign of the cross, thanked the invisible priest and left as quickly as she could, relieved to have it behind her, a weight lifted from her shoulders.

Cruz wiped the sweat from his brow where he sat like a caged tiger in the enclosed, airless cubicle. He'd almost had the words out of his mouth to reveal his identity to her when she spoke of her husband. He'd kept silent, hoping to learn more about Cameron Layton. He knew she would assume that he was Father Auguste and then it had been too late for his admission. She was already telling him about her "sin," a sin in which he had participated, which, in fact, he had initiated, and for which he was primarily responsible. He was to blame, not Cassie Layton. He should have been the one seeking forgiveness.

So he had kept silent and allowed his identity to remain a secret. But it had been one of the hardest things he'd ever done. He wanted to reach out to her, to assure her she'd done nothing wrong. He admired her courage for being able to admit it.

What he wanted to do more than anything was to hold her and make love to her again, just as he had on the night that was the subject of her confession. He wanted to tell her the truth about everything, and spend every minute of the day making it all up to her.

This whole thing was a complication he hadn't counted on and didn't need. It made him feel guilty as hell. He was the one at fault here, not her. She had done nothing.

He had to put an end to this, before she was hurt more than she already had been. He would do something to make sure she no longer cared for him, something that would drive her away from him, so that there was no way back for either of them.

But before Cruz could find a way to end his relationship with Cassie, word came to him of the theft of a priceless piece of art from one of the other parish churches, the chapel called San Miguel, that lay in the southern part of town. Immediately, he set out to learn everything he could about what might have happened and who was responsible. He was dressed in regular clothes and did not take the time to don his robes before he sped away out the door of the church.

This painting had disappeared from under his very nose, so to speak, and it made him furiously angry. Apparently, the fact that it was common knowledge that the Mexican government had sent a spy into Santa Fe to investigate the thefts had done nothing to slow or intimidate the thieves, still greedily stripping the churches of their treasures. He had to find them and put an end to this once and for all.

Cassie, who had been in the schoolroom and watched him hurry by the door without glancing inside, knew something was going on. His haste and his appearance were clue enough. This might be her chance to find out something about him, maybe even about Cameron's death.

Giving rapid instructions to the two older children on how to tutor the younger ones, making them promise to see everyone home safely before dark if necessary, she grabbed her shawl and struck out after him.

Cassie was beginning to entertain occasional doubts about Delgado's being a priest at all. Her suspicions didn't just stem from wishful thinking. She wondered if the priestly robes weren't just a disguise of some sort. He had an official reason for being in Santa Fe not connected to his business with the church. Wasn't it remotely possible he only used the priesthood as a cover from his enemies?

The slight possibility she could be on the right track had her heart pounding, her pulse racing as she sped along. If he really weren't a priest, then. . . .

Scarcely daring to hope that she might be right about him, she watched him as he strode along, unaware he was being observed. He was dressed in tight buckskin breeches that outlined his strong, muscular legs, high polished black boots with silver spurs, a wide Mexican hat and a great black cape rather than his usual priestly garb. He was strikingly handsome.

Someone who knew him less well would doubt it was the same man at all.

What was there about the way he looked and the way he walked, the way he carried himself, that disturbed her so?

He walked like a gunslinger, a *vaquero*, perhaps, but there was nothing in his stalking gait that even distantly resembled the meek priestly shuffle one might expect.

He was a priest, wasn't he? What was wrong with her? She couldn't make hasty judgments about a man by the way he *walked*, for goodness' sake!

Was it desperate, clutching at straws thinking? Did she want him so badly not to be a priest, that she would wish it to be so? She brushed that unacceptable thought aside. Surely she had more good sense and more moral fiber than a lovesick lass who would hope by wishing alone to make things other than they were.

He was stopped by a lovely young *señorita* who came running out, put her hand on his arm and stood looking up at him and talking animatedly, her white teeth flashing. Cassie heard him reply in what sounded like pure Castilian, rather than the more common Spanish spoken by those of mixed blood in Santa Fe. The words rolled off his tongue effortlessly and, though she couldn't understand most of the words, the sounds and rhythms were intriguing. She could see the lass falling under his hypnotic spell, hanging on his every word.

And she thought he looked like the devil himself with his tousled raven hair and blazing blue eyes, his compelling charm. She had to admit there was a power and vitality in his gaze, and a sensuous laziness in his movements completely out of character in a priest.

Was he aware of it, or was it an unconscious thing? She couldn't be sure.

The young girl stood gazing up at him in awe and was practically throwing herself at him, sidling up to him and fluttering long eyelashes at him. He appeared not to be returning her attentions and seemed, more than anything, to be in a hurry to continue on his way.

What was the magnetic attraction this priest had for all the women in town? She had seen others behave in the same way, many of them mature and even married women. They all groveled at his feet! Shameless hussies!

As if she wasn't one of them herself! She could still *taste* his lips on hers, and she pined to have his arms around her again. She had recently come from confession; how could she entertain such sinful thoughts again so soon?

If only he weren't a priest . . . then everything would be so different. Or would it? There would still be things to stand between them, to keep them apart. With an impatient shake of her head, she banished the recalcitrant thoughts. No more would she allow her mind to wander off in that direction. He was a priest and that was that, she told herself heatedly. She would work with him and accept whatever help he was willing to give her, and that would be the end of it! She would try to be content with just his friendship, if that was all she could have of him.

At a distance, she continued following him, after he'd freed himself from the clinging young woman, through the backroads and alleys, across the river and continuing southward until he turned into De Vargas street in the old settlement of Analco. Cassie was careful to duck into open doorways or seek another kind of cover when he paused and might have looked back, catching her following him. After greeting several people along the uneven roadway, he strode through the entrance into the chapel of San Miguel, the oldest church in Santa Fe. She lagged behind purposely, noting fallow fields adjacent to the chapel that would be cultivated in maize in season and used to supply food to the parishioners. These people were poor, but hardworking, much like those with whom she worked.

Built in 1610, the simple church had stood for centuries as a testament to the religious fervor of the early Spanish settlers of New Mexico. Ravaged by a fire set by rebels in a pitched conflict with colonials in the late seventeenth century, it had been restored and now stood watch over the community, the plain cross on top proclaiming its purpose and reason for existence.

So, her priest had made his way from the *parroquia* in the main part of town to another church! Nothing suspicious in that. A priest entering a church. Nothing more. What could be more natural? Her hopes of discovering something about him were dashed. What had she hoped to learn? She wasn't quite sure. Anything but this. She was more disappointed than she would have dreamed possible.

What more likely place to find a real priest . . . than in another of the parish churches? Simply carrying out his religious duties, though he was not dressed traditionally now, and he *had* left in a precipitous rush. Often, though, he didn't conduct himself in the manner of a religious leader. Still, he had probably been here oftentimes before, and there was nothing more to be made out of it.

Out of idle curiosity more than anything else, and because she'd come this far, Cassie stepped through the entryway. She hesitated in the shadows just inside the door until her eyes accustomed themselves to the dim interior.

Paper flowers and the usual array of statuary decorated the dimly lit chapel, along with scattered gilt candlesticks and a few ornaments of burnished silver.

Cruz was speaking with Evan Hamilton, his back to her. This seemed like a strange place for the two men to meet, even though it was common knowledge that they were friends and had gone to school together back East. Holding her breath and pressing herself into the wall so she wouldn't be seen, she listened, unashamed of her blatant eavesdropping. But she heard only a smattering of the conversation.

". . . another one?"

"This time . . . a Goya."

"Damn!"

"Yes."

". . . watch . . . Perego."

Cassie was frustrated she couldn't hear more. They were discussing paintings. Another one had been stolen? Was that what had brought Delgado to New Mexico? And what brought him now to the church of San Miguel? It certainly seemed a possibility that this meeting had everything to do with the thefts.

Or, as a local priest, would Cruz have every right to be concerned and interested in the thefts and devoted to preventing further looting of treasures from the coffers of the churches?

But what part did Evan Hamilton play in all of this?

And she had heard the name of Perego mentioned between them. Again, she wondered if Cruz were supportive of and in cahoots with the despicable Spaniard. Her heart fell at the thought.

She didn't think she could live with that. There had to be another explanation for the times she'd seen them together, a logical explanation that wouldn't implicate Cruz in the man's almost certain criminal dealings.

Hamilton handed Cruz a small bag. She could barely see, but it looked like one Cameron had possessed at one time. With a sinking of her heart, she heard him say, "Layton . . . CML. Read the name. What do you make of this?"

Cruz pulled a small sheaf of paper out of the bag and unfolded it, the crinkling of its pages echoing loudly in the high-ceilinged, quiet church.

What did this mean?

She knew Cameron had had no dealings with Perego. He could never have been involved in the thefts, yet Cruz and now Evan Hamilton seemed to think there was a connection. She had to prove to them that they were wrong about Cameron.

She would step up her campaign to prove his innocence and she would do it, too, if it was the last thing she ever did.

The two men shook hands and seemed to be about

to leave. She slipped out the door and fled around to the side of the building so she wouldn't be seen.

They left soon afterward, going off in different directions. Cassie waited a few minutes longer before heading back to the church and the children, distracted and troubled by what she'd seen and heard. She sped through the streets of town, stopping for nothing along the way. Cruz would, no doubt, beat her back with his headstart.

Out of breath and her hair flying in all directions, she reached the schoolroom, only to find Cruz in the middle of the children, coaching them in their lessons and listening to them recite. He looked as though he belonged there, surrounded by wide-eyed children who clearly adored him.

He looked up at her, a question in his eyes, while she returned her shawl to its place on the hook by the children's coats, and smoothed her hands over her hair nervously.

"I . . . I . . . forgot something at home," she stuttered, explaining before he could ask. She had never before left the children in the middle of the day. They both knew it, making her departure today and its timing, coming so soon after his own, even more suspicious.

He looked at her empty hands and a raised eyebrow showed his doubts about the validity of her excuse. The inscrutable mask covered his features and he said nothing more, did not question her any further.

Cassie was reminded that there was a side to this man that she didn't know at all.

"Well, children," she began, eager for him and his questioning eyes to be gone, the tension that filled the room dissipated. "Let's get on with our lessons, shall we?"

But, maddeningly, he stayed, watching and listening without apology or comment, while she caught up with what had been done in her absence and went on with the remainder of the lessons planned for the day. The tension steadily increased and her unease along with it. The air in the room became stifling before he finally stood and left, not ever once glancing back over his shoulder in her direction. His feelings were as much a mystery to her as the puzzle of his identity.

Chapter Eleven

"Cass! You won't believe what I've found out! Just from listening to my customers. I told you I could learn something! And you told me not to get involved. But when have I ever listened to you? You can find out so damned much from listening, you know. Cassie, are you listening to me?"

"Yes, I always listen to you, Luci." Cassie laughed, enjoying her friend's disjointed ramblings, even while she kept her eyes on the constant stream of people who seemed to come and go on the plaza. She carefully avoided telling her friend about following Cruz the preceding day.

"No, you don't!" she came back with a snort. "But this time it's really important. I found out something about—"

Before Luci could share her information, they were interrupted by a big man in the uniform of the governor's personal guard.

"*Señorita* Lucita," the big man was apologetic, holding his hat in his hands. "I beg your pardon for interrupting you, but my wife and I need to talk with you immediately. Would you please come with me?"

235

"Right now? But can't you see I'm busy—?"

"But this is *muy importante, por favor.* I will pay you double." His eyes were lowered and he seemed agitated, very disturbed about something.

He went on in a rush before she could answer, "She is waiting for us at your house. You must come with me!"

Lucita hesitated only a moment, before she nodded and indicated that she would go with him.

"All right, *Señor Lopez,* if it is that important."

"But, Luci—" Cassie began.

"No, it's all right, really. He's a customer. I'll see you in an hour or so, Cass."

The chance gone for sharing her confidence, Luci whispered to Cassie before she left, "I will tell you later. You are just positively not going to believe it."

Like a hummingbird, Luci flitted from one place to another, and now she was gone again, leaving Cassie shaking her head and wondering about what Luci had started to tell her.

Feeling vaguely uneasy about the encounter, Cassie watched them walk away, her friend talking nonstop as usual, gesturing with her hands, until they were well out of sight. The quiet after Luci's departure was noticeable. It always was. For a few minutes, Cassie enjoyed sitting and watching the bustle of the plaza, the comings and goings of the citizens of Santa Fe.

Emerson called to her from a storefront across the road, "Miz Cassie. How ya doin' this fine day? That was some special fine dinner t'other night. Sure was!" He ambled over and sat down beside her.

236

"Why, thank you, Emerson. Having you to dinner at my home was certainly my pleasure."

"Everything all right with Miss Luci? Nobody botherin' her none or nothin', are they? She sure left here in one awful rush!"

"No, there've been no more incidents, not since that one time. I think those parents understood it wasn't Luci's fault. I hope it will all die down and go away."

"I heard they understood, all right, after you had a few choice words for them," he said with an appreciative chuckle. "But it will die down only if nobody stirs it up," he went on, a frown on his wrinkled face.

"I know. I plan to speak with Perego about it. I am almost certain he must have put them up to it."

"You'd better be leavin' this Perego feller alone, Miz Cassie. He's low-down scum. Don't you trifle with that one."

"That description fits the Spaniard admirably well," she said with a smile for Emerson, "But I *will* talk to him."

Perego had seemed to be avoiding her, a circumstance that was unusual in itself. Did he already know that she would accuse him? Probably. He was a coward of the worst sort, an unfeeling bully as well, when it came to confrontations.

Luci at first had been too full of excitement about what she had to tell Cassie to notice anything malevolent about the man who held her arm, urging her forcefully to a faster pace. He had only explained that he needed a fortune told for his wife who would be waiting for them at Luci's house. Since she had done sessions for both of them before, she didn't find that too strange. But now his nervous haste had her wondering what he was up to!

"Take it easy there, *Señor* Lopez. What's the big hurry? We'll be there in plenty of time to solve all your marital problems." Luci smiled at him, hoping with her bawdy humor to ease the building tension, but he didn't respond with a smile. His expression was glum, his face tight and closed.

Instead of a verbal response, he grunted and propelled her along even faster, until her feet were skimming over the ground. His grip on her arm tightened until it had become painful.

"Let me go!" she ordered.

But he didn't.

Now she was truly frightened. His behavior was not normal. Something was very wrong here. Luci planted her heels and dug in, resolved to halt his headlong pace, to buy herself some time. Dust kicked up around them, and he slowed reluctantly. He didn't, however, loosen his hold on her.

"Now, just a damned minute!" She glanced around them, while he regrouped to get a better grip on her, seeking help of any kind. No one stirred in the narrow side street, deserted except for a stray mongrel and a couple of lazy burros dozing in the sun. It was the quiet of mid-afternoon . . . siesta time. It would be unusual to find anyone out and about during this time, or for at least another couple of hours.

Luci threw a glance back over her shoulder. They had come much too far for her screams to reach Cassie, or anyone else on the plaza who might help. She was, for all intents and purposes, alone with this big ruffian who had more on his mind than having his fortune told. She was not strong enough to fight him, so she would have to find a way to outsmart him.

"Come along peacefully, *Señorita*. I will not hurt you," he growled. She didn't find the promise comforting, not in the least.

Now he had his arm under hers and yanked her up to his side so hard it knocked the breath from her body.

"Sure I will!" she huffed. "And my name's Governor Armijo!"

At the mention of the powerful Spanish official's name, Lopez faltered, but only for a minute. He dragged her another hundred yards or so, before turning into an alleyway littered with garbage and hidden from the sight of anyone who might happen by.

He shoved her to the ground, holding her down with a strong hand on her shoulder. "He'll be here soon." His breathing was ragged, his sour breath coming in gasps that nauseated her.

She didn't turn away, but looked him straight in the eye with a fierce need to know what was going on. "For God's sake, *who?* Lopez, tell me who! Why are you doing this?"

"For the silver, *Señorita*."

"But who would pay you to do such a thing? I

239

know of no one who would do that. Take me home, Lopez, and I'll do a reading for you *and* your wife, with no charge! Just take me home right now and we'll forget this ever happened. I promise, Lopez, I will never breathe a word of it."

"I cannot do that. I am sorry."

There was more fear than regret in his expression, she thought, watching him closely. Lopez was afraid. But of whom?

"Well, I am sorry, too, and I'll just be on my way."

Before Luci had finished speaking, she gave a heave with all her strength and unseated him. Rolling over, she managed to slide out from under the grip of his big hands, and lurched to her feet. He grabbed for her, but he was too slow.

Luci tore away from him and ran as fast as she could toward the far end of the alley. It was not a great distance, but before she'd taken a half dozen steps, she heard the man's heavy steps pounding behind her. He was gaining on her fast. She would never make it.

Whatever his reasons, he was doing his best to stop her from getting away. And she had a sudden, sinking feeling that he would succeed.

A cat screamed when she stepped on its tail and she hesitated only a heartbeat, but it was enough to give him the advantage he needed. A muscular arm wrapped around her midriff like an iron band and the breath left her body in a gust of air. Her hopes of any escape were gone, too, dashed by the burly strength of the man who held her pinned against his chest.

"I wouldn't do that if I were you," he snarled, panting into her ear, out of breath from the chase, but no less strong. "It might not be too healthy. I think maybe you should just be nice to me to make up for all the trouble you've caused me." His free hand stretched around to take hold of her breast, still heaving from her exertion.

"No!" she cried out. "Please don't! I won't run again. I promise. Just let me go."

"Uh uh. I think I'll just keep you real close. You feel good." He squeezed his hand like a vise on her breast, and she cried out in pain and even more, in terror.

"Let her go, Lopez."

The voice that came from behind them was authoritative and familiar. Luci couldn't quite place where she'd heard it before. But she didn't care who'd come to her rescue, as long as someone could make this big oaf release her and take his hands off her.

Thankfully, the big hands loosened and his arm dropped away, releasing the lock he'd been holding on her lungs. She gasped for air and fought the stars that danced in front of her eyes.

"Go on, Lopez," the voice ordered. "I don't need you anymore."

The man who'd been tormenting her did as he was ordered. Before her vision cleared, he disappeared completely from the alley.

Luci turned, ready to thank her rescuer and make her own hasty exit.

"Lieutenant Mendez." Luci was surprised and

would not have expected such gallantry from one of Perego's henchman. She was about to express her gratitude when she saw the hard, bitter look in his black eyes that raked insolently over her.

"Señorita."

His voice was as cold as his eyes and deep and menacing, in a way the other's had not been. She knew in that instant that she was in more trouble than ever. The other man might have raped her without a second thought, but this one could kill her, would do so if it suited his purpose.

Once more, she whirled around and made a final, desperate attempt to get away from him. Out of breath, she staggered and took only a couple of steps before her skirts wrapped around her legs, sending her tumbling facedown into the smelly dirt of the alley.

Before she could get up, he was on top of her, his knees straddling her. With a flat, open hand, as hard as steel, he struck her hard on the side of the head. She moaned and threw up her arm to protect her face and head, but he grabbed it and yanked it painfully up behind her back.

"Do not scream," he commanded, speaking slowly and accenting each word.

Scream, she thought, *when I can barely breathe?* No, she wouldn't scream, but she would fight him, as long and as hard as she could. He hadn't succeeded in killing her spirit yet.

Luci threw her other arm up and back at him, but it flailed uselessly in the air. He was much stronger and had the upper hand. Still, she wriggled and thrashed as much as she could, making him angrier and more violent with each sign of her resistance.

"Stop it, *bruja!*" he commanded, his voice surly.

He had both her hands pulled up behind her, and a knee in her back. Luci couldn't move, couldn't fight him anymore. Her strength ebbed away.

He struck her again. The last thing she heard before the blackness overcame her were his harsh words. "You'll . . . never . . . tell . . . anyone, *bruja.* This will be our little secret. . . . Forever."

Luci had one last, lucid thought. She knew why this was happening to her. Perego. What she knew about Perego would go no further than this dark back alley.

When Luci did not return to the plaza, Cassie decided the session with Lopez and his wife must have been more involved than she'd expected. The more she thought about it, the more intrigued she was by what Luci had been about to tell her. She would stop by Luci's on her own way home and give her another chance to share her news.

When Cassie reached her friend's square adobe house, all was as still and quiet as a tomb. No customers. No Luci.

Maybe she had finished up their readings and taken the coins back to the plaza for some shopping. Luci could never resist shopping. But it was nearly dark and it was unsafe for a single woman to be abroad alone after nightfall. Luci knew that as well as she did. Besides, Cassie would surely have seen her if she'd headed back in the direction of the plaza.

Cassie wavered between going home herself before it got any later and going back to the plaza to search for her friend. Who was that soldier who'd taken her away in such an awful hurry? Luci had called him Lopez. Cassie figured he was one of her regulars with some kind of personal problem. But he had seemed very agitated, now that she thought about it.

And didn't she remember having seen him before in the company of Lieutenant Mendez, or even Perego himself? Was he involved with that ring of criminals? Had there been a sinister motive behind the soldier's abrupt request? Could Luci be in danger? All kinds of thoughts rolled around in her mind. She tried to remain sensible, but was becoming more frightened by the minute.

All the fears she'd ever had for her friend's safety came hurtling back at her. Did this have something to do with what Luci was about to tell her before Lopez interrupted and spirited her away? Was there a connection with Lieutenant Mendez, or possibly even with Perego himself?

Cassie turned and ran as hard as she could back to the center of town, only slowing down long enough to ask anyone she saw along the way if they'd seen Luci. She had no luck. No one had seen her friend since the two of them sat there together earlier.

Emerson reached out for her from a doorway

when she would have run right by without seeing him.

"Whoa, now! What's this here bee in your bonnet, Miz Cassie?"

"It's Luci, Emerson. She went with some man called Lopez."

Cassie was breathing hard, barely able to get the words out, but she struggled on. "But they never got to her house. It must have all been a trick. I'm so afraid he might hurt her!"

"Hold on," he said, putting his arm around her shoulders. "Take some deep breaths, and let's think for a minute. Which way did she go when she left with him?"

Cassie pointed to the northeast corner of the plaza, where a narrow road led away from the main part of town.

"Down . . . that . . . way, I think!"

"All right, you jest set yourself down right here and I'll mosey on down there and find her for you."

"No! I'm going with you."

He knew better than to waste time and energy arguing with her when she had her mind made up. "All right. All right. Come on, then."

Hurriedly, with fear giving flight to their feet, they sped up and down one road and then another in the direction Cassie had seen Luci go, checking every alley, every vacant lot and asking the few people they saw. Sometimes, they split up to cover more territory and met up again at the end of a street. Nothing. There was no sign of Luci or of the soldier.

It was completely dark, and still they searched with only the meager light that spilled out of scattered houses to help them find their way. Often, they groped along in the dark, holding onto each other to keep from stumbling and falling flat on their faces.

"Listen!" Emerson admonished her, stopping in his tracks. "Do you hear that?" He was talking about the continuous barking of a dog nearby.

"Yes, I think I do. Oh, Emerson! Do you think . . ." Cassie was afraid to think about what it might mean to her friend. "Let's go! Over this way." He urged her along, as fast as they could go, drawing nearer to the ceaseless, agitated barking. "Around here."

A thin shaft of moonlight fell into the narrow alleyway and they saw the mangy cur whose barking had led them to this deserted place.

At their muddy feet lay the battered, crumpled body of Lucita Chavez.

"Oh my God! Emerson! It's Luci!" Cassie cried, falling to her knees beside her friend. With his help, she gently turned her over and smoothed a hand tenderly over the bruised and scratched skin of her friend's face.

"Luci! Luci! Can you hear me? Open your eyes, Luci. Please." Cassie's voice rose with her growing fear and her pleading eyes looked up at Emerson.

He put a finger to the vein in Luci's throat and detected a thready pulse. "She's alive, Miz Cassie. She's just unconscious."

Only the sound of the uninterrupted barking of the dog and their labored breathing broke the stillness of the night.

"Let's get her home."

Carefully, Emerson lifted Luci's body up in his arms and they turned toward Luci's house. Tears filled Cassie's eyes, but she brushed them aside. There was no time for that. They had to get Luci home and be sure she was all right.

"You will be all right, Luci," she whispered and hoped with all her heart that she was making a promise that would come true.

Despite all they did over the long hours between midnight and dawn, Luci never stirred toward consciousness. She lay deep in another dimension, far from their loving attentions. Cassie had tended to her face with cool cloths and they made her as comfortable as they could. The doctor was sent for and examined her thoroughly. He found no outward sign of trauma other than the marks on her face. Finally, he said that all they could do was wait to see if she would come out of it.

With the first light of dawn, Cassie could stand it no longer. "Emerson, there's something I have to do."

"Now, Miz Cass—" he began.

"No, it's all right," she reassured him. "It's just an errand," she went on vaguely, "something I should have done before now. I won't be gone long. And I'll send Sarah back to sit with her."

She could not tell Emerson what she planned to do or he would never allow her to leave the house.

Cassie was on her way out the door, and the older man had little choice but to do as she asked. He cursed his helplessness and worried about what she might be up to. He didn't believe her story for a minute. Emerson knew it was no idle errand that drew her away from her friend's bedside. He turned to look at the small, still body on the bed. There was no sign of life or of a return to consciousness.

When Sarah arrived about a half hour later, he hurried back to the plaza, determined to find Cassie and keep an eye on her. She could only be up to something that would bring more trouble upon her.

It had been hard to leave Luci's side, but Cassie had a blinding need to confront Perego and to learn what he had to do with the attack on Luci. She also wanted to find out, if she could, what Luci had been about to tell her. It was beginning to appear that it must have been very important, indeed.

As soon as she had solicited Sarah's help and filled her in on Luci's condition, Cassie headed directly for the plaza with determined steps. Her weakness from not having eaten in twenty-four hours and her exhaustion from the efforts of the night before forgotten, she thought only of Perego.

The man who had almost certainly been responsible for the murder of her husband had now nearly killed her best friend. It was time for some answers and time for him to pay for what he'd done. It was time for all of this to stop.

She had expected to have to face him in his office, but as she turned the corner onto the east side of the plaza, they almost collided.

"Perego!"

248

The loathing in her voice stunned him momentarily, and he took a protective step backwards.

"*Señora* Layton?" His voice asked a question accentuated by the lifting of one black eyebrow.

"You know very well what I want, and you have some answering to do. I want . . . to . . . know . . ." she said, biting out the words slowly as her eyes drilled holes into him, "why . . . you had your henchmen attack my friend? What did you expect to accomplish? Did you mean to kill her, to silence her forever, the same way you did Cameron?"

"Now, *Señora*," he began placating her, holding up a hand as though in his own defense.

Instead of calming her as he'd intended, his actions made her even more furious.

"Don't try to deny it. I know everything! It is much too late for denials!"

Her voice was growing louder and he began to look concerned about the scene she was making in this very public place. He had his image to consider.

"Now, *Señora*," he said once more, his voice no longer softening in an attempt to calm her, but filled with a cold anger of his own. "You must stop this."

His eyes darted about. Seeing no one near enough to hear the gist of the heated discussion, he clasped a strong hand around her elbow and steered her around a corner.

"If you'll be so kind as to come with me," he ground out, clearly giving her no choice in the matter.

Before she had a chance to scream, he clamped a

hand over her mouth and tightened his grip on her arm. He dragged her along beside him and she saw only a blur of passing buildings, but not a soul who might come to her rescue.

He shoved a brawny shoulder into a door that opened off the narrow road. Before she knew what was happening, she found herself alone in a large, almost empty warehouse with her hated enemy, who now arranged the bulk of his body between her and the only exit from the semi-dark room.

He took a threatening step toward her, but she refused to back up. She was sick to death of his bullying. It was time things were finally settled between them. She stiffened her back and stood her ground. She was not afraid of him and her face showed her lack of fear.

His expression was inscrutable, dark and very dangerous. It indicated he was a man at the end of his rope. But he stood where he was, not taking another step toward her.

"Why did you do that to Lucita?" she demanded again.

"I, *Señora?* I have done nothing. I was in my office doing paperwork for the entire evening."

"No! You hired someone to do your dirty work for you. You're much too big a coward to have done it yourself." The words were hurled at him angrily.

"Is that right? And I suppose I'm too big a coward to tend to a troublesome little problem such as yourself?"

His hand snaked inside his coat front and she wasn't sure if he was reaching for a gun or a knife, but fully expected to see it emerge with some kind of weapon.

"No," she said slowly, still looking straight into his small, pale eyes. "A bully with a woman who is much smaller than he in a deserted building would surely have no need to show any cowardice."

His face darkened. Every word she spoke only served to make him more furious. She had been a thorn in his side for months. It was time something was done about her. He muttered curses, but otherwise did not respond outwardly. His hand remained hidden inside his jacket, and he hardly moved a muscle.

Their eyes met and held, neither willing to back away or give ground.

"You have nothing to lose, then," she pointed out, "by telling me the truth now. What happened to my husband?"

"He died, I believe, in some rather questionable circumstances," he said with a faint smirk, unwilling even now to give her the answers she needed.

"No!" she cried. "You murdered him!"

This time, Cassie flew at him. The rage that had built up in her over the last months exploded in a frenzy at this man who could stand here so calmly and proclaim that her husband had died and yet still not admit his part in it.

Her small fists beat ineffectually at his wide chest. With an oath and a grunt, he stumbled backward, but quickly collected himself. He grabbed her wrists, and spun her about until she was against the wall, the bulk of his body pinning her in place.

The silver of a knife blade flashed in his right hand while his left forearm across her neck held her in place against the wall. Cassie tasted fear when she looked into the dead coldness of his reptilian eyes. She had been a fool and now she would have to pay the price with her life. The worst part was that she had learned nothing. Salty tears of frustration stung her eyelids and she fought for each painful breath. His arm cut off the air to her lungs. She would probably suffocate before he had time to use the knife he now held to her throat.

Emerson had been in his usual place by the storefront on the west side of the plaza, watching for Cassie when he witnessed her confrontation with Perego. Instantly, he knew she was in a lot of trouble, and his old heart had almost stopped when Perego took her arm and hauled her away around the corner and out of his sight. Cassie hadn't screamed, but maybe she hadn't been able to. He had seen enough to know that she had not gone with the man willingly and more than enough to know that she was in great danger.

He hurried across the street, looked down the rutted road, and watched while Perego dragged her inside the deserted building. He knew he needed help, that he was not strong enough to save her from Perego by himself.

One day in his youth he would have been able to, but now. . . . He knew a man, though, who could save her and who cared enough about her to put his own life on the line for her. Cruz Delgado.

Emerson ran the few blocks to the church where he hoped to find the priest. He reached it breathless, his heart pounding so hard he was afraid he might not live long enough to get Cassie the help she needed.

He leaned against the wooden doorjamb, hand on his chest, trying to calm his racing heart and his ragged breathing.

"Emerson, what is it?"

Delgado was there beside him in an instant. He put a comforting hand on the older man's shoulder. "What's wrong? Is it Luci? Is she worse? Am I needed there?"

He had visited during the night and done what he could to comfort those who watched the inert figure of the young woman who lay so still on her narrow bed. Especially Cassie, whose beautiful face had been drawn with fear for her friend and with her own fatigue.

"No!" Emerson gasped out, "It's . . . Cassie!"

"What is it about Cassie?"

Cruz tightened his grip on the older man's shoulder, concern etched in his face. "What's happened to her?"

His body was still in a gathering of strength.

"Where is she?"

"With Perego . . ." he managed between huge gulps of air. "In a deserted building . . . north of the plaza . . . about midway down the block."

Cruz didn't wait for anything more, but stripped off his robe that was worn over his trousers and shirt and flew down the uneven steps. He couldn't see, he couldn't think straight. He only knew he had to get to her before Perego could hurt her. The image of Luci's bruised and torn face flashed in front of his eyes. Whoever had done that to her had intended for the damage to be permanent. They would do that to Cassie, and worse, if he didn't get there in time.

"Cassie!" his soul cried out, even as his steps pounded in his headlong flight. His heart twisted in agony at the thought of her lying wounded, or even worse, lying dead in a deserted building!

"Perego!" The despised name exploded from his lips. "Bastard! You will pay for this!"

He ran without wavering or slowing, in the direction Emerson had indicated. He pounded on the first door he came to. When there was no answer, he threw his weight against the door and sent it crashing open.

Empty! Heated curses escaped his lips. Where were they? Would he find them in time?

"Cassie!" he shouted.

There was no reply.

So he ran on. The next door yielded the same result. This was apparently a street of deserted warehouses and she could be in any one of them. Where? Which one? God help him, which one?

The sound of a scuffle drew his pounding steps across the road to an adobe building. His feet barely touched the walk, and he hurtled off the ground, his body colliding with the door, smashing it inward.

A soft, glad cry and an angry snarl greeted his entry into the room. He had found them! Thank

God! She was still alive.

But Cruz Delgado lost all control when he saw Perego with a knife poised at Cassie's throat, his body crushing hers against the wall.

He saw in his mind the same knife blade cleanly slice the throat of his father, wielded by the same four-fingered hand. He heard the terrible screams of his mother. The time for his vengeance had come.

"Perego!"

The word was an accusation and a threat of immense proportions.

"Goddamn it, Perego. Turn her loose."

Caught off guard, the Spaniard had dropped his arm from her neck. He stood facing the full fury of Delgado with nothing but a knife in his hand. Not nearly enough defense against such a ferocious, blindly angry opponent.

Chapter Twelve

When Cruz burst through the door, he flew into the room with the full force of a killer tornado. Perego didn't have time to blink, much less do anything to defend himself before Cruz was on him, big fists flying. A sharp downward blow to the heavier man's wrist sent the knife sailing across the room. He never had time to reach for his gun.

Cruz yanked the man away from Cassie before he had a chance to grab her and use her as a shield. He fought like a man possessed, a wild fury driving him and giving him superhuman strength.

Perego made an abortive attempt to defend himself, but he was no match for the much taller, much stronger, and much younger man who fought as though his whole existence was being brought into question, as though his life and future depended upon the outcome, as well they might.

Cruz reached out, grabbed Perego's shoulder, whirled him all the way around, and slammed his fist into the man's gaping mouth.

A tooth flew out and blood spurted. The burly

man uttered a colorful oath and whaled into Cruz with both fists. When his blows were deflected and he couldn't land even one, he bent over double and threw himself at the younger man, intent on using his head as a battering ram.

Deftly, Cruz dodged aside. Perego stumbled past him and went crashing down to his knees. Cruz stepped over him, locked onto his collar with one strong hand, and hauled the overweight man to his feet.

With his left hand, Perego tried to reach around behind his back. His right hand slithered beneath his coat to get his hand on the cold steel of his firearm, but Cruz was too fast for him. Before he could draw his weapon, Cruz clasped his wrist and twisted hard.

Perego yelled and dropped the gun, watching it fall with a thud to the floor several feet away, out of his reach.

Perego's eyes, when he looked up, showed all too clearly his fear and his knowledge that he was facing a man with nothing to lose. He was battling a foe who didn't mind spilling his own blood or losing his life, as long as he could take his opponent's life in the process. He saw hate and unbridled loathing in Delgado's icy silver eyes and a firm, deadly set to his jaw that meant trouble, plain and simple.

The same silver-blue eyes of a much older man flashed into his mind. But that man's name had not been Delgado, it had been . . . What had it been? It was such a long time ago. No, but the resemblance was there, the same aristocratic good looks, the same icy blue eyes. But that man was dead, killed by his own hand many years ago.

Could it be that this man was from that same family and set on revenge? His eyes widened and Cruz saw the knowledge there.

"Yes. I see that you understand. It was my family that you brutally murdered. I am Antonio de la Cruz Santiago Reyes. Now you will pay, Perego." Cruz spit out the name with hatred, his eyes burning with deadly fire.

Perego cowered, sank to his knees, hung his head. "Please, I beg you, spare me." Cruz glanced down at him with disdain, reached for the other man's gun lying on the ground and raised it, holding it point blank to his chest. His hand was steady and his eyes as cold and hard as the steel in his fingers.

"Get up," he growled. "I could never shoot a man on his knees."

Perego, crazy with fear, turned white-rimmed eyes on Cassie, who had listened to the exchange without taking a breath. He scrambled to his feet, afraid to do as the man commanded and afraid not to.

"He will do it, *Señora*. He will, by damn, kill me, right here and now, in cold blood. Do not let him! Only you can stop him. Please, *Señora*."

Perego grabbed hold of Cruz's wrist with the trembling four-fingered hand. Cruz looked down at the hand and a shudder went through him. In front of him was the man he'd followed all the way from Mexico, the man who, in the worst night of his life, had systematically murdered his family. As Cruz became lost in his thoughts, his lips were a thin, tight line and his dark brows drew together.

In horror, Cassie watched him. He was a different man than she'd ever seen before. This was not her gentle priest. This man was a dark stranger with murder in his eyes, eyes now the opaque color of gun metal, eyes that burned with bitter hatred. An unleashed violence proclaimed itself in his stance, wide-legged and unflinching and in the bunched muscles of his shoulders, the steady gaze from those flinty eyes that drilled holes into the trembling Perego.

He was mere seconds away from ending the man's life. Cassie had no doubt whatsoever about that. Unless she did something and unless Cruz would listen to her, Perego would be a dead man in the space of a few heartbeats.

She wasn't at all sure she could stop him. There was more here than just what Perego had almost done to her: a deeper grudge, a darker loathing, a lifetime of hate.

But she had to try. He couldn't shoot a man down like that. She didn't care about Perego; he deserved his fate for all the despicable things he'd done. But she couldn't let Cruz do this to himself, not without trying to do something to stop him.

"Don't," she said tightly, not pleading, but speaking reasonably, appealing to the sensible and sensitive side of the man, a side of him that she'd seen so many times. She had to try to get past the potent, chilling anger that controlled him.

"Don't do this, Cruz. You can't kill a man in cold blood. Even this one." But she knew he could, as easily as he might bat an eye. "You will be the one to lose, don't you see? Settle your differences with him legally. He didn't hurt me . . . look at me! Please look at me, Cruz."

His eyes met hers, moved over her, examining her closely, to be sure she was telling him the truth, that she was unharmed.

A softer look flickered in the icy blue depths of his eyes, then was gone, but it was enough to give her hope that he might do as she asked. The remnant of the man she knew still remained beneath that dangerous exterior.

"I couldn't live with myself if you killed him because of me."

He gritted his teeth, the muscle in his jaw flexing rapidly with his driving compulsion to pull the trigger, to put an end to this miserable man's existence. His finger twitched and his chest heaved. This was what he'd vowed to do, what he'd wanted for so long, what he'd promised his dead family. It had been the driving purpose in his life for as long as he could remember.

And he had more reason than ever now, for what Perego had been about to do to Cassie. The scene that had met his eyes when he'd burst into the warehouse flashed through his mind, along with the crippling terror that Perego would harm her before he could stop him. If he had hurt her in any way,

Perego would be lying dead on the ground at this very moment.

Watching the play of emotions in the blue eyes, Perego edged back, flattening himself against the wall, sure he was already a dead man. His eyes were a faded gray, like the ash of a cold campfire, and his lips began to mouth his last request of his god.

Steely blue eyes pinned the shaking Spanish official to the wall like a fly, but no deafening roar echoed from the gun held to his chest.

Seconds ticked away, one by one. No one moved. No one spoke. A deadly silence hung in the room.

At last, Cruz dropped Perego's collar that he had twisted up and held tightly in his left hand. With a final shove as though he found even touching the man distasteful, he thrust him away.

Perego sprawled out in the dirt, whimpering in relief, hands over his head. He stayed there for a long time, waiting for Delgado's wrath to fall on him again, fully expecting it. When it became clear to him that he had been given a reprieve and was not going to be shot where he lay, he scrambled up and crawled away on all fours, before Delgado could change his mind.

Cassie ran to Cruz, threw her arms around him, and clung to him tightly, relief flowing through her. He had listened to her and he hadn't shot Perego, even though she thought she knew how much he'd wanted to. She felt his trembling, even after he'd dropped the gun and returned her embrace fiercely.

* * *

His sweet relief from knowing she was safe and unharmed was chased away by a steadily increasing anger at her for putting herself into such a predicament. Even while he knew in his heart he shouldn't blame her, he could do nothing to extinguish the fury that burned in him. He cared for her far too much. Dropping his arms, he scowled down at her.

"How could you let this happen? How could you put yourself into such a dangerous situation?" he said, his words clipped and harsh.

Cassie stepped back as though she had been struck. His anger was as sudden and unexpected as a thunderstorm in a New Mexico winter.

"What?!" she cried, trying to grab hold of her emotional bearings, to follow his abrupt change in mood, his unreasonable anger with her. "What on earth do you mean?"

"I mean," he ground out, "I mean . . . what were you doing here alone with that beast? He could have raped you." His temper worsened even more at the thought of those lecherous hands on her. "He might even have killed you."

Cruz shook her shoulders hard and backed her against the wall, looming over her, where only minutes ago he had pinned his enemy.

Now it was as though she had become his enemy, too. Cassie was baffled and hurt. But her anger, too, was building. Her eyes blazed with an angry inferno of their own.

"How dare you treat me like this? I am not your

enemy. I haven't wronged you, Cruz Delgado."

Cassie was breathing heavily and her chest rose and fell with the effort before she went on, "I don't answer to you, *Father* Delgado. I will go anywhere I want and with whomever I choose. No one has named you my guardian. I didn't ask you to come here."

She knew even as she hurled the words at him that she was being unreasonable. This man had risked his own life to save her from Perego. But his self-righteous, possessive attitude had angered her.

His eyes, the silver of midnight stars, showed that her rebuttal was having an effect on him. But instead of backing away as she might have expected, he took a step closer, still making no apology for his actions, his eyes now dangerous in a completely different way.

Her breath caught in her throat and she wondered if she hadn't done a foolish thing by lashing out at him that way. He was so tall, towering over her as he did, his shoulders blocked out the dim light that filtered in through the room's single window. She saw only shadows, not the expression on his face.

The room grew more stifling with each passing, agonizing minute and seemed to be growing smaller. She felt trapped, like a horse in a box canyon with one way out and that exit blocked most effectively.

She sympathized with how Perego must have felt facing such a deadly serious adversary. Surely, Cruz would not do her any physical harm, but that was not the true nature of her fear. It came from something more primal, more personal, and infinitely more frightening.

His low chuckle was throaty, filled with a dangerous quality that sent a shiver racing through her. The sound did little to comfort her nerves, to settle her racing pulse. His body spoke to hers with a language all its own. He was tense, unmovable, and as still as a statue carved in stone. He was so close to her, their breaths mingled and she inhaled the manly fragrance that was so singularly his.

His actions today only served to affirm her growing suspicions about his true identity. A priest would not react violently as Cruz had in dealing with Perego, but would have been more reasonable and law abiding, not so quick to take the law into his own hands. A man of God would seek other means, would respond in more peaceful ways. And a priest would not press himself so brazenly into a woman as he was doing at this moment, would not grin at her in such a thoroughly maddening way, would not goad her into such an unreasonable, angry reaction.

Who was he, then, this Cruz Delgado? She had just found out that the name she knew him by was not his real name. Was he not truly a priest, either, then? She remembered again his walk when she'd followed him to the chapel at San Miguel and his furtive meeting with Evan Hamilton, a swaggering walk that had seemed so unpriestly.

A priest would not stalk about with that long-legged stride as he had done, and a priest would not slug it out with his fists. A holy man would not come within inches of killing a man, as he had this night with Perego.

Come to think of it, his priestly robes had always appeared to belong to someone else. He had never looked comfortable in them. They never quite seemed to fit . . . more than just in size.

He had certainly not resembled a priest in his buckskins with shiny black boots, silver spurs and wide-brimmed hat. Only as she thought about these things did she notice that he had discarded his priestly robes today. Once again, he was clad in a simple shirt with full sleeves, tight-fitting breeches, and those familiar, polished black boots.

This man was no priest. *Surely*, he was not a priest. Lord help her if he was not a priest, and Lord help her if he was!

If he was not a priest, as he claimed, then he had been brazenly deceiving her and was still carrying on the deception. Cassie vowed that she would find out the truth, if it was the last thing she ever did. Were there two men where only one should be? Was he very adept at playing a part?

This fierce man whose flat, taut belly and lower body pressed her so tightly to the wall and whose strong arms placed on either side of her head kept her from moving so much as an inch . . . this man could not be the same one who had tenderly cared for the sick children, and the same one who had gloriously brought her spirit back with his loving the same night. She had thought she knew him well then, but the tough and violent nature she'd seen in him today could not be reconciled with that other, gentler man.

No, this man was lethal and deadly . . . dangerous . . . exciting.

And he was, little by little, taking her prisoner to the desire she saw in his eyes, the demands of the pressures of his body. At some point, the fury consuming him had given way to the passions that now flared hotly in his moonlit eyes.

Cassie had seen it and she, too, burned, consumed by the hunger he aroused in her. She wondered at the response of her body to him, at the longing so fierce, so blindingly intense, it drove all else from her mind.

His head lowered and he kissed her with a savage expertise. His tongue plundered her mouth, drawing from her an unwilling, but fervent response. Her need for him was a living thing, devouring in a heartbeat all her doubts and her reservations. Nothing else mattered except the two of them, that they were alive and together. For now, it was enough.

With a moan of pleasure and hating herself for her weakness, she wrapped her arms around his neck and moved against him, wanting to be closer.

He inhaled sharply and his arms swept down hers, holding her to him, driving himself against her. A white heat stormed through his veins, settling unmercifully between his legs. He could protract the loving only a little while longer or he'd surely die from the excruciating longing.

He pulled open the laces on her bodice and her

blouse slid off her shoulders, down her arms. She was clad only in her chemise from the waist up. His hands trembled as he stroked the smooth silkiness of her skin over the rounded softness of her womanly breasts, then drifted lower, slipping under the band of her skirt to move over the tautness of her flat stomach.

He had to make her his. In a very real way, she was his already, and she had taken him captive as well. He had been so wild with terror when he'd found out what terrible danger she was in. And then, when it was over, he'd been relieved and unreasonably angry with her.

She'd been so desirable when her eyes flashed in outrage at him, he'd been unable to keep his distance, to keep his hands off her. He wanted her more than anything. But could he put an end to her longings and his own as well and be the man she thought he was? Maybe not.

He had no choice, though, regardless of what his doubts might be. He was ruled by the passions that flowed through him and those that answered back from her. She wanted him just as badly as he wanted her. He couldn't turn away from this, no matter what tomorrow might bring.

Cruz swept her up into his arms, their bodies molding together, her arms moving around him, clasping him tightly. Her acceptance was enough for him and he could no longer stop himself from claiming her as his own. They were wild with their needs.

Their lovemaking was as brief and nearly as violent as the encounter with Perego. He ground his hips into hers and she met his assault thrust for thrust. She was every bit as hungry as he. With her arms and legs, indeed, her whole body moving with him, she told him clearly she wanted him just as badly as he wanted her.

His muscular legs that straddled hers were like strong tree trunks and he bore her entire weight when she leaned into him and clung to him. He had no patience for disrobing either of them further, but pushed up her skirts in his fiery haste; his other hand tugged her pantalets down until they lay around her feet. He yanked open the fastenings of his trousers and eased his rigid, pulsing shaft into her until he was buried within her, smoothly stroking.

Despite the lack of foreplay, he was gratified to find her damp and ready for him. He sheathed himself deeply in her and she rode him passionately, sliding up and down, guided and assisted by his hands spanning her hips. They reached a pounding climax simultaneously and clung to each other, spent by their passions, at its conclusion.

It was the most glorious lovemaking of his life and had been as inevitable as the coming of the dawn, as hauntingly beautiful as the last brilliant rays of sunset.

"Thank you," she whispered into his ear, her breath still coming in soft pants.

He smiled and set her back the slightest bit so he could look into her eyes. "No. It is I who must thank you, my love."

His lips turned up at the corners and she answered him with a smile of her own, a womanly, satisfied smile that thrilled him with its intimacy and sweet promise. Their eyes connected and, in that look, they shared their deepest feelings, the desires of their hearts.

She pulled her blouse up, sliding her arms into the sleeves, and made some attempt to cover the outward signs of their consuming passions. He helped her, efficiently fastening the buttons with fingers surprisingly agile, smoothing her rumpled skirt, his eyes never leaving her. He was so inexpressibly glad she was safe and in his arms, near enough to be touched by him.

She spoke at last. "Thank you for coming after me. You were right. He would have killed me."

"No," he said slowly, shaking his head as though coming out of a fog. "Thank you for saving me from myself, from doing something I would always be sorry for. And I am sorry I was so angry with you. I was just so damned scared something terrible had happened to you. When I saw that bastard standing there over you with that knife, I just exploded. Afterward, I felt that I had to blame someone other than myself for my loss of control, and you were handy."

He was also relieved that he hadn't taken his revenge on the poor excuse for a human being who had scrabbled out of the hovel, disappearing like a bad dream, at his first opportunity. It didn't seem that important anymore. His biggest concern was

Cassie and whether or not she'd been hurt.

Cruz had stared his hatred and his past in the face and had done the right thing, thanks to her. In her beseeching brown eyes, he had seen the destruction his revenge could bring . . . not to his enemy, but to himself. He trembled to think what he would have done if she had not pleaded with him to spare Perego.

The skunk didn't deserve killing; a simple death was too good, too easy for him. He deserved a very, very long sentence in a dark, unforgiving Mexican jail.

And then, the wild loving that followed the rescue was more than he'd ever imagined such a thing could be. It was sweeter and more potent than the best vintage French wine. She had given him a gift more precious than any he'd ever received.

The wild, passionate side of the woman had been his for the taking. Returning stroke for stroke, caress for caress and devouring kisses in kind, she'd been as out of control as he. Their union was beyond any dream, fraught with desires and out of bound passions, building up to an inferno of rapture that consumed them both.

He had been lost in her and, for a while, so far beyond time and space that he'd thought he might never come back to earth. It had been magnificent in its fiery intensity. His skin still burned from the heat of her touch; his body continued to throb with a relentless need for her.

"We'll make him pay," she promised, "for all he's

done to you, to Luci, and to me. We'll do it together, Cruz. From inside the law. He will be punished every bit as much as he deserves, you'll see."

"Cassie, love," he'd said, tenderly holding her to him, smoothing the satiny softness of her hair beneath his fingers. "You are wonderful."

She laughed lightly. "That's not what you were saying a few minutes ago," she teased.

"No," he said slowly. "But a man is entitled to change his mind, is he not?"

She raised an eyebrow at him. "I thought that was a woman's privilege."

Then a shadow passed over her face, as she remembered why she'd come after Perego in the first place. "Luci! I have to get back to her."

"I will go with you."

He put his hand on her elbow and they turned for the door together. She stood on her toes and kissed him. It was a long, lingering kiss that left them both weak.

Chapter Thirteen

"The little *problema* we discussed is taken care of," Lieutenant Mendez assured his superior, Juan Perego, in a furtive and secret meeting far from their offices at the Governor's Palace. "*Señorita Chavez* will tell no one of what she has learned."

The third person present in the hovel that was the lieutenant's quarters, was Lopez, who shook his large head in complete agreement with the lieutenant's statement.

"Good," Perego growled. "We'll meet tonight then, as planned. I have taken care of a little 'trouble' myself this morning."

He would not reveal that he had come out on the losing end of the confrontation with Delgado and his lady friend. Or that he was not finished with what he'd started, not by a long shot. They didn't have to know everything.

Neither underling mentioned Perego's missing tooth and split lip. They didn't dare, but it was obvious that he had been in some kind of scrape.

Lopez sported a few bruises and scratches of his

own from his encounter with the feisty little fortune-teller. He wished Mendez had been a little longer getting there, though. He might have had himself some fun with her.

Perego continued, "As soon as our 'cargo' is on its way to Mexico, we can sit back and wait for the money to roll in. Soon, we shall all be wealthy men. No one will ever be able to prove we had anything to do with any of it."

"What about Delgado?" the lieutenant asked.

"What about him?" Perego spoke sharply, a frown darkening his face at the mention of that despised name.

"Is he not almost certainly the spy sent here from Mexico by *el presidente?*" Mendez had given up on his threats against Cassie since they had not had the desired effect. She had not been frightened enough to back off her investigation. But he had still been watching her and had seen her the day she followed Delgado to his meeting with Evan Hamilton. Suspicions that he'd harbored since the priest's appearance in Santa Fe had been solidified, and he was almost sure Delgado was the man they'd been seeking.

Perego looked surprised that Lieutenant Mendez knew so much. "It would seem so. He arrived here about the same time and that is suspicious, of course. Additionally, I have some interesting personal knowledge of the good priest indicating that he is not all that he claims to be."

"Then we should take care of him, no?" The

young lieutenant thrived on action and would be impetuous enough to go up against Delgado alone.

Let him try it, Perego thought, but aloud he said, "Yes, we will take care of him. But later. First, we have some important business this night. The American has said that he will handle that one, Delgado. The *padre* is loved and trusted by the people here in Santa Fe, so we dare not do anything openly against him, in any event." Perego was thoughtful, his voice more quiet than usual, while he remembered the drumming he'd taken at the hands of Delgado, whose real name was Antonio de la Cruz Santiago Reyes.

So, the past had caught up with him after all these years. Well, he'd lived comfortably for a very long time on the lands that had belonged to the Reyes family. He had practically gone through their entire fortune, which had been considerable. He had never thought to see any of them again, had not even known that another son existed to hunt him down.

"Then you believe he is the spy?" Lieutenant Mendez was anxious to uncover the spy sent by the Mexican government.

Perego said nothing further on the subject, but flexed his aching arm and rotated his neck as much as he was able. His muscles were stiff and painful. The ferocious man who'd torn into him and who would have gladly killed him, except for the *señora's* intercession, could not be, by any stretch of the imagination, a priest.

"There is *no* doubt," he repeated, emphasizing the words. "The robes are a disguise only. But do not worry. We will soon be rid of him. And I hope he enjoys his last meal on this earth tonight and his last night in the arms of the beautiful *señora*." Perego snickered. He had noticed something pass between Delgado and the beautiful widow.

No matter. It would be over soon and the "priest" out of their way for good. But first, they must conduct the night's important business.

"The bastard will die tomorrow."

Across town, Cassie sat by the side of her unconscious friend, refusing to leave until there was some change in her condition. She tried not to think about Cruz or Perego, to dismiss from her mind the troublesome events of the past twenty-four hours. But she could have more easily sprouted wings and flown with the eagles. She could not control the wanderings of her mind.

Cassie had been moved and forever changed by Cruz's gallant rescue and the passions of their love-making, by the emotions they'd so willingly shared, the other side of him she'd come to know. She had not wanted to leave him afterward and she could tell he felt the same. Only concern for her reputation had driven him to leave her, and he'd said as much.

They were navigating in dangerous waters and headed for ultimate and painful disaster, but they couldn't seem to help themselves.

Still, she had her doubts and she wondered about him, especially after what she'd seen and heard in the warehouse. She could not forget her promise to herself to find out the truth about him. Her heart was understandably heavy, and not filled with the joy it should have been.

She set herself on an unswerving course that would reveal his deception, if the priesthood were merely a disguise, but either way she was aware that she would lose. If he were indeed a priest as he claimed, he was lost to her forever by the nature of his calling and his position in the church. And if he were not, then he had been deceiving her all along and could never earn her trust or respect, so he was lost to her just as surely by the nature of his betrayal.

Her heart told her not to pursue this hurtful course, to allow things to go along as they had been, to leave well enough alone until such time as she would have to face the truth. But something in her would not allow her to let it rest. She had to know and she had to know *now*, regardless of the results or the magnitude of the loss to her heart.

Girding herself in the robes of her resolve and summoning as much courage as she could muster, she embarked upon her mission. She vowed to find something that would put her doubts and fears at ease and bring a final answer to this question that plagued her about Cruz Delgado and his identity. Whatever it took, she was willing to do it. She had to know the truth, regardless of what the answer turned out to be, regardless of how much it hurt her.

In the meanwhile, she was committed to Luci and prayed without ceasing for her friend's recovery. For another long day she stayed by her side, refusing to leave as long as her friend lay unconscious.

She studied Luci's face and watched her hands and her body closely for any signs of life. For hours, there was no change, not the slightest movement.

Cassie was very close to giving up hope. She was near complete exhaustion. When hopelessness had dulled her spirit, she was finally rewarded by a flicker of an eyelid and a faint movement of Luci's fingertips where they lay on the woven blanket that covered her.

Cassie was instantly on her feet, leaning over the bed, begging for even more response. "That's it! Luci! Can you hear me? It's Cassie." Praying she hadn't imagined it, she rubbed her friend's hands and repeated, "Luci, it's Cassie. Can you hear me?"

"I know it's you, Cassie," came the blessedly familiar voice. Surprisingly, it was as strong as though nothing had happened and the past day had been but a dream. "You don't have to shout. I am right here."

Brown eyes blinked twice and then opened. Luci looked straight up into her friend's startled face and smiled. She was out of the comatose state in an instant, as quickly as she'd entered it.

"Who else would be silly enough to sit here, talking to a person who doesn't talk back?" she went on, returning the pressure Cassie was putting on her hand.

Cassie thought her smile was the most beautiful thing she'd ever seen, and told her so.

"I didn't know you were so sentimental. I am sorry not to return the compliment, but you do not look so good, my friend. You have dark circles under your eyes and your face is too thin. What is going on here?"

Cassie quickly explained about the attack. The smoldering look in Luci's dark eyes showed that her memory of that day remained quite clear and that she knew, as well, exactly who had done this to her.

"And you have been here, unconscious, for over twenty-four hours now. We thought we'd lost you." Cassie's voice broke and tears of relief streamed down her face.

"Oh, Cass . . ." Luci's eyes, too, filled with tears. "And I suppose you have been here ever since, haven't you? No wonder you are exhausted. I have been resting, and you have been playing nursemaid, wearing yourself out, on my account. My dear friend, you are in need of a good, long sleep. Go home now, please."

"Soon. Not quite yet, Luci. But I'll go soon, I promise. I'm just so glad you're really okay! I can't tell you what I've gone through, worrying about you."

Cassie leaned down and hugged her as hard as

she dared, almost afraid to turn her loose, to tempt the good fortune that had brought her friend back. After Cassie coaxed her to drink a bit of tea and sip some broth, they spoke quietly about Lopez's trickery and the arrival of Lieutenant Mendez, who'd beaten her and left her in the alley for dead. Finally, speaking more slowly, Luci told Cassie of the reason behind the incident.

"It's all about what I was going to tell you, Cassie. They wanted to silence me. Can you imagine," she asked, showing some of her old flash, "the nerve of anyone to think they could silence me!?"

Cassie shook her head, aware of how close Mendez had come to doing just that.

"I'm fine, Cass. Really," Luci hastened to reassure her, seeing her worried look. "I feel a little tired and sore, that's all. But I have to tell you what I found out about Perego—"

"I *knew* it was about him!" Cassie said, interrupting her.

"Of course. And you were right about him all along. Lopez slipped during one of our sessions and told me a lot more than he meant to, about Perego and Lieutenant Mendez. He had been drinking and I don't think he realized what he'd done until later. I should have known better than to go with him when he came for me on the plaza."

"Luci! We have to get you away from here until this is all over. He might come back for you, if he knew you survived the attack."

"I don't think that's necessary, Cass."

"This is one time you're not arguing with me," Cassie said, trying to think of some place. Her own house would not be a good idea, as Lopez and Perego would look there first.

"There is somewhere I can go, if you insist." Luci mentioned a mutual friend who lived nearby and Cassie heartily agreed with that idea.

"But I have more to tell you first," Luci went on rapidly. "He told me something about a payroll . . . and a valuable painting stolen from the San Miguel chapel. It is hidden out at Perego's *hacendado,* south of town. And he mentioned something about a meeting out there on Saturday night."

"It is Saturday today, Luci."

"Oh."

Luci's wide eyes acknowledged the passing of time when she had been unaware of it.

"They're meeting tonight, then," Cassie observed, her voice quiet.

"Yes, I suppose. Cass, you must go to the authorities. Do you hear me? Get some help. I *know* that look, but you can't do this by yourself. These are dangerous, desperate men. They will stop at nothing to get what they want, Cassie. Cassie! Are you listening to me? Will you *please* just listen to me for once? Just look what he did to me!"

"Of course, I am listening, Luci. How could I not?" She smiled at her friend warmly, so glad to hear the constant babble of her voice, now back to normal and so glad to see the familiar piercing, dark-eyed gaze regarding her, demanding she listen

280

and heed Luci's words of wisdom.

Luci now sat propped up in the center of several pillows, her eyes showing her continuing suspicion that Cassie was lying to her and was silently making her own plans about how she could bring Perego down.

"Cassie! Cass, are you in here? It's me, Sarah."

A whisper came from the doorway, as the freckled face of Cassie's sister peeped around the corner. Her eyes widened at the sight of Luci sitting up and talking animatedly.

"Luci!" she cried loudly. "You're awake! I'm so glad. I can't tell you how good it is to see you. Are you really, truly all right?"

Luci winked at Cassie and teased, "She talks almost as much as I do, doesn't she?"

"Yes, she does," said Cassie, giving her sister a hug. "She always has."

Sarah explained, "I came by this afternoon, but Cassie refused to leave you even for a few minutes."

"I suspected as much," Luci said, frowning at Cassie, who was doing her best to stand up straight and to hide how tired she really was.

"Go home, Cass. I'll stay with Luci now that she's back to normal," Sarah offered.

"You have to get some rest, Cass," Luci urged, too.

"I think I will." Cassie smiled at the two of them, her mind already somewhere else. She had no intention of going home. Luci's recovery and the information about the meeting at Perego's had rejuvenated her and given her a new burst of energy.

First, she would see that Luci was safe and she would ask Sarah to stay with her. Then, she would be there at the meeting at Perego's *hacendado* that very evening, but she had no intention of going alone. She would take Luci's advice and ask for help. Her first thought had been of Cruz Delgado. He would go with her and would probably be very upset if she didn't ask. They had a common goal: to find enough evidence on Perego that he could be stripped of his position and power and thrown into jail, along with the companions who had worked with him to steal and to murder. They had agreed to work together.

This was their chance to catch him in the very act . . . to get all the proof they needed! She sped over to the church, certain she'd find him there. It was quiet there, and the young priest nowhere to be found. His living quarters, too, were unoccupied, and Father Auguste claimed not to know where he was.

Her disappointment was immense. Where could he be?

The hour was growing late, daylight fast waning toward night, and there was no more time to search for him. She couldn't tarry any longer. She would have to do this on her own.

Wavering, she thought about the men involved, seeing their evil faces in her mind. Perego's expression when he'd held the knife to her throat was still vivid in her mind. It was not something she ever wanted to see again in her lifetime.

She could only imagine what they'd do to her if they caught her spying on them. With a determined shake of her head, she dismissed any doubts. She had to accomplish this.

She thought of Emerson. He would go with her if she asked. But he had been through too much lately, and he wasn't a young man any longer. She couldn't drag him into the night's intrigues, whatever they might turn out to be. She couldn't even risk letting him know where she was going.

Rushing over to the stable, Cassie made the decision to take Cameron's horse, rather than her own, since the big black had not been exercised in some time and had more stamina and strength than her own bay horse.

Napoleon, unlike his French namesake, was long-legged and well-built. Part-Arabian, the gelding was strong and wiry and had been bred for speed. Cameron had trained him and he was completely dependable. He was inky black with just a flash of a white marking on his chest. Cassie asked Joey, the stable hand, to saddle him while she went home to retrieve a few, essential items.

"It's just you and me," she whispered to the big horse, her words whipped away by the cold night wind that blew into her face as she galloped out of town only a half hour or so later. She hoped no one other than the groom had noticed her abrupt departure. Joey was young and not extremely bright.

No doubt, he would waste no time worrying about her, or mentioning it to anyone else.

Perego's *hacendado* was not far and she knew the way well; it lay along the route she'd taken so many times to her own summer cabin. She would reach there shortly after dark, which suited her purpose and could work to her advantage. She wanted to see without being seen, to listen without being heard, and she wanted to get away without being discovered.

Dressed in her darkest riding outfit and astride the midnight-colored horse, she blended in with the deepening nightfall. She was an invisible wraith, a fleeting spirit bent on dark justice. She had even concealed her bright hair beneath a wide-brimmed black hat. No one would pick her out of the darkness, or so she fervently hoped. She kept to the shadows along the edges of the road, just to be sure.

When she was within sight of the Spaniard's elegant home, she pulled up and dismounted, slipping quietly to the ground. She tied the horse to a tree and made her way on foot past the western edge of the sprawling house. She couldn't help noticing that the impressive hacienda was a very nice property, more elaborate than one could be expected to afford on the governor's payroll alone. It was becoming clear to her just where he'd been finding additional funds to support such a grand life-style.

The huge barn rose up in front of her, yellow light spilling out from a few scattered windows and from beneath a large, double doorway on the far side of the massive, two-story building. Two horses were tied to a rail alongside the front entrance.

Her heartbeat accelerated with the certainty that the men she sought and the evidence she needed were separated from her only by the thickness of the wall. Careful not to make a sound, she eased her way down the length of the barn to a shutterless window. Encouraged by the sound of muffled voices drifting out, she was frustrated when she couldn't make out the words.

When she could hear more clearly, she was appalled to realize the men were speaking only in Spanish, even though she admitted that was the normal thing for them to do. Only scattered words and bits of phrases were recognizable to her. It wasn't enough!

Then she saw the painting. It was a striking Goya in brilliant reds and blacks depicting a Spanish don and his lady. It fit the description of the one recently removed from the San Miguel chapel. Even though Luci had mentioned the painting, Cassie was still surprised to see it here in plain sight and in the possession of these ruffians.

She seethed. These unprincipled men were stealing from the churches on top of all their other assorted crimes. They were also the men who had murdered Cameron and beaten her best friend senseless. One of them had murdered Cruz's family in cold blood many years ago. She looked from one face to another. They were all there.

Perego. Lieutenant Mendez. Even Lopez, who seemed to be a minor player in the drama. These were the men she'd known to be involved, though she'd suspected there might be a fourth, a man smarter and more powerful than any of these three, an American perhaps. But she could have been wrong about that.

Their activity and the air of excitement told her that something big was about to happen, but she couldn't understand enough of the words to know what that was. She listened harder, straining to pick out more words she knew, slipping in closer and sneaking a peek inside from time to time to see what they were doing inside the barn.

Her heart jumped to her throat, though, when she heard a deep and sweetly familiar voice interrupt the proceedings with a shouted command.

"Throw down your guns, gentlemen."

A glance inside confirmed her very worst fears. Cruz Delgado stood facing the men. He was alone.

The men had stopped talking and were eyeing him warily. Their hands were out from their sides, not moving a muscle, but not making a move to do as he had ordered.

He held a five-shot Colt revolver on them, which had their full attention and apparently their respect, as well. But his eyes had an even more chilling effect. A hard ruthlessness in their cool blue depths had warned far braver men than these to beware of his wrath.

Their eyes darted from one to the other, searching for an option, some way out of this life threatening dilemma.

"Drop your weapons now! You have only three seconds. And kick them over here!"

There was no denying the authority in his ringing voice. They began to comply reluctantly, one by one, dropping their own weapons into the hay at their feet and kicking them in his direction.

His gun trained on Perego's heart, Cruz bent with an athletic grace and retrieved their firearms from the ground to toss them well out of their reach behind him.

Cassie breathed easier. He seemed to have it under control. He had outsmarted the three of them, and herself as well. She wasn't surprised. She had seen this undercurrent of strength and brittle toughness in him before and had come to respect it. At times like this, she could appreciate it, but she didn't suppose she would ever understand it.

Afraid to call out for fear of distracting him, she watched quietly as he moved from one of them to the next, tying their hands securely behind their backs. He paused then for a glance at the painting and had a few more harsh words for them in fluent Spanish. Whatever he'd said had their faces contorting with impotent anger.

He laughed and the wintry sound of it chilled her down to her bones. It was not the soft, gentle laughter of the man she'd come to know and love. It was the laughter of a man who had suffered and who thirsted for revenge. It sliced her heart open.

The hopeless echo of it rang in her ears long after he'd clamped his lips tightly together, cutting off the sound.

Cruz Delgado was as much a tormented man as the three Spaniards manacled in front of him. But he was in control. Cassie was about to call out to him, to reveal her presence and offer to help, when a new arrival stopped her.

A cultured American voice broke the extended stillness that followed the laughter. The words were clipped and straightforward.

"Throw down the gun, Cruz, and turn around very slowly. It's all over."

Cruz hesitated, and Cassie was terrified that he would ignore the order and face the man's gun, bringing almost certain death to himself in the action. The silence stretched tightly between the two men. Perego and his co-conspirators watched with undiluted interest, afraid to move.

Cruz did exactly as she feared he would. He whirled, raising his gun in the same motion. What happened next was so fast, the action seemed to blur in front of Cassie's horror-stricken eyes.

A puff of smoke was the first indication that the man's gun had been fired. The noise of percussion followed and then a grunt from Cruz, whose own gun flew out of his hand.

He grabbed his wrist which showed a ribbon of bright blood and looked the man in the eye without a sign of emotion and with no sign of pain.

"You always were the best shot in the East," he

said with the same evidence of hardness in his voice that had been in his laughter seconds earlier. "But I never thought you would be shooting at me."

Cruz's eyes were steady and gave away none of what he was thinking, but Cassie felt his pain at this final betrayal. The man who stood there, aiming for his wide chest, was his close friend, Evan Hamilton.

"I don't want to have to kill you, Cruz." Evan's eyes and hand were steady, too. It was clear that he would shoot if he had to.

"No, I don't suppose you would want to, but I do create a problem for you, don't I?" Cruz challenged.

"I'll have to think about it," he muttered, moving quickly from one Spaniard to the next to release their bonds, keeping his gun trained on Cruz the entire time.

"Kill him and we'll throw him in the ravine out back. The buzzards will make a feast of his bones long before anybody finds him." Perego's words were predictable, as was the complete lack of sentiment behind them.

Evan Hamilton shook his handsome blond head sadly. "No," he said. "Tie him up, Mendez, and make sure the ropes are good and tight. He's strong and he's smart. I don't want him getting loose."

Mendez grunted as he bent to his task with relish.

Cruz's eyes of blue steel were once more unreadable and did not stray from his former friend.

Cassie shivered, unable to believe this final, hateful turn of events. But, of course, it all made sense. Evan must be the one who had put Perego in touch with American merchants, who would offer cash for the stolen paintings. Evan had systematically betrayed all of them: herself; Sarah, who had come to care for him; but most of all, Cruz, who had trusted him.

"So what happens now, *compadre?*" The Spanish word for "friend" was a barbed dart that missed its mark, leaving Hamilton unmoved. The use of it gave Cruz some satisfaction, nevertheless. "Do you kill me and leave me for the buzzards, as our esteemed colleague has so thoughtfully suggested?"

"No!" Evan shouted, revealing that he felt some discomfort with the bizarre turn of events that had brought friend against friend. "No," he said more quietly, "I will not sanction your death, *compadre,* if there is another solution."

He repeated the word spoken by Cruz quietly, as though he meant it, but he went on, "I have another plan."

Instead of revealing it immediately to Cruz, he turned to the other three. In a low conversation that neither Cassie nor Cruz was able to overhear, Evan told them his solution to the problem Cruz presented for them.

The three Spanish men shared long pulls from a flask of Taos Lightning and soon a lighter spirit filled the barn. Only Evan Hamilton remained aloof, his eyes never straying for long from his prisoner tied up in the corner. The other three talked, joked, drank, and occasionally cursed at one another. Becoming bored, they even set up a makeshift target and took turns throwing their knives at it.

Another hour passed. Cassie rose up on her toes to watch whenever she felt safe in doing so, but nothing much happened inside the barn. The men seemed to be waiting for something or someone. After what seemed like ages, Cassie heard the rattle of wagon wheels nearing the barn. The door was thrown open and several men Cassie had never seen before sauntered in. These five men, too, had been drinking heavily.

Greetings were dispensed quickly. Perego, speaking rapidly in Spanish, motioned to the painting, a stack of goods resting in a corner of the barn, and finally to Cruz. The strangers nodded agreeably and shook hands with the four men who had been waiting for them in the barn. A deal had been struck.

Cassie was terrified of what it might mean to Cruz; even though Evan Hamilton, who seemed to be their leader and was thus the missing piece in the puzzle, had promised not to kill him.

Would he keep his word? What would they do with Cruz? Would they listen to Evan? They couldn't just turn him loose to go straight to the authorities. That much was certain.

The men set to work loading the goods into the waiting wagon, and Cassie heard the word "Chihuahua" tossed about in the conversation. One of the men whistled pleasantly and picked up the heavy, ornately framed original oil painting.

Perego shouted at him for his cavalier manner in handling the valuable painting. After that, he exerted a bit more care, but not much.

It took four strong men to subdue Cruz and move him out the door and into the wagon, even though he was still bound hand and foot. Cassie watched him fight and admired his strength, even while her breath caught in her throat.

He cursed and railed at them, promising retribution of all kinds, in this life and into the next. One of them angrily stuffed a dirty rag into his mouth. After that, only his vicious mutterings could be heard. The men with the task of loading him had bruises and scrapes to show for it afterwards. By the time it was done, they were cursing, too.

It was clear he would not give up nor go down easily, but would most surely fight to the death if necessary. Wherever they were taking him, it would never be far enough that they would be safe from his wrath and retribution, should he escape and come back for them.

Did they intend to transport him along with their valuable cargo all the way to Mexico? No! She wouldn't let that happen. She might not be able to stop them now, but she could follow them and try to find a way to free him. It didn't occur to her until much later what a foolish and headstrong thing to do that had been, and how much danger she'd put them both in by following such a course without help of any kind.

Still, in her own defense, there really hadn't been time to do anything else. If she had ridden back to town, they would have been long gone and catching up with them on the trail not a likelihood.

As she watched, the wagon joined a line of four others outside the arched entryway to the *hacendado*. The small caravan journeyed off in a southeasterly direction, well under the cover of darkness, with several hours yet remaining before sunrise.

Cassie trailed along, staying close enough to keep their shadowed outlines in sight, hoping they'd never think to look behind them for pursuit. *Pursuit!* The word indicated some kind of action, a threat, she thought with wry humor. She definitely posed neither one. A lone woman with no weapon save a small knife and a rifle she wasn't very skilled at using. She boasted no reinforcements; she only possessed an overriding desire to free at all costs the man they held prisoner.

She pulled her collar up, hunkered down into it, and tied a scarf she pulled from her pocket snugly around her head and ears. She was ready for a long, cold ride, if that's what it took. She would go all the way to Mexico, if she had to, but she didn't plan on it taking anywhere near that long before finding a way to free Cruz.

Cruz cursed himself roundly for letting Hamilton slip up on him that way. Now that he had the leisure to think back on the past few weeks' events, he could see that he should have put scattered bits of information together and been looking more diligently for the American connection in the smuggling ring. But would he have looked in the direction of the man he considered a very good friend, even if he had? Probably not.

The men charged with getting him and the cargo to Mexico had not been cruel in their treatment of him, thus far. In fact, they had very nearly ignored him. He had been bound hand and foot for the majority of the time. They untied his hands only twice for him to eat and drink and to relieve himself in the bushes along the trail. They seemed not to worry that he might manage to free himself from the bonds and escape.

Cruz was bruised and sore from the bouncing wagon and from his inability to move around much in order to find a more comfortable position, tied up as he was. He was stiff and cold, his fingers and toes almost numb and he was getting hungry.

It would be a long, miserable trip to Mexico. But he had made up his mind he wouldn't be going that far. He would keep his eyes open for the first opportunity to escape. The next time they untied him, he'd find a way to make a break for it.

The caravan traveled all night without stopping and on through the next day. With their load of contraband, they apparently intended to put as much distance between themselves and Santa Fe as possible.

In the daylight, Cassie dropped farther back with

only the dust kicked up by their wheels to point the way. She was bone weary and could hardly keep her eyes open. She prayed they would stop soon to rest, or she was afraid there was no way she could keep going.

Once, she thought she'd lost them. Her eyes must have drifted shut and she had slept sitting up long enough for her horse to stray from the trail. She could no longer see them in the distance. When she doubled back, there was no sign of them for well over two hours.

She was horrified that she could have let such a thing happen. Not only would Cruz continue to be their prisoner and end up deep in Mexico somewhere, but in the miles they had already covered, she had become disoriented and didn't know where she was or how to find her way back. She would be alone out here.

The men with the wagons seemed to be travelling south to southeast, as a rule, she'd decided by watching the track of the sun during the day. So, she kept on in that general direction, urging her tired horse into a lope, determined to catch them.

It was nearly dusk when, thankfully, she caught sight of the white cloth of their wagon covers flapping in the waning light, and heard the echoes of their shouting.

She was so unspeakably glad to have them in sight again, she could hardly contain herself. She slowed her horse back to a walk and trained her eyes on them, determined not to allow a repetition of her carelessness.

At that moment, she knew she would move heaven and earth to see Cruz again, to hold him, to know that he lived and was safe from harm.

When the caravan finally halted for the night, her body ached in every joint and muscle as she slid limply to the ground. The unexpected jolt jarred its way up through her feet and legs and into her chest and her head, which already pounded miserably. Her legs felt permanently bowed in the shape of the horse, and her bottom was blistered from the unaccustomed long hours in the saddle.

Her game horse, too, had expended his store of energy and was badly in need of food. They'd crossed a stream a few miles back where he'd been able to get much needed water, but there had been no grass or hay since they left Perego's barn behind the previous day. The steady pace had been grueling for the animal.

Cassie unfastened the cinch and eased the saddle to the ground. Using the blanket, she rubbed the horse's damp coat and undoubtedly sore muscles before she slumped to the ground to begin tending to her own needs.

With the sounds of the commotion of the men securing their wagons and animals for the night just beyond the rise, she laid her head wearily against the saddle for a few minutes' desperately needed rest.

She awoke with a start to a starlit darkness and a quiet so vast it seemed the whole world must lay sleeping. It was time to move. She had waited for this moment, planning what action she would take. She knew which wagon Cruz had been kept in, and there had been only one other man in it for most of the trip.

If she could only sneak up to him quietly and untie him, they could slip out together and be gone before anyone knew she was in the camp. If only it would prove to be that easy, but she knew that all kinds of things could happen to foil her plan.

Treading as softly as she could, she worked her way up to the edge of the camp before she saw the guard. He sat high on a flat mesa no more than a hundred feet away, but on the other side of the wagons.

She dropped silently to her knees before he could see her, hidden by the bulk of the wagon in front of her. She would have to work her way carefully around to the back of the wagon third from the end and be careful not to be seen or heard in the process. Her knees cramped from the unnatural squatting position and her feet were nearly numb from the cold and the long hours spent in the saddle. She put a hand behind her wearily to rub her aching back and her sore bottom, praying she could hold on long enough to follow this thing through, to free Cruz and be on their way back to Santa Fe.

Then another man called out to the man standing guard. The guard rose and stretched, retrieving the rifle propped beside him, obviously happy to be relieved.

The guard was being changed. Rested eyes would take over and Cassie would have to be more careful than ever. This new man was not likely to doze off anytime soon.

The wagons were circled and now they all looked alike. She could no longer tell which had been third in line, which one held Cruz inside.

Cassie rubbed her head, willing her eyes to stay open and her tired body to cooperate for just a while longer, begging her fuddled brain to think clearly. Which one!? She couldn't make a mistake now, not when she was so close she could almost reach out and touch him. But which one?

If she entered the wrong one, their figurative goose was cooked. Had there been anything distinctive about the wagon carrying Cruz, other than its previous place in line? Think, Cassie, think! she admonished herself.

The five wagons were nearly identical, certainly from the distance at which she had been following them. Try as hard as she could, Cassie remembered nothing to distinguish one from the other. She hadn't ever really been that close.

Footsteps shuffling toward her sent her scrambling for some cactus cover, hoping her flight hadn't been as loud in their ears as it had been in her own. She held her breath in her panic, watching warily.

Two men, including the guard who'd just been relieved, passed within a few feet of her hiding place. Since one was American, she could follow the conversation fairly well. They mentioned the name of Cruz Delgado. One of them had a bowl of beans and some bread. Could he be on his way to feed the prisoner? It was worth the risk of following him to find out what was happening and if he were truly on his way to Cruz. She had to know where he was. She could not do anything until she found him.

The two men split up, heading for different wagons. Going with her hunch, Cassie crept along in the shadows near the man with the food. He pulled up a flap and ducked into one of the wagons. She heard him mutter something and then he was back outside, without the bowl! She had guessed right! Cruz must be in this very wagon.

It had grown very dark and the only light in the camp was from the fire in the center of the circled wagons. It reflected off the sides of the wagons facing inside, leaving their outer side swathed in darkness, which would work to her advantage.

But if one of the men chanced to look in her direction, he might easily see her feet beneath the wagon. And when she made a move to enter the wagon, she would be exposed for those few seconds it took her to scramble inside. Also, she faced the problem of getting him untied and the two of them escaping the same way without being seen or heard. She waited impatiently, her eyes on the men squatting around the campfire. When they seemed otherwise occupied, she made her move.

As silent as a shadow, she whipped around the

back of the wagon, her hand reaching for the bottom of the flap. Eyes trained on the men and willing them not to look, she yanked it up. It was very dark inside, but she scuttled under the canvas as quickly as she could.

She was lying flat on her stomach in the pitch black interior of the wagon. There was no sound and no movement. She felt around her in the dark. *Nothing*. Had she chosen the wrong wagon after all? Would she have to do it again, if they didn't catch up with her first?

"Cruz," she whispered. A muttering from the corner had her scrambling in that direction. "Is that really you?"

She felt a muscled length of leg, then her hands groped, moving across a wide chest and strong shoulders. One of her hands flew to his face and felt the blessedly familiar contours of his nose and high cheekbones.

"Cruz!"

Fumbling in the darkness, she felt the gag tied around his head. She slid her hands behind his head to work the tight knot loose.

"Cassie!" His voice was rough and deep, but did not rise above a whisper. "What are . . . ?"

"Shh!" He hadn't sounded a bit glad to scc her, but that didn't matter in the least. "Be still," she admonished him, while she sawed at the ropes that held his hands securely behind his back. Her knife was not as sharp as it might have been, and the task took longer than it should have.

He spoke into her ear, then, and she wished he hadn't. "Cass . . . I could throttle you!"

"That's the thanks I get for risking my life for you!" she shot back in a quiet whisper, but she was smiling. "Ingrate."

The ropes fell to the ground and she rubbed his wrists until the feeling returned. Then he took the knife from her and made quick work of the ropes that held his feet together.

"Is this the only weapon you have, love?"

"Damn! I left the rifle back on my horse."

"How far?"

"About a hundred yards."

"Oh, boy."

He flexed his ankles, groaning when she bent to rub them as well.

"Can you walk?" Cassie was truly concerned.

"I think so. At least, I'd better be able to. Or we'll never get out of here."

They would have to move fast and there was no way they could take the paintings or any of the other stolen goods with them. If they got away safely, they could send someone back for the contraband goods on the wagon train.

Cassie's sweet breath brushed Cruz's face when she spoke to him so softly, and her leg slid along his when she bent to rub his stiff legs. The feeling returned with a rush, not just to his legs, but to all parts of his body. He was appalled to feel an unexpected and singularly unwelcome swelling against his trousers. He wanted her!

What in God's name could his renegade body be doing to him now? This was neither the time nor the place. One sound could give them away and spoil his escape, but that seemed to make no difference. He squirmed, trying to keep her from knowing the source of his discomfort.

"Cassie."

"Yes?"

"It's nothing. I . . ."

"Do you hurt somewhere? Does your wrist hurt from the gunshot?"

In panic, she remembered the bright blood and instinctively moved to find his arm in the darkness, leaning across him.

He groaned.

"I'm sorry," she apologized quickly. "Did I hurt you?"

"No!" he shot back in an agitated whisper. She had no idea what she was doing to him, lying across him as she was.

His arm lay around her waist and before he knew what he was doing or could put a halt to it, his fingers splayed out across her spine, pulling her down closer to him.

Cassie stilled and ceased groping for his injured wrist when she realized he had other things on his mind than making his escape. He was about to kiss her! Her heart slammed against her chest, and she gasped for a breath before his full, sensuous lips played over hers.

"Cruz . . ." she began. "We have to—"

Her protests were stifled by a deepened kiss that swept all rational thought from her head. Her heart sang. He was alive and well and here in her arms.

Only the shaking of the wagon was sufficient cause to break off the kiss that could have gone on and on. He held her away from him and put a finger to his lips, though they both knew she was not about to utter a sound that would give them away. They were rocked from side to side. Somebody was climbing up into the front of the wagon!

They scarcely dared to breathe while they waited for whatever would happen next. The silver flash of the knife in Cruz's hand was the only thing to be seen in the wagon's darkness until the man up front struck a match and lit a lantern suspended just above their heads, but outside the canvas.

"When he climbs down," Cruz whispered in her ear, "slip out the back and head straight back to your horse. Wait for me there. I'll be right behind you."

"But—" she began, her words cut off by his lips that again brushed hers.

"Shhh. Do as I say." His lips barely moved, but she heard the words and waited.

Minutes later, the swaying of the wagon that indicated the man was climbing down spurred her into action. She crawled quickly to the back, slipped out from under the flap on the side of the wagon farthest away from the campfire, and then ducked behind a tree. She hid only a second or two before the burly man shuffled around the back of the wagon, holding the lantern high over his head. He climbed inside, cursing and losing his footing more than once, so that he almost fell backward onto the hard ground. He sang a few bars of a cattle driving song when he could breathe well enough.

The lantern remained lit where he hung it on a nail inside while he spread his pallet and took off his boots with a loud grunt. His pants dropped to the floor in a pile on top of the boots.

Cassie's head pounded while she watched the silhouettes inside. Cruz did not move and she guessed he was pretending to be tied up and asleep. If the man looked closely, he would have to see that his prisoner's feet were unbound. There was no telling what he might do then. He would almost surely raise an alarm that would bring the others running. At the very least, he would tie Cruz securely and he wouldn't have a chance of getting away. She could only pray he was drunk enough that he wouldn't notice.

The heavyset man was humming happily to himself, probably the result of more than one trip to the flask this night. He didn't seem to be paying any attention to Cruz where he lay in the corner of the wagon, hardly even glanced over at him. Extinguishing the light, the man fell onto his makeshift bed and was instantly snoring loudly.

Cassie stood outside, afraid to go back to her horse as Cruz had instructed. He might not be able to find his way in the darkness without her to guide him, and she wasn't leaving there without him.

Time seemed swallowed into a bottomless vacuum while she stared at the wagon and waited. Night birds called and she heard the crackling of the campfire and smelled the smoke as it drifted out to her. Every so often a voice could be heard calling out and another answering in reply.

Not all the men in the camp were asleep. Any one of them might notice when Cruz tried to slip out of the wagon and make his escape. While she watched, the shadowed outline of a booted foot descended slowly from the wagon and then another, followed by a length of leg. He was on the ground in one graceful leap and moving with the stealth of a wildcat, only steps away from her.

"Hey!" came a shout from one of the men.

Cruz halted, frozen in his tracks. Cassie was sure it was all over for them. They had been found out and would probably be on their way to Mexico and an uncertain future.

The two of them had no weapons other than the small knife, and it was of little use against the high caliber guns favored by the merchants. Her horse and the rifle on her saddle were much too far away to do them any good. The men could shoot them down where they stood in the shadows, if they wished.

Cruz's body tensed like a finely coiled spring, a clear sign that he wouldn't go easily, wouldn't give up what they'd gained without a fight. Even if it was a fight to the death.

Expecting gunfire or more shouted commands, they were surprised when nothing followed. No sound, no movement. Nothing.

It was once more reasonably quiet in the camp. Everyone had settled down. The call had not been a sign that the escape attempt had been discovered, but merely a drunken shout from one to another of the merchants.

Cassie motioned to him to keep coming when she was sure no one was watching them from behind him. He reached her in a few long strides and took her hand. He indicated with a motion of his head that he would follow her, for her to lead on through the brush. She knew he would probably let her have it later on for disobeying him again.

They reached her horse without further incident and mounted up, with her in back, clinging to him. If they could only get a mile or two away without being discovered, they might stand a chance.

Cruz knew the men were well armed and that they had a stake in seeing him delivered all the way down to Mexico. They would fight to take him back, if they had to. Cassie must have used utmost care to reach him without alerting them in any way. He couldn't believe she'd followed them for a day and a night, all by herself. He would have to confront her about it later. But now, their first goal was to get safely away from the camp, as quickly as possible.

There was a good chance that if they hadn't already been detected, they would not be, at least not until morning light. He would not rest easy, however, until they put some distance between themselves and these men.

Cassie's rifle hung on the saddle, and it was the only weapon they had, except for the small knife, which he had stuck in his belt. It would not be enough if there was pursuit from the camp.

He felt the muscular horse beneath them leap up and step out in long strides when he put the spurs to its side. Cassie's blue-black horse had a lot of heart and was fast, but carrying two was a disadvantage for any mount. They had a long way to travel through unfamiliar territory and with the real possibility that they would be pursued.

Chapter Fourteen

The two of them pressed on a horse, snugly together, brought back all too vivid memories of their first horseback ride into Santa Fe. It seemed such a very long time ago and so very much had happened to them since then. Riding next to him, even under the worst of conditions, was surprisingly pleasant for Cassie. She remembered being so comfortable and at ease on that other trip that she'd drifted off to sleep leaning against him. She could do that again; she was so tired and his back so straight and strong.

Cassie relaxed and soon slept, held in place by his firm grip on her hands that were clasped tightly across his stomach. They rode on for several miles and were well away from the camp and out of danger, at least for the moment, when he found a secluded place where they could stop for a few hours' rest. He knew she needed the rest and would soon collapse without it. She had tended to Luci and had slept little. Then, without a second thought and with no rest, she had set off after him. How had she managed to do it?

With as much care as a father for a young child,

he helped her off the horse. Wearily, she leaned into him and slid along his length. He enjoyed the feel of her in his arms for only a few seconds before he turned to spread pine needles and the blanket from the horse under an overhanging rock. He settled her there on the makeshift bed, making her as comfortable as he could. Sitting down beside her, he leaned back against a tree and pulled her close, easing her head down on his shoulder. She didn't complain, but murmured her appreciation sleepily.

Her eyes drifted shut and she was asleep in an instant. She was as light as a feather in his arms. He smiled and allowed himself to sleep, as well, confident that she was comfortable and safe. When Cassie awoke, she wasn't aware that she'd moved so much as a muscle, but he was instantly awake, too, his arm tightening protectively around her.

"Are you all right, Cass?"

"Mmmhmm," she murmured, warm and sleepy, secure in the circle of his arms.

"Thank you for coming after me."

"You're welcome," she answered, a bit surprised that he hadn't scolded her. But his next words were exactly what she expected, knowing him as she did.

"But you shouldn't have, you know. You took a terrible risk." His face was dark and he squeezed her shoulder hard, his fear for her conveyed quite clearly in the gesture. "How did you know what was happening with Perego and the others, anyway?" he went on, without slackening his hold on her, his eyes still troubled.

She told him about Luci's sudden recovery, and

what she'd learned when her friend had finally been able to talk to her, about the thefts and the planned meeting between Perego and the others. She also told him how she had looked for him all over town.

"I am glad Luci is all right." His voice was deep and sincere; she could tell that he meant it. "So, you believed what she told you about the meeting, and you rode out to Perego's alone?"

"I had no other choice."

"I see." He thought about that for a moment. Perhaps she hadn't had a choice. It had truly been a brave, if foolhardy, thing she'd done. "Well, then, thank you again."

He dropped a kiss on the top of her head and slid his arm out from around her. "You must be starving." Reaching inside a coat pocket, he pulled out a small bag, giving her two cold, square biscuits and a strip of jerked beef he had snatched up on his way out of the wagon.

"Mmm. This is really good."

She ate ravenously, relishing every crumbly bite of the hardened bread and the strongly flavored stick of dried meat, licking her lips in satisfaction.

"I have some water," she choked out, pointing to her saddlebags.

Instantly, he sprang to his feet and found the canteen. "Here," he offered, holding it up to her lips. She drank her fill.

"Now you," she said, pushing it toward him.

He took a few sips and then returned the canteen to the saddlebags. For a few minutes, they sat in

310

companionable silence, glad to be alive and together again.

Without warning, he reached for her and, drawing her in to him, leaned down and kissed her. There was an edge of desperation in him as his lips moved over hers, his tongue teasing the corners of her mouth, venturing inside when her lips parted willingly for him. He tasted her, tracing the contours of her mouth, coaxing a response from her tongue, and felt wild with heat when it played back and tangled with his own.

Dancing along the contours of his full lips, her tongue found its way to the waiting cavern of his mouth, drawing a sigh from deep inside him. She melted against him helplessly, a fiery warmth racing through her. All during the time when she'd followed after the wagons, thoughts of kissing him and holding him had tormented her mind. She couldn't believe he'd actually kissed her in the wagon, with the men who were his jailers all around them. She hadn't exactly backed away from it, either, she remembered with a smile.

Cruz was tough and mysterious and more man than anyone she'd ever known. He was an experienced fighter and lover, rough and at times even dangerous. He'd even seemed to be adept at undoing the buttons and fastenings on her clothing, something that surely came with experience: *experience* that no *priest* should have had. He knew how to do all this, did it with practiced ease, the same way he handled a gun and fought. He was schooled in a great many things, other than religion and the church.

311

"You're not a priest, are you?" she blurted out, pulling away from him and looking up into those startlingly blue eyes that never failed to have an effect on her. They could be imperious eyes, used to commanding and being obeyed. Now the usual light silver-blue had darkened to a deep cobalt, nearly the color of the midnight sky.

At last, she was asking the question that had plagued her consciousness for so long. And she wished she could snatch the words back. She didn't want to know the answer. God help her, she was better off not knowing.

"No."

The answer was inevitable, implacable, the truth undeniable. The fact that it was spoken in that voice she loved, the same one that did such wonderful things to her, made it not one whit easier to accept. She wanted to shout at him to deny it, to keep on lying to her, anything rather than admit to such deception, but instead she stared at him quietly.

Cruz knew it would not do to lie to her any longer. He had always known that when she asked him, he would have to tell the truth, no matter the cost. He couldn't bear to lie to her any longer, not even to protect his mission, to continue his cover. None of that was worth losing her over; nothing was more important than the two of them.

Besides, it would do no good to argue, because she knew! He could tell from the hurt look in her big, haunted brown eyes. He had waited too late to tell her the truth, he realized with a sinking feeling in the pit of his stomach.

"I never meant to lie to you. I wanted to tell you the truth in the very beginning, but I couldn't, Cass. I just couldn't. You see, I had to protect you as well as myself and my mission. I suspected Cameron's involvement and I didn't know what you might know."

Her heart sank. No matter how much she loved him, she could never trust him again. He had used her and lied to her. Now, he was lost to her, as surely as if Perego had killed him back in the warehouse. Once they'd become friends and then even lovers, why couldn't he have trusted and confided in her then?

"He's dead, Cruz! Cameron is dead! You're the liar here! He's innocent. I'll never believe anything bad about him. I don't care what you say. You can't convince me he had anything to do with those awful men and their thievery."

"Such loyalty!"

He, too, was growing angry. She had never cared about him the way she still cared for a dead man! He'd been a fool to think she ever could. For her, it was always Cameron, and it always would be, even if the man hadn't deserved such devotion. She would never love anyone else like she had loved her husband, least of all him.

"Your dear, dead husband lied to you, Cass. He gave money to Perego, lots of it. I can prove it to you. I have the receipt, signed by the both of them."

"No, I won't listen," she cried, putting her hands over her ears.

He pulled her hands down and spoke firmly but

not unkindly, looking at her so she couldn't turn away. "You *will* listen, Cassie. This is important. You have to hear what I'm saying. I know how much he meant to you, but these are facts. They're real! It's time to let go of all that, to get on with your life."

She listened, but it was obvious that it was not her choice to do so. Her eyes were still closed. She refused to look at him and he could tell she was denying the truth of everything he was telling her. He was furious with her, for her rejection of him as much as for her steadfast defense of Cameron Layton

"I suppose you never lied to me with your body, your caresses, never once offered me, through your actions, anything that was never yours to give." His temper cooled a little and he went on, speaking more softly, the pain evident in his rich voice, ". . . or mine to take."

He looked at her long and hard with the clear and hurtful knowledge that he could have found her only to lose her in this one, long night. Her eyes still sparked with angry fire and her chest heaved from the turbulent emotions sweeping through her. He thought she had never looked more beautiful. His hungry eyes drank in the features of her fine-boned face, the delicate arch of her brow, her wide-set, dark brown eyes, as rich and warm as sable. She was indescribably lovely and he longed to reach out and touch her, to pull her into his arms and never let her go.

But she wouldn't welcome his touch. Not now.

Perhaps not ever. He hurt deep inside for the pain he'd unintentionally caused her. Her calm good sense and courage had saved his life once, and she had earned him his freedom tonight. All he had to give her in return was the painful, damaging truth. He shuddered to think of the unbreachable rift it would cause between them.

Cruz Delgado found himself thinking like a man in love. He wanted to share his thoughts with her, reveal his identity and make love to her slowly and so thoroughly she would cry out with joy. He wanted to feel her nails rake across his bare skin, to sink into her moist warmth, making her completely his, for now and for always. He thought with longing of her passions that could match his own, the way she had loved him without reservation.

What waited in her heart was the answer to the deepest longings of his soul, the quest of his lifetime: the need to belong, to find a place that was well and truly his. Was it never to be? For, surely he couldn't give in to his desires. Though she may want him as much as he wanted her, Cassie Layton was as unattainable to him as the sun and as far away as the midnight stars. It was best for the both of them that she remain there, just beyond his reach.

He scowled and stuffed his hands into his pockets to keep from hitting something or ravishing her where she stood, without a word of apology. Bit by bit, he was coming apart. He could feel himself losing control.

Thoughts of her had tormented his dreams when they'd been apart. That agony didn't compare to what he felt now when he was with her, yet separate, unable to touch, to reach out to her. He was so near now he could feel the warmth of her body, but they might as well have been miles apart.

"Cassie, I'm sorry. I couldn't tell you the truth, as much as I might have wanted to."

"Why not, Cruz? You couldn't trust me to keep your secret? Haven't I been keeping secrets for you from the very beginning? Haven't I lied for you more than once? Protected you? What else could I have done to convince you I was trustworthy?" Her voice was sarcastic now and filled with hurt and anger.

He saw in a blinding flash his mistake. He could have trusted her; *should* have trusted her with the truth from the beginning. Cassie Layton was a strong, courageous woman and she would have been well able to keep his secret, to deal with anything that might have come along. If he had told her, perhaps now she wouldn't hate him, perhaps there would still be a chance for them.

But he had been too stupid and blind to do the wise and honorable thing. Now all was in ruins. All that was left of the glorious love they might have shared was chaff, to be blown about by the winter winds. There was nothing left of substance, nothing on which to cling. With a sinking certainty, he could see cold, lonely nights stretching out ahead of him, nights he would spend alone.

How could he have been such a complete fool? Wasn't a truth untold the same as a lie, even if one had every intention of telling the truth when the time was right? He didn't blame her for her anger. It was a righteous anger, and he doubted there was anything he could do to diffuse it.

There would be no mercy, no quarter given, but he'd never expected any, not when she finally learned the truth about him. She would never understand the deep need or the good intentions that had driven him to deceive her, nor how he had agonized over the decision, tried to find some way out of lying to her.

But could he walk away and leave her now, even if she demanded it? A jagged, excruciating pain pierced his heart at that thought. Yet he would be leaving soon, though it was the last thing he would ever in this world choose to do. He wanted to stay with her. He *wanted* her.

God help him, he loved her with everything that was in him. Since he'd made that shattering discovery about his feelings, it had been a continuous, enlarging, gnawing pain in his gut. He hurt deep down inside and the flask of Taos Lightning he'd been swigging did little to blunt the hard edges of the pain.

She had been in his every conscious thought. Though he'd known he shouldn't kiss her in the wagon tonight, there had been no way he could stop himself. Every effort to eradicate her from his thoughts had failed, just as completely as his attempts to chase her out of the corners of his heart. Lord, how she could charm a man, bring him crashing to his knees with no conscious effort on her part.

If he were ever to get over her, only time would

help, not distance. He didn't think he had enough time, not even if he lived to be a very old man.

Cassie wanted to tell him to go away for good and leave her alone. But when she opened her mouth, the words refused to come out.

Dear God! Could he be right in his suspicions about Cameron? Had Cam given money to Perego? Cruz said he could prove it, and she recalled the part of the conversation between him and Evan Hamilton that she had overheard. They had mentioned Cameron's name and she'd seen the pouch that had belonged to him. If Cameron had done that, if he'd had dealings with Perego, he'd kept it all a secret from her. He had never mentioned a word about any of that.

Had he been involved with the ring of criminals? Could it be possible? Was he not the honorable man she thought she'd married and thought she knew?

Had she been aware on some level of consciousness, but refused to believe it? Could she have loved a man who would keep secrets from her and do such terrible things?

If so, then she must not be a very good judge of character. Were all men liars who only used their women for their own purposes?

Added to her growing doubts about Cameron was the excruciating pain of Cruz's betrayal. She had been a fool where he was concerned from the very beginning. She had made a decision from that first night and the arrival of Lieutenant Mendez to pro-

318

tect him, to cover for him and to lie for him. She had never wavered from that even when it looked as though she might be wrong about him. Now that no longer mattered.

It was over, except for tonight, this last night. After they got back to Santa Fe, he would surely leave and she would never see him again. If he could leave her like that without looking back, he didn't love her the way she loved him, the way she wanted to be loved.

Cruz watched as the turmoil crossed her beautiful face. Tentatively, he reached out a hand and stroked her cheek with the back of his knuckles, sending a shiver from her head to her toes. His forefinger under her chin, he tilted her head up until she was looking into his face.

The sheen of tears in her eyes nearly undid him. With a cry of anguish, he hauled her into his arms, against his chest, clutching her tightly. She put a hand up to his face and felt the dampness of his tears.

Her eyes wide with this new knowledge, she pulled away and looked up at him. "Cruz."

The pathos in the sound of his name echoed in the night and in his heart long after she had spoken the single word.

Cassie had been alone for so long. His comforting embrace was a shelter from any storm, and it felt so good that she couldn't break away. She couldn't send him away, not tonight. She couldn't turn away from him nor deny what he asked of her. It didn't matter what he'd done.

Sensing her hesitation, he turned her to him. His mouth moved down toward hers, hovering, not quite touching, but so near, so compelling. Finally his lips touched hers like the gentle feathering of a butterfly's wing. The sweet, leisurely stroking of his lips evoked a heated response. Suddenly she was on fire, hungry for his loving, desperate for his touch, returning his kiss in a frenzy.

They were meant to be together, and destined to love each other, even if it was only for this one brief moment. They would be one, complete in the love they shared. And she wouldn't have to be alone, at least for this one night. Maybe they could make enough memories to last them for a lifetime of loneliness.

She prayed it would be a long night, that some angel or deity could see fit to hold back the dawn. For tonight, she could not deny him a kiss, a caress, anything he wanted from her. She sensed that he knew that as well.

But, dear God! he was a priest. No, he wasn't. Her mind spiralled from turmoil; she could not differentiate truth from fiction after weeks of self-torment. Cruz had lied to her, deceived her with his every word and action over the past weeks, ever since the night when she saved his life. Those were the facts. Had his betrayal *finally* stopped?

None of that mattered a whit! She loved this man. She ached with a consuming longing for him and had no control over her body or her heart where he was concerned.

"You love me, Cassie," he whispered. "You cannot turn your back on that and walk away."

"Oh, yes, I—" she began to protest.

"Look at me."

She wanted that least of all, and tried to turn her head away. His gentle, persistent hands held her shoulders immobile until she could find nowhere else to look. She had to look up into those silvery, moonlit eyes.

"Cruz."

Her resistance melted. She was betrayed, not by him this time, but by her own body and soul. She cried out his name once more before she opened her arms and her lips and gave her body willingly to him. Propriety fled from her mind, along with any thoughts about tomorrow. All was chased away by the flames of passion that engulfed her.

"We shouldn't do this," she said, but her protest was whispered and meek.

"I know," he agreed, his voice husky with longing as he tilted his head back to look at her. When he saw the shimmering sparkle of love in her eyes, he was lost to any further resistance.

He grabbed her again and they clung together, unleashed passion sweeping them both up in its compelling spell. Neither of them wanted to surrender so easily. They would, perhaps, have kept on fighting it if they could. But they would have lost in the end.

What they felt was stronger than what they were.

They were powerless against the onslaught of passion and theirs was a bittersweet surrender after a battle with no clear winners and no losers. Each of them took and each gave, in a slow kiss that unleashed a burst of sweeping desire that overwhelmed all reasonable thought. A mindless urgency drove them.

His hands were all over her, as though he would memorize her curves. The strength in his touch was testimony to the man, to what he could do, to what he would never do, to what he could make her feel. The tension of past days when they'd tried to stay apart, tried to deny what they truly felt, exploded around them like compressed gunpowder.

The kiss ended at last, but the emotions that prompted and fueled it did not. She looked up at him, studying the face dearer to her than her life, and her heart expanded with love for him.

What was it that compelled her to accept his embraces, to return them so wholeheartedly? He was so very handsome, he sometimes stole the breath right out of her body. He was well-muscled and strong, his body perfectly formed and beautifully bronzed by nature rather than the sun. Striking blue eyes that smoldered with passion were framed by the blackest of lashes and a black slash of aristocratic brow. His square jaw, high cheekbones and chiseled features gave his face character and strength, a timeless and very masculine beauty.

And he was blessed with that remarkable voice that did such crazy things to her heart. He was her beautiful, dark angel. But that wasn't why she loved him. It was much, much more than that. It was the way his eyes darkened to the grayish silver of mercury when he looked at her. It was the longing that crept into his voice when he wasn't aware of it. It was the way he listened to the poor who came to him with their problems, and the way he did everything he could to help them. It was the strength of character etched into the lines of his weathered face, defining his eyes and bracketing his full lips.

His was the face of a man who'd lived near half a lifetime already. But with that experience, he still maintained the enthusiasm and the fresh good looks of his youth. His wild nobility and his innate goodness captured her. It was all of those things and more that held her spellbound.

Cruz Delgado was a good, kind man with the courage to be who he was, to make commitments and stick with them. Under a tough exterior, he was as gentle and soft as the underside of a rose. Regardless of what had happened between the two of them, she knew these things to be true about him. And it was also true that the very sight of him could send her heart skittering out of control.

His perfectly shaped mouth moved over hers in a kiss that sizzled with passion. It ignited fires in her, and she burned hotly from it. She opened her mouth to the soft invasion of his tongue and felt a persistent pulling on a spring deep inside her. His touch was like a match set to tinder. She couldn't deny it, couldn't deny him, not if her life depended on it. It didn't matter what he'd done or what he hadn't done. He was the man she loved above any other. Tonight they would make love with no thoughts of tomorrow.

Sometime before morning Cruz slipped from her arms while she slept. He had shared her passion, but could ask nothing more of her. His job in Santa Fe was still not done, but when it was complete, he would leave there. He would leave her. He must.

Cassie Layton deserved a man who was whole and complete, without these demons tearing at him. He should never have let Perego go, not when he had the chance to avenge himself and his family. But he had done it for her.

No, she would be happier with one of her own people, someone like Cameron.

For her own sake, he had to put as much distance as possible between them and deny all that they'd been to each other, all that they might ever be.

Cassie awoke to find him gone from her arms. She realized all too well that it had been only a sweet dream, never a reality. It was only a midnight dream to be chased away by the rays of the morning sun.

He had merely been caught in the throes of passion and had never meant his sweet words of love. If he had, he could never have left her arms, could not be making plans to leave her for good. His words of love had been as much of a sham as his identity. Such a man could never be trusted with one's heart, with one's future.

Nothing had changed. Nothing at all.

She rolled over and stretched out an arm. The place where he'd been beside her was cold. As cold as her heart. As cold as the icy wind that had begun to howl during the night. She had not felt it when his body had cushioned and shielded her. But now she felt it all the way to her soul.

She was alone. How would she bear it? She buried her head in her hands. A moment passed, and she felt two eyes boring into her. She looked up hesitantly . . . into Cruz's face.

Cruz was torn. He wanted to hurry back and see to it that Evan Hamilton and his henchmen, particularly Perego, were locked up. Conversely, he wanted to prolong the trip as long as possible, to be alone with Cassie. This was definitely the last time they had the chance. He knew he had to tell her goodbye and walk away from her for real . . . eventually. He'd already brought enough trouble and pain into her life.

They rode through areas of thick timber and towering mountain peaks, and he told himself that it was necessary to go slowly, since neither of them knew the territory well. He had been trussed up in the back of a covered wagon on the trip south. Cassie had told him that she'd focused so much of her attention on keeping the wagons in sight, she hadn't paid enough attention to the trail.

At times, the wagons had followed a worn roadway with its deep, icy ruts. At other times, it had seemed to strike out across country, on some short-cut or other, across bluffs or meadows. The merchants had made this trip often before and they obviously knew the best trails to follow.

Unfortunately, neither Cassie nor Cruz had a sure notion of how to find their way back by the shortest route. He presumed that they would eventually find Santa Fe if they continued traveling to the northwest, and so they kept on, with the sun as their guide.

Occasionally, Cassie recognized a landmark she had seen before and they would be encouraged they were headed in the right direction. They found berries to eat and, with the jerked beef she had stuffed in her saddlebags, they managed to keep from going hungry. They had also, thankfully, found grass to sustain the horse. Despite a threatening future of separation, they worked as a team now: assisting, cooperating, and caring.

Chapter Fifteen

Sarah awoke to an unnaturally quiet house. No sounds came from the kitchen or the other room where her sister slept.

Where was Cassie?

Usually at this time of the morning she was up and stirring about, preparing some breakfast and getting ready to go to the church and meet with her students. The two sisters had shared the morning meal every morning when it was possible for them to do so.

Sarah reached for her robe and wrapped it around her freckled shoulders before leaving the room where she'd been sleeping. Cassie was nowhere to be seen and the fire had not been laid for breakfast.

Sarah was deeply troubled. This was so unlike Cassie. Had her sister become ill during the night? Had she gotten the terrible sickness, scarlatina, after all? Her heart pounding in fear, she ran to the other room that opened off the sitting room, pushed against the door that stood ajar, and looked inside.

No one was in there. Cassie's bed was smoothly

made up. It was hard to tell if she'd slept there the night before.

"Cassie!" she cried, running to the door opening out the back of the house. Maybe her sister had gone out back for some reason. But the backyard, too, was empty and quiet.

Dressing as quickly as she could, her fingers fumbling with buttons and lacings, Sarah whipped out the door and ran off up the path in the direction of the church. Maybe Cassie had gone there without following her usual routine. Perhaps she'd awakened late and had no time for a fire or breakfast. But that was so unlike her sister that troubled doubts continued to plague Sarah even as she hurried along in that direction.

Her fears multiplied when Father Auguste said that he had seen neither Cassie nor Cruz since the previous day. It had occurred to Sarah as she asked about the young priest, that perhaps he and Cassie were together. She had seen something between them, was intuitive enough to see the attraction that they both refused to admit. Though she would have been surprised to find that Cassie had spent the night with him, it was a possibility to be considered. And discarded.

Cassie would never do such a thing. But it seemed strange that the priest was missing, too. What was going on? Not knowing where else to turn, Sarah continued on to the plaza, hopeful of locating Evan or Emerson, who might have some information or who would, for sure, be willing to help her find her sister.

Emerson lounged in his usual place where he had

a clear view of the entire plaza. He missed little that went on there, and enjoyed spending his days watching the people come and go. He saw her as soon as she rounded the corner. Sarah headed straight for him, her red hair flying around her in a cloud.

"Mornin' Miss Sarah," he drawled. "Somethin' wrong?" he went on to ask when she skidded to a stop and tried to regain her breath. She looked a lot like she had on the evening she'd come to him needing an escort to Santa Fe, determined and frightened.

"Yes! That is, I'm not sure, but I'm afraid something is very wrong, Emerson. It's Cassie. She's missing. She wasn't at the house when I woke up this morning and it looks like she might not have come in all night. That's not like her at all. Have you seen her today?"

"Well, no, Miss Sarah, I sure ain't. But that don't mean they's somethin's wrong, now, does it? She's a grown woman and there might be a lot of purely logical explanations as to where she might be, don't you reckon?"

Sarah had to admit he was right and that she was more than likely overreacting. She hoped she was. But for some reason, she just couldn't let it go. She knew her sister too well and knew what she was likely to do. Cassie would not go away for an entire night without telling anyone. Sarah was as certain of that fact as she could be about anything.

"Something must have happened to her, Emerson. I am sure she wouldn't have stayed out without telling me. And Father Delgado is missing, too, it seems."

Evan Hamilton, ever vigilant, had been watching the exchange and ambled over to learn more. They filled him in on Sarah's concerns and he tried to reassure her, putting an arm around her shoulders. But the news troubled him, as well. Could it be connected to what had happened the previous night out at Perego's *hacendado?*

It seemed impossible, yet he'd seen Cassie Layton sticking her cute little nose in places it didn't belong before. If she had somehow found out about the meeting at Perego's, it wouldn't have been unlike her to nose around out there. She could have seen what went on in the barn.

And if she did, she very likely would have been impetuous enough to strike out after the caravan, determined to rescue Cruz. With a sinking feeling, he realized she just might succeed, if she could catch the few men on the caravan unaware. Yes, she just might succeed.

"I'll do some checking," he promised, taking Sarah's hand in his. "Stay here with Emerson. I'll be right back."

He strode quickly over to the stable and found one of Cassie's two horses gone. The stable hand told him what time she had ridden out the day before and that she had not returned the horse to the stable that evening. The lad assumed she had merely stabled it at her house, which she sometimes did, and had thought nothing more about it.

A hurried trip to Cassie's home confirmed Evan's worst fears. The horse was not there, either. Cassie Layton was gone from Santa Fe and he felt sure he knew exactly where she was.

The very attractive little widow had gone out riding, all alone. She could easily destroy his carefully made plans. If Cruz was able to make his way back to town safely with her help, that would be the end of everything. Delgado would go directly to the authorities and Evan's profitable little game would be over. He and Perego, all of them, would be in prison before nightfall.

Knowing that Emerson would doubtless ride out looking for the young widow, he decided it would be to his advantage to go along. It would look bad if he brought Lopez or Perego, so he'd have to do this without his partners. But he could handle Cruz, one on one, especially if he could use the element of surprise. The old man was really not a problem.

Evan recalled with satisfaction the way he'd gotten the drop on Cruz in the barn and the surprised look on his friend's face. It had felt good to have the upper hand in that relationship for once. Ever since he'd known him, Cruz Delgado had always been just a bit better at everything. A faster draw. A straighter shot. A better student. More admired by the ladies.

Evan had liked Cruz, he really had. That hadn't been an act. But he'd always been jealous; he'd wanted to be more like him, but had fallen far short and became more and more angry with each time he failed to measure up.

Now, for the first time, he had the chance to come out on top. If he had to kill Cruz to do it, he would; he would do whatever was necessary.

This job meant enough cash to line his pockets for the rest of his natural life. He would never have to work for the United States government again. He would never have to work for anyone again. He could retire in luxury, move farther west, or even down into Mexico. He would live the life he'd only dared to dream of before.

When he returned to Emerson and the attractive redhead waiting for him on the plaza, he told them tersely what he had found out.

"I'm going after her, then," Emerson declared, heading for the stable. "Sarah, you go back home and stay there, in case she comes back."

She nodded her head in agreement but looked to Evan, who quickly assured her that he would be riding along.

"Of course, I'll go. Don't worry, Sarah. We'll bring her back." He gave her a quick kiss and watched her hurry back to Cassie's house. It was too bad he'd be leaving town before he got to know her better.

Seeing that they would be riding out immediately, Evan realized he had no time to let Perego and the others know where he was going. It was just as well he handled this quietly and on his own, anyway. The less they knew, the better off they all might be. It would all be taken care of in a very few hours and no one would have to be the wiser.

"Let's go, Emerson," he said with a friendly pat on the back for the older man. "She's probably just ridden out to her cabin in the mountains, and forgotten to tell anyone."

"I'm not so sure. I don't rightly think she'd do that." The toothpick held between Emerson's teeth barely wiggled when he talked. His teeth were clenched and a worried look added lines to his wrinkled face. "It's not like Miz Cassie to do such as that. I come by the church, already. Delgado ain't been around this mornin', neither." It was obvious that he didn't know what to make of that.

Emerson knew that if the two of them had left town together, all was well. He would have trusted Cruz Delgado with his life. But his gut instincts told him there had been some foul play, that he didn't know everything that was going on, and that Cassie could be alone and in grave danger. His heart pounded painfully in his chest, and he was having trouble getting his breath.

"You're not up to this, Emerson," Evan said, noting the other man's red face and putting a hand on his reins. "Why don't you stay here? I'll find her."

"No!" Emerson barked, sitting up straighter in the saddle. Something in the younger man's eyes troubled him. He couldn't explain it, but he didn't like it one bit. "I'm a'goin'. Now, come on, let's go!"

"Okay. Okay," Evan said with a shrug of his wide shoulders. Emerson Smith would not be that much of a problem, so it was all the same to Evan whether he tagged along or not. They rode out together, an unlikely pair set on an uncertain venture, each with his own private thoughts and personal agenda.

Evan set a brisk pace and the trip was long and hard on Emerson, who wondered several times if he had really done the wise thing to come along. But he couldn't have done anything else. He had come to care for the two McPherson sisters a great deal, and he supposed he would do anything necessary to save either of them. He only hoped they would be able to find Cassie in time.

His traveling companion seemed to know exactly

which route to take and that was a puzzle to Emerson, who personally had no idea where Cassie might have gone, if not to her cabin. But they had not even gone in that direction.

Evan seemed to be following tracks and Emerson hoped he knew what he was doing. He had no other recourse than to follow him. He didn't know how to read signs very well himself, except the most obvious ones.

Reluctantly, Evan called a halt to the search when it grew dark. They were about to dismount and wait until the first light of dawn to continue when Emerson pointed a little distance up ahead and asked, "Ain't that a campfire?"

Evan tensed, reining in his horse to have a good look. It was, indeed, the distinctive light of a campfire. He was almost certain that it had to be Cassie and Cruz Delgado, on their way back to Santa Fe, having escaped the wagon train.

"Maybe it's her! Miz Cassie! Let's go on in and see." Emerson was excited at the prospect of finding her alive and well and ready to move.

"Not so fast. It could be anybody. We'll have to sneak up on them and see who it is and what they're up to before we go riding in."

Emerson's face registered his surprise. He was having a hard time understanding Evan's reasoning. "No! I'm going on in! It's Cassie and I'll call out to her before I get all the way there." He turned to look at the younger man who sat on his horse so quietly next to him. Something about his posture and the expression on his face told Emerson what he'd been denying throughout the long hours they'd ridden together.

"You! You're in with Perego and the others!" Emerson gathered up his reins and reached for his gun before he went on, "I won't let you hurt her!"

"You don't have a choice, old man! There's nothing you can do to stop me!"

Evan Hamilton whipped out his gun before Emerson could unholster his. He struck the old man a blow to the side of the head that caught him off guard. Emerson slumped and slid off his horse, landing in a crumpled heap on the ground alongside the narrow road.

Emerson's horse, spooked by the unexpected action, bolted off down the road before Evan could get a hand on him to stop him from crashing through the underbrush.

He cursed. They would be sure to hear the horse and be forewarned. But there was no help for it. He glanced down at the twisted body on the ground. Emerson did not move and his eyes were closed.

"Nosy old man. Good enough for you." He chuckled. "Since you have no horse, I guess you can stay right here until someone comes along. Of course, it may be a while and by then it will be much too late for you to help your friends."

Keeping the campfire in his sights, he bore off to his left, walking his horse slowly so as not to make any unnecessary noise. His plan was to circle them, coming up on them from the other side. He hoped he could catch them unaware; it might be as easy as shooting at ducks in a pond.

When he was close enough to smell the smoke from the fire and then to see into the clearing, he decided it was going to be even easier than he'd imagined.

Cassie Layton was alone, sitting motionless near the fire. She had a worried frown on her lovely face and a rifle lying across her skirts. All he had to do was to get around behind her and grab her before she had a chance to see him coming and turn the gun on him.

Apparently, Cruz had heard Emerson's horse bolt and had gone to investigate. It couldn't have worked out better if he'd planned the whole thing.

When they had stopped for a second night's rest, Cruz knew they couldn't be far from Santa Fe. They had escaped any pursuit from the wagon train and would soon be back home. When they got into town, they would go straight to the authorities and have Juan Perego and his partners locked away in the jail.

In the camp they made that night, there was a feeling of isolation. They were miles from anywhere or anyone. It was peaceful and comfortable. The two of them were alone together, the fire cozy and warm. They were safe from prying eyes.

"Did you know it was Perego all along?" she asked.

"Yes," he replied, "I just needed evidence to prove he was involved in the thefts of the artwork and the army payroll."

"And he was also the man who murdered your

family?"

"Yes." Pain etched furrows in his face.

"I am so sorry." She reached out and placed her hand on top of his.

They sat that way for a very long time.

"I swore that one day he would pay. And when I learned his identity, I followed him here. The four-fingered hand was the conclusive sign. I knew he was the one."

"He *will* pay, Cruz. You did the right thing by not killing him when you had the chance."

How could he admit he'd done it for her? That she was the reason he hadn't blown the Spaniard all the way back to Mexico. His love for her had been stronger than his abiding need to avenge the deaths of his family. But he couldn't tell her that.

"I felt so guilty when they died, my mother and father and my brother. As though I should have done something to stop it. I should have run for help, yelled out, done something. But I stood there like a statue, unable to move. I did nothing while he killed them!"

"You were just a child," she said, her voice strangled with sympathy for his pain, her hand stroking his that lay so still in hers. "You were nothing more than a boy, Cruz. Anyone would have done the same. You were terrified."

"I know, but knowing that hasn't helped. It has taken me a long time to find him, but I kept myself going by knowing that when I did, I could make up for it somehow. Do you understand?"

"Of course I do. I have a need to see him punished, too, you know."

Her brown eyes were clear, and focused without wavering on his face.

"I know," he answered.

"And I, too, feel guilt. I spent months wondering what I could have done to prevent Cam's death, wanting to make up for arguing with him that morning, wishing I'd gone after him, wanting to find some way to reverse everything and bring him back."

He put a comforting arm around her and drew her up close to him. "It's all right, little love. There was nothing you could have done, either. It's all over now."

The promise seemed to be made as much to himself as to her. The healing had begun in him, finally. "Perego will spend the rest of his life behind bars and you can go on with your life and put all that behind you," he said.

Cassie noticed that he had mentioned nothing about a life for the two of them. She loved him and knew that he loved her, too, but the things that kept them apart were things that must be reckoned with. It would not be an easy battle, and perhaps not one they could win.

The night had fallen silent, dead silent in the space of a heartbeat. Even the small, chill breeze that stirred the air earlier had quieted. The peaceful mood they had shared was disrupted by a new tension crackling in the air. It was an ominous quiet, an expectant stillness, as though something were about to happen.

Cassie caught her breath and Cruz listened, quietly alert, a tense readiness apparent in every line of his muscled body. At times like this, when she looked at him, she was surprised all over again at how big he was. He was comfortingly large. She knew that he could protect her from whatever might be out there.

"Stay here," he cautioned, leaping to his feet as gracefully and as quietly as a tiger ready to pounce.

"Cruz."

"I mean it, Cass," he whispered. "Stay right here. I heard something. I'll just go check it out." His shadow loomed over her, but she could still see the blue blaze of his eyes.

He put the gun in her hands and took only the knife for himself.

"If anyone comes, shoot first and ask questions later."

"I'm not sure I—"

"Of course you can do it."

She nodded. She was ruffled by the deep timbre of his voice. As intimate as a caress, it wrapped around her heart, the way it always did.

"Be careful," she urged him, her blood pounding through her veins, her throat tight with fear.

A quick nod of his head and he was gone, swallowed up in the thick darkness. One moment he was there and the next he had completely disappeared into the shadows.

The silence lengthened, unbroken by the call of an insect or bird. Whatever noise they had heard had been swallowed up by the night, too. There was no repetition of it or any other night sound.

Cruz was as silent as a cat, stealthily making his

way through the stand of trees into which he'd disappeared.

Cassie was anxious and uneasy while she waited. She could not bear to remain behind, and to stay perfectly still and quiet was difficult. All she wanted was to stay by his side, to fight with him if need be. She didn't want him out of her sight. She detested the notion of waiting idly in the small clearing to see what would happen.

But every time she'd failed to listen to him before, she had gotten into trouble. She knew she would be wise to do exactly as he'd said. Still, the temptation was strong. . . .

What in God's name was happening out there? Had someone followed them? Were they in danger of being recaptured by the men of the wagon train? She had been so sure that threat was well behind them. Had the men discovered his absence and set off after them?

Cruz had seemed so certain they had gotten away without being noticed. But if it was not the men from the wagons, who could be out there? Were they in danger from some unknown source? Perego and his henchmen? Evan Hamilton?

Or maybe Cruz had only thought he heard something. Soon, he would be back and they'd be laughing about it together. She hoped that would be the case, but she knew he was a man not easily fooled. If he believed something or someone was out there, he was more than likely right.

She heard the slightest of noises in the brush behind her and whirled, her rifle aimed at an invisible target in the darkness. A cold knot of fear coiled in her stomach and the chill spread through her as she listened. Her hand on the rifle shook and she fought for control of her nerves. She could not shoot until she knew it wasn't Cruz, who might be returning from a different direction. It didn't matter that he'd told her to shoot. She would not take a chance of hitting him by mistake.

"Cruz?" The whispered question was soft and there was no reply.

The night's quiet was unbroken with no further repetition of the sound she'd heard, but it had served to heighten the unease she had felt ever since Cruz left her. She would be more watchful.

She sat back down, but remained alert, her eyes searching, her ears listening for the slightest sound, ready to shoot like he'd told her the minute she knew it was an enemy and not the man she loved.

In that moment of fear for him, the enormity of what she felt for Cruz Delgado crashed in on her until she felt weak from it. Her heart pounded with worry for him, out there in the darkness with only a small knife for defense.

She should have insisted he take the gun. But there had been no arguing with him, not with those steely blue eyes drilling into her.

As she called his image to mind, her fears grew even stronger. Desperately, she felt the pressing need to go after him.

Cruz had hated to leave her alone and he didn't intend to stray very far. He would stay close enough that he could hear her if she became frightened and called out to him. He set off in the direction from which he'd thought the sound had come. It had been the sound of a rustling of branches and could have been merely a wild animal and nothing more, but he had to find out. He couldn't risk someone sneaking in and catching him off guard. He had more than himself to consider.

There was Cassie.

He would die if anything happened to her.

Faint moonlight illuminated his way and he searched through the stand of trees, weaving back and forth, never too far away from the campfire where Cassie waited for him with her rifle ready.

A shadowy shape loomed up in front of him and startled him. He stood without moving or even daring to breathe, slipping his knife to his fingertips, in readiness, should he need it. With a feeling of relief, he realized it was only a riderless horse that stood there in the moonlight. Movement of the animal must have been what had alarmed him earlier.

Moving cautiously closer and trying not to spook the animal, he made sure there was no one around. Then, on closer examination, he realized that the mare was Emerson's horse. But the older man was nowhere to be seen. He must have come out from town after Cassie and had an accident before he could find her.

Cruz called out to him, hoping he wasn't too far away and that he could find Emerson in time to help him. No longer feeling that he was personally in any danger, he tramped through the underbrush, calling out, "Emerson! Emerson Smith, are you out there?"

At last, he was rewarded with a faint answer and

strode off in the direction of the sound. He stumbled over a fallen tree trunk, righted himself with a curse, and plunged on. The underbrush was thick and he had to use his knife more than once to cut through vines that twisted around his ankles, hampering his progress.

Over a short rise and down a gentle incline, he came upon the crumpled body of the older man, lying off the edge of the roadway. Cruz felt lucky to have found him. It appeared to him that Emerson was unconscious. He did not respond to Cruz's efforts to talk to him and he lay very still.

Knowing that he had to get him back to the light and warmth of the fire and find out how badly he'd been hurt, Cruz slid the knife back into his belt, bent down, and hefted the man's large body up in his arms. Gingerly, he carried him back, picking his way through the night, not wanting to injure him any further. It seemed a much longer distance back than he had thought, and he began to worry about Cassie long before he came to the clearing.

Chapter Sixteen

Without warning, a man stepped silently into the clearing beside Cassie and snatched the rifle from her hands before she had a chance to react.

"Oh, God, no!" she cried, whirled around and began to run. A strong grip on her wrist halted her in mid-step.

"Not so fast, Cassie."

Evan Hamilton's voice cut through the silence. She gasped, panting in terror. His arm fastened around her midriff, cutting off her breath so she couldn't shout the warning that had been on her lips. He wrenched her head back and she cried out then, but bit off the scream, realizing Cruz would hear it and come crashing back, straight into danger.

It was probably too late anyway. Cruz might have heard her cry of surprise. She had to warn him somehow. Grabbing for breath, she called out, "Cruz, look—"

He clamped a hand over her mouth and cut off any further sound.

"Easy now. We want him back here, but it would be better if he didn't know I was here. We'll just wait here quietly and see what happens."

Cassie was sure that if Cruz returned to the clearing, Evan Hamilton would shoot him down without a second thought. The man who had her in a vise-like grip was furious and desperate. There was no telling what he might do.

Becoming more desperate about Cruz walking into a trap, she twisted her mouth and bit down hard on the fingers of the hand across her mouth. Hamilton let out a howl and hit her a stunning blow to the head that sent her reeling.

Cassie lurched, but regained her balance, fought off the blackness that threatened to engulf her and flew at him before he knew what was happening. She crashed into him and they both tumbled to the ground, rolling over in a confusion of arms and legs. Cassie tried desperately to evade him, and Hamilton did his best to get a hold on her before she could get up and away from him. His hand fastened on her elbow, but she drew back her leg and landed a booted kick on his shin.

"You little bitch!" he snarled, throwing himself at her.

She was too quick for him and rolled away, scrambling quickly to her feet. One of his hands snaked out and grabbed her ankle, keeping her from moving any farther away. She drew back her other leg to kick him again, but he yanked her leg hard before she could. He sent her crashing down on her bottom.

345

"Oof!" she grunted, watching stars dance crazily in front of her eyes.

"Cassie!" A worried voice boomed out and Cruz burst into the clearing with an unconscious Emerson in his arms.

The blood drained from Cassie's face in shock when she looked up and saw Cruz unarmed, cradling Emerson's wounded body in his arms up next to his chest.

In an instant, she understood what must have happened. The dear old man had come all the way out here to find her. Sarah must have noticed that she was missing and gone to him. Either Evan had followed him, or Emerson had been traveling with their enemy without knowing it. There was no way he could have known about Evan Hamilton's involvement with Perego and the others.

"Well, well. I sorta thought her little scream might bring a certain *padre* running to her rescue. Looks like you've already been out on a rescue mission."

Hamilton's voice was sharp and sarcastic. His unwavering look of hatred revealed he was through offering Delgado special treatment. This had become a deadly game, a battle of wits he was set on winning.

His rifle, though, was trained not on Cruz, who was laying Emerson out so carefully on the ground, but on Cassie, sitting between them, her eyes filled with concern for Emerson.

He spoke reasonably, the words clipped. "I think the smart thing for you to do would be to drop that knife from your belt and sit down over there."

Cruz continued to examine Emerson's crumpled

body and his anger flared. "What have you done to him?" he ground out, dropping his weapon and kneeling to pick up Emerson's head and cradle it gently in his arms.

His anger was a very real and potent force in the clearing. Even though he had no weapon in his hand, Evan had second thoughts about squaring off with him. Only the repeating rifle in his hand gave him the courage he needed not to cut and run as fast as he could.

Evan's tone was relatively calm in spite of his growing anxiety and the knot in his stomach. "He's all right," he said. "Just taking a little nap. He's a nosy, meddlesome old codger, and he kept on getting in my way."

Cruz ascertained that Emerson was, indeed, breathing normally, though he still seemed to be unconscious. He gently laid his head back down before turning his attention to his adversary.

"He needs a doctor, Ham." Cruz, too, tried to conceal his feelings of hostility in hopes he could still appeal to Hamilton's reasonable side.

"Not so fast. Nobody's leaving here. We have a little unfinished business, the four of us." Evan waved the gun wildly to include Cassie and the two men on the ground a few feet away from her.

"You are certainly right about that. *You*," Cruz said, pointing an accusing finger at Evan Hamilton, "you left him out there to die." In spite of all his attempts to control his feelings, Cruz's anger had built until he could hardly contain it. His eyes blazed an icy blue fire.

Evan was undaunted. "He's just a meddlesome old man, past his prime, of use to no one anymore. Leave him be."

The gun leveled at Cruz's head said he meant business, but Cruz was not easily intimidated. He would not leave Emerson's side as long as he thought there might be something else he could do for him.

Cassie crawled over to the unconscious man.

Her lips tightened when she saw the deeply bruised and cut side of his face.

"What have you done to him?" she gritted between clenched teeth. "This wound needs cleansing," she announced, ripping off a strip of petticoat and walking with a determined step to her canteen. She soaked the soft cloth with water and returned to Emerson, never once looking at Evan or asking his permission.

Cruz had to admire her grit every bit as much as her kindness and compassion. He watched Evan closely and would have been on him in an instant if he'd even begun to make a threatening move toward either Cassie or Emerson.

"It's not as bad as it looks," she said with a sigh of relief. "But he needs a doctor."

Quickly, she cleaned the blood and bathed the wound, tore off another strip of petticoat, and wrapped his head tightly to stop any further bleeding.

While she worked, Cruz studied the man who had once been his friend. Evan's face was shadowed with a two days' growth of beard, though he had been clean-shaven ever since Cruz had known him. His beard, like his clothing, showed a recent lack of attention and concern about his looks. The uniform of the American military, in which he'd looked so handsome, had been discarded in favor of well-worn, almost shabby, buckskins and a floppy hat pulled down over his dishwater blond hair. Even his eyes seemed to have undergone a change and were darker and less lively. Had this happened overnight, or more gradually? Had Cruz merely failed to notice until now?

"If you've done him any harm, you'll answer to me," Cruz growled at him, a swift shadow of anger darkening his features. He was formidable, even unarmed and at a disadvantage.

"Is that so? I would say that you, my friend, are hardly in a position to be making threats. Neither you, nor your lady friend there."

Evan Hamilton laughed and the eerie sound sent chills up Cassie's spine. His words brought her even more consternation when he went on. "You're a dead man, *compadre*. And your little playmate, too. You both know way too much to live."

Turning to Cassie, he continued, "For your information, Mrs. Layton, your dear, departed husband is the one who caused so much of the trouble in Santa Fe. If it hadn't been for him snooping around, and his threats of notifying Washington, I wouldn't have had to come out here from the East. And you, my dear lady, wouldn't be a widow today."

"You!?" Cassie gasped. "It was *you* who killed Cameron?"

"I'm afraid so. And if Cameron hadn't stirred up

349

things, Cruz would never have been sent here, and it would never have come to this particular sad state of affairs that has set us against one another."

She shot him a look of pure contempt, but his eyes were now on Cruz who spoke up, "The receipts you showed me signed by Perego and Cameron Layton were bogus then?"

"Oh, no!" he said smoothly. "They were one hundred per cent real."

"What, then . . . ?"

"It seems our fine upstanding American citizen, Cameron Layton, went out of his way to help the struggling Spanish government of Santa Fe with a generous loan from out of his own pocket. It was intended to help them meet their payroll. Very noble of him, you must admit." His voice was filled with mockery.

"But it never reached the soldiers, did it, Ham?" Cruz guessed, watching the other man closely. "And at San Miguel, that was all an act, wasn't it, to keep me from being suspicious of you?"

"Very shrewd thinking, my good man. I had to make you think I was really investigating and on your side, as you had been led to believe by my government and yours."

"And all the time you were a traitor to your own government and busy lining your own pockets," Cruz cut in.

A lifted eyebrow attested to the truth of the observation and to Hamilton's total lack of remorse or guilt. "Too bad you couldn't have put it together and figured it out before now, though, isn't it? Then you

350

might not be in this predicament. I really didn't want to hurt you. But, you see, *compadre,* I greatly fear that this time I have no recourse whatsoever. I shall have to shoot you. I can't risk our organization and my future, even for you. I tried to spare you, you'll have to admit that I did. I even arranged safe passage for you back home to Mexico. But the nosy *seōra* took care of that, didn't she?"

"Let her go, Ham. She doesn't deserve to die."

Cruz knew his argument was futile. Cassie knew too much, as did he and Emerson, who chose that moment to raise his head. He was watching now with disbelief in his rheumy eyes and one hand over his heart.

Cassie leaned over and spoke to him softly, trying to calm him.

"You'll have to kill us all," Cruz observed, looking from them back to Evan. His former friend seemed to enjoy hearing the sound of his own voice and was inclined to draw out the job he planned to do. If they could keep him talking until Cruz could think of a way to make a move to free them without any endangerment, they might have a chance to live through this.

"I've waited a long time for this," the young American went on with a smirk marring his handsome features.

"For what, Ham? Is money that important to you? Is it worth betraying your country and your friends. Is it worth kidnapping and even murder? Is it worth spending the rest of your life in prison?"

"We're talking about a lot of money, Cruz, more

351

than a man could ever expect to see in a lifetime."

"But are you certain Perego can be trusted to give you your share? He's double-crossed men before. He's a thief and a murderer. He has no morals and no honor."

"He wouldn't dare double-cross me. He needs me too much for that."

"Not any more. Not after we're out of the way. And the cargo is now safely on its way to Mexico. You'll be the only one standing in his way, then. You will be expendable, don't you see that?"

"No! You're wrong. All I have to do is wait for the money to reach here from Mexico, just like he said. We'll all be rich."

"How will you explain our disappearance to the authorities?" Cruz asked, changing tactics. "You'd better think about that. One of us could be explained perhaps, but not all three. Think about it, Ham, before you make a tragic mistake."

"Shut up, Delgado! You're just trying to save your skin and that of your beautiful widow friend."

"Maybe, but it's the only way out for you, too, Evan. Quit before you get in any deeper."

"I'm in over my head already."

Cruz gave up talking. Ham was right. He'd already gone over the edge and there was no use trying to reason with him.

Out of the corner of his eye, he could still see Cassie tending to Emerson, who was coming around little by little. But he kept his attention riveted on Evan Hamilton, who might decide to start shooting them at any minute.

Cruz took a furtive step, edging over to his left, hoping to put himself between Evan and the other two, but the raised eyebrow of his adversary and the lowering of his rifle, pointed directly at Cassie, put a quick end to any thoughts in that direction.

He had to do something. He could not stand there and watch Evan shoot them all, one by one.

Cassie stood up and smoothed her hands down over her wrinkled wool riding skirt. She looked very tired. He could see fatigue in the swaying of her slight body while she did her utmost to hold herself upright, and he saw it in the darkening circles under her eyes and in new lines in her lovely face.

She had put her life in jeopardy to save him for the second time. He would see to it that Evan Hamilton did nothing to hurt her.

Too late, though, he noticed the angry sparks in her brown-gold eyes when she looked at Evan and saw what she intended to do. "I'm leaving," she announced firmly. "Someone has to go for a doctor."

"Cass—" Cruz began.

"No!" Evan barked. "No one leaves!"

It was a standoff and Cassie appeared to be in no mood to back down, or even to negotiate. She whirled, oblivious to Evan's repeated threats, and began to walk quickly over to her big, blue-black horse.

"Cassie, be still! Don't move."

She heard a voice ring out, a voice she'd learned to heed. Instantly, she did as he commanded. While she stood there motionless, she could not see what was happening behind her, but she heard a flurry of movement. Then, a bullet whined through the air, within inches of her head. She could bear it no longer and turned to see what was happening between the two men.

The bullet that had come so close it would have struck her, had she not done exactly as Cruz ordered, had lodged itself with a thud in the center of Evan Hamilton's wide chest. A surprised look crossed his handsome face. Without uttering a sound, he put his hand to his chest and it came away bloody. His eyes grew large. The circle of red was spreading ominously across his shirt.

Time and motion seemed suspended while they watched him standing there, and then he began to lean to one side.

Finally, after an interminably long time, he toppled sideways to the ground and did not move again.

Cruz walked over to him. "He's dead," he announced with no emotion coloring his words, but his shoulders had slumped and his head was bowed.

"I'm sorry," she said, moving up next to him and placing her hand on the arm that still held the smoking rifle. "I know he was once your friend."

"Or I only thought he was my friend. But he never was, not really." Shifting his attention from the dead back to the living, he said, "Let's get our friend over there to a doctor. And then we have some important business in town. We can send someone back for his body." With a flick of his wrist, he indicated the body of Evan Hamilton.

Cruz fashioned a crude travois for Emerson from

some branches, strips of leather, and the extra saddle blanket from Evan's horse. He rigged it so he could pull it behind Cassie's muscular horse. He would walk beside it to be sure they found the smoothest track so that Emerson's injury wouldn't be worsened by a rough ride.

Though they weren't far from Santa Fe, according to Emerson, it was still shaping up to be a very long ride at the slow pace he would be forced to set for them.

Cassie and Cruz had no more time, opportunity, or even the energy for talking. When they reached the outskirts of town at first light Cruz first took Emerson to the doctor's house, where he left him under his care. Then, he directed the horse to Cassie's and soon had put her to bed. She was too tired even to argue with him.

He'd summoned up enough strength to pay a visit to the governor and fill him in on Perego's activities. What he managed to tell him was enough to start the wheels of justice turning.

Armijo promised to take care of things, round up the men, and hold them for trial. He would also send two soldiers back out after the body of Evan Hamilton.

Later, Cruz and Cassie would both be asked to appear before him with complete details. The governor assured Cruz that they would also be called to testify at the trial.

Finally, Cruz dragged himself to his own quarters and fell across his narrow bed for a few hours' sleep.

Chapter Seventeen

Spring arrived slowly, more often than not, in the New Mexico mountains. The month of March could be as much a part of winter as of spring. Nevertheless, the month brought with it thoughts of the arrival of spring and, eventually, summer.

The weather was no colder than Cassie's heart, though, when she said goodbye to Sarah and Emerson who left to go back East. She wanted to beg Sarah to stay, but she understood her sister's need to get back home and put her life back together in familiar circumstances in the midst of her family. The betrayal of Evan Hamilton had hit Sarah hard, but she was strong. With the support of her family, she could handle it.

Now they were gone, and Cruz, too, would soon be leaving. He might even be gone by now, for all Cassie knew.

The political situation in Santa Fe was turbulent. Change was imminent. In the December just past, Texas had become a state and it was said that President James K. Polk intended to annex California. Rumors had been flying that Mexico had even agreed to sell New Mexico to the United States.

On January 12, 1846, General Zachary Taylor had brought his four thousand man army to the disputed area along the Rio Grande. It was a volatile situation and only a spark was required to set it off.

Finally, in March, Manuel Armijo was appointed commander general. He had been organizing patrols and sending out unsuccessful pleas for monies to fill the government's coffers ever since.

The Mexican government in control of Santa Fe was unstable, to say the least, and in need of reformation. But it had not suffered from the removal from office of Juan Perego, Lieutenant Mendez, and Lopez. The three Mexican crooks were confined in the jail located in the Governor's Palace and would likely be there for quite some time.

Cassie and Cruz had jointly presented an overwhelming case with all the necessary evidence in front of Armijo, who listened to them intently and graciously and had, thankfully, acted quickly to jail the guilty men.

Cameron Layton's name was cleared for good, in the process. It had been proven that he'd had no part in the criminal activities. In fact, he had done all he could to help the government, to make Santa Fe a better place to live for Spanish and American alike.

Some of the paintings and other artifacts were returned to the churches from where they'd been stolen. A patrol had been sent out quickly as promised, and the wagon train was intercepted before it could reach Mexico. The contraband they were transporting was returned, to be distributed to its rightful owners.

Though she had never liked the man, Cassie was glad that Father Auguste proved to have taken no active part in the thefts. He had offered no willing compliance in the schemes, but had merely found himself, on occasion, in some very bad company and used by those men without conscience. He was charged with no crime and continued to be as much of a priest as he'd ever been, though he was only slightly better than no clergy at all.

Luci recovered nicely and went about her life and her business with lusty enthusiasm and good will. She, too, had been disappointed at the departure of Emerson and Sarah, who had been good friends to her.

Cassie would miss Sarah and Emerson desperately, but they had both expressed the need to go home. Emerson said he'd prefer to live out his last days where things were a little more peaceful. He'd had enough excitement for a lifetime, he said. He was limping as they left, but otherwise, showed no sign that he was the worse for wear after his encounter with Evan Hamilton. Sarah did her best to talk him into going all the way to Boston with her. Though he was having a hard time saying "no" to her as he always had, he thought Boston might be too "high falutin'" for his tastes.

* * *

Soon after their departure, Cassie fled Santa Fe for the refuge of her cabin, a place where she could be alone and try to find some way to put it all behind her, to work out the tangled skeins of her life.

The end of winter was nearing, and it was almost time to prepare the cabin for the lovely days of spring. So she set out on Napoleon, now her favorite of the two horses she owned. The big horse had shown his heart on the expedition to rescue Cruz from the wagon train, although she tried not to let her thoughts linger too much on that adventure.

She left behind the political situation boiling in town that made it a hotbed of intrigue and tension-filled. She worried about what would happen to her adopted home before the conflict was settled between the Spanish and the Americans.

A cold blast of air to her face when she opened the door to the mountain cabin brought memories hurtling back, memories best forgotten. The wind slammed the door back hard into the wall.

Looking around at the familiar furnishings, she could not keep herself from thinking back to the night she had half-carried, half-dragged the mysterious priest back from the ravine through the blinding snowstorm. She remembered, too, how she had cared for him and how she had begun, even then, to fall slowly in love with him. Now, she recalled Luci's prediction about how she would find love, but much trouble, as well.

It had been a truly incredible thing for her to have done, going out into the storm like that. It was like a distant, beautiful dream, gone as surely as a blanket of fog burned away by the rising of the early morning sun. So much had passed between the two of them since then.

Her beautiful home in the mountains failed to bring her the comfort it usually did, even after she settled in and had a fire blazing and coffee brewing. Cassie felt bereft and so alone, the pain was almost physical. Her dearest sister and the irrepressible Emerson were gone.

Cruz would no doubt be leaving for Mexico soon. They would all be gone. And she would be truly alone. She had hurt when she lost Cameron, but this pain was far worse, an aching hurt that wouldn't stop, that she feared might never stop. A feeling of desperate dread and blinding sorrow swept through her. Cruz would be gone from her just as surely as if he'd died, but she would have the hurtful knowledge that somewhere in the world he still lived and breathed and perhaps loved again.

God! How could she bear it? Had she done something to deserve this pain? These days, she found herself thinking only of Cruz, remembering far too clearly every moment of the times they'd spent together.

But once more, she was left with only Luci and the children to console her in Santa Fe. At least, she had gotten the vindication for Cameron she'd longed for and worked for. The men responsible for his death were all either behind bars or dead.

Why, then, didn't she feel the satisfaction she'd expected? Why was she experiencing such a letdown, this terrible, overwhelming depression? Why did she feel like her life was over?

She knew the answers to those questions even as she asked them. She felt that way because she had lost the one person dearer than any other to her. Cruz, who meant more than life itself.

She hadn't spoken his name aloud, had only thought it, but now he stood there in the doorway, as though summoned by her, looking strong and masculine and so unbelievably handsome. She caught and held her breath while she looked steadily at him.

The priestly disguise had been discarded for good. His white lawn shirt was open at the collar, setting off his dark coloring in a dramatic way, and revealing a line of dark chest hair. Tailored trousers hugged his long, muscular legs like a second skin. A gun belt rode low on his hips and shiny, black boots came nearly to his knees. He was tall, whipcord lean, and his dark good looks stole her breath away.

His hat had been pushed back on his head, and inky-black hair shone in the day's dying sun like a raven's wing. He was every inch the dark and mysterious stranger Luci had warned her about from the very beginning.

And her life had, indeed, been turned upside down by his arrival in Santa Fe and in her life. She had to drag her eyes away from him to keep from staring with an open mouth. It was incredible that he could have such an effect on her.

Why hadn't her friend included in her warning that this handsome stranger would break her heart and leave her in the end?

As usual, Luci had been only half right in her predictions. Cassie smiled at the thought.

Cruz answered with a smile of his own, a brilliant flash of white teeth, and the crinkling at the corners of his eyes that had so captivated her. Then the smile was gone as quickly as it had come and his face serious once more.

"Cassie."

He was still the same, the man she loved, whose voice did all those wickedly wonderful things to her heart. The gooseflesh she felt was not from the cold. She rubbed her arms, not willing to let him see the effect he was having on her.

Foolish woman. She had thought she could make it all stop, make it go away, just by saying so, just by wishing. She hadn't known he could still make her feel like this. She had thought—no, she had even dared to hope—that her life could go on as before. But her heart had not been a part of that pact.

"Cruz." Her voice was soft and revealed none of her thoughts.

"I wanted to say," he began, speaking slowly, "that I am glad your husband was not involved with Perego and the others. I see now that he was an honorable man, just as you said all along."

Cruz thought Cameron had been a very lucky

man to engender such devotion, a devotion that lived on even after he was gone. Cassie loved her family back East, but had stayed on in Santa Fe out of a sense of duty to her husband even after he was dead. That knowledge made Cruz feel hurt, anger, and a pining jealousy that she would never care about him that much.

He had not intended to come out here. In fact, he had been on his way back to Mexico, but something had drawn him and he hadn't been able to resist. Though he hadn't expected to find her there, he couldn't say he was sorry to see her one more time. To have the chance to look at her one last time was worth any price.

Now as he stood there so close to her, his body responded in answer to his heart as it always had, every time he'd ever been near her. She was extraordinarily lovely, her delicate ivory skin accentuated by the autumn blaze of her hair, caught up in a single, fat braid that lay sedately over her shoulder. The gray-blue wool frock she wore fit snugly around her waist and midriff, and was cut just low enough to show off the creamy skin of her throat and rounded outline of the tops of her breasts.

A cameo pin lay at the "v" in the shadowy crease and drew his eyes to the spot where he longed to place his lips. A pair of matching ear clips adorned her ears and his eyes lingered there, as well. She clutched the soft, cashmere shawl that lay around her shoulders and he saw that her fingers trembled.

His heart jumped and his loins tightened with an

unconscious response that he was helpless to fight. He had no control over himself, never had, where this delicate minx was concerned. She had curled her way around his heart insidiously, had burrowed in to stay. His mind was constantly besotted with thoughts of her, lying satisfied in his arms, standing up to Perego and fighting back, nursing the dying children and her friend Luci, rescuing him from the wagon train, riding like the wind through the night. . . . He had to make himself stop this painful pointless thinking . . .

"Thank you for saying that about Cameron," Cassie answered quietly, her brown eyes luminous. Strangely enough, Cameron's guilt or innocence no longer seemed as important to her as it had once been.

The rest of Luci's prediction came back to her and she recalled that her friend had said, "When you find a way to let go of the past, then you will find the future."

"I'm different now, Cruz."

"I can see that."

"Santa Fe and the children are important to me."

"I know that, Cass."

"I can do good by staying here."

"Yes."

"Monosyllables. We're talking in monosyllables again."

"It's me."

"What?"

"I'm the one speaking in monosyllables."

"Well."

"Well, what? Now you're doing it, too."

She laughed, but he thought the sound of it was not a happy one. He knew he had brought too much pain into her life. His leaving would only be the last.

The difference she described showed in her face. It was more mature, showed more understanding and compassion. There were a few fine lines around those warm gold-brown eyes and bracketing her full lips that hadn't been there before. There was a new, quiet strength in her. He had only to look at her and begin to grow hard.

Wanting her was a constant, unrelenting pain in him. It wouldn't go away. So he would.

He'd made the decision. Now he had only to find the strength in himself to carry it out. By staying and loving her, he could destroy her and himself, all at the same time.

"I am leaving Santa Fe. My mission here is complete."

His voice, though deep and familiar, was without expression and gave no insight into his true feelings.

Cassie had always known that one day he would be leaving. Since the night they'd spent together after her rescue of him from the wagon train, she had known that it would be soon. He had already begun to leave her that morning when she'd awakened and he had no longer been in her arms. It had been in his eyes, in the taut lines of his body.

Why, then, did the truth of it seem now to be

hurled at her out of nowhere and crush her so completely with its stunning reality? Somewhere along the way, she had come to love these people of New Mexico, this place known as Santa Fe, and to claim them as her own. She would stay, regardless of what anyone else chose to do. Even Cruz.

She never wanted to leave here. But *he* was leaving. His coming had been only temporary from the beginning, and she'd known that he'd never meant to stay. Even what he felt for her was not enough to keep him so far from home, away from his life.

She didn't dare to think what his answer would be if she asked him to stay. She could never do that. They'd come from different lands, different cultures. She had to admit to herself, no matter what it cost her, they could never be together the way she wanted. She could never have the future she'd always dreamed of. They would never have children. They would never share a home . . . peace . . . and love, the forever kind, the kind one could build a life around.

All those things were only shadows dancing in the night, distortions of candlelight, the whimsy of an over-romantic nature. Such dreams gave way to sanity in the light of day. To the harsh realities of life.

It was over. Her mind knew the certainty of that fact, though her heart rejected it defiantly. It wanted to fight for him, for what they could have. It wanted to struggle until the very end, until he was gone for good from her life.

This was the end. The words were so clear she

might have spoken them aloud. Even though she hadn't, they seemed to echo through the empty cavernous room.

It was all over. It was over. Over. Over. . . .

She dropped her head and the tears coursed freely and unheeded down her cheeks, dampening the top of her shirtwaist. Nothing mattered any more. Before she looked up, she brushed the tears away furtively, not wanting him to know how much she could still be moved by him. Desperately, she tried to think more clearly, to find some way to cope with what was happening and with what lay ahead for her.

But she could never think straight when he was around. His presence filled the corners of her mind so thoroughly, there was no room left for rational thought.

Was that why she'd been such a fool repeatedly where he was concerned?

"And you will be returning to Mexico?" Her voice held barely a clue of the turmoil that filled her mind and heart. It was cool and unruffled, the result of an extreme, nearly painful, effort on her part.

They shared a look that showed him she had known for some time that his story about San Antonio had not been true. He looked chagrined.

"I never wanted to lie to you, Cass. I wish you could find it in your heart to believe me." But he saw that she couldn't. He went on in reply to her question, fully aware that she deserved answers, had deserved them from the beginning. "Yes, I will go back to Mexico City and then home to Spain, I expect." His voice lacked conviction when he said he'd leave her.

What waited for him in either place was uncertain and returning there was far from the truest desire of his heart. He wasn't sure he could find the strength to ride away from her. More than anything, he wanted to be wherever she was.

"Oh." Her voice was soft and small.

"And you?"

"I'll be staying on here." She now spoke firmly, secure in the fact that her decision to stay in Santa Fe was the right one for her. That, in spite of anything else, it was what she had to do, what she wanted to do.

"Oh?" A black eyebrow shot up. "Alone?"

"I have Luci . . . and the children."

"Is that enough?"

No! she thought. It wasn't. It wasn't nearly enough. But she wasn't ready to admit that to him.

"It will have to be. Santa Fe is my home now, and I have no wish to return to Boston."

"Oh." Now his voice was soft and low, heavy with remorse.

They couldn't seem to get past those silly monosyllables. Was there nothing more to be said, then? Had it all come down to this? All the passion, all the pain, all for nothing?

"Cassie, I owe you so much. I just wanted to say thank you."

"You don't owe me anything, Cruz."

"Only my life," he replied quietly. "I want you to have this." He reached inside his pocket and pulled out a delicate heart-shaped pendant on a fine gold chain. "Please say you'll accept it." He had planned to leave it there for her to find, later.

Hesitantly, she reached out and held it in her fingers. The featherweight of it against her palm was like a caress, and she wished she'd never touched it. His hand lingered on hers, warm and so familiar, so dear.

"Open it," he urged, his voice little more than a whisper, the entreaty in it all too clear.

With trembling fingers, she released the clasp and the heart opened, revealing a tintype likeness of two of the people dearer than all the world to her.

"It's Sarah and Emerson," she said in awe. "Did you do this for me?"

"Yes," he answered, "I felt you needed something of them, after they'd gone. So, I got them to pose for it just before they pulled out of town."

He didn't say how much he had longed to have one made of her as well, but he knew in his heart that he really had no need of it. Her image would be hauntingly clear in his mind until his dying day, no matter how far apart they were.

Cassie's eyes filled with tears at what he'd done for her. He had understood the pain she'd felt at their leaving and had done this thoughtful thing to help her through it. She would keep the locket. It was the only thing of him that was hers. He'd given it to her, as he'd never given her what she wanted most, the gift of himself.

"I wish—" she began.

"Wish what?" he blurted, hoping to prolong the conversation, even as uncomfortable as it had been. He could not bear to turn and walk away from her.

"I wish," she said, and then continued slowly, "I wish that things could have been different."

Dear God! he thought, so do I!

"I am so sorry, Cass. I should have told you the truth from the beginning. I should have trusted you more."

"You're right. You shouldn't have deceived me."

She remembered all the guilt and all the hurt she'd felt for her feelings and conduct with a priest. And he'd had the information that could have put an end to all of that. With just a word of truth, he could have relieved her terrible anxiety and guilt she'd harbored.

"No. I deeply regret it. I would do anything I could to change it, Cassie. Anything. But I cannot go back and do it differently, any of it, as much as I might want to. There is no way I can ever make it up to you, love." He had played the devil incarnate to this angel. She deserved better. He would leave quickly, as he planned. It was the only answer.

"No."

He spoke and the words were dredged up from his very soul, "All in this world I can do, Cassie, is to tell you how very much I love you and that I would spend the rest of my life trying to make it up to you, if you would only give me the chance."

He wondered what in the world he was saying? What happened to his decision to go away and leave her for good? What had happened to his firm resolve not to be moved into doing something romantic and foolish? He knew now that he could never leave her.

Her eyes never left his face and her bottom lip began that quivering he'd never been able to resist, that pulled so at the strings of his heart, that made him want to grab her and hold her to his heart forever.

"Cass . . . please, don't . . . I . . . I love you," he said, his voice soft as a baby's breath. "I'll love you for years, for all my life. Can't you find it in your heart to love me back? There's nothing else on earth I want as much, Cassie. Can't love be enough?"

But even as he said the words, he knew that sometimes love just wasn't enough. It had to be accompanied by trust, certainly by forgiveness. And she had been used and so badly hurt by him, he wouldn't blame her if she could never come to trust him again.

"Forgive me, Cassie. Please. Can't you find it in your heart?" He took the locket from her hands, and while she held her braid to the side, he fastened it around the column of her neck. Then, he reached for her hands and when she didn't resist, clasped them both in his and held them over his heart, his blue eyes never leaving hers.

If forgiveness were granted, trust would surely follow over time. Her eyes were wide, dark pools filled with her remaining doubts and fears. In their depths, he saw something else flicker.

He waited for her answer silently, the moments stretching out endlessly between them. Her hands were still warm and soft in his and she hadn't moved to withdraw them, a small sign he would grasp and hold onto.

An expectant tension held him rooted to the spot where he stood. Her answer meant everything to him. *To them*. To their future. She never looked away and made no attempt to avoid his steady gaze, nor did she seem to be purposely postponing her answer. He knew she wouldn't do that. She simply needed more time. He was willing to give her that and much, much more.

Cassie's heart reverberated in her chest, though she looked at him unwaveringly. His gaze was the brilliant blue of a cloudless afternoon sky and focused entirely on her as though his very life depended on her. He seemed to touch her with his eyes everywhere he looked at her. Something reached deep inside and pulled at her soul.

He deserved an answer, and she knew how important it was to both of them. She also knew she had to be, above all things, true to herself and honest about her feelings.

She thought she had never heard sweeter words than his straightforward testimony of love. Her heart melted its stony resistance, overcome by his simple vow of love. She wanted him more than her life, wanted to be with him wherever he was.

His finger traced the thin gold line of the necklace that lay on her neck, his touch lighting sparks in her, his own naked desire showing in his eyes.

"We shouldn't do this." Her protest was whispered softly and weak.

"I know," he agreed, his voice deep and husky with longings long repressed, his eyes filled with love for her.

"Oh, Cruz, hold me."

She would do it. No longer the prim and proper widow, tonight she was all woman, from the crown of her golden red hair to the soles of her feet.

His need was like a living force in him, showing itself in his eyes, in the tension that gathered and thundered through him, holding his body taut and still.

Cassie stepped willingly into his arms and folded her arms around him, her sable eyes awash with tears, but somehow sparkling in spite of them.

"I do love you so. And I forgive you, my love."

Propriety fled from her thoughts, chased away by the hot flames of passion that engulfed her. She could and she would put it all behind them and look forward only to the future they could build together.

Cassie was ready to go forward into the dawn, with her hand securely in his.

A dam of feelings long restrained burst open, flooding her with sensations so strong the current swept her away. It was a river of feelings: wild, restless, unsatiable.

"I'll stay with you, my love, if you want me. I'll

never leave." His words thrilled her heart.

"Promise me." But it didn't matter, for in her heart, she knew that she would go with him anywhere.

"I promise."

Clinging to each other, they rode the torrent of their encompassing feelings, enjoying the power, reveling in the serene completion.

When he started to say something more, she quieted him.

"Shh!" she said, placing a finger on his lips, stroking their moist softness. "No more words of regret or of forgiveness. Not tonight. Not ever."

Her tears and the quivering lip had been the last straw for him. He could not leave her. God help him. He could never leave! And he could not stop himself from kissing her. He needed her loving so desperately. He tipped her face up with a finger under her chin, and his head lowered until his lips were on hers, stroking and tasting.

Joyfully, he felt her return his kiss, her lips moving under his, her mouth accepting the tentative invasion of his tongue. He drank of her sweet nectar. It was exhilarating and refreshing like a dip in a cold mountain stream. It served only to deepen his yearning and did nothing to quench the fires burning inside him.

The kiss held far more than passion alone. It was a claiming kiss, a lasting kiss, a lifetime kiss.

She was light and joy. She was his life. She was the future and she was the past. She was all around him; day to his night, light to his darkness, joy to his sorrow and comfort to his suffering. In a blinding flash of intuition usually reserved for the fairer sex, he saw his life without her stretching into the future, barren and futile. He also saw clearly what life could be like with her by his side. She would be all the family, all the home he'd ever need in this life.

Together, anywhere in the world, they would be complete and at peace. Was there, finally, a dream that might come true? He hardly dared to hope, he'd been disappointed so many times in the past. But her sweet words of forgiveness, longing, and love he would carry with him until his dying day.

Forgiveness could be granted by a loving heart, but her trust must be earned, day by day. He would do his part, would spend his whole life showing her she could depend upon him and his word. He would never betray her or lie to her again.

If two people loved each other, really loved each other, they could overcome obstacles and forge ever ahead, never looking back. That was his fondest dream for the two of them.

"Cassie, my love, my life," he spoke into her ear so softly she barely heard, his arms squeezing her so tightly she could hardly catch her breath. He clung to her, as though afraid someone or something might snatch her out of his embrace. He held her as if by holding onto her tightly enough, he could yet make his dreams a reality.

"Oh, Cruz, I do love you so." Her tawny eyes

were filled to overflowing with the wonder of their love.

The repetition of the blessed words brought a peace and contentment to his soul and a full measure of healing in a heartbeat. Even if there were never a future, it was enough for now to hear the words, to know that she loved him like that. To know that she had forgiven him.

In her arms, through the magic of her love for him, there was a way for him to find himself, a port for his drifting soul, and all the things he needed most from this life.

"I love you, my darling."

His lips covered hers then, cutting off further conversation; no more words were needed between them. Their bodies and hearts were doing all their talking and speaking eloquently, words of the soul.

His hands splayed downward, cupping her bottom and pulling her into him so that they both felt the hardness of his arousal against her. Her fingers played through the heavy midnight silk of his hair and caressed the firm column of his neck, then spread out to knead muscular shoulders that flexed beneath the soft fabric of his shirt.

She was glad he no longer dressed as a priest, but rather as a man; the man she loved, the man she desired above all others. She would be his, if he wanted her. She had made up her mind and there would be no turning back and no regrets.

His hands stroked her lazily and then in a more demanding way. He reached around her back to seek buttons and fastenings that gave way to his impatient fingers. Her dress slid off her shoulders and her full breasts sprang free, revealed to his seeking eyes.

Unheeded, the dress and then her chemise, dropped to the floor at their feet. He loosened the ribbon holding her fiery hair in its single braid and gently moved his fingers through that red gold satin until it cascaded down over her ivory shoulders. Her locks framed her face so beautifully it hit him with the force of a sharp blow to the stomach.

A white heat roared through his veins, settling unmercifully between his legs. He loved her so much, and she was so exceedingly lovely. He could protract the tender loving only a little while longer, or he'd surely die from the longing. His hands trembled as he stroked the smooth silkiness of her skin over the rounded softness of womanly breasts and drifted lower over the tautness of her flat stomach.

The heated magic they made together had commenced.

He was spellbound each time she touched him, hypnotized every time she called his name. She would be his; she had made that clear. And he wanted her more than life itself.

With a groan, he gave in to the overwhelming, driving need of his aching loins and slid into her, captured and held by her tight heat. Together, they moved in the rhythms of love, fast and heated, mindless, still standing, her legs wrapped securely around him, he bearing her slight weight in his arms.

Nothing else in the world mattered, save the two of them and their love for each other.

In the isolated cocoon of the mountain cabin, they spent the long hours of evening and nighttime; loving and sharing, unable to get enough. They did not sleep.

The first gray light of early dawn found them ensconced in her bed, lying on their backs, his hand lazily sliding over her in an intimate caress. Spent from a night of loving, they still could not pull themselves away.

"How do you feel about Cameron now, Cass?" Cruz knew it was not a fair question and that his timing was probably all wrong, but he had to have the answer or die. "Is there room in that generous, loving heart of yours for another man?"

The silence was blissfully short; he didn't have to wait long for her answer to his question.

"Yes, oh yes, Cruz! There's more than enough room for you in this heart!" she exclaimed, taking his hand and placing it over her pounding heart. "Ever since that first night when I found you, I think that's been true. I just wasn't able to admit it, even to myself, until now. There will always be room for you in here."

"And enough room to spare for all the beautiful children we will make together?"

Her answer was immediate and completely physical. She threw herself on top of him, slid her arms tightly behind his head, pulled it up to her, and kissed him long and hard.

"There!" she announced after they had to stop for a breath of air. "Do you have any more questions, sir?"

"Perhaps one or two," he retorted with raised eyebrows, "but they could best be answered without words."

"Is that a proposition, sir?"

"Now who is asking questions?" he growled, clutching her tightly to him.

"No more questions," she murmured into his neck.

"Only one," he replied, his lips brushing hers.

"And what might that be?"

"Will you marry me, my love?"

"Yes! Oh, yes!"

She pulled away, but only slightly. Her smile was wide, her eyes softly mocking. "Do you think you can find a priest who would do the job?"

"I suspect Father Auguste will be more than happy to oblige."

His happiness made his eyes the clearest, purest blue she'd ever seen.

Epilogue

During the unrest of that long spring of 1846, Cassie and Cruz were in Mexico City, where he made his report to the President. As he had promised, he also requested the assignment of a new priest to be sent to New Mexico. Father Auguste would retire and return to Mexico, his last official act having been to perform their wedding ceremony.

Cassie was enthralled with Mexico City. Cruz proudly showed her around the capital city, but they were both anxious to return to the place they now considered home, Santa Fe.

They arrived back there in early summer when there was still confusion and the government unsettled. They worked to make the inevitable overthrow of the Spanish by the Americans as painless as possible. Cruz had always known that the future of Santa Fe lay under the American flag.

It was not until August 18, 1846, that an American army of four thousand men commanded by General Stephen Watts Kearny arrived and claimed New Mexico for the United States.

To the delight of most of the citizens of Santa Fe, it was an entirely peaceful occupation and no blood was spilled on either side. Jubilant celebrations followed, complete with fireworks and fandangos, enjoyed by people of all the diverse cultures that made up the settlement.

Santa Fe was now a good place for Americans, Spanish, and Indians alike to make their homes and raise their children in peace.

As part of his required restitution, Juan Perego had been forced to deed to Cruz his lands and his *hacendado,* which became the home for the happy couple.

Carmelita de la Cruz Santiago Reyes made her arrival there shortly after the beginning of a new year in January of 1847. She would grow up as an American, but proud of her Spanish heritage, along with a brother and sister, soon to follow, and adored by her doting parents.

Cassie continued her rewarding work with the children until Cruz decided to resume his educational training for the medical profession. After a stint of a few years in the East, they returned to Santa Fe, to live their lives among those people they loved, tending to their needs in every way they could. Cruz took care of their bodies and Cassie their minds with her patient teaching.

Author's Note

The position of *aesesor* occupied by Juan Perego in this story was a real one, but rarely filled due to the difficulty of finding qualified men. Perego is, of course, totally fictional, based on no real individual, living or dead. The Goya mentioned is also imaginary, although such paintings were, on occasion, hung on the walls of parish churches in New Mexico.

DISCOVER DEANA JAMES!

CAPTIVE ANGEL   (2524, $4.50/$5.50)
Abandoned, penniless, and suddenly responsible for the biggest tobacco plantation in Colleton County, distraught Caroline Gillard had no time to dissolve into tears. By day the willowy redhead labored to exhaustion beside her slaves . . . but each night left her restless with longing for her wayward husband. She'd make the sea captain regret his betrayal until he begged her to take him back!

MASQUE OF SAPPHIRE   (2885, $4.50/$5.50)
Judith Talbot-Harrow left England with a heavy heart. She was going to America to join a father she despised and a sister she distrusted. She was certainly in no mood to put up with the insulting actions of the arrogant Yankee privateer who boarded her ship, ransacked her things, then "apologized" with an indecent, brazen kiss! She vowed that someday he'd pay dearly for the liberties he had taken and the desires he had awakened.

SPEAK ONLY LOVE   (3439, $4.95/$5.95)
Long ago, the shock of her mother's death had robbed Vivian Marleigh of the power of speech. Now she was being forced to marry a bitter man with brandy on his breath. But she could not say what was in her heart. It was up to the viscount to spark the fires that would melt her icy reserve.

WILD TEXAS HEART   (3205, $4.95/$5.95)
Fan Breckenridge was terrified when the stranger found her near-naked and shivering beneath the Texas stars. Unable to remember who she was or what had happened, all she had in the world was the deed to a patch of land that might yield oil . . . and the fierce loving of this wildcatter who called himself Irons.

Available wherever paperbacks are sold, or order direct from the Publisher. Send cover price plus 50¢ per copy for mailing and handling to Zebra Books, Dept. 3948, 475 Park Avenue South, New York, N.Y. 10016. Residents of New York and Tennessee must include sales tax. DO NOT SEND CASH. For a free Zebra/Pinnacle catalog please write to the above address.